From *Swan Song* to *Boy's Life* to *The Queen of Bedlam*,
New York Times bestselling author
Robert McCammon is
"a master who keeps his audience spellbound with
every sentence" (*Clarion-Ledger,* Jackson, MS)

Praise for Robert McCammon and

BOY'S LIFE

"Wonderful. . . . Recaptures the magic of being a child in a world
of possibilities and promise."

—The Atlanta Journal-Constitution

"Enthralling. . . . Teeming with smartly realized characters. . . .
A cornucopia of bittersweet fantasy storytelling that is by far
McCammon's finest book."

—Kirkus Reviews

"For sheer screwball storytelling exuberance, McCammon's book
is hard to top."

—Entertainment Weekly

"McCammon captures the joys and fears of late childhood with
sure strokes."

—San Francisco Chronicle

"Entertaining. . . . A powerful story about the magic inherent in
everyday life, about the many wonders and pains of growing up,
about the strange beauty around us that we so often miss."

—BookPage

For more "first-rate entertainment by a world-class storyteller" (*Locus*), be sure to read these superb Pocket Books novels from Robert McCammon

THE QUEEN OF BEDLAM

"[A] spellbinding sequel to *Speaks the Nightbird*. . . . McCammon brilliantly captures colonial New York and closes with a tantalizing cliffhanger that suggests more exciting sleuthing to come."
—*Publishers Weekly* (starred review)

"McCammon keeps the story moving. Fans of *Speaks the Nightbird* will certainly enjoy this . . . [as will] new readers."
—*Library Journal*

"McCammon skillfully re-creates early-eighteenth-century America. . . . He paints a picture of a vastly different time without letting research overwhelm his storytelling. . . . The revelations [are] gratifying."
—OnyxReviews.com

SPEAKS THE NIGHTBIRD

"An excellent story, full of tension and suspense. . . . Thoughtful as well as entertaining—think *Burn, Witch, Burn* crossed with Arthur Miller's *The Crucible*. . . . The week I spent listening to the nightbird every evening between eight and eleven was a very fine one."
—Stephen King

"No one can paint word pictures as vividly as Robert McCammon, and never has his palette had such depth as in *Speaks the Nightbird*. Told with matchless insight into the human soul, this novel makes for a deeply satisfying read."

—Sandra Brown, *New York Times*
bestselling author of *Play Dirty*

"Powerful and tense, thrilling and atmospheric."

—*The Clarion-Ledger* (Jackson, MS)

"A fine detective story . . . an exposé into the dark side of human nature. . . . Will keep readers glued to the pages."

—*Rocky Mountain News* (Denver)

"Disturbing. . . . McCammon tells a compelling story."

—*Library Journal* (starred review)

"Compulsively readable. . . . [An] absorbing historical mystery."

—*Publishers Weekly*

SWAN SONG

"A broad, compelling story. . . . A long, satisfying look at hell and salvation."

—*Publishers Weekly*

"A wild ride into terror. . . . A grand and disturbing adventure."

—Dean R. Koontz

"A chilling vision that keeps you turning pages to the shocking end."

—John Saul

Books by Robert McCammon

Published by POCKET BOOKS

BOY'S LIFE

ROBERT McCAMMON

POCKET BOOKS
New York London Toronto Sydney

Pocket Books
A Division of Simon & Schuster, Inc.
1230 Avenue of the Americas
New York, NY 10020

This Pocket Books trade paperback edition July 2008

POCKET and colophon are registered trademarks of
Simon & Schuster, Inc.

For information about special discounts for bulk purchases,
please contact Simon & Schuster Special Sales at 1-800-456-6798
or business@simonandschuster.com.

Designed by Claudia Martinez

Manufactured in the United States of America

10 9 8 7 6 5 4 3 2 1

ISBN-13: 978-1-4165-7778-2
ISBN-10:   1-4165-7778-5

We ran like young wild furies,
where angels feared to tread.
The woods were dark and deep.
Before us demons fled.
We checked Coke bottle bottoms
to see how far was far.
Our worlds of magic wonder
were never reached by car.
We loved our dogs like brothers,
our bikes like rocket ships.
We were going to the stars,
to Mars we'd make round trips.
We swung on vines like Tarzan,
and flashed Zorro's keen blade.
We were James Bond in his Aston,
we were Hercules unchained.
We looked upon the future
and we saw a distant land,
where our folks were always ageless,
and time was shifting sand.
We filled up life with living,
with grins, scabbed knees, and noise.
In glass I see an older man,
but this book's for the boys.

Foreword to the 2008 Edition

Why I Wrote *Boy's Life*

I FIND IT EASIER to write a book than to write *about* a book I've already written.

Does that make sense? It's because, I guess, for me a book I've already written is cast in stone. There's nothing more to be added or subtracted, everything is there where it needs to be. Or not. Because the writer, if he's lucky, is not yet cast in stone and keeps on going, which means learning more about *how* to write. So sometimes it's difficult to look back at earlier works, because inevitably you find something you'd like to subtract or you wish you could add, but stone cannot be moved.

Having said that, when I look back at *Boy's Life* I don't really find a lot I would have changed. I always believed that when you finished a book, if it was fifty percent of what you'd hoped it would be when it began, it would be good. I found to my amazement that when I finished *Boy's Life* it was about ninety percent of what I'd hoped it would be.

I don't, and never did, write with an outline. I have what I call "signpost scenes," something that happens at the beginning, the middle and toward the end, that hopefully keep me going in the right direction, but the only time I did try to use an outline I didn't finish the book. I already knew everything that was going to happen, so what was the point?

I guess what I'm trying to say is that I write, number one, for myself. I want to be the "first reader." I want to write books that I would read for fun, if I were not working so hard to write them. *Huh?* But it does make sense, at least to me, and approaching the writing in this way has always given me something to look forward to.

Well, if you have this new edition of *Boy's Life* in your hands now and are looking over this particular patch of rambling, you might either have already read the book or be thinking of reading it for the first time. I thought I'd fill you in on why I wrote the book, but first let me tell you the answer to a question I'm often asked concerning the book.

The question being: Is *Boy's Life* autobiographical?

The answer is: Yes, and I do consider myself a character in the book, but I'm *not* Cory, the lead character.

Who do I most identify with in *Boy's Life*? I'll let you know a little farther along.

About the book. It began as a murder mystery in a small Southern town, and was going to involve a secret in a *second* town that had been flooded and was underneath the lake. The main character was going to be the sheriff, and . . . oh gosh, I almost went to sleep right there!

So I took a long, hard look at the two hundred pages I'd already done and decided it just wasn't going to work. The painting never came to life. I'd had in mind for several years the story of a boy who wanted to be a writer, and the things happening in his hometown that influenced his life, but I'd kept putting that on the back burner. But now, here I was with a Southern town and a murder in mind, and I thought . . . okay, let's try out the book about the boy.

I started writing *Boy's Life* with no outline, but a lot of ideas. And suddenly the painting came to life. Not only that, but the painting came to a *fierce* life that I had rarely felt before in my work. I flew through the writing. Now, not to say it wasn't hard and I didn't have to do a lot of thinking and work many hundreds of hours, but *Boy's Life* was really moving and I just sort of turned the steering wheel to direct it, or so it sometimes seemed to me.

This is the thing about writing. *The* thing. When the writing isn't going well, there's nobody on God's earth who can help you. Not spouse, not brother or sister, not best friend, not editor. Nobody. Because no one understands the work as you do. If there's a problem, you have to deal with it, and you alone.

Conversely, when the work is going well . . . what can I say? That you hear angels singing? Or you hear the music of the spheres or something? That every fortune you get in your cookie says "Great Success Is Ahead, If You Don't Mess It Up"?

Something like that, I suppose. But when the work is going well, and you see the painting coming to life, and the people are real and you know them and see their faces and realize you are creating Life, in a way, then . . . I don't think there's any better satisfaction in the world.

When I finished *Boy's Life,* I was very high on what I'd done. I sent it to my publisher thinking, *Rick, they're going to call you, and they're going to be so excited, and they're going to say, Rick we didn't know you had it in you, and this is so different, and we're so excited, and you've done a very, very good job.*

I waited. I waited. And then I did get the phone call.

Rick. Listen. Um . . . you know . . . about the book. We really like it and everything, but . . . you know . . . the story is really about the murder, and you're going to confuse your readers by making them think this is autobiographical, and . . . you know . . . you probably should cut all that out about the town and the people and focus on the murder.

I'm sorry. I'm sorry. I just . . . I just . . . something's wrong with the phone, I think. I'm sorry.

When I got myself together, I called back and said, *Hold that thought. I'll be in your office tomorrow.* And then I went to the airport, me a guy from Birmingham, Alabama, without really a great literary education but a love of reading and writing and the feeling that this time—this time—I had to stand up for what I believed, and I flew to New York to face the big dogs.

I said I couldn't change the book. I said I would have to break the contract I had with them if they insisted on these changes, and the ashes would have to fall from the merry bonfire that used to be my career.

They cited me some business facts and figures from the chart on the wall, about how bad things happen to writers who try to step out of their boxes, but then they said okay. Fine. Your book is your book. If you believe that strongly in it, then so do we.

That was great. Just great. But, still . . . you know, when somebody looks at your child and says, *Oh, very lovely, very good and strong. If you say so* . . . a little bit of the joy of creation flies away. A little bit of what made you want to be a writer just gets up, very quietly, and goes out the door.

Boy's Life was not written for a young audience, but in the years since its first publication it has found a huge audience among younger readers. I don't know the exact figures, but it's taught in high schools across the country. I know, because I've been to many of them to speak to the English classes and the students in their gyms and auditoriums. On one day, I got a letter from a Scottish gentleman in his eighties and one from a boy in Seattle who was thirteen, both telling me how much they enjoyed the book. I think it's worldwide now. To see a Japanese cover with a rendition of Cory standing on the edge of the lake . . . it's just amazing.

One letter I got, I just have to mention, because to me this one was . . . well, how can I describe the feeling?

A woman wrote me several years ago to tell me that her elderly father had passed away, and that she wanted me to know he had asked that a copy of his favorite book be buried with him.

He had read it over and over, she said. So many times that it was no longer a book. It was a constant companion.

Not long ago I went into a chain bookstore—not, incidentally, in my hometown—and I walked over to what they called the "Classics Table." On that table were novels by Dickens, Hugo, Steinbeck, Twain, Verne, Updike, Vonnegut . . . basically everybody teachers try to get students to read and that they *ought* to read, just for the sake of the world's future.

And right there. Right there amid all those books with all those names was *Boy's Life*.

My child.

I doubt if I'll ever write another book that is fit to be on that table. God knows I'm going to keep trying. But I do have one book there, and I think one is enough.

The character I most closely identify with in *Boy's Life*?

You probably already know. It's Vernon, whose dream ended because he was broken by the weight of a chart on the wall. Because he did not stand up, in that office in New York. Because he came home to Zephyr without a fight, and closed his eyes to the world beyond.

He woke up, and he was still alive.

I've always wanted to use that line somewhere. This seems the right place.

If you are reading *Boy's Life* for the first time, I hope you enjoy it. I hope it takes you to some places you never knew existed . . . or to places that you may have forgotten ever did exist.

If this is your second or third reading, I welcome you back to Zephyr. To the life of Cory and his world. To summer days everlasting, to glorious secrets, to hidden places and the magic that is in all of us, but that sometimes just curls up and goes to sleep, waiting for its best friend to come home.

I thank you.

Robert "Rick" McCammon
January 29, 2008
Just after midnight

I WANT TO TELL YOU some important things before we start our journey.

I lived through it all. That's one problem about relating events in first person. The reader knows the narrator didn't get killed. So whatever might happen to me—whatever *did* happen to me—you can be sure I lived through it all, though I might be a little better or worse for the experience, and you can make up your own mind which.

There might be some places where you'll say, "Hey, how come he knows this event right here happened or this person said or did this or that if he wasn't even there?" The answer to that question is that I found out enough later on to fill in the blanks, or in some cases I made up what happened, or in other cases I figured it ought to have happened that way even if it didn't.

I was born in July of 1952. I am approaching my fortieth birthday. Gosh, that's some number, isn't it? I am no longer, as my reviews used to say, a "promising young talent." I am what I am. I have been writing since I was in grammar school, and thinking up stories long before I understood exactly what it was I was doing. I have been a published writer since 1978. Or is it "author"? Paperback writer, as the Beatles said. Hardback author? One thing's for sure: I certainly have developed a hard back. I have suffered kicks and smiled at kindnesses just like any other brother or sister on our spinning home. I have been blessed, to be

able to create characters and worlds out of whole cloth. Writer?
Author?

How about storyteller?

I wanted to set my memories down on paper, where I can hold
them. You know, I do believe in magic. I was born and raised in a
magic time, in a magic town, among magicians. Oh, most everybody else didn't realize we lived in that web of magic, connected
by the silver filaments of chance and circumstance. But I knew it
all along. When I was twelve years old, the world was my magic
lantern, and by its green spirit glow I saw the past, the present,
and into the future. You probably did, too; you just don't recall it.
See, this is my opinion: we all start out knowing magic. We are
born with whirlwinds, forest fires, and comets inside us. We are
born able to sing to birds and read the clouds and see our destiny
in grains of sand. But then we get the magic educated right out
of our souls. We get it churched out, spanked out, washed out,
and combed out. We get put on the straight and narrow and told
to be responsible. Told to act our age. Told to grow up, for God's
sake. And you know why we were told that? Because the people
doing the telling were afraid of our wildness and youth, and because the magic we knew made them ashamed and sad of what
they'd allowed to wither in themselves.

After you go so far away from it, though, you can't really get
it back. You can have seconds of it. Just seconds of knowing and
remembering. When people get weepy at movies, it's because in
that dark theater the golden pool of magic is touched, just briefly.
Then they come out into the hard sun of logic and reason again
and it dries up, and they're left feeling a little heartsad and not
knowing why. When a song stirs a memory, when motes of dust
turning in a shaft of light takes your attention from the world,
when you listen to a train passing on a track at night in the distance and wonder where it might be going, you step beyond who
you are and where you are. For the briefest of instants, you have
stepped into the magic realm.

That's what I believe.

The truth of life is that every year we get farther away from the essence that is born within us. We get shouldered with burdens, some of them good, some of them not so good. Things happen to us. Loved ones die. People get in wrecks and get crippled. People lose their way, for one reason or another. It's not hard to do, in this world of crazy mazes. Life itself does its best to take that memory of magic away from us. You don't know it's happening until one day you feel you've lost something but you're not sure what it is. It's like smiling at a pretty girl and she calls you "sir." It just happens.

These memories of who I was and where I lived are important to me. They make up a large part of who I'm going to be when my journey winds down. I need the memory of magic if I am ever going to conjure magic again. I need to know and remember, and I want to tell you.

My name is Cory Jay Mackenson. My hometown was a place called Zephyr, in south Alabama. It never got too cold there, or too hot. Its streets were shaded with water oaks, and its houses had front porches and screens on the windows. There was a park with two baseball fields, one for the kids and one for the grown-ups. There was a public swimming pool where the water was blue and clear and children plumbed the deep end for pennies. On the Fourth of July there was a barbecue, and at the end of summer a writing contest. When I was twelve years old, in 1964, Zephyr held about fifteen hundred people. There was the Bright Star Cafe, a Woolworth's, and a little Piggly-Wiggly grocery store. There was a house where bad girls lived out on Route Ten. Not every family had a television set. The county was dry, which meant that bootleggers thrived. The roads went south, north, east, and west, and at night a freight train passed through on its way to Birmingham and left the smell of scorched iron in its wake. Zephyr had four churches and an elementary school, and a cemetery stood on Poulter Hill. There was a lake nearby so deep it might as well have been bottomless. My hometown was full of heroes and villains, honest people who knew the beauty of truth and others whose beauty was a lie. My hometown was probably a lot like yours.

But Zephyr was a magic place. Spirits walked in the moonlight. They came out of the grassy graveyard and stood on the hill and talked about old times when Coca-Cola really had a bite and you could tell a Democrat from a Republican. I know. I've heard them. The breeze in Zephyr blew through the screens, bringing the incense of honeysuckle and awakening love, and jagged blue lightning crashed down upon the earth and awakened hate. We had windstorms and droughts and the river that lay alongside my town had the bad habit of flooding. In the spring of my fifth year, a flood brought snakes to the streets. Then hawks came down by the hundreds in a dark tornado and lifted up the snakes in their killing beaks, and the river slinked back to its banks like a whipped dog. Then the sun came out like a trumpet call, and steam swirled up from the blood-specked roofs of my hometown.

We had a dark queen who was one hundred and six years old. We had a gunfighter who saved the life of Wyatt Earp at the O.K. Corral. We had a monster in the river, and a secret in the lake. We had a ghost that haunted the road behind the wheel of a black dragster with flames on the hood. We had a Gabriel and a Lucifer, and a rebel that rose from the dead. We had an alien invader, a boy with a perfect arm, and we had a dinosaur loose on Merchants Street.

It was a magic place.

In me are the memories of a boy's life, spent in that realm of enchantments.

I remember.

These are the things I want to tell you.

One

The Shades of Spring

1

Before the Sun

"Cory? Wake up, son. It's time."

I let him pull me up from the dark cavern of sleep, and I opened my eyes and looked up at him. He was already dressed, in his dark brown uniform with his name—Tom—written in white letters across his breast pocket. I smelled bacon and eggs, and the radio was playing softly in the kitchen. A pan rattled and glasses clinked; Mom was at work in her element as surely as a trout rides a current. "It's time," my father said, and he switched on the lamp beside my bed and left me squinting with the last images of a dream fading in my brain.

The sun wasn't up yet. It was mid-March, and a chill wind blew through the trees beyond my window. I could feel the wind by putting my hand against the glass. Mom, realizing that I was awake when my dad went in for his cup of coffee, turned the radio up a little louder to catch the weather report. Spring had sprung a couple of days before, but this year winter had sharp teeth and nails and he clung to the South like a white cat. We hadn't had snow, we never had snow, but the wind was chill and it blew hard from the lungs of the Pole.

"Heavy sweater!" Mom called. "Hear?"

"I hear!" I answered back, and I got my green heavy sweater from my dresser. Here is my room, in the yellow lamplight and the space heater rumbling: Indian rug red as Cochise's blood, a desk with seven mystic drawers, a chair covered in material as velvety blue-black as Batman's cape, an aquarium holding tiny fish so pale you could see their hearts beat, the aforementioned dresser covered with decals from Revell model airplane kits, a bed with a quilt sewn by a relative of Jefferson Davis's, a closet, and the shelves. Oh, yes, the shelves. The troves of treasure. On those shelves are stacks of me: hundreds of comic books—Justice League, Flash, Green Lantern, Batman, the Spirit, Blackhawk, Sgt. Rock and Easy Company, Aquaman, and the Fantastic Four. There are *Boy's Life* magazines, dozens of issues of *Famous Monsters of Filmland, Screen Thrills,* and *Popular Mechanics.* There is a yellow wall of *National Geographic*s, and I have to blush and say I know where all the African pictures are.

The shelves go on for miles and miles. My collection of marbles gleams in a mason jar. My dried cicada waits to sing again in summer. My Duncan yo-yo that whistles except the string is broken and Dad's got to fix it. My little book of suit cloth samples that I got from Mr. Parlowe at the Stagg Shop for Men. I use those pieces of cloth as carpet inside my airplane models, along with seats cut from cardboard. My silver bullet, forged by the Lone Ranger for a werewolf hunter. My Civil War button that fell from a butternut uniform when the storm swept Shiloh. My rubber knife for stalking killer crocodiles in the bathtub. My Canadian coins, smooth as the northern plains. I am rich beyond measure.

"Breakfast's on!" Mom called. I zipped up my sweater, which was the same hue as Sgt. Rock's ripped shirt. My blue jeans had patches on the knees, like badges of courage marking encounters with barbed wire and gravel. My flannel shirt was red enough to stagger a bull. My socks were white as dove wings and my Keds midnight black. My mom was color-blind, and my dad thought checks went with plaid. I was all right.

It's funny, sometimes, when you look at the people who brought you into this world and you see yourself so clearly in them. You realize that every person in the world is a compromise of nature. I had my mother's small-boned frame and her wavy, dark brown hair, but my father had given me his blue eyes and his sharp-bridged nose. I had my mother's long-fingered hands—an "artist's hands," she used to tell me when I fretted that my fingers were so skinny—and my dad's thick eyebrows and the small cleft in his chin. I wished that some nights I would go to sleep and awaken resembling a man's man like Stuart Whitman in *Cimarron Strip* or Clint Walker in *Cheyenne,* but the truth of it was that I was a skinny, gawky kid of average height and looks, and I could blend into wallpaper by closing my eyes and holding my breath. In my fantasies, though, I tracked lawbreakers along with the cowboys and detectives who paraded past us nightly on our television set, and out in the woods that came up behind our house I helped Tarzan call the lions and shot Nazis down in a solitary war. I had a small group of friends, guys like Johnny Wilson, Davy Ray Callan, and Ben Sears, but I wasn't what you might call popular. Sometimes I got nervous talking to people and my tongue got tangled, so I stayed quiet. My friends and I were about the same in size, age, and temperament; we avoided what we could not fight, and we were all pitiful fighters.

This is where I think the writing started. The "righting," if you will. The righting of circumstances, the shaping of the world the way it should have been, had God not had crossed eyes and buck teeth. In the real world I had no power; in my world I was Hercules unchained.

One thing I do know I got from my granddaddy Jaybird, my dad's father: his curiosity about the world. He was seventy-six years old and as tough as beef jerky, and he had a foul mouth and an even fouler disposition, but he was always prowling the woods around his farm. He brought home things that made Grandmomma Sarah swoon: snakeskins, empty hornets' nests, even animals he'd found dead. He liked to cut things open with a penknife and look at their insides, arranging all their bloody guts out on newspapers. One time he hung up a dead toad from a tree and invited me to watch the flies eat it with him. He brought home a burlap sack full of leaves, dumped them in the front room, and examined each of them with a magnifying glass, writing down their differences in one of his hundreds of Nifty notebooks. He collected cigar butts and dried spits of chewing tobacco, which he kept in glass vials. He could sit for hours in the dark and look at the moon.

Maybe he was crazy. Maybe crazy is what they call anybody who's got magic in them after they're no longer a child. But Granddaddy Jaybird read the Sunday comics to me, and he told me stories about the haunted house in the small hamlet of his birth. Granddaddy Jaybird could be mean and stupid and petty, but he lit a candle of wonder in me and by that light I could see a long way beyond Zephyr.

On that morning before the sun, as I sat eating my breakfast with my dad and mom in our house on Hilltop Street, the year was 1964. There were great changes in the winds of earth, things of which I was unaware. All I knew at that moment was that I needed another glass of orange juice, and that I was going to help my dad on his route before he took me to school. So when breakfast was over and the dishes were cleared, after I had gone out into the cold to say good morning to Rebel and feed him his Gravy Train, Mom kissed both Dad and me, I put on my fleece-lined jacket and got my schoolbooks and off we went in the coughy old pickup truck. Freed from his backyard pen, Rebel followed us a distance, but at the corner of Hilltop and Shawson streets he crossed into the territory of Bodog, the Doberman pinscher that belonged to the Ramseys, and he beat a diplomatic retreat to a drumroll of barks.

And there was Zephyr before us, the town quiet in its dreaming, the moon a white sickle in the sky.

A few lights were on. Not many. It wasn't five o'clock yet. The sickle moon glittered in the slow curve of the Tecumseh River, and if Old Moses swam there he swam with his leathery belly kissing mud. The trees along Zephyr's streets were still without leaves, and their branches moved with the wind. The traffic lights—all four of them at what might be called major intersections—blinked yellow in a steady accord. To the east, a stone bridge with brooding gargoyles crossed the wide hollow where the river ran. Some said the faces of the gargoyles, carved in the early twenties, were representations of various Confederate generals, fallen angels, as it were. To the west, the highway wound into the wooded hills and on toward other towns. A railroad track cut across Zephyr to the north, right through the Bruton area, where all the black people lived. In the south was the public park where a band-shell stood and a couple of baseball diamonds had been cut into the earth. The park was named for Clifford Gray Haines, who founded Zephyr, and there was a statue of him sitting on a rock with his chin resting on his hand. My dad said it looked as if Clifford was perpetually constipated and could neither do his business nor get off the pot. Farther south, Route Ten left Zephyr's limits and wound like a black cottonmouth past swampy woods, a trailer park, and Saxon's Lake, which shelved into unknown depths.

Dad turned us onto Merchants Street, and we drove through the center of Zephyr, where the stores were. There was Dollar's Barbershop, the Stagg Shop for Men, the Zephyr Feeds and Hardware Store, the Piggly-Wiggly grocery, the Woolworth's store, the Lyric theater, and other attractions along the sidewalked thoroughfare. It wasn't much, though; if you blinked a few times, you were past it. Then Dad crossed the railroad track, drove another two miles, and turned into a gate that had a sign above it: GREEN MEADOWS DAIRY. The milk trucks were at the loading dock, getting filled up. Here there was a lot of activity, because Green Meadows Dairy opened early and the milkmen had their appointed rounds.

Sometimes when my father had an especially busy schedule, he asked me to help him with his deliveries. I liked the silence and stillness of the mornings. I liked the world before the sun. I liked finding out what different people ordered from the dairy. I don't know why; maybe that was my granddaddy Jaybird's curiosity in me.

My dad went over a checklist with the foreman, a big crew-cut man named Mr. Bowers, and then Dad and I started loading our truck. Here came the bottles of milk, the cartons of fresh eggs, buckets of cottage cheese and Green Meadows' special potato and bean salads. Everything was still cold from the ice room, and the milk bottles sparkled with frost under the loading dock's lights. Their paper caps bore the face of a smiling milkman and the words. "Good for You!" As we were working, Mr. Bowers came up and watched with his clipboard at his side and his pen behind his ear. "You think you'd like to be a milkman, Cory?" he asked me, and I said I might. "The world'll always need milkmen," Mr. Bowers went on. "Isn't that right, Tom?"

"Right as rain," my dad said; this was an all-purpose phrase he used when he was only half listening.

"You come apply when you turn eighteen," Mr. Bowers told me. "We'll fix you up." He gave me a clap on the shoulder that almost rattled my teeth and did rattle the bottles in the tray I was carrying.

Then Dad climbed behind the big-spoked wheel, I got into the seat next to him, he turned the key, and the engine started and we backed away from the loading dock with our creamy cargo. Ahead of us, the moon was sinking down and the last of the stars hung on the lip of night. "What about that?" Dad asked. "Being a milkman, I mean. That appeal to you?"

"It'd be fun," I said.

"Not really. Oh, it's okay, but no job's fun every day. I guess we've never talked about what you want to do, have we?"

"No sir."

"Well, I don't think you ought to be a milkman just because that's what I do. See, I didn't start out to be a milkman. Granddaddy Jaybird wanted me to be a farmer like him. Grandmomma Sarah wanted me to be a doctor. Can you imagine that?" He glanced at me and grinned. "Me, a doctor! Doctor Tom! No sir, that wasn't for me."

"What'd you start out to be?" I asked.

My dad was quiet for a while. He seemed to be thinking this question over, in a deep place. It occurred to me that maybe no one had ever asked him this before. He gripped the spoked wheel with his grown-up hands and negotiated the road that unwound before us in the headlights, and then he said, "First man on Venus. Or a rodeo rider. Or a man who can look at an empty space and see in his mind the house he wants to build there right down to the last nail and shingle. Or a detective." My dad made a little laughing noise in his throat. "But the dairy needed another milk-man, so here I am."

"I wouldn't mind bein' a race car driver," I said. My dad sometimes took me to the stock car races at the track near Barnesboro, and we sat there eating hot dogs and watching sparks fly in the collision of banged-up metal. "Bein' a detective would be okay, too. I'd get to solve mysteries and stuff, like the Hardy Boys."

"Yeah, that'd be good," my dad agreed. "You never know how things are gonna turn out, though, and that's the truth. You aim for one place, sure as an arrow, but before you hit the mark, the wind gets you. I don't believe I ever met one person who became what they wanted to be when they were your age."

"I'd like to be everybody in the world," I said. "I'd like to live a million times."

"Well"—and here my father gave one of his sagely nods—"that would be a fine piece of magic, wouldn't it?" He pointed. "Here's our first stop."

That first house must've had children in it, because they got two quarts of chocolate milk to go along with their two quarts of plain milk. Then we were off again, driving through the streets where the only sounds were the wind and the barking of early dogs, and we stopped on Shantuck Street to deliver buttermilk and cottage cheese to somebody who must've liked things sour. We left bottles glistening on the steps of most of the houses on

Bevard Lane, and my dad worked fast as I checked off the list and got the next items ready from the chilly back of the truck; we were a good team.

Dad said he had some customers down south near Saxon's Lake and then he'd swing back up so we could finish the rest of the street deliveries before my school bell rang. He drove us past the park and out of Zephyr, and the forest closed in on either side of the road.

It was getting on toward six o'clock. To the east, over the hills of pine and kudzu, the sky was beginning to lighten. The wind shoved its way through the trees like the fist of a bully. We passed a car going north, and its driver blinked the lights and Dad waved. "Marty Barklee deliverin' the newspapers," Dad told me. I thought about the fact that there was a whole world going about its business before the sun, and people who were just waking up weren't part of it. We turned off Route Ten and drove up a dirt drive to deliver milk, buttermilk, and potato salad to a small house nestled in the woods, and then we went south toward the lake again. "College," my dad said. "You ought to go to college, it seems to me."

"I guess so," I answered, but that sounded like an awful long distance from where I was now. All I knew about college was Auburn and Alabama football, and the fact that some people praised Bear Bryant and others worshipped Shug Jordan. It seemed to me that you chose which college to go to according to which coach you liked best.

"Gotta have good grades to get into college," Dad said. "Gotta study your lessons."

"Do detectives have to go to college?"

"I reckon they do if they want to be professional about it. If I'd gone to college, I might've turned out to be that man who builds a house in empty space. You never know what's ahead for you, and that's the—"

Truth, he was about to say, but he never finished it because we came around a wooded bend and a brown car jumped out of the forest right in front of us and Dad yelped like he was hornet-stung as his foot punched the brake.

The brown car went past us as Dad whipped the wheel to the left, and I saw that car go off Route Ten and down the embankment on my right. Its lights weren't on but there was somebody sitting behind the wheel. The car's tires tore through the underbrush and then it went over a little cliff of red rock and down into the dark. Water splashed up, and I realized the car had just plunged into Saxon's Lake.

"He went in the water!" I shouted, and Dad stopped the milk truck, pulled up the hand brake, and jumped out into the roadside weeds. As I climbed out, Dad was already running toward the lake. The wind whipped and whirled around us, and Dad stood there on the red rock cliff. By the faint pinkish light we could see the car wallowing in the water, huge bubbles bursting around its trunk. "Hey!" Dad shouted with his hands cupped around his mouth. "Get out of there!" Everybody knew Saxon's Lake was as deep as sin, and when that car went down into the inky depths it was gone for good and ever. "Hey, get out!" Dad shouted again, but whoever was behind the wheel didn't answer. "I think he's been knocked cold!" Dad told me as he took off his shoes. The car was starting to turn onto its passenger side, and there was an awful howling sound coming from it that must've been the rush of water pouring into the car. Dad said, "Stand back." I did, and he leaped into the lake.

He was a strong swimmer. He reached the car in a few powerful strokes, and he saw that the driver's window was open. He could feel the suction of water moving around his legs, drawing the car down into the unfathomed deep. "Get out!" he hollered, but the driver just sat there. Dad clung to the door, reached in, and grabbed the driver's shoulder. It was a man, and he wore no shirt. The flesh was white and cold, and my dad felt his own skin crawl. The man's head lolled back, his mouth open. He had short-cropped blond hair, his eyes sealed shut with black bruises, his face swollen and malformed from the pressures of a savage beating. Around his throat was knotted a copper piano wire, the thin metal pulled so tightly that the flesh had split open.

"Oh Jesus," my dad whispered, treading water.

The car lurched and hissed. The head lolled forward over the chest again, as if in an attitude of prayer. Water was rising up over the driver's bare knees. My dad realized the driver was naked, not a stitch on him. Something glinted on the steering wheel, and he saw handcuffs that secured the man's right wrist to the inner spoke.

My dad had lived thirty-four years. He'd seen dead men before. Hodge Klemson, one of his best friends, had drowned in the Tecumseh River when they were both fifteen years old, and the body had been found after three days bloated and covered with yellow bottom mud like a crusty ancient mummy. He'd seen what remained of Walter and Jeanine Traynor after the head-on collision six years ago between Walter's Buick and a logging truck driven by a kid eating pep pills. He'd seen the dark shiny mass of Little Stevie Cauley after firemen doused the flames of the crumpled black dragster named Midnight Mona. He had looked upon the grinning rictus of death several times, had taken that sight like a man, but this one was different.

This one wore the face of murder.

The car was going down. As its hood sank, its tail fins started rising. The body behind the wheel shifted again, and my father saw something on the man's shoulder. A blue patch, there against the white. Not a bruise, no; a tattoo. It was a skull with wings swept back from the bony temples.

A great burst of bubbles blew out of the car as more water rushed in. The lake would not be denied; it was going to claim its toy and tuck it away in a secret drawer. As the car began to slide down into the murk, the suction grabbed my father's legs and pulled him under, and standing on the red rock cliff I saw his head disappear and I shouted *Dad!* as panic seized my guts.

Underwater, he fought the lake's muscles. The car fell away beneath him, and as his legs thrashed for a hold in the liquid tomb, more bubbles rushed up and broke him loose and he climbed up their silver staircase toward the attic of air.

I saw his head break the surface. "Dad!" I shouted again. "Come on back, Dad!"

"I'm all right!" he answered, but his voice was shaky. "I'm comin' in!" He began dog-paddling toward shore, his body suddenly as weak as a squeezed-out rag. The lake continued to erupt where the car disturbed its innards, like something bad being digested. Dad couldn't get up the red rock cliff, so he swam to a place where he could clamber up on kudzu vines and stones. "I'm all right!" he said again as he came out of the lake and his legs sank to the knees in mud. A turtle the size of a dinner plate skittered past him and submerged with a perplexed snort. I glanced back toward the milk truck; I don't know why, but I did.

And I saw a figure standing in the woods across the road.

Just standing there, wearing a long dark coat. Its folds moved with the wind. Maybe I'd felt the eyes of whoever was watching me as I'd watched my father swim to the sinking car. I shivered a little, bone cold, and then I blinked a couple of times and where the figure had been was just windswept woods again.

"Cory?" my dad called. "Gimme a hand up, son!"

I went down to the muddy shore and gave him as much help as a cold, scared child could. Then his feet found solid earth and he pushed the wet hair back from his forehead. "Gotta get to a phone," he said urgently. "There was a man in that car. Went straight down to the bottom!"

"I saw . . . I saw . . ." I pointed toward the woods on the other side of Route Ten. "Somebody was—"

"Come on, let's go!" My father was already crossing the road with his sturdy, soggy legs, his shoes in his hand. I jump-started my own legs and followed him as close as a shadow, and my gaze returned to where I'd seen that figure but nobody was there, nobody, nobody at all.

Dad started the milk truck's engine and switched on the heater. His teeth were chattering, and in the gray twilight his face looked as pale as candle wax. "Damnedest thing," he said, and this shocked me because he never cursed in front of me. "Hand-cuffed to the wheel, he was. Handcuffed. My God, that fella's face was all beat up!"

"Who was it?"

"I don't know." He turned the heater up, and then he started driving south toward the nearest house. "Somebody did a job on him, that's for sure! Lord, I'm cold!"

A dirt road turned to the right, and my father followed it. Fifty yards off Route Ten stood a small white house with a screened-in front porch. A rose garden stood off to one side. Parked under a green plastic awning were two cars, one a red Mustang and the other an old Cadillac splotched with rust. My dad pulled up in front of the house and said, "Wait here," and he walked to the door in his wet socks and rang the bell. He had to ring it two more times before the door opened with a tinkle of chimes, and a red-haired woman who made three of my mom stood there wear-ing a blue robe with black flowers on it.

Dad said, "Miss Grace, I need to use your telephone real quick."

"You're all *wet!*" Miss Grace's voice sounded like the rasp of a rusty saw blade. She gripped a cigarette in one hand, and rings sparkled on her fingers.

"Somethin' bad's happened," Dad told her, and she sighed like a redheaded raincloud and said, "All right, come on in, then. Watch the carpet." Dad entered the house, the chimey door closed, and I sat in the milk truck as the first orange rays of sun-light started breaking over the eastern hills. I could smell the lake in the truck with me, a puddle of water on the floorboard beneath my father's seat. I had seen somebody standing in the woods. I knew I had. Hadn't I? Why hadn't he come over to see about the man in the car? And who had the man in the car been?

I was puzzling over these questions when the door opened again and Miss Grace came out, this time wearing a floppy white sweater over her blue gown. She had on sneakers, her ankles and

calves thick as young trees. She had a box of Lorna Doone cookies in one hand and the burning cigarette in the other, and she
walked to the milk truck and smiled at me. "Hey there," she said.
"You're Cory."

"Yes'm," I answered.

Miss Grace didn't have much of a smile. Her lips were thin
and her nose was broad and flat and her brows were black-penciled
streaks above deep-set blue eyes. She thrust the Lorna Doones at
me. "Want a cookie?"

I wasn't hungry, but my folks had always taught me never to
refuse a gift. I took one.

"Have two," Miss Grace offered, and I took a second cookie.
She ate a cookie herself and then sucked on the cigarette and
blew smoke through her nostrils. "Your daddy's our milkman,"
she said. "I believe you've got us on your list. Six quarts of milk,
two buttermilks, two chocolates, and three pints of cream."

I checked the list. There was her name—Grace Stafford—
and the order, just as she'd said. I told her I'd get everything for
her, and I started putting the order together. "How old are you?"
Miss Grace asked as I worked. "Twelve?"

"No ma'am. Not until July."

"I've got a son." Miss Grace knocked ashes from her cigarette.
She chewed on another cookie. "Turned twenty in December. He
lives in San Antonio. Know where that is?"

"Yes ma'am. Texas. Where the Alamo is."

"That's right. Turned twenty, which makes me thirty-eight.
I'm an old fossil, ain't I?"

This was a trick question, I thought. "No ma'am," I decided
to say.

"Well, you're a little diplomat, ain't you?" She smiled again,
and this time the smile was in her eyes. "Have another cookie."
She left me the box and walked to the door, and she hollered into
the house: "Lainie! Lainie, get your butt up and come out here!"

My dad emerged first. He looked old in the hard light of
morning, and there were dark circles under his eyes. "Called the

sheriff's office," he told me as he sat in his wet seat and squeezed his feet into his shoes. "Somebody's gonna meet us where the car went in."

"Who the hell was it?" Miss Grace asked.

"I couldn't tell. His face was . . ." He glanced quickly at me, then back to the woman. "He was beat up pretty bad."

"Must've been drunk. Moonshinin', most likely."

"I don't think so." Dad hadn't said anything over the phone about the car's driver being naked, strangled with a piano wire, and handcuffed to the wheel. That was for the sheriff and not for Miss Grace's or anybody else's ears. "You ever see a fella with a tattoo on his left shoulder? Looked like a skull with wings growin' out of its head?"

"I've seen more tattoos than the Navy," Miss Grace said, "but I can't recall anything like that around here. Why? Fella have his shirt off or somethin'?"

"Yeah, he did. Had that skull with wings tattooed right about here." He touched his left shoulder. Dad shivered again, and rubbed his hands together. "They'll never bring that car up. Never. Saxon's Lake is three hundred feet deep if it's an inch."

The chimes sounded. I looked toward the door with the tray of milk quarts in my arms.

A girl with sleep-swollen eyes stumbled out. She was wearing a long plaid bathrobe and her feet were bare. Her hair was the color of cornsilk and hung around her shoulders, and as she neared the milk truck she blinked in the light and said, "I'm all fucked up."

I think I must've almost fallen down, because never in my life had I heard a female use a word that dirty before. Oh, I knew what the word meant and all, but its casual use from a pretty mouth shocked the fool out of me.

"There's a young man on the premises, Lainie," Miss Grace said in a voice that could curl an iron nail. "Watch your language, please."

Lainie looked at me, and her cool stare made me recall the

time I'd put a fork in an electric socket. Lainie's eyes were chocolate brown and her lips seemed to wear a half smile, half sneer. Something about her face looked tough and wary, as if she'd run out of trust. There was a small red mark in the hollow of her throat. "Who's the kid?" she asked.

"Mr. Mackenson's son. Show some class, hear?"

I swallowed hard and averted my eyes from Lainie's. Her robe was creeping open. It hit me what kind of girl used bad words, and what kind of place this was. I had heard from both Johnny Wilson and Ben Sears that there was a house full of whores somewhere near Zephyr. It was common knowledge at the elementary school. When you told somebody to "go suck a whore," you were standing right on the razor's edge of violence. I'd always imagined the whorehouse to be a mansion, though, with drooping willow trees and black servants who fetched the customers mint juleps on the front porch; the reality, however, was that the whorehouse wasn't much of a step up from a broken-down trailer. Still and all, here it was right in front of me, and the girl with cornsilk hair and a dirty mouth earned her living by the pleasures of the flesh. I felt goose bumps ripple up my back, and I can't tell you the kind of scenes that moved like a slow, dangerous storm through my head.

"Take that milk and stuff to the kitchen," Miss Grace told her.

The sneer won out over the smile, and those brown eyes turned black. "I ain't got kitchen duty! It's Donna Ann's week!"

"It's whose week I say it is, missy, and you know why I ought to put you in the kitchen for a whole *month,* too! Now, you do what I tell you and keep your smart mouth shut!"

Lainie's lips drew up into a puckered, practiced pout. But her eyes did not register the chastisement so falsely; they held cold centers of anger. She took the tray from me, and standing with her back to my dad and Miss Grace, she stuck out her wet pink tongue in my face and curled it up into a funnel. Then the tongue slicked back into her mouth, she turned away from me, and dismissed all of us with a buttstrut that was as wicked as a sword slash. She swayed on into the house, and after Lainie was gone Miss Grace grunted and said, "She's as rough as a cob."

"Aren't they all?" Dad asked, and Miss Grace blew a smoke ring and answered, "Yeah, but she don't even *pretend* she's got manners." Her gaze settled on me. "Cory, why don't you keep the cookies. All right?"

I looked at Dad. He shrugged. "Yes, ma'am," I said.

"Good. It was a real pleasure to meet you." Miss Grace returned her attention to my father and the cigarette to the corner of her mouth. "Let me know how everything turns out."

"I will, and thanks for lettin' me use the phone." He slid behind the wheel again. "I'll pick up the milk tray next trip."

"Ya'll be careful," Miss Grace said, and she went into the white-painted whorehouse as Dad started the engine and let off the hand brake.

We drove back to where the car had gone in. Saxon's Lake was streaked with blue and purple in the morning light. Dad pulled the milk truck off onto a dirt road; the road, both of us realized, was where the car had come from. Then we sat and waited for the sheriff as the sunlight strengthened and the sky turned azure.

Sitting there, my mind was split: one part was thinking about the car and the figure I thought I'd seen, and the other part was wondering how my dad knew Miss Grace at the whorehouse so well. But Dad knew all of his customers; he talked about them to Mom at the dinner table. I never recalled him mentioning Miss Grace or the whorehouse, however. Well, it wasn't a proper subject for the dinner table, was it? And anyway, they wouldn't talk about such things when I was around, even though all my friends and everybody else at school from the fourth grade up knew there was a house full of bad girls somewhere around Zephyr.

I had been there. I had actually seen a bad girl. I had seen her curled tongue and her butt move in the folds of her robe.

That, I figured, was going to make me one heck of a celebrity.

"Cory?" my father said quietly. "Do you know what kind of business Miss Grace runs in that house?"

"I . . ." Even a third-grader could've figured it out. "Yes sir."

"Any other day, I would've just left the order by the front door." He was staring at the lake, as if seeing the car still tumbling slowly down through the depths with a handcuffed corpse at the wheel. "Miss Grace has been on my delivery route for two years. Every Monday and Thursday, like clockwork. In case it's crossed your mind, your mother *does* know I come out here."

I didn't answer, but I felt a whole lot lighter.

"I don't want you to tell anybody about Miss Grace or that house," my father went on. "I want you to forget you were there, and what you saw and heard. Can you do that?"

"Why?" I had to ask.

"Because Miss Grace might be a lot different than you, me, or your mother, and she might be tough and mean and her line of work might not be a preacher's dream, but she's a good lady. I just don't want talk gettin' stirred up. The less said about Miss Grace and that house, the better. Do you see?"

"I guess I do."

"Good." He flexed his fingers on the steering wheel. The subject was closed.

I was true to my word. My celebrityhood took flight, and that was that.

I was about to open my mouth to tell him about the figure I'd seen in the woods when a black and white Ford with a bubble light on top and the town seal of Zephyr on the driver's door rounded the corner and slowed to a stop near the milk truck. Sheriff Amory, whose first name was J.T., standing for Junior Talmadge, got out and Dad walked over to meet him.

Sheriff Amory was a thin, tall man whose long-jawed face made me think of a picture I'd seen: Ichabod Crane trying to outrace the Headless Horseman. He had big hands and feet and a pair of ears that might've shamed Dumbo. If his nose had been any larger, he would've made a dandy weathervane. He wore his sheriff's star pinned to the front of his hat, and underneath it his dome was almost bald except for a wreath of dark brown hair. He pushed his hat back up on his shiny forehead as he and my dad talked at the lake's edge and I watched my father's hand motions as he showed Sheriff Amory where the car had come from and where it had gone. Then they both looked out toward the lake's still surface, and I knew what they were thinking.

That car might've sunken to the center of the earth. Even the snapping turtles that lived along the lakeshore couldn't get far enough down to ever see that car again. Whoever the driver had been, he was sitting in the dark right now with mud in his teeth.

"Handcuffed," Sheriff Amory said, in his quiet voice. He had thick dark eyebrows over deep-set eyes the color of coal, and the pallor of his flesh suggested he had an affinity to the night. "You're sure about that, Tom? And about the wire, too?"

"I'm sure. Whoever strangled that fella did a hell of a job. Near about took his head off."

"Handcuffed," the sheriff said again. "That was so he wouldn't float out, I reckon." He tapped his lower lip with a forefinger. "Well," he said at last, "I believe we've got a murder on our hands, don't you?"

"If it wasn't, I don't know what murder is."

As they talked, I got out of the milk truck and wandered over to where I thought I'd seen that person watching me. There was nothing but weeds, rocks, and dirt where he'd been standing. If it had been a man, I thought. Could it have been a woman? I hadn't seen long hair, but then again I hadn't seen much of anything but a coat swirling in the wind. I walked back and forth along the line of trees. Beyond it, the woods deepened and swampy ground took over. I found nothing.

"Better come on to the office and let me write it up," the sheriff told my father. "If you want to go home and get some dry clothes on, that'd be fine."

My dad nodded. "I've got to finish my deliveries and get Cory to school, too."

"Okay. Seems to me we can't do much for that fella at the bottom, anyhow." He grunted, his hands in his pockets. "A murder. Last murder we had in Zephyr was in 1961. You remember when Bo Kallagan beat his wife to death with a bowlin' trophy?"

I returned to the milk truck and waited for my dad. The sun was up good and proper now, lighting the world. Or, at least, the world I knew. But things weighed heavy on my mind. It seemed to me that there were two worlds: one before the sun, and one after. And if that were true, then maybe there were people who were citizens of those different worlds as well. Some moved easily through the landscape of night, and others clung to the bright hours. Maybe I had seen one of those darktime citizens, in the world before the sun. And—a chilling thought—maybe he had seen *me* seeing him, too.

I realized I had brought mud back into the milk truck. It was smeared all over my Keds.

I looked at the soles, and the earth I had collected.

On the bottom of my left Ked was a small green feather.

2

Down in the Dark

The green feather went into my pocket. From there it found its way into a White Owl cigar box in my room, along with my collection of old keys and dried-up insects. I closed the box lid, placed the box in one of the seven mystic drawers, and slid the drawer shut.

And that was how I forgot about it.

The more I thought about seeing that figure at the edge of the woods, the more I thought I'd been wrong, that my eyes had been scared from seeing Dad sink underwater as the car went down. Several times I started to tell Dad about it, but something else got in the way. Mom threw a gut-busting fit when she found out he'd jumped into the lake. She was so mad at him she sobbed as she yelled, and Dad had to sit her down at the kitchen table and explain to her calmly why he had done it. "There was a man at the wheel," Dad said. "I didn't know he was already dead, I thought he was knocked cold. If I'd stood there without doing anything, what would I have thought of myself after it was over?"

"You could've drowned!" she fired at him, tears on her cheeks. "You could've hit your head on a rock and drowned!"

"I didn't drown. I didn't hit my head on a rock. I did what I had to do." He gave her a paper napkin, and she used it to blot her eyes. A last salvo came out of her: "That lake's full of cotton-mouths! You could've swum right into a nest of 'em!"

"I didn't," he said, and she sighed and shook her head as if she lived with the craziest fool ever born.

"You'd better get out of those damp clothes," she told him at last, and her voice was under control again. "I just thank God it's not your body down at the bottom of the lake, too." She stood up and helped him unbutton his soggy shirt. "Do you know who it was?"

"Never saw him before."

"Who would do such a thing to another human being?"

"That's for J.T. to find out." He peeled his shirt off, and Mom took it from him with two fingers as if the lake's water carried leprosy. "I've got to go over to his office to help him write it up. I'll tell you, Rebecca, when I looked into that dead man's face my heart almost stopped. I've never seen anything like that before, and I hope to God I never see such a thing again, either."

"Lord," Mom said. "What if you'd had a heart attack? Who would've saved *you?*"

Worrying was my mother's way. She fretted about the weather, the cost of groceries, the washing machine breaking down, the Tecumseh River being dirtied by the paper mill in Adams Valley, the price of new clothes, and everything under the sun. To my mother, the world was a vast quilt whose stitches were always coming undone. Her worrying somehow worked like a needle, tightening those dangerous seams. If she could imagine events through to their worst tragedy, then she seemed to have some kind of control over them. As I said, it was her way. My father could throw up a fistful of dice to make a decision, but my mother had an agony for every hour. I guess they balanced, as two people who love each other should.

My mother's parents, Grand Austin and Nana Alice, lived about twelve miles south in a town called Waxahatchee, on the edge of Robbins Air Force Base. Nana Alice was even worse a worrier than Mom; something in her soul craved tragic manna, whereas Grand Austin—who had been a logger and had a wooden leg to show for the slip of a band saw—warned her he would unscrew his leg and whop her upside the head with it if she didn't pipe down and give him peace. He called his wooden leg his "peace pipe," but as far as I know he never used it for any purpose except that for which it was carved. My mother had an older brother and sister, but my father was an only child.

Anyway, I went to school that day and at the first opportunity told Davy Ray Callan, Johnny Wilson, and Ben Sears what had happened. By the time the school bell rang and I walked home, the news was moving across Zephyr like a crackling wildfire. *Murder* was the word of the hour. My parents were fighting off the phone calls. Everybody wanted to know the grisly details. I went outside to ride my rusted old bike and lead Rebel for a chase in the woods, and it came to me that maybe one of those people who called already knew the details. Maybe one of them was just trying to find out if he'd been seen, or what Sheriff Amory knew.

I realized then, as I pedaled my bike through the forest and Rebel ran at my heels, that somebody in my hometown might be a killer.

The days passed, warming into the heart of spring. A week after Dad had jumped into Saxon's Lake, this was the story: Sheriff Amory had found no one missing from Zephyr or from any of the surrounding communities. A front-page article in the weekly Adams Valley *Journal* brought forth no new information. Sheriff Amory and two of his deputies, some of the firemen, and a half-dozen volunteers got out on the lake in rowboats and dragged nets back and forth, but they only came up with an angry catch of snapping turtles and cottonmouths.

Saxon's Lake used to be Saxon's Quarry back in the twenties, before the steam shovels had broken into an underground river that would not be capped or shunted aside. Estimates of its depth ranged from three hundred to five hundred feet. There wasn't a net on earth that could scoop that sunken car back to the surface.

The sheriff came by one evening for a talk with Dad and Mom, and they let me sit in on it. "Whoever did it," Sheriff Amory explained, his hat in his lap and his nose throwing a shadow, "must've backed that car onto the dirt road facin' the lake. We found the tire marks, but the footprints were all scuffed over. The killer must've had somethin' wedged against the gas pedal. Just before you rounded the bend, he released the hand brake, slammed the door, and jumped back, and the car took off across Route Ten. He didn't know you were gonna be there, of course. If you hadn't been, the car would've gone on into the lake, sunk, and nobody would ever have known it happened." He shrugged. "That's the best I can come up with."

"You talked to Marty Barklee?"

"Yeah, I did. Marty didn't see anything. The way that dirt road sits, you can drive right past it at a reasonable clip and never even know it's there."

"So where does that leave us?"

The sheriff pondered my dad's question, the silver star on his hat catching the lamplight. Outside, Rebel was barking and other dogs picked up the tribal call across Zephyr. The sheriff spread his big hands out and looked at his fingers. "Tom," he said, "we have a real strange situation here. We've got tire marks but no car. You say you saw a dead man handcuffed to the wheel and a wire around his throat, but we don't have a body and we're not likely to recover one. Nobody's missin' from town. Nobody's missin' in the whole area, except a teenaged girl whose mother thinks she ran off with her boyfriend to Nashville. And the boy don't have a tattoo, by the way. I can't find anybody who's seen a fella with a tattoo like the one you described." Sheriff Amory looked at me, then my mother, and then back to my dad with his coal-black eyes. "You know that riddle, Tom? The one about a tree fallin' in the woods, and if there's nobody around to hear it, does it make a noise? Well, if there's no body and no one's missin' anywhere that I can tell, was there a murder or not?"

"I know what I saw," Dad said. "Are you doubtin' my word, J.T.?"

"No, I didn't say that. I'm only sayin' I can't do anything more until we get a murder victim. I need a name, Tom. I need a face. Without an identification, I don't even know where to start."

"So in the meantime somebody who killed another man is walkin' around as free as you please and doesn't have to be scared of gettin' caught anytime soon. Is that it?"

"Yep," the sheriff admitted. "That about sums it up."

Of course Sheriff Amory promised he'd keep working on it, and that he'd call around the state for information on missing persons. Sooner or later, he said, somebody would have to ask after the man who had gone down in the lake. When the sheriff had gone, my father went out to sit on the front porch by himself with the light off, and he sat there alone past the time Mom told me to get ready for bed.

That was the night my father's cry awakened me in the dark.

I sat up in bed, my nerves jangled. I could hear Mom talking to Dad through the wall. "It's all right," she was saying. "It was a bad dream, just a bad dream, everything's all right."

Dad was quiet for a long time. I heard water running in the bathroom. Then the squeak of their bedsprings. "You want to tell me about it?" Mom asked him.

"No. God, no."

"It was just a bad dream."

"I don't care. It was real enough."

"Can you get back to sleep?"

He sighed. I could imagine him there in the darkened bedroom, his hands pressed to his face. "I don't know," he said.

"Let me rub your back."

The bedsprings squeaked again, as the weight of their bodies shifted. "You're awful tight," Mom said. "All up in your neck, too."

"That hurts like hell. Right there, where your thumb is."

"It's a crick. You must've pulled a muscle."

Silence. My neck and shoulders, too, had been comforted by my mother's supple hands. Every so often the springs spoke, announcing a movement. Then my father's voice came back. "I had another nightmare about that man in the car."

"I figured so."

"I was lookin' at him in that car, with his face beat all to pulp and his throat strangled with a wire. I saw the handcuff on his wrist, and the tattoo on his shoulder. The car was goin' down, and then . . . then his eyes opened."

I shivered. I could see it myself, and my father's voice was almost a gasp.

"He looked at me. Right at me. Water poured out of his eyeholes. He opened his mouth, and his tongue was as black as a snake's head. And then he said, 'Come with me.'"

"Don't think about it," Mom interrupted. "Just close your eyes and rest."

"I can't rest. I can't." I pictured my father's body, lying like a question mark on the bed as Mom kneaded the iron-tight muscles of his back. "My nightmare," he went on. "The man in the car reached out and grabbed my wrist. His fingernails were blue. His fingers bit hard into my skin, and he said, 'Come with me, down in the dark.' The car . . . the car started sinkin', faster and faster, and I tried to break loose but he wouldn't let me go, and he said, 'Come with me, come with me, down in the dark.' And then the lake closed over my head and I couldn't get away from it and I opened my mouth to scream but the water filled it up. Oh Jesus, Rebecca. Oh, Jesus."

"It wasn't real. Listen to me! It was only a bad dream, and everythin's all right now."

"No," Dad answered. "It's not. This thing is eatin' at me, and it's only gettin' worse. I thought I could put it behind me.

I mean, my God, I've seen a dead person before. Up close. But this . . . this is different. That wire around his throat, the handcuff, the face that somebody had pounded into putty . . . it's different. And not knowin' who he was, or anythin' about him . . . it's eatin' at me, day and night."

"It'll pass," Mom said. "That's what you tell me whenever I want to worry the warts off a frog. Hang on, you tell me. It'll pass."

"Maybe it will. I hope to God it will. But for right now, it's in my head and I can't shake it loose for the life of me. And this is the worst thing, Rebecca; this is what's grindin' inside of me. Whoever did it had to be a local. Had to be. Whoever did it knew how deep the lake is. He knew when that car went in there, the body was gone. Rebecca . . . whoever did this thing might be somebody I deliver milk to. It might be somebody who sits on our pew at church. Somebody we buy groceries or clothes from. Somebody we've known all our lives . . . or *thought* we knew. That scares me like I've never been scared before. You know why?" He was silent for a moment, and I could imagine the way the pulse throbbed at his temple. "Because if it's not safe here, it's not safe anywhere in this world." His voice cracked a little on the last word. I was glad I wasn't in that room, and that I couldn't see his face.

Two or three minutes passed. I think my father was just lying there, letting Mom rub his back. "Do you think you can sleep now?" she finally asked him, and he said, "I'll try."

The springs spoke a few times. I heard my mother murmur something close to his ear. He said, "I hope so," and then they were silent. Sometimes my dad snored; tonight he did not. I wondered if he lay awake after Mom had drifted off, and if he saw the corpse in the car reaching for him to drag him under. What he'd said haunted me: *if it's not safe here, it's not safe anywhere in this world.* This thing had hurt my father, in a place deeper than the bottom of Saxon's Lake. Maybe it was the suddenness of what had happened, or the violence, or the cold-bloodedness of it. Maybe it was the knowledge that there were terrible secrets behind closed doors, even in the kindest of towns.

I think my father had always believed all people were good, even in their secret souls. This thing had cracked his foundations, and it occurred to me that the murderer had handcuffed my father to that awful moment in time just as the victim had been handcuffed to the wheel. I closed my eyes and prayed for Dad, that he could find his way up out of the dark.

March went out like a lamb, but the murderer's work was unfinished.

3

The Invader

T HINGS SETTLED DOWN, as things will.

On the first Saturday afternoon in April, with the trees budding and flowers pushing up from the warming earth, I sat between Ben Sears and Johnny Wilson surrounded by the screaming hordes as Tarzan—Gordon Scott, the best Tarzan there ever was—plunged his knife into a crocodile's belly and blood spurted in scarlet Eastman color.

"Did you see that? Did you see that?" Ben kept saying, elbowing me in the ribs. Of course I saw it. I had eyes, didn't I? My ribs weren't going to last until the Three Stooges short between the double features, that was for certain.

The Lyric was the only movie theater in Zephyr. It had been built in 1945, after the Second World War, when Zephyr's sons marched or limped back home and they wanted entertainment to chase away the nightmares of swastika and rising sun. Some fine town father dug into his pockets and brought a construction man from Birmingham who drew a blueprint and marked off squares on a vacant lot where a tobacco barn used to be. I wasn't there at the time, of course, but Mr. Dollar could tell you the whole story.

Up went a palace of stucco angels, and on Saturday afternoons we devils of the common clay hunkered down in those seats with our popcorn, candy, and Yoo-Hoos and for a few hours our parents had breathing space again.

Anyway, my two buddies and me were sitting watching Tarzan on a Saturday afternoon. I forget why Davy Ray wasn't there; I think he was grounded for hitting Molly Lujack in the head with a pine cone. But satellites could go up and spit sparks in outer space. A man with a beard and a cigar could jabber in Spanish on an island off the coast of Florida while blood reddened a bay for pigs. That bald-headed Russian could bang his shoe. Soldiers could be packing their gear for a trip to a jungle called Vietnam. Atom bombs could go off in the desert and blow dummies out of tract-house living rooms. We didn't care about any of that. It wasn't magic. Magic was inside the Lyric on Saturday afternoons, at the double feature, and we took full advantage of getting ourselves lost in the spell.

I recall watching a TV show—"77 Sunset Strip"—where the hero walked into a theater named the Lyric, and I got to thinking about that word. I looked it up in my massive two-thousand-four-hundred-and-eighty-three-page dictionary Granddaddy Jaybird had given me for my tenth birthday. "Lyric," it said: "Melodic. Suitable for singing. A lyric poem. Of the lyre." That didn't seem to make much sense in regards to a movie theater, until I continued following *lyre* in my dictionary. *Lyre* took me into the story-poems sung by traveling minstrels back when there were castles and kings. Which took me back to that wonderful word: *story*. It seemed to me at an early age that all human communication—whether it's TV, movies, or books—begins with somebody wanting to tell a story. That need to tell, to plug into a universal socket, is probably one of our grandest desires. And the need to hear stories, to live lives other than our own for even the briefest moment, is the key to the magic that was born in our bones.

The Lyric.

"Stab it, Tarzan! Stab it!" Ben yelled, and that elbow was

working overtime. Ben Sears was a plump boy with brown hair cropped close to his skull, and he had a high, girlish voice and wore horn-rimmed glasses. The shirt wasn't made that could stay tucked into his jeans. He was so clumsy his shoelaces could strangle him. He had a broad chin and fat cheeks and he would never grow up to resemble Tarzan in any girl's dream, but he was my friend. By contrast to Ben's chubby exuberance, Johnny Wilson was slim, quiet, and bookish. He had some Indian blood in him that showed in his black, luminous eyes. Under the summer sun his skin turned brown as a pine nut. His hair was almost black, too, and slicked back with Vitalis except for a cowlick that shot up like a wild onion at the crease of his part. His father, who was a foreman at the sheetrock plant between Zephyr and Union Town, wore his hair exactly the same way. Johnny's mother was the library teacher at Zephyr Elementary, so I suppose that's how he got his affinity for reading. Johnny ate encyclopedias like any other kid might eat Red Hots or Lemonheads. He had a nose like a Cherokee hatchet and a small scar warped his right eyebrow where his cousin Philbo had hit him with a stick when we were all playing soldiers back in 1960. Johnny Wilson endured school-yard taunts about being a "squawboy," or having "nigger blood," and he'd been born with a clubfoot to boot, which only doubled the abuse directed at him. He was a stoic before I knew the meaning of the word.

The movie meandered to its conclusion like a jungle river to the sea. Tarzan defeated the evil elephant poachers, returned the Star of Solomon to its tribe, and swung into the sunset. The Three Stooges short subject came on, in which Moe wrenched out Larry's hair by the handfuls and Curly sat in a bathtub full of lobsters. We all had a grand old time.

And then, without fanfare, the second feature began.

It was in black and white, which caused immediate groans from the audience. Everybody knew that color was real life. The title came up on the screen: *Invaders from Mars*. The movie looked old, like it had been made in the fifties. "I'm goin' for popcorn,"

Ben announced. "Anybody want anythin'?" We said no, and he negotiated the raucous aisle alone.

The credits ended, and the story started.

Ben returned with his bucket of buttered popcorn in time to see what the young hero saw through his telescope, aimed at the stormy night sky: a flying saucer, descending into a sand hill behind his house. Usually the Saturday-afternoon crowd hollered and laughed at the screen when there was no fighting going on, but this time the stark sight of that ominous saucer coming down silenced the house.

I believe that for the next hour and a half the concession stand did no business, though there were kids leaving their seats and running for a view of daylight. The boy in the movie couldn't make anybody believe he'd seen a flying saucer come down, and he watched through his telescope as a policeman was sucked down into a vortex of sand as if by a grotesque, otherworldly vacuum cleaner. Then the policeman came to visit the house and assure the boy that no, of course no flying saucer had landed. Nobody else had seen this flying saucer land, had they? But the policeman acted . . . funny. Like he was a robot, his eyes dead in a pasty face. The boy had noticed a weird X-shaped wound on the back of the policeman's neck. The policeman, a jolly gent before his walk to the sand hill, did not smile. He was changed.

The X-shaped wound began to show up on the backs of other necks. No one believed the boy, who tried to make his parents understand there was a nest of Martians in the earth behind his house. Then his parents went out to see for themselves.

Ben had forgotten about the bucket of popcorn in his lap. Johnny sat with his knees pulled up to his chest. I couldn't seem to draw a breath.

Oh, you are such a silly boy, the grim, unsmiling parents told him when they returned from their walk. There is nothing to be afraid of. Nothing. Everything is fine. Come with us, let us go up to where you say you saw this saucer descend. Let us show you what a silly, silly boy you are.

"Don't go," Ben whispered. "Don't go don't go!" I heard his fingernails scrape against the armrests.

The boy ran. Away from home, away from the unsmiling strangers. Everywhere he looked, he saw the X-shaped wound. The chief of police had one on the back of his neck. People the boy had always known were suddenly changed, and they wanted to hold him until his parents could come pick him up. Silly, silly boy, they said. Martians in the ground, about to take over the world. Who would ever believe a story like that?

At the end of this horror, the army got down in a honeycomb of tunnels the Martians had burrowed in the ground. The Martians had a machine down there that cut into the back of your neck and turned you into one of them. The leader of the Martians, a head with tentacles in a glass bowl, looked like something that had backed up out of a septic tank. The boy and the army fought against the Martians, who shambled through the tunnels as if fighting the weight of gravity. At the collision of Martian machines and army tanks, with the earth hanging in the balance . . .

. . . the boy awakened.

A dream, his father said. His mother smiled at him. A dream. Nothing to fear. Go to sleep, we'll see you in the morning.

Just a bad, bad dream.

And then the boy got up in the dark, peered through his telescope, and saw a flying saucer descending from the stormy night sky into a sand hill behind his house.

The End?

The lights came up. Saturday afternoon at the movies was over.

"What's wrong with them?" I heard Mr. Stellko, the Lyric's manager, say to one of the ushers as we filed out.

"Why're they so darned *quiet?*"

Sheer terror has no voice.

Somehow we managed to get on our bikes and start pedaling. Some kids walked home, some waited for their parents to pick them up. All of us were linked by what we had just witnessed, and when Ben, Johnny, and I stopped at the gas station on Ridgeton Street to get air put in Johnny's front tire, I caught Ben staring at the back of Mr. White's neck, where the sunburned skin folded up.

We parted ways at the corner of Bonner and Hilltop streets. Johnny flew for home, Ben cranked his bike with his stumpy legs, and I fought the rusted chain every foot of the distance. My bike had seen its best days. It was ancient when it came to me, by way of a flea market. I kept asking for a new one, but my father said I would have to do with what I had or do without. Money was tight some months; going to the movies on Saturday was a luxury. I found out, sometime later, that Saturday afternoon was the only time the springs in my parents' bedroom could sing a symphony without me wondering what was going on.

"You have fun?" my mother asked when I came in from playing with Rebel.

"Yes ma'am," I said. "The Tarzan movie was neat."

"Double feature, wasn't it?" Dad inquired, sitting on the sofa with his feet up. The television was tuned to an exhibition baseball game; it was getting to be that time of year.

"Yes sir." I walked on past them, en route to the kitchen and an apple.

"Well, what was the other movie about?"

"Oh . . . nothin'," I answered.

Parents can smell a mouse quicker than a starving cat. They let me get my apple, wash it under the faucet, polish it, and then bring it back into the front room. They let me sink my teeth into it, and then my dad looked up from the Zenith and said, "What's the matter with you?"

I crunched the apple. Mom sat down next to Dad, and their eyes were on me. "Sir?" I asked.

"Every other Saturday you burst in here like gangbusters wantin' to tell us all about the movies. We can't hardly stop you from actin' 'em out scene by scene. So what's the matter with you today?"

"Uh . . . I guess I . . . don't know, exactly."

"Come here," Mom said. When I did, her hand flew to my forehead. "Not runnin' a fever. Cory, you feel all right?"

"I'm fine."

"So one movie was about Tarzan," my father plowed on, bulldog stubborn. "What was the other movie about?"

I supposed I could tell them the title. But how could I tell them what it was *really* about? How could I tell them that the movie I had just seen tapped the primal fear of every child alive: that their parents would, in an instant of irreversible time, be forever swept away and replaced by cold, unsmiling aliens? "It was . . . a monster movie," I decided to say.

"That must've been right up your alley, then." Dad's attention veered back to the baseball game as a bat cracked like a pistol shot. "Whoa! Run for it, Mickey!"

The telephone rang. I hurried to answer it before my folks could ask me any more questions. "Cory? Hi, this is Mrs. Sears. Can I speak to your mother, please?"

"Just a minute. Mom?" I called. "Phone for you!"

Mom took the receiver, and I had to go to the bathroom. Number one, thankfully. I wasn't sure I was ready to sit on the toilet with the memory of that tentacled Martian head in my mind.

"Rebecca?" Mrs. Sears said. "How are you?"

"Doin' fine, Lizbeth. You get your raffle tickets?"

"I sure did. Four of them, and I hope at least one is lucky."

"That's good."

"Well, the reason I'm callin' is, Ben got back from the movies just a little while ago and I was wonderin' how Cory is."

"Cory? He's——" She paused, and in her mind she was considering my strange state. "He says he's fine."

"So does Ben, but he acts a little . . . I don't know, maybe 'bothered' is the word I'm lookin' for. Usually he hounds the heck out of Sim and me wantin' to tell us about the movies, but today we can't get him to talk. He's out back right now. Said he wants to make sure about somethin', but he won't tell us what."

"Cory's in the bathroom," my mother said, as if that, too, was a piece of the puzzle. She cast her voice lower, in case I could hear over my waterfall. "He does act a little funny. You think somethin' happened between 'em at the movies?"

"I thought of it. Maybe they had a fallin'-out."

"Well, they've been friends for a long time, but it does happen."

"Happened with me and Amy Lynn McGraw. We were fast friends for six years and then we didn't speak for a whole year over a lost packet of sewin' needles. But I was thinkin', maybe the boys ought to get together. If they've had an argument, maybe they ought to work it out right off."

"Makes sense."

"I was gonna ask Ben if he'd like Cory to spend the night. Would that be all right with you?"

"I don't mind, but I'll have to ask Tom and Cory."

"Wait a minute," Mrs. Sears said, "Ben's comin' in." My mother heard a screen door slam. "Ben? I've got Cory's mother on the phone. Would you like Cory to spend the night here tonight?" My mother listened, but she couldn't make out what Ben was saying over the flush of our toilet.

"He says he'd like that," Mrs. Sears told her.

I emerged from the bathroom, into the well-meaning complicity. "Cory, would you like to spend the night at Ben's house?"

I thought about it. "I don't know," I said, but I couldn't tell her why. The last time I'd spent the night over there, back in February, Mr. Sears hadn't come home all night and Mrs. Sears had walked the floor fretting about where he might be. Ben told me his father took a lot of overnight trips and he asked me not to say anything.

"Ben wants you to come," Mom prodded, mistaking my reluctance.

I shrugged. "Okay. I guess."

"Go make sure it's all right with your father." While I went to the front room to ask, my mother said to Mrs. Sears, "I know how important friendship is. We'll get 'em patched up if there's any problem."

"Dad says okay," I told her when I returned. If my father was watching a baseball game, he would be agreeable to flossing his teeth with barbed wire.

"Lizbeth? He'll be there. 'Round six o'clock?" She put her hand over the mouthpiece and said to me, "They're havin' fried chicken for dinner."

I nodded and tried to summon a smile, but my thoughts were in the tunnels where the Martians plotted the destruction of the human race, town by town.

"Rebecca? How're things goin'?" Mrs. Sears asked. "You know what I mean."

"Run on, Cory," she told me, and I did even though I knew important things were about to be discussed. "Well," she said to Lizbeth Sears, "Tom's sleepin' a little better now, but he still has the nightmares. I wish I could do somethin' to help, but I think he just has to work it out for himself."

"I hear the sheriff's about given it up."

"It's been three weeks without any kind of lead. J.T. told Tom on Friday that he sent word out all over the state, Georgia and Mississippi, too, but he hasn't come up with a thing. It's like the man in that car came from another planet."

"Now, there's a chilly thought."

"Somethin' else," my mother said, and she sighed heavily. "Tom's . . . changed. It's more than the nightmares, Lizbeth." She turned toward the kitchen pantry and stretched the cord as far as it would go so there was no chance of Dad hearing. "He's careful to lock all the doors and windows, where before he didn't care about locks. Up until it happened, we left our doors unlocked most of the time, like everybody else does. Now Tom gets up two or three times in the night to check the bolts. And last week he came home from his route with red mud on his shoes, when it hadn't rained. I think he went back to the lake."

"What on earth for?"

"I don't know. To walk and think, I suppose. I remember when I was nine years old I had a yellow cat that got run over by a truck in front of our house. Calico's blood stayed on the pavement for a long time. That place pulled me. I hated it, but I had to go there and see where Calico died. I always thought that there was somethin' I could've done to keep him alive. Or maybe up until it happened, I thought everythin' lived forever." She paused, staring at pencil marks on the back door that showed the steady progress of my growth. "I think Tom's got a lot on his mind right now."

Their conversation rolled on into the realm of this and that, though at the center of it was the incident at Saxon's Lake. I watched the baseball game with Dad, and I noticed that he kept closing and opening his right hand as if he were either trying to grasp something or free himself from a grip. Then it got time to get ready to go, and I gathered up my pajamas, my toothbrush, and another set of socks and underwear and shoved everything down in my army surplus knapsack. Dad told me to be careful and Mom told me to have fun, but to be back in the morning in time for Sunday school. I rubbed Rebel's head and threw a stick for him to chase, and then I climbed on my bike and pedaled away.

Ben didn't live very far, only a half mile or so from my house at the dead end of Deerman Street. On Deerman Street I pedaled quietly, because guarding the corner of Deerman and Shantuck was the somber gray stone house where the notorious Branlin brothers lived. The Branlins, thirteen and fourteen years of age, had peroxided blond hair and delighted in destruction. Oftentimes they roamed the neighborhood on their matching black bicycles like vultures searching for fresh meat. I had heard from Davy Ray Callan that the Branlins sometimes tried to run cars off the street with their speeding black bikes, and that he'd actually witnessed Gotha Branlin, the oldest, tell his own mother to go to the bad place. Gotha and Gordo were like the Black Plague; you hoped they wouldn't get you, but once they laid a hand on you, there was no escape.

So far I had been insignificant to their careening meanness. I planned for it to stay that way.

Ben's house was much like my own. Ben had a brown dog named Tumper, who got up from his belly on the front porch to bark my arrival. Ben came out to meet me, and Mrs. Sears said hello and asked if I wanted a glass of root beer. She was dark-haired and had a pretty face, but she had hips as big as watermelons. Inside the house, Mr. Sears came up from his woodshop in the basement to speak to me. He was large and round, too, his heavy-jowled face ruddy under crew-cut brown hair. Mr. Sears was a happy man with a buck-toothed grin, woodshavings clinging to his striped shirt, and he told me a joke about a Baptist preacher and an outhouse that I didn't really understand, but he laughed to cue me and Ben said, "Aw, Daddy!" as if he'd heard that dumb joke a dozen times.

I unpacked my knapsack in Ben's room, where he had nifty collections of baseball cards, bottle caps, and wasps' nests. As I got squared away, Ben sat down on his Superman bedspread and said, "Did you tell your folks about the movie?"

"No. Did you?"

"Uh-uh." He picked at a loose thread on Superman's face. "How come you didn't?"

"I don't know. How come *you* didn't?"

Ben shrugged, but thoughts were working in his head. "I guess," he said, "it was too awful to tell."

"Yeah."

"I went out back," Ben said. "No sand. Just rock."

We both agreed the Martians would have a tough time drilling through all the red rock in the hills around Zephyr, if they were to come calling. Then Ben opened a cardboard box and showed me his Civil War bubble gum cards that had gory paintings of guys getting shot, bayoneted, and clobbered by cannon balls, and we sat making up a story for each card until his mother rang a bell to say it was time for fried chicken.

After dinner—and Mrs. Sears's wonderful black bottom pie

washed down with a glass of cold Green Meadows milk—we all played a game of Scrabble. Ben's parents were partners, and Mr. Sears kept trying to pass made-up words that even I knew weren't in the dictionary, like "kafloom" and "goganus." Mrs. Sears said he was as crazy as a monkey in itching powder, but she grinned at his antics just like I did. "Cory?" he said. "Didja hear the one about the three preachers tryin' to get into heaven?" and before I could say "No" he was off on a joke-telling jaunt. He seemed to favor the preacher jokes, and I had to wonder what Reverend Lovoy at the Methodist church would think of them.

It was past eight o'clock and we'd started our second game when Tumper barked on the front porch and a few seconds later there was a knock on the door. "I'll get it," Mr. Sears said. He opened the door to a wiry, craggy-faced man wearing jeans and a red-checked shirt. "Hey, Donny!" Mr. Sears greeted him. "Come on in, you buzzard!"

Mrs. Sears was watching her husband and the man named Donny. I saw her jaw tense.

Donny said something in a low voice to Mr. Sears, and Mr. Sears called to us, "Me and Donny are gonna sit on the porch for a while. Y'll go on and play."

"Hon?" Mrs. Sears drew up a smile, but I could tell it was in danger of slipping. "I need a partner."

The screen door closed at his back.

Mrs. Sears sat very still for a long moment, staring at the door. Her smile had gone.

"Mom?" Ben said. "It's your turn."

"All right." She tried to pull her attention to the Scrabble tiles. I could tell she was trying as hard as she could, but her gaze kept slipping back to the screen door. Out on the porch, Mr. Sears and the wiry man named Donny were sitting in folding chairs, their conversation quiet and serious. "All right," Ben's mother said again. "Let me think now, just give me a minute."

More than a minute passed. Off in the distance, a dog began

barking. Then two more. Tumper took up the call. Mrs. Sears was still choosing her tiles when the door flew open again.

"Hey, Lizbeth! Ben! Come out here, and hurry!"

"What is it, Sim? What's—"

"Just come *out* here!" he hollered, and of course we all got up from the table to see.

Donny was standing in the yard, looking toward the west. The neighborhood dogs were really whooping it up. Lights burned in windows, and other people were emerging to find out what the uproar was about. Mr. Sears pointed in the direction Donny was looking. "You ever seen anythin' like *that* before?"

I looked up. So did Ben, and I heard him gasp as if he'd been stomach-punched.

It was coming down from the night sky, descending from the canopy of stars. It was a glowing red thing, purple spears of fire trailing behind it, and it left a white trail of smoke against the darkness.

In that instant my heart almost exploded. Ben took a backward step, and he might have fallen had he not collided with one of his mother's hips. I knew in my hammering, rioting heart that everywhere across Zephyr kids who had been in the Lyric theater that afternoon were looking up at the sky and feeling terror peel the lips back from their teeth.

I came very close to wetting my pants. Somehow I held my water, but it was a near thing.

Ben blubbered. He made mangled sounds. He wheezed, "It's . . . it's . . . it's . . ."

"A comet!" Mr. Sears shouted. "Look at that thing fall!"

Donny grunted and slid a toothpick into the corner of his mouth. I glanced at him and by the porch light saw his dirty fingernails.

It was falling in a long, slow spiral, ribbons of sparks flaying out in its wake. It made no noise, but people were shouting for other people to look and some of the dogs had started that kind of howling that makes your backbone quiver.

"Comin' down between here and Union Town," Donny observed. His head was cocked to one side, his face gaunt and his dark hair slick with brilliantine. "Comin' down like a sonofabitch."

Between Zephyr and Union Town lay eight miles of hills, woods, and swamp cut by the Tecumseh River. It was Martian territory if there ever was, I thought, and I felt all the circuits in my brain jangle like fire alarms going off. I looked at Ben. His eyes seemed to be bulging outward by the cranial pressure of pure fear. The only thing I could think of when I stared at the fireball again was the tentacled head in the glass bowl, its face serenely evil and slightly Oriental. I could hardly stand up, my legs were so weak.

"Hey, Sim?" Donny's voice was low and slow, and he was chewing on the toothpick. "How about we go chase that bugger down?" His face turned toward Mr. Sears. His nose was flat, as if it had been busted by a big fist. "What do you say, Sim?"

"Yeah!" he answered. "Yeah, we'll go chase it down! Find out where it falls!"

"No, Sim!" Mrs. Sears said. In her voice was a note of pleading. "Stay with me and the boys tonight!"

"It's a comet, Lizbeth!" he explained, grinning. "How many times in your life do you get to chase a comet?"

"Please, Sim." She grasped his forearm. "Stay with us. All right?" I saw her fingers tighten.

"About to hit." Donny's jaw muscles clenched as he chewed. "Time's wastin'."

"Yeah! Time's wastin', Lizbeth!" Mr. Sears pulled away. "I'll get my jacket!" He rushed up the porch steps and into the house. Before the screen door could slam, Ben was running after his father.

Mr. Sears went back to the bedroom he shared with his wife. He opened the closet, got his brown poplin jacket, and shrugged into it. Then he reached up onto the closet's top shelf, his hand winnowing under a red blanket. As Mr. Sears's hand emerged,

Ben walked into the room behind him and caught a glint of metal between his father's fingers.

Ben knew what it was. He knew what it was for.

"Daddy?" he said. "Please stay home."

"Hey, boy!" His father turned toward him, grin in place, and he slid the metal object down into his jacket and zipped the jacket up. "I'm gonna go see where the comet comes down with Mr. Blaylock. I won't be but a little while."

Ben stood in the doorway, between his father and the outside world. His eyes were wet and scared. "Can I go with you, Daddy?"

"No, Ben. Not this time. I gotta go now."

"Let me go with you. Okay? I won't make any noise. Okay?"

"No, son." Mr. Sears's hand clamped down on Ben's shoulder. "You have to stay here with your mother and Cory." Though Ben stiffly resisted, his father's hand moved him aside. "You be a good boy, now," Mr. Sears said as his big shoes carried him toward the door.

Ben made one more attempt by grasping his father's fingers and trying to hold him. "Don't go, Daddy!" he said. "Don't go! Please don't go!"

"Ben, don't act like a baby. Let me go, son."

"No, sir," Ben answered. The wetness of his eyes had overflowed onto his pudgy cheeks. "I won't."

"I'm just goin' out to see where the comet falls. I won't be gone but a little while."

"If you go . . . if you go . . ." Ben's throat was clogging up with emotion, and he could hardly squeeze the words out. "You'll come back *changed*."

"Let's hit the road, Sim!" Donny Blaylock urged from the front porch.

"Ben?" Mr. Sears said sternly. "I'm goin' with Mr. Blaylock. Act like a man, now." He worked his fingers free, and Ben stood there looking up at him with an expression of agony. His father scraped a hand through Ben's cropped hair. "I'll bring you back a piece of it, all right, Tiger?"

"Don't go," the weeping tiger croaked.

His father turned his back on him, and strode out the screen door to where Donny Blaylock waited. I was still standing with Mrs. Sears in the yard, watching the fiery thing in its last few seconds of descent. Mrs. Sears said, "Sim? Don't do it," but her voice was so weak it didn't carry. Mr. Sears did not speak to his wife, and he followed the other man to a dark blue Chevy parked at the curb. Red foam dice hung from the radio antenna, and the right rear side was smashed in. Donny Blaylock slid behind the wheel and Mr. Sears got in the other side. The Chevy started up like a cannon going off, shooting black exhaust. As the car pulled away, I heard Mr. Sears laugh as if he'd just told another preacher joke. Donny Blaylock must've stomped the gas pedal, because the rear tires shrieked as the Chevy tore away up Deerman Street.

I looked toward the west again, and saw the fiery thing disappear over the wooded hills. Its glow pulsed against the dark like a beating heart. It had come to earth somewhere in the wilderness.

There was no sand anywhere out there. The Martians, I thought, were going to have to slog through a lot of mud and waterweeds.

I heard the screen door slam, and I turned around and saw Ben standing on the front porch. He wiped his eyes with the back of his hand. He stared along Deerman Street, as if he were tracking the Chevy's progress, but by that time the car had turned right on Shantuck and was out of sight.

In the distance, probably up in Bruton, dogs were still baying. Mrs. Sears released a long, strengthless sigh. "Let's go in," she said.

Ben's eyes were swollen, but his crying was done. No one seemed to want to finish the game of Scrabble. Mrs. Sears said, "Why don't you boys go play in your room, Ben?" and he nodded slowly, his eyes glazed as if he'd taken a heavy blow to the skull. Mrs. Sears went back to the kitchen, where she turned on the water. In Ben's room, I sat on the floor with the Civil War cards while Ben stood at the window.

I could tell he was suffering. I'd never seen him like this before, and I had to say something. "Don't worry," I told him. "It's not Martians. It was a meteor, that's all."

He didn't answer.

"A meteor's just a big hot rock," I said. "There're no Martians inside it."

Ben was silent; his thoughts had him.

"Your dad'll be okay," I said.

Ben spoke, in a voice terrible in its quiet: "He'll come back changed."

"No, he won't. Listen . . . that was just a movie. It was made up." I realized that as I said this I was letting go of something, and it felt both painful and good at the same time. "See, there's not really a machine that cuts into the backs of people's necks. There's not really a big Martian head in a glass bowl. It's all made up. You don't have to be scared. See?"

"He'll come back changed," Ben repeated.

I tried, but nothing I could say would make him believe any differently. Mrs. Sears came in, and her eyes looked swollen, too. But she managed a brave smile that hurt my heart, and she said, "Cory? Do you want to take the first bath?"

Mr. Sears was not home by ten o'clock, when his wife switched off the light in Ben's bedroom. I lay under the crisp white sheet beside Ben, listening to the night. A couple of dogs still conversed back and forth, and every once in a while Tumper offered a muttered opinion. "Ben?" I whispered. "You awake?" He didn't answer, but the way he was breathing told me he wasn't sleeping. "Don't worry," I said. "Okay?"

He turned over, and pressed his face against his pillow.

Eventually I drifted off. I did not, surprisingly, dream of Martians and X-shaped wounds on the backs of loved ones' necks. In my dream my father swam for the sinking car, and when his head went under, it did not come back up. I stood on the red rock cliff, calling for him, until Lainie came to me like a white mist and took my hand in a damp grip. As she led me away from the lake, I could hear my mother calling to me from the distance, and a figure stood at the edge of the woods wearing a long overcoat that flapped in the wind.

An earthquake woke me up.

I opened my eyes, my heart pounding. Something had crashed; the sound was trapped inside my head. The lights were still off, and the night still reigned. I reached out and touched Ben beside me. He drew in a sharp breath, as if my touch had scared the wits out of him. I heard an engine boom, and I looked out the window toward Deerman Street to see a Chevy's taillights as Donny Blaylock pulled away.

The screen door, I realized. The sound of the screen door slamming had jolted me awake.

"Ben?" I rasped, my mouth thick with sleep. "Your dad's come home!"

Something else crashed down in the front room. The whole house seemed to shake.

"Sim?" It was Mrs. Sears's voice, high-pitched. *"Sim?"*

I got out of bed, but Ben just lay there. I think he was staring at the ceiling. I walked through the hallway in the dark, my feet squeaking the boards. I bumped into Mrs. Sears, standing where the hall met the front room, no lights on anywhere.

I heard a hoarse, terrible breathing.

It was, I thought, the sound a Martian might make as its alien lungs strained on earthly air.

"Sim?" Mrs. Sears said. "I'm right here."

"Right here," a voice answered. "Right . . . here. Right . . . fuckin' . . . here."

It was Mr. Sears's voice, yes. But it was different. Changed. There was no humor in it, no fun, no hint of a preacher joke. It was as heavy as doom, and just as mean.

"Sim, I'm going to turn on the light now."

Click.

And there he was.

Mr. Sears was on the floor on his hands and knees, his head bowed and one cheek mashed against the rug. His face looked bloated and wet, his eyes sunken in fleshy folds. The right shoulder of his jacket was dirty, and dirt was smeared on his jeans as if he'd taken a fall in the woods. He blinked in the light, a silver thread of saliva hanging from his lower lip. "Where is it?" he said. "You see it?"

"It's . . . beside your right hand."

His left hand groped. "You're a goddamned liar," he said.

"Your other hand, Sim," she told him wearily.

His right hand moved toward the metal object lying there. It was a whiskey flask, and his fingers gripped it and pulled it to him.

He sat up on his knees and stared at his wife. A fierceness passed over his face, ugly in its swiftness. "Don't you smart-mouth me," he said. "Don't you open that big fat smart mouth."

I stepped back then, into the hallway. I was seeing a monster that had slipped from its skin.

Mr. Sears struggled to stand. He grabbed hold of the table that held the Scrabble tiles, and it went over in an explosion of vowels and consonants. Then he made it to his feet, and he unscrewed the cap off the flask and licked the bottle neck.

"Come on to bed, Sim," she said; it was spoken without strength, as if she knew full well what the outcome of this would be.

"Come on to bed!" he mocked. "Come on to bed!" His lip curled. "I don't *wanna* come to bed, you fat-assed cow!"

I saw Mrs. Sears tremble as if she'd been stung by a whip. A hand pressed to her mouth. "Oh . . . *Sim,*" she moaned, and it was an awful sound to hear.

I backed away some more. And then Ben walked past me in his yellow pajamas, his face blank of expression but tear tracks glistening on his cheeks.

There are things much worse than monster movies. There

are horrors that burst the bounds of screen and page, and come home all twisted up and grinning behind the face of somebody you love. At that moment I knew Ben would have gladly looked into that glass bowl at the tentacled Martian head rather than into his father's drunk-red eyes.

"Hey, Benny boy!" Mr. Sears said. He staggered and caught himself against a chair. "Hey, you know what happened to you? You know what? The best part of you stayed in that busted rubber, that's what happened."

Ben stopped beside his mother. Whatever emotion tortured him inside, it did not show on his face. He must've known this was going to happen, I realized. Ben had known when his father went with Donny Blaylock, he would come home changed not by the Martians but by the home brew in that flask.

"You're a real sight. The both of you." Mr. Sears tried to screw the cap back on, but he couldn't make it fit. "Standin' there with your smart mouths. You think this is funny, don't you, boy?"

"No sir."

"Yes you do! You can't wait to go laugh and tell everybody, can you? Where's that Mackenson boy? Hey, you!" He spotted me, back in the hall, and I flinched. "You can tell that goddamned milkman daddy of yours to go straight to hell. Hear me?"

I nodded, and his attention wandered away from me. This was not Mr. Sears talking, not really; this was the voice of what the flask flayed raw and bloody inside his soul, what it stomped and kicked and tortured until the voice had to scream for release.

"What'd you say?" He stared at Mrs. Sears, his eyelids swollen and heavy. "What'd you *say?*"

"I . . . didn't say—"

He was on her like a charging bull. Mrs. Sears cried out and retreated but he grabbed the front of her gown with one hand and reared his other hand back, the flask gripped in it, as if to smash her across the face. *"Yes you did!"* he shouted. *"Don't you backtalk me!"*

"Daddy, don't!" Ben pleaded, and he flung both arms around one of his father's thighs and hung tight. The moment stretched, Mr. Sears about to strike his wife, me standing in a state of shock in the hallway, Ben holding on to his father's leg.

Mrs. Sears's lips trembled. With the flask poised to strike her face, she spoke: "I . . . said . . . that we both love you, and that . . . we want you to be happy. That's all." Tears welled up and trickled. "Just happy."

He didn't speak. His eyes closed, and he opened them again with an effort.

"Happy," he whispered. Ben was sobbing now, his face pressed against his father's thigh, his knuckles white at the twining of his fingers. Mr. Sears lowered his hand, and he let go of his wife's gown. "Happy. See, I'm happy. Look at me smile."

His face didn't change.

He stood there, breathing roughly, his hand with the flask in it hanging at his side. He started to step one way and then another, but he couldn't seem to decide which way to go.

"Why don't you sit down, Sim?" Mrs. Sears asked. She sniffled and wiped her dripping nose. "Want me to help you?"

He nodded. "Yeah. Help."

Ben let him go, and Mrs. Sears guided her husband to his chair. He collapsed into it, like a large pile of dirty laundry. He stared at the opposite wall, his mouth hanging open. She drew up another chair close beside him. There was a feeling in the room as if a storm had passed. It might come again, some other night, but for now it was gone.

"I don't think—" He stopped, as if he'd lost what he was about to say. He blinked, searching for it. "I don't think I'm doin' so good," he said.

Mrs. Sears leaned his head gently on her shoulder. He squeezed his eyes shut, his chest heaved, and he began to cry, and I walked out of the house into the cool night air in my pajamas because it didn't seem right for me to be in there, a stranger at a private pain.

I sat down on the porch steps. Tumper plodded over, sat beside me, and licked my hand. I felt an awful long way from home.

Ben had known. What courage it must have taken for him to lie in that bed, pretending to sleep. He had known that when the screen door slammed, long after midnight, the invader who wore his father's flesh would be in the house. The knowing and the waiting must've been a desperate torment.

After a while, Ben came outside and sat on the steps, too. He asked me if I was all right, and I said I was. I asked him if he was all right. He said yeah. I believed him. He had learned to live with this, and though it was a horrible thing, he was grappling with it the best he could.

"My daddy has spells," Ben explained. "He says bad things sometimes, but he can't help it."

I nodded.

"He didn't mean what he said about your daddy. You don't hate him, do you?"

"No," I said. "I don't."

"You don't hate *me,* do you?"

"No," I told him. "I don't hate anybody."

"You're a real good buddy," Ben said, and he put his arm around my shoulders.

Mrs. Sears came out and brought us a blanket. It was red. We sat there as the stars slowly wheeled their course, and soon the birds of morning began to peep.

At the breakfast table, we had bowls of hot oatmeal and blueberry muffins. Mrs. Sears told us that Mr. Sears was sleeping, that he would sleep most of the day, and that if I wanted to I could ask my mother to call her and they'd have a long talk. After I got dressed and packed all my belongings into the knapsack, I thanked Mrs. Sears for having me over, and Ben said he'd see me at school tomorrow. He walked me out to my bike, and we talked for a few minutes about our Little League baseball team that would soon start practicing. It was getting to be that time of year.

Never again would we mention to each other the movie where Martians plotted to conquer the earth, town by town, father by mother by child. We had both seen the face of the invader.

It was Sunday morning. I pedaled for home, and when I looked back at the house at the dead end of Deerman Street, my friend waved so long.

4

Wasps at Easter

THE METEOR, AS IT turned out, must've burned itself to cinders as it flamed down from outer space. A few pine trees had caught fire, but it started raining on Sunday night and the fire hissed away. It was still raining on Monday morning, when the school bell rang, and the rain fell all through that long, gray day. The following Sunday was Easter, and Mom said she hoped the rain—forecast to fall intermittently all week long—didn't spoil the Merchants Street Easter parade on Saturday.

Early on the morning of Good Friday, starting around six o'clock or so, there was always another parade of sorts in Zephyr. It began in Bruton, at a small frame house painted purple, orange, red, and sunburst yellow. A procession of black men in black suits, white shirts, and ties made their way from this house, with a number of women and children in somber clothing following behind. Two of the men carried drums, and beat a slow, steady rhythm to time the paces. The procession wound its way across the railroad track and along Merchants Street, the center of town, and no one spoke to each other. Since this was an annual event, many of Zephyr's white population emerged from their houses to stand along the street and watch. My mother was one of them, though my dad was already at work by that time of the morning. I usually went with her, because I grasped the significance of this event just as everyone else did.

The three black men who led the way carried burlap bags. Around their necks, dangling down over their ties, were necklaces of amber beads, chicken bones, and the shells of small river mussels. On this particular Good Friday, the streets were wet and the rain drizzled down, but the members of the black parade carried no umbrellas. They spoke to no one on the sidewalks, nor to anyone who happened to be so rude as to speak to them. I saw Mr. Lightfoot walking near the parade's center, and though he knew every white face in town he looked neither right nor left but straight ahead at the back of the man who walked before him. An invaluable asset to the interlocked communities of Bruton and Zephyr, Marcus Lightfoot was a handyman who could repair any object ever devised by the human mind though he might work at the pace of grass growing. I saw Mr. Dennis, who was a custodian at the elementary school. I saw Mrs. Velvadine, who worked in the kitchen at our church, and I saw Mrs. Pearl, who was always laughing and cheerful at the Merchants Street Bake Shoppe. Today, though, she was nothing but serious, and she wore a clear plastic rain hat.

Bringing up the very rear of the procession, even behind the women and children, was a spindly man wearing a black tuxedo and a top hat. He carried a small drum, and his black-gloved hand beat it to mark the rhythm. It was this man and his wife whom many had come out on the chilly, rainy morning to see. The wife would arrive later; he walked alone, his face downcast.

We called him the Moon Man, because we didn't know his real name. He was very old, but exactly how old it was impossible to say. He was very rarely seen outside of Bruton, except on this occasion, as was his wife. Either a birth defect or a skin malady had affected one side of his long, narrow face, turning it pale yellow while the other side remained deep ebony, the two halves merging in a war of splotches down his forehead, the bridge of his elegant nose, and his white-bearded chin. The Moon Man, an enigma, had two watches on each wrist and a gilded crucifix the size of a ham hock hanging on a chain around his neck. He was, we presumed, the parade's official timekeeper as well as one of its royal personages.

The parade continued, step by steady step, through Zephyr to the gargoyle bridge over the Tecumseh River. It might take a while, but it was worth being late to school to see, and because of it school never really got into session until around ten o'clock on Good Fridays.

Once the three men with the burlap bags reached the center of the bridge, they stopped and stood like black statues. The rest of the procession got as close as possible without blocking the bridge, though Sheriff Amory had set up sawhorses with blinking lights along the route.

In a moment a Pontiac Bonneville covered hood to trunk with gleaming plastic rhinestones was driven slowly along Merchants Street from Bruton, following the parade's path. When it arrived at the center of the gargoyle bridge, the driver got out and opened the rear door, and the Moon Man took his wife's wrinkled hand and helped her to her feet.

The Lady had arrived.

She was as thin as a shadow, and just as dark. She had a cotton-cloud of white hair, her neck long and regal, her shoulders frail but unbowed. She wore not a costume of outlandish color and design, but a simple black dress with a silver belt, white shoes, and a white pillbox hat with a veil. She wore white gloves to her bony elbows. As the Moon Man helped her from the car, the driver opened an umbrella and held it over her royal, ancient head.

The Lady, it was said, had been born in the year 1858. That made her one hundred and six years old. My mom said the Lady had been a slave in Louisiana, and had run away with her momma into the swamp before the Civil War. The Lady had grown up in a colony of lepers, escaped convicts, and slaves in the bayou below

New Orleans, and that was where she'd learned everything she knew.

The Lady was a queen, and Bruton was her kingdom. No one outside Bruton—and no one inside Bruton, as far as I understood—knew her by any name but "the Lady." It suited her; she was elegance, through and through.

Someone gave her a bell. She stood looking down at the sluggish brown river, and she began to slowly swing the bell back and forth.

I knew what she was doing. My mom did, too. Everyone who watched did.

The Lady was calling the river's monster up from its mansion of mud.

I had never seen the beast that was called Old Moses. One night when I was nine years of age, I did think I heard Old Moses calling after a heavy rain, when the air itself was as thick as water. It was a low rumble, like the deepest bass note from a church's pipe organ, so deep your bones hear it before your ears do. It went up into a hoarse roar that made the town's dogs go crazy, and then the noise was gone. It hadn't lasted but maybe five or six seconds. The next day, that noise was the talk of the school. Train's whistle, was Ben's and Davy Ray's opinion. Johnny didn't say what he thought. At home, my folks said it must've been the train passing through, but we didn't find out until later that the rain had washed away a section of track more than twenty miles from Zephyr and the freight to Birmingham hadn't even run that night.

Such things make you wonder.

A mangled cow washed up, once, under the gargoyle bridge. Missing its head and guts, Mr. Dollar told my father when he and I went to get scalped. Two men netting crayfish along the riverbank just beyond Zephyr spread the story that a human corpse had floated past on the current, the body's chest peeled open like a sardine can and its arms and legs ripped off at the roots, but no corpse was ever found downriver. One October night, something hit a submerged piling of the gargoyle bridge and left cracks in the support columns that had to be filled with concrete. "A big tree trunk" was Mayor Swope's official explanation in the Adams Valley *Journal*.

The Lady rang the bell, her arm working like a metronome. She began to chant and sing, in a voice surprisingly clear and loud. The chant was all African words, which I understood about as much as I grasped nuclear physics. She would stop for a while, her head slightly cocked to one side as if watching or listening for something, and then she'd swing the bell again. She never once said the name "Old Moses." She kept saying "Damballah, Damballah, Damballah," and then her voice would sail upward in an African song again.

At last she ceased ringing the bell, and she lowered it to her side. She nodded, and the Moon Man took it from her. She was staring fixedly at the river, but what she was seeing there I don't know. Then she stepped back and the three men with the burlap bags stood at the edge of the gargoyle bridge. They opened the bags and brought out objects wrapped up in butcher's paper and tape. Some of the paper was bloody, and you could smell the coppery odor of fresh meat. They began to unwrap the gory feast, and as they did they threw the steaks, briskets, and beef ribs down into the swirling brown water. A whole plucked chicken went into the river, too, along with chicken intestines poured from a plastic jar. Calf brains slid out of a green Tupperware bowl, and wet red beef kidneys and liver came out of one of the damp packages. A bottle of pickled pigs' feet was opened, its contents splashing down into the water. A pig's snout and ears followed the feet. The last thing in was a beef heart bigger than a wrestler's fist. It splashed in like a red stone, and then the three men folded up their burlap bags and the Lady stepped forward again, watching her footing on the blood that had dripped onto the pavement.

It occurred to me that an awful lot of Sunday dinners had just gone into the drink.

"Damballah, Damballah, Damballah!" the Lady chanted

once more. She stood there for maybe four or five minutes, motionless as she watched the river move beneath the bridge. Then she breathed a long sigh and I saw her face behind the veil as she turned toward her rhinestone Pontiac again. She was frowning; whatever she had seen or had not seen, she wasn't too happy about it. She got into the car, the Moon Man climbed in after her, the driver closed the door and slid behind the wheel. The Pontiac backed up to a place where it could turn around and then started toward Bruton. The procession began to go back the route it had come. Usually by this time there was a lot of laughing and talking, and people would stop to speak to the white faces along the way. On this particular Good Friday, however, the Lady's somber mood had carried and no one seemed to feel much like laughing.

I knew exactly what the ritual was all about. Everybody in town did. The Lady was feeding Old Moses his annual banquet. When this had started, I didn't know; it had been going on long before I was born. You might think, as Reverend Blessett at the Freedom Baptist church did, that it was pagan and of the devil and should be outlawed by the mayor and town council, but enough white people believed in Old Moses to override the preacher's objections. It was like carrying a rabbit's foot or throwing salt over your shoulder if you happened to spill any; these things were part of the grain and texture of life, and better to do them than not, just in case God's ways were more mysterious than we Christians could grasp.

On the following day the rain fell harder, and thunderclouds rolled over Zephyr. The Merchants Street Easter parade was canceled, much to the dismay of the Arts Council and the Commerce Club. Mr. Vandercamp Junior, whose family owned the hardware and feeds store, had been dressing up as the Easter bunny and riding in the parade's last car for six years, having inherited the task from Mr. Vandercamp Senior, who got too old to hop. This Easter the rain doused all hopes of catching candy eggs thrown by the various merchants and their families from their cars, the ladies of the Sunshine Club couldn't show off their Easter dresses, husbands, and children, the members of Zephyr's VFW unit couldn't march behind the flag, and the Confederate Sweethearts—girls who attended Adams Valley High School—couldn't wear their hoop skirts and spin their parasols.

Easter morning arrived, cloaked in gloom. My dad and I were compatriots in grousing about getting slicked up, putting on starched white shirts, suits, and polished shoes. Mom had an all-purpose answer to our grumbles, much the same as Dad's "Right as rain." She said, "It's only one day," as if this made the stiff collar and the necktie knot more comfortable. Easter was a family day, and Mom phoned Grand Austin and Nana Alice and then Dad picked up the telephone to call Granddaddy Jaybird and Grand-momma Sarah. We would all, as we did every Easter, converge on the Zephyr First Methodist church to hear about the empty tomb.

The white church on Cedarvine Street, between Bonner and Shantuck, was filling up by the time we parked our pickup truck. We walked through the sloppy mist toward the light that streamed through the church's stained-glass windows, all the polish getting soaked off our shoes. People were shedding their raincoats and closing their umbrellas at the front door, beneath the overhanging eaves. It was an old church, built in 1939, the whitewash coming off and leaving gray patches. Usually the church was primed to its finest on Easter day, but this year the rain had defeated the paint brush and lawn mower so weeds were winning in the front yard.

"Come in, Handsome! Come in, Flowers! Watch your step there, Noodles! Good Easter morning to you, Sunshine!" That was Dr. Lezander, who served as the church's greeter. He had never missed a Sunday, as far as I knew. Dr. Frans Lezander was the veterinarian in Zephyr, and it was he who had cured Rebel of the worms last year. He was a Dutchman, and though he still had a heavy accent he and his wife Veronica, Dad had told me, had come from Holland long before I was born. He was in his mid-fifties, stood about five eight, was broad-shouldered and baldheaded and had a neatly trimmed gray beard. He wore natty three-piece suits, always with a bow tie and a lapel carnation, and he made up names for people as they entered the church. "Good morning, Peach Pie!" he said to my smiling mother. To my father, with a knuckle-popping handshake: "Raining hard enough for you, Thunderbird?" And to me, with a squeeze of the shoulder and a grin that shot light off a silver front tooth: "Step right in, Bronco!"

"Hear what Dr. Lezander called me?" I asked Dad once we were inside. *"Bronco!"* Getting a new christening for a day was always a highlight of church.

The sanctuary was steamy, though the wooden ceiling fans revolved. The Glass sisters were up front, playing a piano and organ duet. They were the perfect definition of the word strange. While not identical twins, the two spinster sisters were close enough to be slightly skewed mirrors. They were both long and bony, Sonia with piled-high whitish-blond hair and Katharina with piled-high blondish-white hair. They both wore thick black-framed glasses. Sonia played the piano and not the organ, while Katharina did vice versa. Depending on who you asked, the Glass sisters—who seemed to always be nagging each other but lived together on Shantuck Street in a house that looked like gingerbread—were either fifty-eight, sixty-two, or sixty-five. The strangeness was completed by their wardrobes: Sonia wore only blue in all its varying shades, while Katharina was a slave to green. Which brought about the inevitable. Sonia was referred to by us kids as Miss Blue Glass, and Katharina was called . . . you guessed it. But, strange or not, they sure could play up a storm.

The pews were packed almost solid. The place looked and felt like a hothouse where exotic hats had bloomed. Other people were trying to find seats, and one of the ushers—Mr. Horace Kaylor, who had a white mustache and a cocked left eye that gave you the creeps when you stared at it—came up the aisle to help us.

"Tom! Over here! For God's sake, are you blind?"

In the whole wide world there was only one person who would holler like a bull moose in church.

He was standing up, waving his arms over the milling hats. I could feel my mother cringe, and my dad put his arm around her as if to steady her from falling down of shame. Granddaddy Jaybird always did something to, as Dad said when he thought I wasn't listening, "show his butt," and today would be no exception.

"We saved you seats!" my grandfather bellowed, and he caused the Glasses to falter, one to go sharp and the other flat. *"Come on before somebody steals 'em!"*

Grand Austin and Nana Alice were in the same row, too. Grand Austin was wearing a seersucker suit that looked as if the rain had drawn it up two sizes, his wrinkled neck clenched by a starched white collar and a blue bow tie, his thin white hair slicked back and his eyes full of misery as he sat with his wooden leg stuck out straight below the pew in front of him. He was sitting beside Granddaddy Jaybird, which had compounded his agitation: the two got along like mud and biscuits. Nana Alice, however, was a vision of happiness. She was wearing a hat covered with small white flowers, her gloves white and her dress the glossy green of a sunlit sea. Her lovely oval face was radiant; she was sitting beside Grandmomma Sarah, and they got along like daisies in the same bouquet. Right now, though, Grandmomma Sarah was tugging at Granddaddy Jaybird's suit jacket—the same black suit he wore rain or shine, Easter or funeral—to try to get him to sit down and stop directing traffic. He was telling people in the rows to move in tighter and then he would holler, *"Room for two more over here!"*

"Sit down, Jay! Sit down!" She had to resort to pinching his bony butt, and then he scowled at her and took his seat.

My parents and I squenched in. Grand Austin said to Dad, "Good to see you, Tom," and they shook hands. "That is, if I *could* see you." His spectacles were fogged up, and he took them off and cleaned the lenses with a handkerchief. "I'd say this is the biggest crowd in a half-dozen Eas—"

"Place is packed as the whorehouse on payday, ain't it, Tom?" Granddaddy Jaybird interrupted, and Grandmomma Sarah elbowed him in the ribs so hard his false teeth clicked.

"I sure wish you'd let me finish a single sentence," Grand Austin told him, the red rising in his cheeks. "Ever since I've been sittin' here, I've yet to get a word in edgewi—"

"Boy, you're lookin' good!" Granddaddy Jaybird plowed on, and he reached across Grand Austin to slap my knee. "Rebecca, you feedin' this boy his meat, ain't you? You know, a growin' boy's got to have meat for his muscles!"

"Can't you hear?" Grand Austin asked him, the red now pulsing in his cheeks.

"Hear what?" Granddaddy Jaybird retorted.

"Turn up your hearin' aid, Jay," Grandmomma Sarah said.

"What?" he asked her.

"Hearin' aid!" she shouted, at her rope's end. *"Turn it up!"*

It was going to be an Easter to remember.

Everybody said hello to everybody, and still wet people were coming into the church as rain started to hammer on the roof. Granddaddy Jaybird, his face long and gaunt and his hair a white bristle-brush, wanted to talk to Dad about the murder, but Dad shook his head and wouldn't go into it. Grandmomma Sarah asked me if I was playing baseball this year, and I said I was. She had a fat-cheeked, kind face and pale blue eyes in nests of wrinkles, but I knew that oftentimes Granddaddy Jaybird's ways made her spit with anger.

Because of the rain, the windows were shut tight and the air was really getting muggy. The floorboards were wet, the walls leaked, and the fans groaned as they turned. The church smelled of a hundred different kinds of perfume, shaving lotion, and hair tonic, plus the sweet aromas of blossoms adorning lapels and hats. The choir filed in, wearing their purple robes. Before the first song was finished, I was sweating under my shirt. We stood up, sang a hymn, and sat down. Two overstuffed women—Mrs. Garrison and Mrs. Prathmore—came up to the front to talk about the donation fund for the poverty-stricken families of Adams Valley. Then we stood up, sang another hymn, and sat down. Both of my grandfathers had voices like bullfrogs battling in a swamp pond.

Plump, round-faced Reverend Richmond Lovoy stepped behind the pulpit and began to talk about what a glorious day it
was, with Jesus risen from the dead and all. Reverend Lovoy had
a comma of brown hair over his left eye, the sides of his hair gone
gray, and every Sunday without fail his brushed-back hair pulled
loose from its shellacked moorings and slid down over his face like
a brown flood as he preached and gestured. His wife was named
Esther, their three children Matthew, Luke, and Joni.

As Reverend Lovoy spoke, his voice competing with the thunder of heaven, I realized who was sitting directly in front of me.

The Demon.

She could read minds. That much was an accepted fact. And
just as it dawned on me that she was there, her head swiveled and
she stared at me with those black eyes that could freeze a witch
at midnight. The Demon's name was Brenda Sutley. She was ten
years old, and she had stringy red hair and a pallid face splashed
with brown freckles. Her eyebrows were as thick as caterpillars,
and the untidy arrangement of her features looked like somebody
had tried to beat out a fire on her face with the flat side of a shovel.
Her right eye looked larger than the left, her nose was a beak with
two gaping holes in it, and her thin-lipped mouth seemed to wander from one side of her face to the other. She couldn't help her
heritage, though; her mother was a fire hydrant with red hair and
a brown mustache, and her red-bearded father would've made
a fence post look brawny. With all those red kinks in her back-
ground, it was no wonder Brenda Sutley was spooky.

The Demon had earned her name because she had once
drawn a picture of her father with horns and a forked tail in art
class, and had told Mrs. Dixon, the art teacher, and her classmates that her pappy kept at the back of his closet a big stack
of magazines that showed boy demons sticking their tails in the
holes of girl demons. But the Demon did more than spill her family's closeted secrets: she had brought a dead cat to school in a
shoebox with pennies taped to its eyeballs for show-and-tell; she
had made a graveyard out of green and white Play-Doh for her

art class project, with the names of her classmates and the dates of their deaths on the headstones, which caused more than one child to go into hysterics when they realized they would not live to see sixteen; she had a fondness for bizarre practical jokes that involved dog manure pressed between sandwich bread; and it was widely rumored that she was behind the explosion of pipes in the girls' bathroom at Zephyr Elementary last November, when every toilet was clogged with notebook paper.

She was, in a word, weird.

And now her royal weirdness was staring at *me*.

A slow smile spread across her crooked mouth. I couldn't look away from those piercing black eyes, and I thought *She's got me*. The thing about adults is, when you want them to pay attention to you and intervene, their minds are worlds away; when you want them to be worlds away, they're sitting on the back of your neck. I wanted my dad or mom or anybody to tell Brenda Sutley to turn around and listen to Reverend Lovoy, but of course it was as if the Demon had willed herself to be invisible. No one could see her but me, her victim of the moment.

Her right hand rose up like the head of a small white snake with dirty fangs. Slowly, with evil grace, she extended the index finger and aimed it toward one of her gaping nose holes. The finger winnowed deep into that nostril, and I thought she was going to keep pushing it in until her whole finger was gone. Then the finger was withdrawn, and on the tip of it was a glistening green mass as big as a corn kernel.

Her black eyes were unblinking. Her mouth began to open.

No, I begged her, mind to mind. *No, please don't do it!*

The Demon slid her green-capped finger toward her wet pink tongue.

I could do nothing but stare as my stomach drew up into a hard little knot.

Green against pink. Dirty fingernail. A sticky strand, hanging down.

The Demon licked her finger, where the green thing had been.

I think I must've squirmed violently, because Dad gripped my knee and whispered, "Pay attention!" but of course he never saw the invisible Demon or her act of prickly torment. The Demon smiled at me, her black eyes sated, and then she turned her head away and the ordeal was over. Her mother lifted up a hand with hairy knuckles and stroked the Demon's fiery locks as if she were the sweetest little girl who ever drew God's breath.

Reverend Lovoy asked everyone to pray. I lowered my head and squeezed my eyes shut.

And about five seconds into the prayer, something thumped hard against the back of my skull.

I looked around.

Horror choked me. Sitting directly behind me, their pewter-colored eyes the hue of sharpened blades, were Gotha and Gordo Branlin. On either side of them, their parents were deep in prayer. I imagined they prayed for deliverance from their brood. Both Branlin boys wore dark blue suits, white shirts, and their ties were similar except Gotha's had black stripes on white and Gordo's had red. Gotha, the oldest by one year, had the whitest hair; Gordo's was a little on the yellow side. Their faces looked like mean carvings in brown rock, and even their bones—lower jaws jutting forward, cheekbones about to tear through flesh, foreheads like slabs of granite—suggested coiled rage. In the fleeting seconds that I dared to look upon those cunning visages, Gordo thrust an upraised middle finger in my face and Gotha loaded a straw with another hard black-eyed pea.

"Cory, turn around!" my mother whispered, and she tugged at me. "Close your eyes and pray!"

I did. The second pea bounced off the back of my head. Those things could sting the whine out of you. All during the rest of that prayer, I could hear the Branlins back there, whispering and giggling like evil trolls. My head was their target for the day.

After the prayer was over, we sang another hymn. Announcements were made, and visitors welcomed. The offering plate was passed around. I put in the dollar Dad had given me for this purpose. The choir sang, with the Glasses playing piano and organ. Behind me, the Branlins giggled. Then Reverend Lovoy stood up again to deliver his Easter sermon, and that was when the wasp landed on my hand.

My hand was resting on my knee. I didn't move it, even as fear shot up my spine like a lightning bolt. The wasp wedged itself between my first and second fingers and sat there, its blue-black stinger twitching.

Now let me say a few things about wasps.

They are not like bees. Bees are fat and happy and they float around from flower to flower without a care for human flesh. Yellowjackets are curious and have mood swings, but they, too, are usually predictable and can be avoided. A wasp, however, particularly the dark, slim kind of wasp that looks like a dagger with a head on it, was born to plunge that stinger into mortal epidermis and draw forth a scream like a connoisseur uncorking a vintage wine. Brushing your head against a wasps' nest can result in a sensation akin to, as I have heard, being peppered with shotgun pellets. I have seen the face of a boy who was stung on the lips and eyelids when he explored an old house in the middle of summer; such a swollen torture I wouldn't even wish on the Branlins. Wasps are insane; they have no rhyme or reason to their stingings. They would sting you to the marrow of your bones if they could drive their stingers in that deeply. They are full of rage, like the Branlins. If the devil indeed ever had a familiar, it was not a black cat or monkey or leather-skinned lizard; it was, and always will be, the wasp.

A third pea got me in the back of the head. It hurt a lot. But I stared at the wasp wedged between my first and second fingers, my heart beating hard, my skin crawling. Something flew past my face, and I looked up to watch a second wasp circle the Demon's head and land on her crown. The Demon must've felt a tickle. She reached back and flicked the wasp off without knowing what she was flicking, and the wasp rose up with an angry whir of black wings. I thought sure the Demon was about to be stung, but the wasp must've sensed its brethren because it flew on up to the ceiling.

Reverend Lovoy was really preaching now, about crucified Jesus and weeping Mary and the stone that had been rolled away.

I looked up at the church's ceiling.

Near one of the revolving fans was a small hole, no bigger than a quarter. As I watched, three wasps emerged from it and descended down into the congregation. A few seconds later, two more came out and swirled in the muggy, saccharine air.

Thunder boomed over the church. The noise of the rain almost drowned out Reverend Lovoy's rising and falling voice. What he was saying I didn't know; I looked at the wasp between my fingers again, then back to the hole in the ceiling.

More were coming out, spiraling down into the steamy, closed-up, rain-damp church. I counted them. Eight . . . nine . . . ten . . . eleven. Some of them clung to the fan's slow blades and rode them like a merry-go-round. Fourteen . . . fifteen . . . sixteen . . . seventeen. A dark, twitching fist of wasps pushed through the hole. Twenty . . . twenty-one . . . twenty-two. I stopped counting at twenty-five.

There must be a nest of them up there in the attic, I thought. Must be a nest the size of a football, pulsing in the damp dark. As I watched, transfixed at the sight as Mary must have been when a stranger on the road showed her his wounded side, a dozen more wasps boiled out of the hole. No one else seemed to notice; were they invisible, as the Demon had been when she picked a nose grape? The wasps spun slowly around and around the ceiling, in emulation of the fans. There were enough now to form a dark cloud, as if the outside storm had found a way in.

The wasp between my fingers was moving. I looked at it, and winced as another pea stung the back of my neck where the hair was stubbled. The wasp crawled along my index finger and stopped on the knuckle. Its stinger lay against my flesh, and I felt the tiny little jagged edge of it like a grain of broken glass.

Reverend Lovoy was in his element now, his arms gesturing and his hair starting to slide forward. Thunder crashed outside and rain beat on the roof. It sounded like Judgment Day out there, time to hew some wood and call the animals together two by two. All but the wasps, I thought; this time around we could fix Noah's mistake. I kept watching that hole in the ceiling with a mixture of fascination and dread. It occurred to me that Satan had found a way to slip into the Easter service, and there he was circling above our heads, looking for flesh.

Two things happened at once.

Reverend Lovoy lifted his hands and said, in his loud preacher's cadence, "And on that *glorious* mornin' after the *darkest* day the angels came down and *gakkkk!*" He had raised his hands to the angels, and suddenly he found them crawling with little wings.

My mom put her hand on mine, where my own wasp was, and squeezed in a loving grip.

It got her at the same instant the wasps decided Reverend Lovoy's sermon had gone on long enough.

She screamed. He screamed. It was the signal the wasps had been waiting for.

The blue-black cloud of them, over a hundred stingers strong, dropped down like a net on the heads of trapped beasts.

I heard Granddaddy Jaybird bellow, *"Shitfire!"* as he was pierced. Nana Alice let out an operatic, quavering high note. The Demon's mother wailed, wasps attacking the back of her neck. The Demon's father flailed at the air with his skinny arms. The Demon started laughing. Behind me, the Branlins croaked with pain, the peashooter forgotten. All across the church there were screams and hollers and people in Easter suits and dresses were jumping up and fighting the air as if grappling the devils of the invisible dimension. Reverend Lovoy was dancing in a paroxysm of agony, shaking his multiple-stung hands as if to disconnect them from the wrists. The whole choir was up and singing, not hymns this time but cries of pain as the wasps stung cheeks, chins, and noses. The air was full of dark, swirling currents that flew into people's faces and wound around their heads like thorny crowns. "Get out! Get out!" somebody was shouting. "Run for it!" somebody else hollered behind me. The Glasses broke, running for the exit with wasps in their hair. All at once everybody was up, and what had been a peaceful congregation barely ten seconds before was now a stampede of terror-struck cattle.

Wasps will do that to you.

"My damn leg's stuck!" Grand Austin shouted.

"Jay! Help him!" Grandmomma Sarah yelled, but Granddaddy Jaybird was already fighting his way out into the clogged, thrashing mass of people in the aisle.

Dad pulled me up. I heard an evil hum in my left ear, and the next instant I took a sting at the edge of my ear that caused the tears to jump from my eyes. *"Ow!"* I heard myself shout, though with all the screaming and hollering one little *ow* was of no consequence. Two more wasps, however, heard me. One of them got me in my right shoulder, stinging through my suit coat and shirt; the other darted at my face like an African lance and impaled my upper lip. I gave a garbled shout—*owgollywowwow*—of the kind that speaks volumes of pain but no syllable of sense, and I, too, fought the churning air. A voice squealed with laughter, and when I looked at the Demon through my watering eyes I saw her jumping up and down on the pew, her mouth split in a grin and red whelps all over her face.

"Everyone *out!*" Dr. Lezander hollered. Three wasps clung, pulsing and stinging, to his bald skull, and his gray-haired, stern-faced wife was behind him, her blue-blossomed Easter hat knocked awry and wasps crawling on her wide shoulders. She gripped her Bible in one hand and her purse with the other and swung tremendous blows at the attacking swarms, her teeth gritted with righteous anger.

People were fighting through the door, ignoring raincoats and umbrellas in their struggle to escape from torment into deluge. Coming into church, the Easter crowd had been the model of polite Christian civilization; going out, they were barbarians to the core. Women and children went down in the muddy yard, and the men tripped over them and fell face-first into rain-beaten puddles. Easter hats spun away and rolled like soggy wheels until the torrent slammed them flat.

I helped Dad pry Grand Austin's wooden leg loose from under the pew. Wasps were jabbing at my father's hands, and every time one would sting I could hear his breath hiss. Mom, Nana Alice, and Grandmomma Sarah were trying to get out into the aisle, where people were falling down and tangling up with each other. Reverend Lovoy, his fingers swollen like link sausages, was trying to shield his children's faces between himself and sobbing Esther. The choir had disintegrated, and some of them had left their empty purple robes behind. Dad and I got Grand Austin out into the aisle. Wasps were attacking the back of his neck, and his cheeks were wet. Dad brushed the wasps off, but more swarmed around us in a vengeful circle like Comanches around a wagon train. Children were crying and women were shrieking, and still the wasps darted and stung. "Out! Out!" Dr. Lezander was shouting at the door, shoving people through as they knotted up. His wife, Veronica, a husky Dutch bear, grabbed a struggling soul and all but flung the man through the doorway.

We were almost out. Grand Austin staggered, but Dad held him up. My mother was plucking the wasps out of Grandmomma Sarah's hair like living nettles. Two hot pins jabbed into the back of my neck, one a split second after the other, and the pain felt like my head was going to blow off. Then Dad took hold of my arm and pulled and the rain pounded on my skull. We all got through the door, but Dad slipped in a puddle and went down on his knees in the muck. I grasped the back of my neck and ran around in circles, crying with the pain, and after a while my feet slipped out from under me and my Easter suit met Zephyr's mud, too.

Reverend Lovoy was the last one out. He slammed the church door shut and stood with his back against it, as if to contain the evil within.

Thunder boomed and rolled. The rain came down like hammers and nails, beating us all senseless. Some people sat in the mud; others wandered around, dazed; others just stood there letting the rain pour over them to help cool the hot suffering.

I was hurting, too. And I imagined, in my delirium of pain, that behind the church's closed door the wasps were rejoicing. After all, it was Easter for them, too. They had risen from the dead of winter, the season that dries up wasps' nests and mummifies their sleeping infants. They had rolled away their own stone and emerged reborn into a new spring, and they had delivered to us a stinging sermon on the tenacity of life that would stay with us far longer than anything Reverend Lovoy could have said. We had, all of us, experienced the thorns and nails in a most personal way.

Someone bent down beside me. I felt cool mud being pressed against the stings on the back of my neck. I looked into Granddaddy Jaybird's rain-soaked face, his hair standing up as if he'd been electric-shocked.

"You all right, boy?" he asked me.

He had turned his back on the rest of us and fled for his own skin. He had been a coward and a Judas, and there was no satisfaction in his offering of mud.

I didn't answer him. I looked right through him. He said, "You'll be all right," and he stood up and went to see about Grandmomma Sarah, who huddled with Mom and Nana Alice. He looked to me like a half-drowned, scrawny rat.

I might've punched him if I'd been my father's size. I couldn't help but be ashamed of him, a deep, stinging shame. And I couldn't help but wonder, as well, if some of Granddaddy Jaybird's cowardice might be inside *me,* too. I didn't know it then, but I was going to find out real soon.

Somewhere across Zephyr the bells of another church rang, the sound coming to us through the rain as if heard in a dream. I stood up, my lower lip and shoulder and the back of my neck throbbing. The thing about pain is, it teaches you humility. Even the Branlins were blubbering like babies. I never saw anybody act cocky after they got a hide full of stingers, have you?

The Easter bells rang across the watery town.

Church was over.

Hallelujah.

5

The Death of a Bike

THE RAIN KEPT FALLING.

Gray clouds hung over Zephyr, and from their swollen bellies came the deluge. I went to sleep with rain slamming the roof, and I awoke to the crash of thunder. Rebel shivered and moaned in his doghouse. I knew how he felt. My wasp stings had diminished to red welts, but for day upon day no ray of sunshine fell upon my hometown; only the incessant rain came down, and when I wasn't doing homework I sat in my room rereading old *Famous Monsters* magazines and my stock of comic books.

The house got that rainy smell in it, an odor of damp boards and wet dirt wafting up from the basement. The downpour caused the cancellation of the Saturday matinee at the Lyric, because the theater's roof had sprung leaks. The very air itself felt slick, like green mold growing on damp stones. At the dinner table a week after Easter, Dad put down his knife and fork and looked at the steamy wet windows and said, "We're gonna have to grow gills if this keeps up."

It did keep up. The air was heavy with water, the clouds cutting all light to a dim, swampy murk. Yards became ponds, and the streets turned into streams. School started letting out early, so everyone could get home, and on Wednesday afternoon at seventeen minutes before three o'clock my old bike gave up the ghost.

One second I was trying to pedal through a torrent on Deerman Street. The next second my bike's front wheel sank into a crater where the pavement had broken and the shock thrummed through the rust-eaten frame. Several things happened at once: the handlebars collapsed, the front wheel's spokes snapped, the seat broke, the frame gave way at its tired old seams, and suddenly I was lying on my belly in water that flooded into my yellow rain slicker. I lay there, stunned, trying to figure out how the earth had knocked me down. Then I sat up, wiped the water out of my eyes, and looked at my bike, and just like that I knew it was dead.

My bike, old in the ways of a boy's life long before it had reached my hands by merit of a flea market, was no longer a living thing. I felt it, as I sat there in the pouring rain. Whatever it is that gives a soul to an object made by the tools of man, it had cracked open and flown to the watery heavens. The frame had bent and snapped, the handlebars hanging by a single screw, the seat turned around like a head on a broken neck. The chain was off its sprockets, the front tire warped from its rim, and the snapped spokes sticking up. I almost cried at the sight of such carnage, but even though my heart hurt, I knew crying wouldn't help. My bike had simply worn out; it had come to the end of its days, pure and simple. I was not its first owner, and maybe that made a difference, too. Maybe a bike, once discarded, pines away year after year for the first hand that steered it, and as it grows old it dreams, in its bike way, of the young roads. It was never really mine, then; it traveled with me, but its pedals and handlebars held the memory of another master. Maybe, on that rainy Wednesday, it killed itself because it knew I yearned for a bike built for me and me alone. Maybe. All I knew for sure at that moment was that I had to walk the rest of the way home, and I couldn't drag the carcass with me.

I pulled it up onto somebody's yard and left it under a dripping oak tree, and I went on with my drenched knapsack on my back and my shoes squeaking with water.

When my father, who was home from the dairy, found out about the bike, he packed me into the pickup truck, and off we went to fetch the carcass on Deerman Street. "It can be fixed," he told me as the wipers slogged back and forth across the windshield. "We'll get somebody to weld it together or somethin'. That'll be cheaper than a new bike, for sure."

"Okay," I answered, but I knew the bike was dead. No amount of welding was going to revive it. "The front wheel was messed up, too," I added, but Dad was concentrating on his driving.

We reached the place where I'd pulled the carcass up under the oak tree. "Where is it?" Dad asked. "Was this the place?"

It was, though the carcass was gone. Dad stopped the truck, got out, and knocked on the front door of the house we sat before. I saw the door open, and a white-haired woman peered out. She and Dad talked for a minute or so, and I saw the woman point toward the street. Then my dad came back, his cap dripping water and his shoulders hunched in his wet milkman's jacket. He slid behind the wheel, closed the door, and said, "Well, she walked out to get her mail, she saw the bike lyin' there under her tree, and she called Mr. Sculley to come pick it up." Mr. Emmett Sculley was Zephyr's junkman, and he drove around in a bright green truck with SCULLEY'S ANTIQUES and a telephone number painted on the sides in red. My dad started the engine and looked at me. I knew that look; it was hard and angry, and I could read a grim future in it. "Why didn't you go to that woman's door and tell her you were gonna come back for your bike? Didn't you think of that?"

"No, sir," I had to admit. "I didn't."

Well, my dad pulled the truck away from the curb and we started off again. Not toward home, but heading west. I knew where we were going. Mr. Sculley's junk shop lay to the west, past the wooded edge of town. On the way, I had to endure my father's tale, the one that began like this: "When I was your age, I had to walk if I wanted to get somewhere. I wish I'd had a bike back then, even a *used* one. Heck, if my buddies and me had to walk two or three miles, we didn't think a thing about it. And we were healthier for it, too. Sun, wind, or rain, it didn't matter. We got where we were going on our own two le—" And so on, you know the kind of speech I mean, the generational paean of childhood.

We left the town limits behind us, and the glistening road wound through the wet green forest. The rain was still coming down, pieces of fog snagged on the treetops and drifting across the road. Dad had to drive slowly because the road around here was dangerous even when the pavement was dry. My dad was still going on about the dubious joys of not having a bike, which I was beginning to realize was his way of telling me I'd better get used to walking if my old ride was unfixable. Thunder boomed off beyond the hazy hills, the road deserted before us as it curved beneath the tires like a wild horse fights a saddle. I don't know why I chose that moment to turn my head and look back, but I did.

And I saw the car that was coming up fast behind us.

The hair on the back of my neck stood up, and the skin beneath it tingled like the scurrying of ants. The car was a black, low-slung, mean-looking panther with gleaming chrome teeth, and it rocketed around the long curve my father had just negotiated with an uneasy alliance of brake and accelerator. The pickup truck's engine was sputtery, but I could hear no sound from the black car that closed on us. I could see a shape and a pale face behind the wheel. I could see red and orange flames painted on the slope of the ebony hood, and then the car was on our tail and showed no sign of slowing or swerving and I looked at my father and shouted, *"Dad!"*

He jumped in his seat and jerked the wheel. The truck's tires slewed to the left, over the faded centerline, and my father fought to keep us from going into the woods. Then the tires got a grip again, the truck straightened out, and Dad had fire in his eyes when he swung his face in my direction. "Are you crazy?" he snapped. "You want to get us killed?"

I looked back.

The black car was gone.

It hadn't passed us. It hadn't turned off anywhere. It was just gone.

"I saw . . . I saw . . ."

"Saw *what? Where?*" he demanded.

"I . . . thought I saw . . . a car," I told him. "It was . . . about to hit us, I thought."

He peered into the rearview mirror. Of course he saw only the same rain and empty road I was seeing. He reached out, put his hand against my forehead, and said, "You feelin' all right?"

"Yes sir." I didn't have a fever. Of that, at least, I was certain. My father, satisfied that I was not building up heat, pulled his hand away and refastened it to the steering wheel. "Just sit still," he said, and I obeyed him. He fixed his attention on the tricky road again, but his jaw muscle clenched every few seconds and I figured he was trying to decide whether I needed to go see Dr. Parrish or get my butt busted.

I didn't say anything more about the black car, because I knew Dad wouldn't believe me. But I had seen that car before, on the streets of Zephyr. It had announced itself with a rumble and growl as it roamed the streets, and when it had passed you could smell the heat and see the pavement shimmer. "Fastest car in town," Davy Ray had told me as he and I and the other guys had lounged around in front of the ice house on Merchants Street, catching cool breezes from the ice blocks on a sultry August day. "My dad," Davy Ray had confided, "says nobody can outrace Midnight Mona."

Midnight Mona. That was the car's name. The guy who owned it was named Stevie Cauley. "Little Stevie," he was called, because he stood only a few inches over five feet tall though he was twenty years old. He chain-smoked Chesterfield cigarettes, and maybe those had stunted his growth.

But the reason I didn't tell my dad about Midnight Mona streaking up behind us on that rain-slick road was that I remembered what had happened on a night last October. My dad, who used to be a volunteer fireman, got a telephone call. It was Chief Marchette, he'd told Mom. A car had wrecked on Route Sixteen, and it was on fire in the woods. My dad had hurried out to help, and he'd come home a couple of hours later with ashes in his hair and his clothes smelling of burnt timber. After that night, and what he'd seen, he hadn't wanted to be a fireman anymore.

We were on Route Sixteen right now. And the car that had wrecked and burned was Midnight Mona, with Little Stevie Cauley behind the wheel.

Little Stevie Cauley's body—what was left of it, I mean—lay in a coffin in the cemetery on Poulter Hill. Midnight Mona was gone, too, to wherever burned-up cars go.

But I had seen it, racing up behind us out of the mist. I had seen someone sitting behind the wheel.

I kept my mouth shut. I was in enough trouble already.

Dad turned off Route Sixteen and eased the truck onto a muddy side road that wound through the woods. We reached a place where rusted old metal signs of all descriptions had been nailed to the trees; there were at least a hundred of them, advertisements for everything from Green Spot Orange Soda to B.C. Headache Powders to the Grand Ole Opry. Beyond the signpost forest the road led to a house of gray wood with a sagging front porch and in the front yard—and here I mean "sea of weeds" instead of yard as ordinary people might know it—a motley collection of rust-eaten clothes wringers, kitchen stoves, lamps, bedframes, electric fans, iceboxes, and other smaller appliances was lying about in untidy piles. There were coils of wire as tall as my father and bushel baskets full of bottles, and amid the junk stood the metal sign of a smiling policeman with the red letters STOP DON'T STEAL painted across his chest. In his head there were three bullet holes.

I don't think stealing was a problem for Mr. Sculley, because as soon as my dad stopped the truck and opened his door two red hound dogs jumped up from their bellies on the porch and began baying to beat the band. A few seconds later, the screen door banged open and a frail-looking little woman with a white braid and a rifle came out of the house.

"Who is it?" she hollered in a voice like a lumberjack's. "Whadda ye want?"

My father lifted his hands. "It's Tom Mackenson, Mrs. Sculley. From Zephyr."

"Tom *who?*"

"Mackenson!" He had to shout over the hound dogs. "From Zephyr!"

Mrs. Sculley roared, *"Shaddup!"* and she plucked a fly swatter from a hook on the porch and swung a few times at the dogs' rumps, which quieted them down considerably.

I got out of the truck and stood close to my dad, our shoes mired in the boggy weeds. "I need to see your husband, Mrs. Sculley," Dad told her. "He picked up my boy's bike by mistake."

"Uh-uh," she replied. "Emmett don't make no mistakes."

"Is he around, please?"

"Back of the house," she said, and she motioned with the rifle. "One of them sheds back there."

"Thank you." He started off and I followed him, and we'd taken maybe a half-dozen steps when Mrs. Sculley said, "Hey! You trip over somethin' and break your legs, we ain't liable for it, hear?"

If what lay in front of the house was a mess, what lay behind it was nightmarish. The two "sheds" were corrugated metal buildings the size of tobacco warehouses. To get to them, you had to follow a rutted trail that meandered between mountains of castaway things: record players, broken statuary, garden hose, chairs, lawn mowers, doors, fireplace mantels, pots and pans, old bricks, roof shingles, irons, radiators, and washbasins to name a few. "Have mercy," Dad said, mostly to himself, as we walked through the valley between the looming hills. The rain spilled and spattered over all these items, in some places running down from the metallic mountaintops in gurgling little streams. And then we came to a big twisted and tangled heap of things that made me stop in my tracks because I knew I had found a truly mystical place.

Before me were hundreds of bicycle frames, locked together with vines of rust, their tires gone, their backs broken.

They say that somewhere in Africa the elephants have a secret grave where they go to lie down, unburden their wrinkled gray bodies, and soar away, light spirits at the end. I believed at that moment in time that I had found the grave of the bicycles, where the carcasses flake away year after year under rain and baking sun, long after the spirits of their wandering lives have gone. In some places on that huge pile the bicycles had melted away until they resembled nothing more than red and copper leaves waiting to be burned on an autumn afternoon. In some places shattered headlights poked up, sightless but defiant, in a dead way. Warped handlebars still held rubber grips, and from some of the grips dangled strips of colored vinyl like faded flames. I had a vision of all these bikes, vibrant in their new paint, with new tires and new pedals and chains that snuggled up to their sprockets in beds of clean new grease. It made me sad, in a way I couldn't understand, because I saw how there is an end to all things, no matter how much we want to hold on to them.

"Howdy, there!" somebody said. "Thought I heard the alarms go off."

My dad and I looked at a man who pushed a large hand-cart before him through the muck. He wore overalls and muddy boots, and he had a big belly and a liver-spotted head with a tuft of white at its peak. Mr. Sculley had a wrinkled face and a bulbous nose with small broken veins showing purple at its tip, and he wore round-lensed glasses over gray eyes. He was grinning a square grin, his teeth dark brown, and on his grizzled chin was a mole that had sprouted three white hairs. "What can I do for you?"

"I'm Tom Mackenson," my dad said, and offered his hand. "Jay's son."

"Oh, yeah! Sorry I didn't recognize you right off!" Mr. Sculley wore dirty canvas gloves, and he took one of them off to shake my father's hand. "This Jay's grandson?"

"Yep. Cory's his name."

"Seen you around, I believe," Mr. Sculley said to me. "I remember when your daddy was your age. Me and your grandpa go back a piece."

"Mr. Sculley, I believe you picked up a bike this afternoon," Dad told him. "In front of a house on Deerman Street?"

"Sure did. Wasn't much to it, though. All busted up."

"Well, it was Cory's bike. I think I can get it fixed, if we can have it back."

"Oops," Mr. Sculley said. His square grin faltered. "Tom, I don't think I can do that."

"Why not? It *is* here, isn't it?"

"Yeah, it's here. *Was* here, I mean." Mr. Sculley motioned toward one of the sheds. "I took it in there just a few minutes ago."

"So we can get it and take it back, can't we?"

Mr. Sculley sucked on his lower lip, looked at me, and then back to Dad. "I don't believe so, Tom." He pushed the handcart aside, next to the mound of dead bikes, and he said, "Come on and have a look." We followed him. He walked with a limp, as if his hip worked on a hinge instead of a ball-and-socket.

"See, here's the story," he said. "Been meanin' to get rid of those old bikes for over a year. Tryin' to clean the place up, ya see. Got to make room for more stuff comin' in. So I said to Belle— that's my wife—I said, 'Belle, when I pick up one more bike I'm gonna do it. Just one more.'" He led us into an open doorway, into the building's cool interior. Lightbulbs hanging on cords threw shadows between more mounds of junk. Here and there larger things rose up from the gloom like Martian machines and presented a glimpse of mysterious curves and edges. Something squeaked and skittered; whether mice or bats, I don't know. The place sure looked like a cavern, where Injun Joe would feel right at home.

"Watch your step here," Mr. Sculley cautioned us as we went through another doorway. Then he stopped beside a big rectangular machine with gears and levers on it and he said, "This here crusher just ate your bike about fifteen minutes ago. It was the first one in." He prodded a barrel full of twisted and crumpled metal pieces. Other barrels were waiting to be filled. "See, I can sell this as scrap metal. I was waitin' for one more bike to start breakin' 'em up, and yours was the one." He looked at me, the overhead bulb shining on his rain-wet dome, and his eyes were not unkind. "Sorry, Cory. If I'd known anybody was gonna come claim it, I'd have held on to it, but it was dead."

"*Dead?*" my father asked.

"Sure. Everythin' dies. It wears out and can't be fixed for love nor money. That's how the bike was. That's how they all are by the time somebody brings 'em here, or somebody calls me to come pick 'em up. You know your bike was dead long before I put it in that crusher, don't you, Cory?"

"Yes sir," I said. "I do."

"It didn't suffer none," Mr. Sculley told me, and I nodded.

It seemed to me that Mr. Sculley understood the very nucleus of existence, that he had kept his young eyes and young heart even though his body had grown old. He saw straight through to the cosmic order of things, and he knew that life is not held only in flesh and bone, but also in those objects—a good, faithful pair of shoes; a reliable car; a pen that always works; a bike that has taken you many a mile—into which we put our trust and which give us back the security and joy of memories.

Here the ancient hearts of stone may chortle and say, "That's *ridiculous!*" But let me ask a question of them: don't you ever wish—even for just a fleeting moment—that you could have your first bike again? You remember what it looked like. You remember. Did you name it Trigger, or Buttermilk, or Flicka, or Lightning? Who took that bike away, and where did it go? Don't you ever, ever wonder?

"Like to show you somethin', Cory," Mr. Sculley said, and he touched my shoulder. "This way."

My dad and I both followed him, away from the bike-crushing machine into another chamber. A window with dirty glass let in a little greenish light to add to the overhead bulb's glare. In this room was Mr. Sculley's desk and a filing cabinet. He opened a closet and reached up onto a high shelf. "I don't show this to just anybody," he told us, "but I figure you fellas might like to see it." He rummaged around, moving boxes, and then he said, "Found it," and his hand emerged from dark into light again.

He was holding a chunk of wood, its bark bleached and dried mollusks still gripping its surface. What looked like a slim ivory dagger, about five inches long, had been driven into the wood. Mr. Sculley held it up to the light, his eyes sparkling behind his glasses. "See it? What do you make of it?"

"No idea," Dad said. I shook my head, too.

"Look close." He held the wood chunk with its embedded ivory dagger in front of my face. I could see pits and scars on the ivory's surface, and its edges were serrated like a fishing knife.

"It's a tooth," Mr. Sculley said. "Or a fang, most likely."

"A *fang?*" Dad frowned, his gaze jumping back and forth between Mr. Sculley and the wood chunk. "Must've been a mighty big snake!"

"No snake, Tom. I cut this piece out of a log I found washed up along the river when I was huntin' bottles three summers ago. See the shells? It must be from an old tree, probably laid on the bottom for quite a while. I figure that last flood we had pulled it up from the mud." He gingerly ran a gloved finger along the serrated edge. "I do believe I've got the only evidence there is."

"You don't mean . . ." Dad began, but I already knew.

"Yep. This here's a fang from the mouth of Old Moses." He held it in front of me once more, but I drew back.

"Maybe his eyesight ain't so good anymore," Mr. Sculley

mused. "Maybe he went after that log thinkin' it was a big turtle. Maybe he was just mean that day, and he snapped at everythin' his snout bumped up against." His finger tapped the fang's broken rim. "Hate to think what this thing could do to a human bein'. Wouldn't be pretty, would it?"

"Can I see that?" Dad asked, and Mr. Sculley let him hold it. Mr. Sculley went to the window and peered out as Dad examined what he held, and after another moment Dad said, "I swear, I believe you're right! It *is* a tooth!"

"Said it was," Mr. Sculley reminded him. "I don't lie."

"You need to show this to somebody! Sheriff Amory or Mayor Swope! Heck, the *governor* needs to see it!"

"Swope's already seen it," Mr. Sculley said. "He's the one advised me to put it in my closet and keep the door shut."

"Why? Somethin' like this is front-page news!"

"Not accordin' to Mayor Swope." He turned away from the window, and I saw that his eyes had darkened. "At first Swope thought it was a fake. He had Doc Parrish look at it, and Doc Parrish called Doc Lezander. Both of them agreed it's a fang from some kind of reptile. Then we all had a sit-down talk in the mayor's office, with the doors closed. Swope said he'd decided to put a lid on the whole thing. Said it might be a fang or it might be a fraud, but it wasn't worth gettin' folks upset over." He took the pierced wood chunk back from my father's hands. "I said, 'Luther Swope, don't you think people would want to see real evidence that there's a monster in the Tecumseh River?' And he looked at me with that damn pipe in his mouth and he says, 'People already know it. Evidence would just scare 'em. Anyway,' Swope says, 'if there's a monster in the river, it's *our* monster, and we don't want to share it with nobody.' And that's how it ended up." Mr. Sculley offered it to me. "Want to touch it, Cory? Just so you can say you did?"

I did, with a tentative index finger. The fang was cool, as I imagined the muddy bottom of the river must be.

Mr. Sculley put the piece of wood and the fang back up on the closet shelf, and he closed the door. The rain was coming down hard again outside, banging on the metal roof. "All this water pourin' down," Mr. Sculley said, "must make Old Moses mighty happy."

"I still think you ought to show somebody else," Dad told him. "Like somebody from the newspaper in Birmingham."

"I would, Tom, but maybe Swope's got a point. Maybe Old Moses *is* our monster. Maybe if we let everybody else know about him, they'd come try to take him away from us. Catch him up in a net, put him in a big glass tank somewhere like an overgrown mudcat." Mr. Sculley frowned and shook his head. "Nah, I wouldn't want that to happen. Neither would the Lady, I reckon. She's been feedin' him on Good Friday for as long as I can remember. This was the first year he didn't like his food."

"Didn't like his food?" Dad asked. "Meanin' what?"

"Didn't you see the parade this year?" Mr. Sculley waited for Dad to say no, and then he went on. "This was the first year Old Moses didn't give the bridge a smack with his tail, same to say 'Thanks for the grub.' It's a quick thing, it passes fast, but you get to know the sound of it when you've heard it so many years. This year it didn't happen."

I recalled how troubled the Lady looked when she left the gargoyle bridge that day, and how the whole procession had been so somber on the march back to Bruton. That must have been because the Lady hadn't heard Old Moses smack the bridge with his tail. But what did such a lack of table manners mean?

"Hard to say what it means," Mr. Sculley said as if reading my mind. "The Lady didn't like it, that's for sure."

It was starting to get dark outside. Dad said we'd better be getting home, and he thanked Mr. Sculley for taking the time to show us where the bike had gone. "Wasn't your fault," Dad said as Mr. Sculley limped in front of us to show us the way out. "You were just doin' your job."

"Yep. Waitin' for one more bike, I was. Like I said, that bike couldn't have been fixed anyhow."

I could've told my dad that. In fact, I did tell him, but one sorry thing about being a kid is that grown-ups listen to you with half an ear.

"Heard about the car in the lake," Mr. Sculley said as we neared the doorway. His voice echoed in the cavernous room, and I sensed my father tightening up. "Bad way for a man to die, without a Christian burial," Mr. Sculley continued. "Sheriff Amory got any clues?"

"None that I know of." My father's voice was a little shaky. I was sure that he saw that sinking car and the body handcuffed to the wheel every time he lay down in bed and closed his eyes.

"Got my own ideas about who it was, and who killed him," Mr. Sculley offered. We reached the way out, but the rain was still falling hard onto the mountains of old dead things and the last of the sunlight had turned green. Mr. Sculley looked at my father and leaned against the door frame. "It was somebody who'd crossed the Blaylock clan. Must've been a fella who wasn't from around here, 'cause everybody else in their right mind knows Wade, Bodean, and Donny Blaylock are meaner'n horny rattlers. They got stills hidden all up in the woods around here. And that daddy of theirs, Biggun, could teach the devil some tricks. Yessir, the Blaylocks are the cause of that fella bein' down at the bottom of the lake, and you can count on it."

"I figure the sheriff thought of that already."

"Probably did. Only trouble is, nobody knows where the Blaylocks hide out. They show up now and again, on some errand of meanness, but trackin' 'em to their snake hole is another thing entirely." Mr. Sculley looked out the door. "Rain's easin' up some. Reckon you don't mind gettin' wet."

We trudged through the mud toward my dad's truck. I looked again at the mound of bikes as we passed, and I saw something I hadn't noticed before: honeysuckle vines were growing in the midst of the tangled metal, and the little sweet white cups were sprouting amid the rust.

My father's attention was snagged by something else that lay over beyond the bikes, something we had not seen on the way in. He stopped, staring at it, and I stopped, too, and Mr. Sculley, limping ahead, sensed our stopping and turned around.

"I wondered where they brought it," Dad said.

"Yeah, gonna haul it off one of these days. Gotta make room for more stuff, y'know."

You couldn't tell much about it, really. It was just a rusted mass of crumpled metal, but some of the metal still held the original black paint. The windshield was gone, the roof smashed flat. Part of the hood remained, though, and on it was a ripple of painted flames.

This one had suffered.

Dad turned away from it, and I followed him to the pickup. Real close, I might add.

"Come back anytime!" Mr. Sculley told us. The hound dogs bayed and Mrs. Sculley came out on the porch, this time without her rifle, and Dad and I drove home along the haunted road.

6

Old Moses Comes to Call

MOM HAD PICKED UP the phone when it rang, past ten o'clock at night about a week after our visit to Mr. Sculley's place.

"Tom!" she said, and her voice carried a frantic edge. "J.T. says the dam's burst at Lake Holman! They're callin' everybody together at the courthouse!"

"Oh, Lord!" Dad sprang up from the sofa, where he'd been watching the news on television, and he slid his feet into his shoes. "It'll be a flood for sure! Cory!" he called. "Get your clothes on!"

I knew from his tone that I'd better move quick. I put aside the story I was trying to write about a black dragster with a ghost at the wheel and I fairly jumped into my jeans. When your parents get scared, your heart starts pounding ninety miles a minute. I had heard Dad use the word *flood*. The last one had been when I was five, and it hadn't done a whole lot of damage except stir up the swamp snakes. I knew, though, from my reading about Zephyr that in 1938 the river had flooded the streets to the depth of four feet, and in 1930 the spring flood had risen almost to the rooftops of some of the houses in Bruton. So my town had a history of being waterlogged, and with all the rain we and the rest of the South had been getting since the beginning of April, there was no telling what might happen this year.

The Tecumseh River fed out of Lake Holman, which lay about forty miles north of us. So, being as it is that all rivers flow to the sea, we were in for it.

I made sure Rebel would be all right in his dog run behind the house, and then my mom, dad, and I jammed into the pickup truck and headed for the courthouse, an old gothic structure that stood at the terminus of Merchants Street. Most everybody's lights were on; the message network was in full operation. It was just drizzling right now, but the water was up to the pickup's wheel rims because of the overloaded drainpipes and some people's basements had already flooded. My friend Johnny Wilson and his folks had had to go live with relatives in Union Town for that very reason.

Cars and pickup trucks were filling up the courthouse's parking lot. Off in the distance, lightning streaked across the heavens and the low clouds lit up. People were being herded into the courthouse's main meeting room, a large chamber with a mural painted on the ceiling that showed angels flying around carrying bales of cotton; it was a holdover from when cotton crop auctions used to be held here, twenty years ago, before the cotton gin and warehouse were moved to floodproof Union Town. We found seats on one of the splintery bleachers, which was fortunate because the way other folks were coming in, there soon wasn't going to be room enough to breathe. Somebody had the good sense to turn on the fans, but the hot air emanating from people's mouths seemed inexhaustible. Mrs. Kattie Yarbrough, one of the biggest chatterboxes in town, squeezed in next to Mom and started jabbering excitedly while her husband, who was also a milkman at Green Meadows, trapped my father. I saw Ben come in with Mr. and Mrs. Sears, but they sat down across the room from us. The Demon, whose hair looked as if it had just been combed with grease, entered trailing her monstrous mother and spindly pop.

They found places near us, and I shuddered when the Demon caught my repulsed gaze and grinned at me. Reverend Lovoy came in with his family, Sheriff Amory and his wife and daughters entered, the Branlins came in, and so did Mr. Parlowe, Mr. Dollar, Davy Ray and his folks, Miss Blue Glass and Miss Green Glass, and plenty more people I didn't know so well. The place got jammed.

"Quiet, everybody! Quiet!" Mr. Wynn Gillie, the assistant mayor, had stepped up to the podium where the cotton auctioneer used to stand, and behind him at a table sat Mayor Luther Swope and Fire Chief Jack Marchette, who was also the head of Civil Defense. "*Quiet!*" Mr. Gillie hollered, the veins standing out on his stringy neck. The talking died down, and Mayor Swope stood up to speak. He was tall and slim, about fifty years old, and he had a long-jawed, somber face and gray hair combed back from a widow's peak. He was always puffing on a briar pipe, like a locomotive burning coal up a long, steep haul, and he wore perfectly creased trousers and shirts with his initials on the breast pocket. He had the air of a successful businessman, which he was: he owned both the Stagg Shop for Men and the Zephyr Ice House, which had been in his family for years. His wife, Lana Jean, was sitting with Dr. Curtis Parrish and the doctor's wife, Brightie.

"Guess everybody's heard the bad news by now," Mayor Swope began. He had a mayorly appearance, but he spoke as if his mouth was full of oatmeal mush. "We ain't got a whole lot of time, folks. Chief Marchette tells me the river's already at flood stage. When that water from Lake Holman gets here, we're gonna have us a real problem. Could be the worst flood we've ever had. Which means Bruton'll get swamped first, it bein' closest to the river. Vandy, where are you?" The mayor looked around, and Mr. Vandercamp Senior raised his rickety hand. "Mr. Vandercamp is openin' up the hardware store," Mayor Swope told us. "He's got shovels and sandbags we can use to start buildin' our own dam between Bruton and the river, maybe we can hold the worst of the flood back. Which means everybody's gonna have to work: men, women, and children, too. I've called Robbins Air Force Base, and they're sendin' some men to help us. Folks are comin' over from Union Town, too. So everybody who can work oughta get over to Bruton and be ready to move some dirt."

"Hold on just one damn minute, Luther!"

The man who'd spoken stood up. You couldn't miss him. I think a book about a white whale was named after him. Mr. Dick Moultry had a florid, puffed face and wore his hair in a crew cut that resembled a brown pincushion. He had on a tent-sized T-shirt and blue jeans that might've fit my dad, Chief Marchette, and Mayor Swope all at the same time. He lifted a blubbery arm and aimed his finger at the mayor. "What you're tellin' us to do, it seems to me, is to forget about our own homes! Yessir! Forget about our own homes and go to work to save a bunch of nig-gers!"

This comment was a crack in the common clay. Some hollered that Mr. Moultry was wrong, and some hollered he was right.

"Dick," Mayor Swope said as he pushed his pipe into his mouth, "you know that if the river's going to flood, it always starts in Bruton. That's the lowland. If we can hold it back there, we can—"

"So where are the Bruton people?" Mr. Moultry asked, and his big square head ratcheted to right and left. "I don't see no dark faces in here! Where are they? How come they ain't in here beggin' us for help?"

"Because they *never* ask for help." The mayor spouted a plume of blue smoke; the locomotive's engine was starting to stoke. "I guarantee you they're out on the riverbank right now, tryin' to build a dam, but they wouldn't ask for help if the water came up to their roofs. The Lady wouldn't stand for it. But they do need our help, Dick. Just like last time."

"If they had any sense, they'd move out of there!" Mr. Moul-try insisted. "Hell, I'm sick and tired of that damn Lady, too! Who does she think she is, a damn *queen?*"

"Sit down, Dick," Chief Marchette told him. The fire chief

was a big-boned man with a chiseled face and piercing blue eyes. "There's no time to argue this thing."

"The hell you say!" Mr. Moultry had decided to be stubborn. His face was getting as red as a fireplug. "Let the Lady come over here to white man's land and *ask* us for help!" That brought a storm of assenting and dissenting shouts. Mr. Moultry's wife, Feather, stood up beside him and hollered, "Hell, yes!" She had platinum-blond hair and was more anvil than feather. Mr. Moultry bellowed over the noise, "I ain't breakin' my ass for no niggers!"

"But, Dick," Mayor Swope said in a bewildered way, "they're *our* niggers."

The shouting and hollering went on, some people saying it was the Christian thing to keep Bruton from being flooded and others saying they hoped the flood was a jimdandy so it would wash Bruton away once and for all. My folks kept quiet, as most of the others did; this was a war of the loudmouths.

Suddenly a quiet began to spread. It began from the back of the chamber, where people were clustered around the doorway. Somebody laughed, but the laugh was choked off almost at once. A few people mumbled and muttered. And then a man made his way into the chamber and you'd have thought the Red Sea was parting as folks shrank back to give him room.

The man was smiling. He had a boyish face and light brown hair cresting a high forehead.

"What's all this yelling about?" he asked. He had a Southern accent, but you could tell he was an educated man. "Any problem here, Mayor Swope?"

"Uh . . . no, Vernon. No problem. Is there, Dick?"

Mr. Moultry looked like he was about to spit and scowl. His wife's face was red as a Christmas beet under her platinum locks. I heard the Branlins giggle, but somebody hushed them up.

"I hope there's no problem," Vernon said, still smiling. "You know how Daddy hates problems."

"Sit *down,*" Mayor Swope told the Moultrys, and they did. Their asses almost busted the bleacher.

"I sense some . . . disunity here," Vernon said. I felt a giggle about to break from my throat, but my father grasped my wrist and squeezed so hard it went away. Other people shifted uneasily in their seats, especially some of the older widow women. "Mayor Swope, can I come up to the podium?"

"God save us," my father whispered, and Mom shivered with a silent laugh beating at her ribs.

"Uh . . . I . . . suppose so, Vernon. Sure. Come on up." Mayor Swope stepped back, pipe smoke swirling around his head.

Vernon Thaxter stepped up to the podium and faced the assembly. He was very pale under the lights. All of him was pale.

He was stark naked. Not a stitch on him.

His doodad and balls hung out in full view. He was a skinny thing, probably because he walked so much. The soles of his feet must've been as hard as dried leather. Rain glistened on his white flesh and his hair was slick with it. He looked like a picture of a dark Hindu mystic I'd seen in one of my *National Geographic*s, though, of course, he was neither dark nor Hindu. I'd have to say he was no mystic, either. Vernon Thaxter was downright, around-the-bend-and-through-the-woods crazy.

Of course, walking around town in his birthday suit was nothing new for Vernon Thaxter. He did it all the time, once the weather started warming up. You didn't see him very much in late autumn or winter, though. When he first appeared in spring, it was always a start; by July nobody gave him a second glance; by October the falling leaves were more interesting. Then it came spring again, and there was Vernon Thaxter with his private parts on public display.

You might wonder why Sheriff Amory didn't stand up right then and there and haul Vernon off to jail for indecent exposure. The reason he did not was because of Moorwood Thaxter, Vernon's father. Moorwood Thaxter owned the bank. He also owned Green Meadows Dairy and the Zephyr Real Estate Company. Just about every house in Zephyr was mortgaged through Moorwood Thaxter's bank. He owned the land the Lyric theater stood on, and the land where this courthouse had been built. He owned every crack in Merchants Street. He owned the shotgun shacks of Bruton, and his own twenty-eight-room mansion at the height of Temple Street. The fear of Moorwood Thaxter, who was in his seventies and rarely seen, was what kept Sheriff Amory in his seat and had kept forty-year-old Vernon naked on the streets of my hometown. It had been this way as long as I remembered.

Mom told me that Vernon used to be all right, but he'd written a book and gone to New York with it and a year later he was back home wandering around nude and nutty.

"Gentlemen and ladies," Vernon began. "And children, too, of course." He reached out his frail arms and grasped the podium's edges. "We have here a very serious situation."

"Momma!" the Demon suddenly squalled. "I can see that feller's dingdo—"

A hand with hairy knuckles clamped over her mouth. I guess the elder Thaxter owned their house, too.

"A very serious situation," Vernon repeated, oblivious to everything but his own voice. "Daddy sent me here with a message. He says he expects the people of this town to show true brotherhood and Christian values in this time of trouble. Mr. Vandercamp Senior, sir?"

"Yes, Vernon?" the old man answered.

"Will you kindly keep a record of the names of those ablebodied and good-thinking men who borrow digging utensils from you for the purpose of helping the residents of Bruton? My daddy would appreciate it."

"Be glad to," Mr. Vandercamp Senior said; he was rich, but not rich enough to say no to Moorwood Thaxter.

"Thank you. That way my daddy can have a list at hand when interest rates go up, as they are bound to do in this unsettled age. My daddy has always felt that those men—and women—who aren't loath to work for their neighbors are deserving of extra considerations." He smiled, gazing out at his audience. "Anyone else have anything to say?"

No one did. It's kind of difficult to talk to a naked man about anything but why he won't wear clothes, and nobody would dare bring up such a sensitive subject.

"I think our mission is clear, then," Vernon said. "Good luck to all." He thanked Mayor Swope for letting him speak, and then he stepped down from the podium and walked out of the chamber the way he'd come. The Red Sea parted for him again, and closed at his back.

For a minute or so everybody sat in silence; maybe we were waiting to make sure Vernon Thaxter was out of earshot. Then somebody started laughing and somebody else picked it up, and the Demon started screaming with laughter and jumping up and down, but other people were hollering for the laughers to shut up and the whole place was like a merry glimpse of hell. "Settle down! Settle down, everybody!" Mayor Swope was yelling, and Chief Marchette stood up and bellowed like a foghorn for quiet.

"It's damn blackmail!" Mr. Moultry was on his feet again. "Nothin' but damn blackmail!" A few others agreed with him, but Dad was one of the men who stood up and told Mr. Moultry to shut his mouth and pay attention to the fire chief.

This is how it got sorted out: Chief Marchette said that everybody who wanted to work should get on over to Bruton, where the river flowed against the edge of town on its way to the gargoyle bridge, and he'd have some volunteers load the shovels, pickaxes, and other stuff into a truck at Mr. Vandercamp's hardware store. The power of Moorwood Thaxter was never more evident when Chief Marchette finished his instructions: everybody went to Bruton, even Mr. Moultry.

Bruton's narrow streets were already awash. Chickens flapped in the water, and dogs were swimming. The rain had started falling hard again, slamming on the tin roofs like rough music. Dark people were pulling their belongings out of the wood-frame houses and trying to get to higher ground. The cars and trucks coming over from Zephyr made waves that rolled across submerged yards to crash foam against the foundations. "This," Dad said, "is gonna be a bad one."

On the wooded riverbank, most of the residents of Bruton were already laboring in knee-deep water. A wall of mud was going up, but the river was hungry. We left the pickup near a public basketball court at the Bruton Recreation Center, where a lot of other vehicles were parked, then we slogged toward the river. Fog swirled over the rising water, and flashlight beams crisscrossed in the night. Lightning flashed and thunder boomed. I heard the urgent cries of people to work faster and harder. My mother's hand gripped mine, and held on tightly while Dad went on ahead to join a group of Bruton men. Someone had backed a dump truck full of sand to the riverbank, and a Bruton man pulled Dad up into it and they started filling little burlap bags and tossing them down to other rain-soaked men. "Over here! Over here!" somebody yelled. "It ain't gonna hold!" someone else shouted. Voices crisscrossed and merged like the flashlight beams. They were scared voices. I was scared, too.

There is something about nature out of control that touches a primal terror. We are used to believing that we're the masters of our domain, and that God has given us this earth to rule over. We need this illusion like a good night-light. The truth is more fearsome: we are as frail as young trees in tornadoes, and our beloved homes are one flood away from driftwood. We plant our roots in trembling earth, we live where mountains rose and fell and prehistoric seas burned away in mist. We and the towns we have built are not permanent; the earth itself is a passing train. When you stand in muddy water that is rising toward your waist and you hear people shouting against the darkness and see their figures struggling to hold back the currents that will not be denied, you realize the truth of it: we will not win, but we cannot give up. No one on that disappearing riverbank, there in the pouring rain, thought the Tecumseh was going to be turned aside. It had never been so. Still, the work went on. The truck full of tools came from the hardware store, and Mr.

Vandercamp Junior had a clipboard where people signed their names as they accepted a shovel. Walls of mud and sandbags were built up, and the river surged through the barricade like brown soup through a mouthful of weak teeth. The water rose. My belt buckle submerged.

Lightning zigzagged down from the heavens, followed by a crash of thunder so loud you couldn't hear the women scream. "That hit somethin' close!" said Reverend Lovoy, who held a shovel and resembled a mud man. "Lights are goin' out!" a black woman shouted a few seconds later, and indeed the power was failing all over Bruton and Zephyr. I watched the lights flicker and disappear from the windows. Then my hometown lay in darkness, and you couldn't tell sky from water. In the distance I saw what looked like a candle glowing in the window of a house about as far from Bruton as you could get and still be within Zephyr's boundaries. As I watched, the light moved from window to window. I realized I was looking at Mr. Moorwood Thaxter's mansion up at the high point of Temple Street.

I sensed it before I saw it.

A figure stood to my left, watching me. Whoever it was wore a long raincoat; his hands in his pockets. The wind shrilled in off the thunderstorm and moved the wet folds of the coat, and I almost choked on my heart because I remembered the figure in the woods opposite Saxon's Lake.

Then whoever it was started wading past my mother and me toward the laborers. It was a tall figure—a man, I presumed— and he moved with purposeful strength. Two flashlight beams seemed to fence in the air for a few seconds, and the man in the raincoat walked into their conflict. The battling lights did not reveal the man's face, but did reveal something else.

The man wore a drenched and dripping fedora. The band of that hat was secured by a silver disc the size of a half-dollar, and a small decorative feather stuck up from it.

A feather, dark with wet, but a feather with a definite glint of green.

Like the green feather I'd found on the bottom of my sneaker that morning.

My mind raced. Might there have been *two* green feathers in that hatband, before the wind had plucked one out?

One of the beams, defeated, drew back. The other pranced away. The man walked in darkness.

"Mom?" I said. "Mom?"

The figure was wading away from us, and had passed no more than eight feet from me. He reached up with a white hand to hold the hat on his head. "Mom?" I said again, and she finally heard me over the noise and answered, "What is it?"

"I think . . . I think . . ." But I didn't know what I thought. I couldn't tell if that was the person I'd seen across the road, or not.

The figure was moving off through the brown water, step after step.

I pulled my hand free from my mother's, and I went after him.

"Cory!" she said. "Cory, take my hand!"

I heard, but I didn't listen. The water swirled around me. I kept going.

"Cory!" Mom shouted.

I had to see his face.

"Mister!" I called. It was too noisy, what with the rain and the river and the working; he couldn't hear. Even if he did, he wouldn't turn around. I felt the Tecumseh's currents pulling at my shoes. I was sunken waist-deep in cold murk. The man was heading toward the riverbank, where my dad was. Flashlights bobbed and weaved, and a shimmering reflection danced up and struck the man's right hand as he pulled it from his pocket.

Something metallic glinted in it.

Something with a sharp edge.

My heart stuttered.

The man in the green-feathered hat was on his way to the riverbank for an appointment with my father. It was an appointment, perhaps, that he'd been planning ever since Dad dove in after the sinking car. With all this commotion, all this noise, and in all this watery dark, might not the man in the green-feathered hat find a chance to drive that blade into my father's back? I couldn't see my dad; I couldn't make out anyone for sure, just glistening figures straining against the inevitable.

He was stronger against the current than I. He was pulling away from me. I lunged forward, fighting the river, and that was when my feet slipped out from under me and I went down, the muddy water closing over my head. I reached up, trying to grab something to hold on to. There was nothing solid, and I couldn't get my feet planted. My mind screamed that I'd never be able to draw a breath again. I splashed and wallowed, and then somebody had gripped me and was lifting me up as the muddy water oozed from my face and hair.

"I've got you," a man said. "You're all right."

"Cory! What's wrong with you, boy?" That was my mother's voice, rising to new heights of terror. "Are you *crazy?*"

"I believe he stepped in a hole, Rebecca." The man set me down. I was still standing in waist-deep water but at least my feet were touching earth. I wiped clots of mud from my eyes and looked up at Dr. Curtis Parrish, who wore a gray raincoat and a rainhat. The hat had no band, therefore it had no silver disc and no green feather. I turned around, looking for the figure I'd been trying to reach, but he had merged with the other people nearer the river's edge. He and the knife he'd drawn from his pocket.

"Where's Dad?" I said, working up to another fever pitch. "I've gotta find Dad!"

"Whoa, whoa, settle down." Dr. Parrish took hold of my shoulders. In one hand he held a flashlight. "Tom's right over there." He pointed the flashlight's beam toward a group of mud-died men. The direction he indicated was not the direction in which the man with the green-feathered hat had gone. But I saw my father over there, working between a black man and Mr. Yar-brough. "See him?"

"Yes sir." Again I searched for the mysterious figure. Vanished.

"Cory, don't you run away from me like that!" Mom scolded. "You scared me almost to death!" She took my hand again in a grip of iron.

Dr. Parrish was a heavyset man, about forty-eight or forty-nine years old, with a firm, square jaw and a flattened nose that reminded everyone he'd been a champion boxer when he was a sergeant in the army. With the same hands that had scooped me from the hole at my feet, Dr. Parrish had delivered me from my mother's womb. He had thick dark eyebrows over eyes the color of steel, and beneath his rainhat his dark brown hair was gray on the sides. Dr. Parrish said to Mom, "I heard from Chief Marchette a little while ago that they've opened up the school gym. They're puttin' in oil lamps and bringin' in some cots and blankets. Most of the women and children are goin' over there to stay, since the water's gettin' so high."

"Is that where we ought to go, then?"

"I think it'd be the wise thing. There's no use you and Cory standin' out here in this mess." He pointed with the flashlight again, this time away from the river and toward the swampy basketball court where we'd parked. "They're pickin' up whoever wants to go to the shelter over that way. Probably be another truck along in a few minutes."

"Dad won't know where we are!" I protested, still thinking of the green feather and the knife.

"I'll let him know. Tom would want you both in a safe place, and I'll tell you the truth, Rebecca: the way this is goin', we'll be catchin' catfish in attics before mornin'."

We didn't need much prodding. "Brightie's already over there," Dr. Parrish said. "You ought to go catch the next truck. Here, take this." He gave Mom the flashlight, and we turned away from the swollen Tecumseh and started toward the basketball court. "Keep hold of my hand!" Mom cautioned as the floodwaters swept around us. I looked back, could see only the lights moving in the darkness and glittering off the roiling water. "Watch your step!" Mom said. Farther along the riverbank, past where my father was working, voices rose in a chorus of shouts. I did not know it then, but a frothy wave had just swamped over the highest part of the earthen dam and the water churned and foamed and men suddenly found themselves up to their elbows in trouble as the river burst through. A flashlight's beam caught a glimpse of brown-mottled scales in the muddied foam, and somebody hollered, "Snakes!" In the next second, the men were bowled over by the twisting currents, and Mr. Stellko, the Lyric's manager, aged by ten years when he put his hand out to seize a grip and felt a log-sized, scaly shape moving past him in the turbulence. Mr. Stellko was struck dumb and peed in his pants at the same time, and when he could find his voice to scream, the monstrous reptile was gone, following the flood into the streets of Bruton.

"Help me! Somebody help me!"

We heard the voice of a woman from nearby, and Mom said, "Wait."

Someone carrying an oil lamp was splashing toward us. Rain hissed on the lamp's hot glass and steamed away. "Please help me!" the woman cried.

"What is it?" Mom turned the light onto the panic-stricken face of a young black woman. I didn't know her, but Mom said, "Nila Castile? Is that you?"

"Yes ma'am, it's Nila! Who's that?"

"Rebecca Mackenson. I used to read books to your mother."

This was before I was born, I presumed.

"It's my daddy, Miz Rebecca!" Nila Castile said. "I think his heart's give out!"

"Where is he?"

"At the house! Over there!" She pointed into the darkness, water swirling around her waist. I was about chest-deep by now. "He can't stand up!"

"All right, Nila. Settle down." My mother, a framework of

little terrors with skin stretched over it, was amazingly calm when someone else needed calming. This, as I understood it, was part of being a grown-up. When it was truly needed, my mother could reveal something that was sorely lacking in Granddaddy Jaybird: courage. "You lead the way," she said.

Water was rushing into the houses of Bruton. Nila Castile's house, like so many others, was a narrow gray shotgun shack. She led us in, the river surging around us, and she shouted in the first room, "Gavin! I'm back!"

Her light, and Mom's light, too, fell on an old black man sitting in a chair, the water up around his knees and newspapers and magazines swirling in the current. He was clutching his hand to his wet shirt over his heart, his ebony face seamed with pain and his eyes squeezed shut. Standing next to him, holding his other hand, was a little boy maybe seven or eight years old.

"Grandpap's cryin', Momma," the little boy said.

"I know he is, Gavin. Daddy, I've brought some help." Nila Castile set the lamp down on a tabletop. "Can you hear me, Daddy?"

"Ohhhhh," the old man groaned. "Hurtin' mighty bad this time."

"We're gonna help you stand up. Gonna get you out of here."

"No, honey." He shook his head. "Old legs . . . gone."

"What're we gonna *do?*" Nila looked at my mother, and I saw the bright tears in her eyes.

The river was shoving its way in. Thunder spoke outside and the lightning flared. If this had been a television show, it would've been time for a commercial.

But real life takes no pauses. "Wheelbarrow," my mother said. "Have you got one?"

Nila said no, but that they'd borrowed a neighbor's wheelbarrow before and she thought it might be up on their back porch. Mom said to me, "You stay here," and she gave me the oil lamp. Now I was going to have to be courageous, whether I liked it or not. Mom and Nila left with the flashlight, and I stood in the flooding front room with the little boy and the old man.

"I'm Gavin Castile," the little boy said.

"I'm Cory Mackenson," I told him.

Hard to be sociable when you're hip-deep in brown water and the flickering light doesn't fill up the room.

"This here's my grandpap, Mr. Booker Thornberry," Gavin went on, his hand locked with the old man's. "He ain't feelin' good."

"How come you didn't get out when everybody else did?"

"Because," Mr. Thornberry said, rousing himself, "this is my *home*, boy. My home. I ain't scared of no damned river."

"Everybody else is," I said. *Everybody with sense,* is what I meant.

"Then everybody else can go on and run." Mr. Thornberry, whom I was beginning to realize shared a stubborn streak with Granddaddy Jaybird, winced as a fresh pain hit him. He blinked slowly, his dark eyes staring at me from a bony face. "My Rubynelle passed on in this house. Right here. I ain't gonna die in no white man's hospital."

"Do you *want* to die?" I asked him.

He seemed to think about this. "Gonna die in my own home," he answered.

"Water's gettin' deep," I said. "Everybody might get drowned."

The old man scowled. Then he turned his head and looked at the small black hand he was clutching.

"My grandpap took me to the movies!" Gavin said, attached to the thin dark arm as the water rose toward his throat. "We seen a Looney Tune!"

"Bugs Bunny," the old man said. "We seen ol' Bugs Bunny and that stutterin' fella looks like a pig. Didn't we, boy?"

"Yes sir!" Gavin answered, and he grinned. "We gone go see another one real soon, ain't we, Grandpap?"

Mr. Thornberry didn't answer. Gavin didn't let go.

I understood then what courage is all about. It is loving someone else more than you love yourself.

My mother and Nila Castile returned, lugging a wheelbarrow.
"Gonna put you in this, Daddy," Nila told him. "We can push you
to where Miz Rebecca says they're pickin' up people in trucks."

Mr. Thornberry took a long, deep breath, held it for a few
seconds, and then let it go. "Damn," he whispered. "Damn old
heart in a damn old fool." His voice cracked a little bit on that
last word.

"Let us help you up," Mom offered.

He nodded. "All right," he said. "It's time to go, ain't it?"

They got him in the wheelbarrow, but real soon Mom and
Nila realized that even though Mr. Thornberry was a skinny
thing, they were both going to have a struggle pushing him and
keeping his head above water. I saw the predicament: out beyond
the house on the underwater street, Gavin's head would be submerged. A current might whisk him away like a cornhusk. Who
was going to hold him up?

"We'll have to come back for the boys," Mom decided. "Cory,
you take the lamp and you and Gavin stand up on that table."
The tabletop was awash, but it would keep us above the flood. I
did as Mom told me, and Gavin pulled himself up, too. We stood
together, me holding the lamp, a small pinewood island beneath
our feet. "All right," Mom said. "Cory, don't move from there. If
you move, I'll give you a whippin' you'll remember for the rest of
your life. Understand?"

"Yes ma'am."

"Gavin, we'll be back directly," Nila Castile said. "We've got
to get Grandpap to where people can help him. Hear?"

"Yes ma'am," Gavin answered.

"You boys mind your mothers." Mr. Thornberry spoke up, his
voice raspy with pain. "I'll whip both your butts if you don't."

"Yes sir," we both said. I figured Mr. Thornberry had decided
he wanted to live.

Mom and Nila Castile began the labor of pushing Mr. Thornberry in the wheelbarrow against the brown water, each supporting one handle and Mom holding the light. They tilted the wheelbarrow up as high as they could, and Mr. Thornberry lifted his head up, the veins standing out in his scrawny neck. I heard my mother grunt with the effort. But the wheelbarrow was moving, and they pushed it through the water that was swirling around the open doorway and across the flooded porch. At the foot of the two cinderblock steps, the water came up to Mr. Thornberry's neck and splashed into his face. They moved away, the current at their backs helping them push the wheelbarrow. I had never thought of my mother as being physically strong before. I guess you never know what a person can do until that person has to do it.

"Cory?" Gavin said after a minute or so.

"Yeah, Gavin?"

"I cain't swim," he said.

He was pressed up against my side. He was starting to shiver now that he didn't have to be so brave for his grandpap. "That's okay," I told him. "You won't have to."

I hoped.

We waited. Surely they'd be back soon. The water was lapping up over our soggy shoes. I asked Gavin if he knew any songs, and he said he knew "On Top of Old Smoky," which he began to sing in a high, quavering yet not unpleasant voice.

His singing—more of a yodel, actually—attracted something that suddenly came paddling through the doorway, and I caught my breath at the noise and swung the light onto it.

It was a brown dog, matted with mud. Its eyes gleamed wildly in the light, its breathing harsh as it swam across the room toward us, through the flotsam of papers and other trash. "Come on, boy!" I said. Whether it was a boy or girl was incidental; the dog looked like it needed a perch. "Come on!" I gave Gavin the lamp, and the dog whimpered and yelped as a slow wave slipped through the door and lifted the animal up and down again. Water smacked the walls.

"Come on, boy!" I leaned down to get the struggling dog. I

grasped its front paws. It looked up into my face, its pink tongue hanging out in the dank yellow light, as a born-again Christian might appeal to the Savior.

I was lifting the dog out by its paws, and I felt it shudder.

Something went *crunch*.

As fast as that.

And then its head and shoulders were coming out of the dark water and suddenly there was no more of the dog beyond the middle of its back, no hindquarters, no tail, no hind legs, nothing but a gaping hole that started spilling a torrent of black blood and steaming guts.

The dog made a little whining sound. That's all. But its paws twitched and its eyes were on me, and the agony I saw in them will last in my mind forever.

I cried out—and what I said I will never know—and dropped the mess that had once been a dog. It splashed in, went under, came back up, and the paws were still trying to paddle. I heard Gavin shout something; *wannawaterMars?* it sounded like. And then the water thrashed around the half of a carcass, the entrails streaming behind it like a hideous tail, and I saw the skin of something break the surface.

It was covered with diamond-shaped scales the colors of autumn leaves: pale brown, shimmering purple, deep gold, and tawny russet. All the shades of the river were there, too, from swirls of muddy ocher to moonlight pink. I saw a forest of mussels leeched to its flesh, gray canyons of scars and fishhooks scarlet with rust. I saw a body as thick as an ancient oak twist slowly around in the water, taking its own sweet time. I was transfixed by the spectacle, even as Gavin wailed with terror. I knew what I was looking at, and though my heart pounded and I could hardly draw a breath, I thought it was as beautiful as anything in God's creation.

Then I recalled the jagged fang driven like a blade into the chunk of wood at Mr. Sculley's. Beautiful or not, Old Moses had just torn a dog in half.

He was still hungry. This happened so fast, my mind hardly had time to see it: a pair of jaws opened, fangs glistened, and an old boot was in there impaled on one of them along with a flopping silver fish. The jaws sucked the remaining half of the dog's carcass in with a snarling rush of water and then closed delicately, as one might savor a lemonhead candy at the Lyric theater. I caught a quick glimpse of a narrow, pale green cat's-eye the size of a baseball, shielded with a gelatinous film. Then Gavin fell back off the table into the water, and the lamp he was holding hissed out.

I didn't think about being brave. I didn't think about being scared.

I cain't swim.

That's what I thought about.

I jumped off the table to where Gavin had gone in. The water was heavy with mud, and up to my shoulders, which meant Gavin was nostrils-deep. He was flailing and kicking, and when I grabbed him around the waist he must've thought it was Old Moses because he almost jerked my arms off. I shouted, "Gavin! Stop kickin'!" and I got his face up out of the water. "Humma hobba humma," he was babbling, like a rain-soaked engine trying to fire its plugs.

I heard a noise behind me, in that dark and soggy room. The noise of something rising from the water.

I turned around. Gavin yelped and grabbed hold with both arms around my neck, all but throttling me.

I saw the shape of Old Moses—huge, horrible, and breathtaking—coming up from the water like a living swamp log. Its head was flat and triangular, like a snake's, but I think it was not just a snake because it seemed to have two small arms with spindly claws just below what would have been the neck. I heard what must have been its tail thwacking against a wall so hard the house shook. Its head bumped the ceiling. Gavin's grip was making my face balloon with blood.

I knew without seeing that Old Moses was looking at us, with eyes that could spot a catfish through murky water at midnight. I felt its appraisal of us, like a cold knife blade pressed against my forehead. I hoped we didn't look much like dogs.

Old Moses smelled like the river at noon: swampy, steaming, and pungent with life. To say I respected that awesome beast would be quite an understatement. But right at that moment I wished I was anywhere else on earth, even in school. But I didn't have much time for thinking, because Old Moses's snaky head began to descend toward us like the front end of a steam shovel and I heard the hiss of its jaws opening. I backed up, hollering at Gavin to let go, but he would not. If I'd been him, I wouldn't have let go, either. The head came at us, but just then I backed out of the front room into a narrow corridor—which I certainly didn't know was there—and Old Moses's jaws slammed against the door frame on either side of us. This seemed to make him mad. He drew back and drove forward again, with the same result, except this time the door frame splintered. Gavin was crying, making a *whoop whoop whoop* sound, and a frothy wave from Old Moses's agitations splashed into my face and over my head. Something jabbed my right shoulder, scaring a ripple up my spine. I reached for it, and found a broom floating in the debris.

Old Moses made a noise like a locomotive about to blow its gaskets. I saw the awful shape of its head coming at the corridor's entrance, and I thought of Gordon Scott's Tarzan, spear in hand, fighting against a giant python. I picked up the broomstick, and when Old Moses hit the doorway again I jammed that broom right down its gaping, dog-swallowing throat.

You know what happens when you touch your finger to the back of your throat, don't you? Well, the same thing happens, evidently, to monsters. Old Moses made a gagging noise as loud as thunder in a barrel. The head drew back and the broom went with it, cornstraw bristles jammed in the gullet. Then, and this is the only way I can describe it, Old Moses puked. I mean it. I heard the rush of liquid and gruesome things flooding from its mouth. Fish, some still flopping and some long dead, went flying all around us along with stinking crayfish, turtle shells, mussels, slimy stones, mud, and bones. The smell was . . . well, you can imagine it. It was a hundred times worse than when the kid in school throws up his morning oatmeal on the desk in front of you. I dunked my head underwater to get away from it, and of course Gavin had to go, too, whether he liked it or not. Underneath there, I thought that Old Moses ought to be more particular about what he scooped off the Tecumseh's bottom.

Currents thrashed around us. I came up again, and Gavin took a gasping breath and yelled his head off. At that point I started yelling, too. "Help!" I shouted. "Somebody help us!"

A light speared through the front door, over the choppy water, and hit me in the face.

"*Cory!*" came the sound of judgment. "*I told you not to move, didn't I?*"

"Gavin? *Gavin?*"

"Lord God!" my mother said. "What's that smell?"

The water was settling down. I realized Old Moses was no longer between the two mothers and their sons. Dead fish floated in a slimy brown sludge on the surface, but Mom's attention was on me. "I'm gonna tan your hide, Cory Mackenson!" she shouted as she waded in with Nila Castile behind her.

Then they walked right into the floating monster disgorgement, and from the sound she made I don't believe my mother was thinking about whipping me anymore.

Lucky me.

7

A Summons from the Lady

NONE OF MY FRIENDS believed me, of course.

Davy Ray Callan just laughed and shook his head, and he said he couldn't have made up a better story if he'd tried. Ben Sears looked at me like I had seen one too many monster movies at the Lyric. Johnny Wilson thought about it awhile, in that slow, deliberating way of his, and then he gave his opinion: "Nope. Didn't happen."

"It did!" I told them as we sat on the porch of my house in the shade under a clear blue sky. "It really did, I swear it!"

"Oh yeah?" Davy Ray, the feisty one of our group and the one who was most likely to make up astounding tales, cocked his brown-haired head and stared at me through pale blue eyes that always held a hint of wild laughter. "Then how come Old Moses didn't just eat you up? How come a monster ran from a kid with a *broom?*"

"Because," I answered, flustered and angry, "I didn't have my monster-killin' ray gun with me, that's why! I don't know! But it happened, and you can ask—"

"Cory," my mother said quietly from the doorway, "I think you'd better stop talkin' about this now."

So I did. And I understood what she meant. There was no use trying to make anybody believe it. My mom herself couldn't quite grasp it, though Gavin Castile had sputtered the whole story to his mother. Mr. Thornberry, incidentally, was all right. He was alive and getting stronger day by day, and I understand he wanted to get well so he could take Gavin to see more Looney Tunes.

My friends would have believed it, though, if they could've smelled my clothes before Mom threw them in the garbage. She threw her own tainted clothes away, too. Dad listened to the tale, and he nodded and sat there with his hands folded before him, bandages on his palms and fingers covering huge blisters that had been raised by the shoveling.

"Well," Dad said, "all I can say is, there're stranger things on this earth than we can ever figure out if we had a hundred lifetimes. I thank God the both of you are all right, and that nobody drowned in the flood. Now: what's for dinner?"

Two weeks passed. We left April and moved through the sunny days of May. The Tecumseh River, having reminded us who was boss, returned to its banks. A quarter of the houses in Bruton weren't worth living in anymore, including Nila Castile's, so the sound of sawing and hammering in Bruton was almost around the clock. There was one benefit of the rain and the flood, though; under the sunshine, the earth exploded in flowers and Zephyr blazed with color. Lawns were deep emerald, honeysuckle grew like mad passion, and kudzu blanketed the hills. Summer was almost upon us.

I turned my attention to studying for final exams. Math was never my strongest subject, and I was going to have to make a high grade so I wouldn't have to go to—and the mere thought of this made me choke—summer school.

In my quiet hours, I did wonder how I'd managed to beat Old Moses away with a bristle-brush broom. I had been lucky in jamming it down the monster's throat, that was for sure. But I figured it might have been something else, too. Old Moses, for all his size and fury, was like Granddaddy Jaybird; he could holler a good game, but at the first sting he took off running. Or swimming, as the case might be. Old Moses was a coward. Maybe Old Moses had gotten used to eating things that didn't fight back, like catfish and turtles and scared dogs paddling for their lives. With that broomstick in his throat, Old Moses might have figured there was easier prey where he came from, down at the bottom of the river in that cool, muddy banquet hall where nothing bites back.

At least, that's my theory. I don't ever want to have to test it again, though.

I had a dream about the man in the long coat and the green-feathered hat. I dreamed I was wading toward him, and when I grasped his arm he turned his face toward me and it was a man with not human skin but diamond-shaped scales the color of autumn leaves. He had fangs like daggers and blood dripping down his chin, and I realized I had interrupted him in the process of eating a small brown dog, the upper half of which he held struggling in his left hand.

It was not a pleasant dream.

But maybe there was some truth in it. Somewhere.

I was a walker in these days, bereft of two wheels to call my own. I enjoyed walking to and from school, but all my friends had bikes and I definitely had lost a step or two of status. One afternoon I was pitching a stick to Rebel and rolling around in the green grass with him when I heard a clankety sound. I looked up, Rebel looked up, and there was a pickup truck approaching our house.

I knew the truck. It was splotchy with rust and its suspension sagged, and the noise it made caused dogs to bay in its wake. Rebel started barking, and I had a time getting him quiet. The truck had a metal frame thing bolted in the bed from which hung, clattering like asylum inmates, a bewildering array of tools, most of which looked as antique and worthless as the truck. On the driver's door was stenciled, not very neatly, LIGHTFOOT'S FIX-IT.

The truck stopped in front of the house. Mom came out on

the porch, alerted by the clamor, but Dad wouldn't be home from work for another hour or so. The truck's door opened, and a long, skinny black man wearing dusty gray overalls got out, so slowly it seemed that movement might be painful for him. He wore a gray cap, and his dark skin was smoky with dust. He came slowly toward the porch, and I have to say that even if a bull had suddenly come charging up behind him, Mr. Marcus Lightfoot probably wouldn't have hurried his pace.

"Good afternoon, Mr. Lightfoot," Mom said, her apron on. She had been working in the kitchen, and she wiped her hands on a paper towel. "How are you?"

Mr. Lightfoot smiled. His small, square teeth were very white, and gray hair boiled up from under his cap. This is how he spoke, in a voice like a slow leak from a clogged pipe: "Good   afternoon to   you,   too,   Miz Mackenson.   Hey there, Cory."

This was a good-paced conversational clip for Mr. Lightfoot, who had been a handyman in Zephyr and Bruton for more than thirty years, picking up the task from his father. Mr. Lightfoot was renowned for his skill with appliances, and though he was slow as a toothache, he always got the job done no matter how baffling the problem. "Mighty fine." He stopped, looking up at the blue sky. The seconds ticked past. Rebel barked, and I put my hand over his muzzle.

"Day," Mr. Lightfoot decided.

"Yes, it is." Mom waited for him to speak again, but Mr. Lightfoot just stood there, this time looking at our house. He reached into one of his many pockets, brought out a handful of penny nails, and clicked them around, as if he were waiting, too. "Uh . . ." Mom cleared her throat. "Can I help you with anythin'?"

"Jus'   passin'," he replied, slow as warm molasses. "Wonderin' if   you"—and here he paused to study the nails in his hand for a few seconds—"might   need   somethin'   fixed?"

"Well, no, not really. I can't think of—" She stopped, and her expression told me she *had* thought of something. "The toaster.

It went out on me day before yesterday. I was gonna call you, but—"

"Yes'm, I know." Mr. Lightfoot nodded sagely. "Time sure does fly."

He went back to the truck to get his toolbox, an old metal fascination filled with drawers and every kind of nut and bolt, it seemed, under the workman's sun. He strapped on his tool belt, from which hung several different kinds of hammers, screwdrivers, and arcane-looking wrenches. Mom held the door open for Mr. Lightfoot, and when he walked into the house she looked at me and shrugged, her statement being: *I don't know why he's here, either*. I left Rebel the gnawed stick and went into the house, too, and in the cool of the kitchen I drank a glass of iced tea and watched Mr. Lightfoot stare down the toaster.

"Mr. Lightfoot, would you care for somethin' to drink?" Mom asked.

"Nome."

"I've got some oatmeal cookies."

"Nome, thank you kindly." He took a clean white square of cloth from another pocket and unfolded it. He draped the cloth over the seat of one of the chairs to the kitchen table. Then he unplugged the toaster, set it on the table alongside his toolbox, and sat down on the white cloth. All this had been done at an underwater pace.

Mr. Lightfoot chose a screwdriver. He had the long, graceful fingers of a surgeon, or an artist. Watching him work was a form of torture for the patience, but no one can say he didn't know what he was doing. He opened the toaster right up, and sat staring at the naked grills. "Uh-huh," he said after a long moment of silence. "Uh-huh."

"What is it?" Mom peered over his shoulder. "Can it be fixed?"

"See there? Little ol' red wire?" He tapped it with the screwdriver's edge. "Done come a'loose."

"Is that all that's wrong? Just that little wire?"

"Yes'm, that's." He began to carefully rewind the wire around its connection, and watching him do this was like a strange kind of hypnosis. "All," he finally finished. Then he put the toaster back together again, plugged it in, pushed down the timer prongs, and we all saw the coils start to redden. "Sometimes," Mr. Lightfoot said.

We waited. I think I could hear my hair growing.

"Just the."

The world turned beneath us.

"Little things." He began to refold the white cloth. We waited, but this particular line of thought had either derailed or reached its dead end. Mr. Lightfoot looked around the kitchen. "Anythin' else need fixin'?"

"No, I think we're in good shape now."

Mr. Lightfoot nodded, but I could tell that he was searching for problems like a bird dog sniffing game. He made a slow circle of the kitchen, during which he delicately placed his hands on the icebox, the four-eyed stove, and the sink's faucet as if divining the health of the machinery through his touch. Mom and I looked at each other, puzzled; Mr. Lightfoot was certainly acting peculiar.

"Icebox kinda stutterin'," he said. "Want me to take a peek?"

"No, don't bother with it," Mom told him. "Mr. Lightfoot, are you feelin' all right today?"

"Surely, Miz Mackenson. Surely." He opened a cupboard and listened to the slight squeak of the hinges. A screwdriver was withdrawn from his tool belt, and he tightened the screws in both that cupboard door and the next one, too. Mom cleared her throat again, nervously this time, and she said, "Uh . . . Mr. Lightfoot, how much do I owe you for fixin' the toaster?"

"It's," he said. He tested the hinges of the kitchen door, and then he went to my mother's MixMaster blender on the countertop and started examining that. "Done paid," he finished.

"*Paid?* But . . . I don't understand." Mom had already reached up on a shelf and brought down the mason jar full of dollar bills and change.

"Yes'm. Paid."

"But I haven't given you any money yet."

Mr. Lightfoot's fingers dug into another pocket, and this time emerged with a white envelope. He gave it to Mom, and I saw that it had The Mackenson Family written across its front in blue ink. On the back, sealing it, was a blob of white wax. "Well," he said at last, "I 'spect I'm done for." He picked up his toolbox. "Today."

"Today?" Mom asked.

"Yes'm. You know." Mr. Lightfoot now started looking at the light fixtures, as if he longed to get into their electrical depths. "My number," he said. "Anythin' needs fixin', you." He smiled at us. "Jus' call."

We saw Mr. Lightfoot off. He waved as he drove away in the clankety old pickup, the tools jangling on their hooks and the neighborhood dogs going crazy. Mom said, mostly to herself, "Tom's not gonna believe this." Then she opened the envelope, took a letter from it, and read it. "Huh," she said. "Want to hear?"

"Yes ma'am."

She read it to me: "'I'd be honored if you would come to my house at seven o'clock this Friday evening. Please bring your son.' And look who it's from." Mom handed the letter to me, and I saw the signature.

The Lady.

When Dad got home, Mom told him about Mr. Lightfoot and showed him the letter almost before he could get his milkman's cap off. "What do you think she wants with *us?*" Dad asked.

"I don't know, but I think she's decided to pay Mr. Lightfoot to be our personal handyman."

Dad regarded the letter again. "She's got nice handwritin', to be so old. I would've thought it'd be crimped up." He chewed on his bottom lip, and just watching him I could tell he was getting edgy. "You know, I've never seen the Lady close up before. Seen her on the street, but . . ." He shook his head. "No. I don't believe I want to go."

"What're you *sayin'?*" Mom asked incredulously. "The Lady wants us to come to her *house!*"

"I don't care." Dad gave her back the letter. "I'm not goin'."

"Why, Tom? Give me one good reason."

"Phillies are playin' the Pirates on radio Friday night," he said as he retired to the comfort of his easy chair. "That's reason enough."

"I don't think so," Mom told him, setting her jaw.

Here we came to a rare fact of life: my parents, though I believe they got along better than ninety-nine percent of the married couples in Zephyr, did have their go-rounds. Just as no one person is perfect, no marriage of two imperfects is going to be without a scrape of friction here and there. I have seen my father blow his top over a missing sock when in fact he was mad he didn't get a raise at the dairy. I have seen my usually placid mother steam with anger over a muddy bootmark on the clean floor when in fact the root of her discontent lay in a rude remark from a neighbor. So, in this tangled web of civilities and rage riots that we know as life, such things will happen as now began to take shape in my parents' house.

"It's because she's colored, isn't it?" Mom threw the first punch. "That's the real reason."

"No, it's not."

"You're as bad as your daddy about that. I swear, Tom—"

"*Hush!*" he hollered. Even I staggered. The comment about Granddaddy Jaybird, who was to racism as crabgrass is to weeds, had been a very low blow. Dad did not hate colored people, and this I knew for sure, but please remember that Dad had been raised by a man who saluted the Confederate flag every morning of his life and who considered black skin to be the mark of the devil. It was a terrible burden my father was carrying, because he loved Granddaddy Jaybird but he believed in his heart, as he taught me to believe, that hating any other man—for any reason—was a sin against God. So this next statement of his had more to do with pride than anything else: "And I'm not takin' charity from that woman, either!"

"Cory," Mom said, "I believe you have some math homework to do?"

I went to my room, but that didn't mean I couldn't hear them.

They weren't really loud, just intense. I suspected this had been brewing awhile, and came from a lot of different places: the car in the lake, the wasps at Easter, the fact that Dad couldn't afford to buy me a new bike, the dangers of the flood. Listening to Dad tell Mom that she couldn't put a rope around his neck and drag him into the Lady's house, I got the feeling that it all boiled down to this: the Lady scared him.

"No way!" he said. "I'm not goin' to see somebody who fools with bones and old dead animals and—" He stopped, and I figured he'd realized he was describing Granddaddy Jaybird. "I'm just not," he finished on a lame note.

Mom had decided she had run this horse to death. I could hear it in her sigh. "I'd like to go find out what she has to say. Is that all right with you?"

Silence. Then, in a quiet voice: "Yeah, it's all right."

"I'd like to take Cory, too."

This started another flare-up. "Why? You want him to see the skeletons hangin' in that woman's closet? Rebecca, I don't know what she wants and I don't *care!* But that woman plays with conjure dolls and black cats and God knows what all! I don't think it's right to take Cory into her house!"

"She asks, right here in the letter, that we bring Cory. See?"

"I see it. And I don't understand it, either, but I'm tellin' you: the Lady is not to be messed with. You remember Burk Hatcher? Used to be assistant foreman at the dairy back in 'fifty-eight?"

"Yes."

"Burk Hatcher used to chew tobacco. Chewed gobs of it, and he was always spittin'. Got to be a bad habit he hardly even knew he had, and—don't you dare tell anybody this—but a couple of times he forgot himself and spat right in a milk vat."

"Oh, Tom! You don't mean it!"

"Right as rain, I do. Now, Burk Hatcher was walkin' down Merchants Street one day, had just got his hair cut at Mr. Dollars's—and he had a full, thick head of hair he could hardly pull a comb through—and he forgot himself and spat on the sidewalk. Only the tobacco wattle never hit the sidewalk, 'cause it got on the Moon Man's shoes. Smack dab all over 'em. Wasn't on purpose, as I understand it. The Moon Man was just walkin' past. Well, Burk had a weird sense of humor, and this thing struck him as funny. He started laughin', right there in the Moon Man's face. And you know what?"

"What?" Mom asked.

"A week later Burk's hair started to fall out."

"Oh, I don't believe it!"

"It's true!" The adamance of my father's voice indicated that he, at least, believed it. "Within one month after Burk Hatcher spat tobacco juice on the Moon Man's shoes, he was balder'n a cue ball! He started wearin' a wig! Yes ma'am, he did! He almost went crazy because of it!" I could imagine my father leaning forward in his chair, his face so grim my mother was having to struggle to keep from laughing. "If you don't think the Lady had somethin' to do with that, you're crazy!"

"Tom, I swear I never knew you put so much faith in the occult."

"Faith, smaith! I saw Burk's bald head! Heck, I can tell you a lot of things I've heard about that woman! Like frogs jumpin' out of people's throats and snakes in the soup bowl and . . . uh-uh, no! I'm not settin' foot in that house!"

"But what if she gets mad at us if we *don't* go there?" Mom asked.

The question hung.

"Mightn't she put a spell on us if I don't take Cory to see her?"

I could tell Mom was jiving my dad a little, from her tone of voice. Still, Dad didn't answer and he was probably mulling over the potential disasters of snubbing the Lady.

"I think I'd better go and take Cory, too," Mom went on. "To show that we respect her. Anyway, aren't you the least bit curious why she wants to see us?"

"No!"

"Not the tiniest least bit?"

"Lord," Dad said after another bout of thinking. "You could argue the warts off a toad. And the Lady's probably got bottles full of those, too, to go along with her mummy dust and bat wings!"

The result of all this was that on Friday evening, as the sun began to slide down across the darkening earth and a cool wind blew through the streets of Zephyr, my mother and I got in the pickup truck and left our house. Dad stayed behind, his radio tuned to the baseball game he'd been awaiting, but I believe he was with us in spirit. He just didn't want to make a mistake and offend the Lady, in manner or speech. I have to say I was no solid rock myself; under my white shirt and the clip-on tie Mom had made me wear, my nerves were frazzling mighty fast.

Work was still going on in Bruton, the dark people sawing and hammering their houses back together. We passed through Bruton's business center, a little area with a barbershop, grocery store, shoe and clothing store, and other establishments run by the locals. Mom turned us onto Jessamyn Street, and at the end of that street she stopped in front of a house from which lights glowed through every window.

The small frame house, as I've already mentioned, was painted in a blaze of orange, purple, red, and yellow. A garage was set off to the side, where I figured the rhinestone-covered Pontiac was stored. The yard was neatly trimmed, and a sidewalk led from the curb to the porch steps. The house appeared neither scary nor the residence of royalty; it was just a house and, except for its coat of many colors, very much like every other house on the street.

Still, I balked when Mom came around and opened my door.

"Come on," she said. Her voice had tightened, though her nervousness didn't show in her face. She was wearing one of her best Sunday dresses, and her nice Sunday shoes. "It's almost seven."

Seven, I thought. Wasn't that supposed to be a voodoo number? "Maybe Dad was right," I told her. "Maybe we ought not to do this."

"It's all right. Look at all the lights on."

If this was supposed to make me feel at ease, it didn't work.

"There's nothin' to be afraid of," Mom said. This, from a woman who fretted that the gray insulation they'd recently sprayed above the ceiling of the elementary school might be bad for your breathing.

Somehow I got up the porch steps to the door. The porch light was painted yellow, to keep bugs away. I'd imagined the door's knocker might be a skull and crossbones. It was, instead, a little silver hand. Mom said, "Here goes," and she rapped on the door.

We heard muffled talking and footsteps. It occurred to me that our time to flee was running out. Mom put her arm around me, and I thought I could feel her pulse beating. Then the door's knob turned, the door opened, and the Lady's house offered entry. A tall, broad-shouldered black man wearing a dark blue suit, a white shirt, and a tie filled up the doorway. To me he looked as tall and burly as a black oak. He had hands that looked as if they could crush bowling balls. Part of his nose appeared to have been sliced off with a razor. His eyebrows merged together, thick as a werewolf's pelt.

In seven mystic words: he scared the crap out of me.

"Uh . . ." Mom began, and faltered. "Uh . . ."

"Come right in, Miz Mackenson." He smiled. With that smile his face became less fearsome and more welcome. But his voice was as deep as a kettledrum and it vibrated in my bones. He stepped aside, and Mom grasped my hand and pulled me across the threshold.

The door closed at our backs.

A young woman with skin the hue of chocolate milk was there to greet us. She had a heart-shaped face and tawny eyes, and she took my mother's hand and said with a smile, "I'm Amelia Damaronde, and I'm so verra pleased to meet you." She had bangle bracelets covering her forearms and five gold pins up the edges of each of her ears.

"Thank you. This is my son, Cory."

"Oh, this is the young man!" Amelia Damaronde turned her attention to me. She had an electricity about her that made me feel as if the air between us was charged. "A pleasure to meet you, too. This is my husband, Charles." The big man nodded at us. Amelia stood about up to his armpits. "We take care of things for the Lady," Amelia said.

"I see." Mom was still holding on to my hand, while I was busy looking around. The mind is a strange thing, isn't it? The mind concocts spiderwebs where there are no spiders, and darkness where the lights are bright. The living room of the Lady's house was no temple to the devil, no repository of black cats and bubbling cauldrons. It was just a room with chairs, a sofa, a little table on which knickknacks rested, and there were shelves with books and framed, vividly colored paintings on the walls. One of the paintings caught me: it showed the face of a bearded black man, his eyes closed in either suffering or ecstasy, and on his head was a crown of thorns.

I had never seen a black Jesus before, and this sight both knocked me for a loop and opened up a space in my mind that I'd never known needed light.

The Moon Man suddenly walked through a hallway into the room. Seeing him so close caused a start for both my mother and me. The Moon Man wore a light blue shirt with the sleeves rolled up, a pair of black trousers, and suspenders. Tonight he had only one wristwatch on, and the white rim of a T-shirt showed instead of his chain and huge gilded crucifix. He wasn't wearing his top hat; the splotchy division of pale yellow and ebony flesh continued up his high forehead and ended in a cap of white wool. The white beard on his chin was pointed, and curled slightly upward. His dark, wrinkle-edged eyes rested on first my mother and then me, and he smiled faintly and nodded. He lifted a thin finger and motioned us into the hallway.

It was time to meet the Lady.

"She's not been feelin' well," Amelia told us. "Dr. Parrish's been loadin' her up with vitamins."

"It's not anythin' serious, is it?" Mom asked.

"The rain got in her lungs. She doesn't get along so good in damp weather, but she's doin' better now that the sun's been out."

We came to a door. The Moon Man opened it, his shoulders, frail and stooped. I smelled dusty violets.

Amelia peered in first. "Ma'am? Your callers are here."

Sheets rustled within the room. "Please," said the shaky voice of an old woman, "send them in."

My mother took a breath and walked into the room. I had to follow, because she gripped my hand. The Moon Man stayed outside, and Amelia said, "If you need anythin', just call," before she gently closed the door.

And there she was.

She lay in a bed with a white metal frame, her back supported by a brocaded pillow, and the top sheet pulled up over her chest. The walls of her bedroom were painted with green fronds and foliage, and but for the polite drone of a box fan, we might have been standing in an equatorial jungle. An electric lamp burned on the bedside table, where magazines and books were stacked, and within her reach was a pair of wire-rimmed glasses.

The Lady just stared at us for a moment, and we at her. She was almost bluish-black against the white bed, and not an inch of her face looked unwrinkled. She reminded me of one of those apple dolls whose faces shrivel up in the hard noonday sun. I had seen handfuls of fresh snow scraped off the Ice House's pipes; the Lady's soft cloud of hair was whiter. She was wearing a blue gown, the straps up around her bony shoulders, and her collarbone jutted in such clear relief against her skin that it appeared painful. So, too, did her cheekbones; they seemed sharp enough to slice a peach. To tell the truth, though, except for one feature the Lady wouldn't have looked like much but an ancient, reed-thin black woman whose head trembled with a little palsy.

But her eyes were green.

I don't mean any old green. I mean the color of pale emeralds, the kind of jewels Tarzan might have been searching for in one of the lost cities of Africa. They were luminous, full of trapped and burning light, and looking into them you felt as if your secret self might be jimmied open like a sardine can and something stolen from you. And you might not even mind it, either; you might *want* it to be so. I had never seen eyes like that before, and I never have since. They scared me, but I could not turn away because their beauty was like that of a fierce wild animal who must be carefully watched at all times.

The Lady blinked, and a smile winnowed up over her wrinkled mouth. If she didn't have her own teeth, they were good fakes. "Don't you both look nice," she said in her palsied voice.

"Thank you, ma'am," Mom managed to answer.

"Your husband didn't want to come."

"Uh . . . no, he's . . . listenin' to the baseball game on the radio."

"Was that his excuse, Miz Mackenson?" She lifted her white brows.

"I . . . don't know what you mean."

"Some people," the Lady said, "are scared of me. Can you beat that? Scared of an old woman in her one hundred and sixth year! And me layin' here can't even keep no supper down! You love your husband, Miz Mackenson?"

"Yes, I do. Very much."

"That's good. Love strong and true can get you through a lot of dookey. And I'm here to tell you, honey, you got to walk through many fields of dookey to get to be my age." Those green, wonderful, and frightening eyes in that wrinkled ebony face turned full blaze on me. "Hello, young man," she said. "You help your momma do chores?"

"Yes'm." It was a whisper. My throat felt parched.

"You dry the dishes? Keep your room neat? You sweep the front porch?"

"Yes'm."

"That's fine. But I bet you never had call to use a broom like you used one at Nila Castile's house, did you?"

I swallowed hard. Now I and my mother knew what this was about.

The Lady grinned. "I wish I'd been there. I swanee I do!"

"Did Nila Castile tell you?" Mom asked.

"She did. I had a long talk with little Gavin, too." Her eyes stayed fixed on me. "You saved Gavin's life, young man. You know what that means to me?" I shook my head. "Nila's mother, God keep her, was a good friend of mine. I kind of adopted Nila. I always thought of Gavin as a great-grandchild. Gavin has a good life ahead of him. You made sure he'll get there."

"I was just . . . keepin' from gettin' eaten up myself," I said.

She chuckled; it was a gaspy sound. "Run him off with a broomstick! Lawd, Lawd! He thought he was such a mean ole thing, thought he could swim right up out of that river and snatch him a feast! But you gave him a mouthful, didn't you?"

"He ate a dog," I told her.

"Yeah, he *would*," the Lady said, and her chuckling died down. Her thin fingers intertwined over her stomach. She looked at my mother. "You did a kindness for Nila and her daddy. That's why whenever you need somethin' fixed, you call Mr. Lightfoot and it's done. Your boy saved Gavin's life. That's why I want to give him somethin', if I have your permit."

"It's not necessary."

"Ain't nothin' *necessary*," the Lady said, and she showed a little flare of irritation that made me think she would've been plenty tough when she was young. "That's why I'm gone do it."

"All right," Mom said, thoroughly cowed.

"Young man?" The Lady's gaze moved to me again. "What would you like?"

I thought about it. *"Anything?"* I asked.

"Within reason," Mom prodded.

"Anythin'," the Lady said.

I thought some more, but the decision wasn't very difficult. "A bike. A new bike that's never belonged to anybody before."

"A new bicycle." She nodded. "One with a lamp on it?"

"Yes'm."

"Want a horn?"

"That'd be fine," I said.

"Want it to be a fast one? Faster'n a cat up a tree?"

"Yes'm." I was getting excited now. "I sure do!"

"Then you'll have it! Soon as I can get my old self up from here."

"That's awfully nice of you," Mom said. "We sure appreciate it. But Cory's father and I can go pick up a bike from the store, if that's—"

"Won't come from a store," the Lady interrupted.

"Pardon?" Mom asked.

"Won't come from a store." She paused, to make sure my mother understood. "Store-bought's not good enough. Not *special* enough. Young man, you want a real special bicycle, don't you?"

"I . . . guess I'll take what I can get, ma'am."

At this, she laughed again. "Well, you're a little gentleman! Yessir, Mr. Lightfoot and I are gone put our heads together and see what we can come up with. Does that suit you?"

I said it did, but in truth I didn't quite understand how this was going to bring me a brand-new bicycle.

"Step closer," the Lady told me. "Come around here real close."

Mom let me go. I walked to the side of the bed, and those green eyes were right there in front of me like spirit lamps.

"What do you like to do besides ride a bicycle?"

"I like to play baseball. I like to read. I like to write stories."

"Write *stories?*" Her eyebrows went up again. "Lawd, Lawd! We gots us a *writer* here?"

"Cory's always liked books," Mom offered. "He writes little stories about cowboys, and detectives, and—"

"Monsters," I said. "Sometimes."

"Monsters," the Lady repeated. "You gone write about Old Moses?"

"I might."

"You gone write a book someday? Maybe about this town and everybody in it?"

I shrugged. "I don't know."

"Look at me," she said. I did. "Deep," she said.

I did.

And then something strange happened. She began to speak, and as she spoke, the air seemed to shimmer between us with a pearly iridescence. Her eyes had captured mine; I could not look away. "I've been called a monster," the Lady said. "Been called worse than a monster. I saw my momma killed when I wasn't much older than you. Woman jealous of her gift killed her. I swore I was gone find that woman. She wore a red dress, and she carried a monkey on her shoulder that told her things. Woman's name was LaRouge. Took me all my life to find her. I've been to Lepersville, and I've rowed a boat through the flooded mansions." Her face, through that shimmering haze, had begun to shed its wrinkles. She was getting younger as I stared at her. "I've seen the dead walkin', and my best friend had scales and crawled on her belly." Her face was younger still. Its beauty began to scorch my face. "I've seen the maskmaker. I've spat in Satan's eye, and I've danced in the halls of the Dark Society." She was a girl with long black hair, her cheekbones high and proud, her chin sharp, her eyes fearsome with memories. "I have *lived*," she said in her clear, strong voice, "a hundred lifetimes, and I'm not dead yet. Can you see me, young man?"

"Yes'm," I answered, and I heard myself as if from a vast distance. "I can."

The spell broke, quick as a heartbeat. One second I was looking at a beautiful young woman, and the next there was the Lady as she really was, one hundred and six years old. Her eyes had cooled some, but I felt feverish.

"Maybe someday you'll write my life story," the Lady told me. It sounded more like a command than a comment. "Now, why don't you go on out and visit with Amelia and Charles while I talk to your momma?"

I said I would. My legs were rubbery as I walked past Mom to the door. Sweat had crept around my collar. At the door, a thought hit me and I turned back to the bed. "'Scuse me, ma'am?" I ventured. "Do you . . . like . . . have anythin' that would help me pass math? I mean like a magic drink or somethin'?"

"*Cory!*" Mom scolded me.

But the Lady just smiled. She said, "Young man, I do. You tell Amelia to get you a drink of Potion Number Ten. Then you go home and you study *hard,* harder'n you ever did before. So hard you can do them 'rithmatics in your sleep." She lifted a finger. "That ought to do the trick."

I left the room and closed the door behind me, eager for magic.

"Potion Number Ten?" Mom asked.

"Glass of milk with some nutmeg flavorin' in it," the Lady said. "Amelia and me got a whole list of potions worked out for folks who need a little extra courage or confidence or what have you."

"Is that how all your magic's done?"

"Most all. You just give folks a key, and they can rightly open their own locks." The Lady's head cocked to one side. "But there's other kinds of magic, too. That's why I need to talk to you."

My mother was silent, not understanding what was about to come.

"Been dreamin'," the Lady said. "Been dreamin' asleep and awake. Things ain't right here no more. Things are tore up on the other side, too."

"The other side?"

"Where the dead go," she said. "Across the river. Not the Tecumseh. The broad, dark river where I'm gonna be goin' before too much longer. Then I'll look back and laugh and I'll say, 'So *that's* what it's all about!'"

Mom shook her head, uncomprehending.

"Things are tore up," the Lady went on. "In the land of the livin' and the world of the dead. I knew somethin' was wrong when Damballah denied his food. Jenna Velvadine told me what happened at your church Easter mornin'. That was the spirit world at work, too."

"It was *wasps*," Mom said.

"To you, wasps. To me, a message. Somebody's in terrible pain on the other side."

"I don't—"

"Understand," the Lady finished for her. "I know you don't. Sometimes I don't either. But I know the language of pain, Miz Mackenson. I grew up speakin' it." The Lady reached over to her bedside table, opened a drawer, and took out a piece of lined note-book paper. She gave it to my mother. "You recognize this?"

Mom stared at it. On the paper was the pencil sketch of a head: a skull, it looked to be, with wings swept back from its temples.

"In my dream I see a man with that tattoo on his shoulder. I see a pair of hands, and in one hand there's a billy club wrapped up with black tape—we call it a crackerknocker—and in the other there's a wire. I can hear voices, but I can't tell what's bein' said. Somebody's yellin', and there's music bein' played real loud."

"Music?" Mom was cold inside; she had recognized the winged skull from what Dad had told her about the corpse in the car.

"Either a record," the Lady said, "or somebody's beatin' hell out of a piano. I told Charles. He recalled me a story I read in the *Journal* back in March. Your husband was the one who saw a dead man go down in Saxon's Lake, ain't that right?"

"Yes."

"Might this have anythin' to do with it?"

Mom took a deep breath, held it, and then let it out. "Yes," she said.

"I thought so. Your husband sleepin' all right?"

"No. He . . . has bad dreams. About the lake, and . . . the man in it."

"Tryin' to reach your husband," the Lady said. "Tryin' to get his attention. I'm just pickin' up the message, like a party line on a telephone."

"Message?" Mom asked. "What message?"

"I don't know," the Lady admitted, "but that kind of pain can sure 'nuff drive a man out of his mind."

Tears began to blur my mother's vision. "I . . . can't . . . I don't . . ." She faltered, and a tear streaked down her left cheek like quicksilver.

"You show him that picture. Tell him to come see me if he wants to talk about it. Tell him he knows where I live."

"He won't come. He's afraid of you."

"You tell him," the Lady said, "this thing could tear him to pieces if he don't set it right. You tell him I could be the best friend he ever had."

Mom nodded. She folded the notebook paper into a square and clenched it in her hand.

"Wipe your eyes," the Lady told her. "Don't want the young man gettin' upset." When my mother had gotten herself fairly composed, the Lady gave a grunt of satisfaction. "There you go. Lookin' pretty again. Now, you go tell the young man he'll have his new bicycle soon as I can manage it. You make sure he studies his lessons, too. Potion Number Ten don't work without a momma or daddy layin' down the law."

My mother thanked the Lady for her kindness. She said she'd talk to my father about coming to see her, but she couldn't promise anything. "I'll expect him when I see him," the Lady said. "You take care of yourself and your family."

Mom and I left the house and walked to the truck. The corners of my mouth still had a little Potion Number Ten in them. I felt ready to tear that math book up.

We left Bruton. The river flowed gently between its banks.

The night's breeze blew softly through the trees, and the lights glowed from windows as people finished their dinners. I had two things on my mind: the hauntingly beautiful face of a young woman with green eyes, and a new bike with a horn and headlight.

My mother was thinking about a dead man whose corpse lay down at the bottom of the lake but whose spirit haunted my father's dreams and now the Lady's dreams as well.

Summer was close upon us, its scent of honeysuckle and violets perfuming the land.

Somewhere in Zephyr, a piano was being played.

Two

Summer of Devils and Angels

1

Last Day of School

*T*ICK . . . *TICK* . . . *TICK.*

In spite of what the calendar says, I have always counted the last day of school as the first day of summer. The sun had grown steadily hotter and hung longer in the sky, the earth had greened and the sky had cleared of all but the fleeciest of clouds, the heat panted for attention like a dog who knows his day is coming, the baseball field had been mowed and white-lined and the swimming pool newly painted and filled, and as our homeroom teacher, Mrs. Selma Neville, intoned about what a good year this had been and how much we'd learned, we students who had passed through the ordeal of final exams sat with one eye fixed to the clock.

Tick . . . tick . . . tick.

In my desk, alphabetically positioned between Ricky Lembeck and Dinah Macurdy, half of me listened to the teacher's speech while the other half longed for an end to it. My head was full up with words. I needed to shake some of them out in the bright summer air. But we were Mrs. Neville's property until the last bell rang, and we had to sit and suffer until time rescued us like Roy Rogers riding over the hill.

Tick . . . tick . . . tick.

Have mercy.

The world was out there, waiting beyond the square metal-rimmed windows. What adventures my friends and I would find this summer of 1964, I had no way of knowing, but I did know that summer's days were long and lazy, and when the sun finally gave up its hold on the sky the cicadas sang and the lightning bugs whirled their dance and there was no homework to be done and oh, it was a wonderful time. I had passed my math exam, and escaped—with a C-minus average, if truth must be known—the snarling trap of summer school. As my friends and I went about our pleasures, running amuck in the land of freedom, we would pause every so often to think of the inmates of summer school—a prison Ben Sears had been sentenced to last year—and wish them well, because time was moving on without them and they weren't getting any younger.

Tick . . . tick . . . tick.

Time, the king of cruelty.

From the hallway we heard a stirring and rustling, followed by laughter and shouts of pure, bubbling joy. Some other teacher had decided to let her class go early. My insides quaked at the injustice of it. Still, Mrs. Neville, who wore a hearing aid and had orange hair though she was at least sixty years old, talked on, as if there were no noise of escape beyond the door at all. It hit me, then; she didn't want to let us go. She wanted to hold us as long as she possibly could, not out of sheer teacher spite but maybe because she didn't have anybody to go home to, and summer alone is no summer at all.

"I hope you boys and girls remember to use the library during recess." Mrs. Neville was speaking in her kindly voice right now, but when she was upset she could spit sparks that made that falling meteor look like a dud. "You mustn't stop reading just because school is out. Your minds are made to be used. So don't forget how to think by the time September comes around a—"

RINGGGGGGG!

We all jumped up, like parts of the same squirming insect.

"One moment," Mrs. Neville said. "One moment. You're not excused yet."

Oh, this was torture! Mrs. Neville, I thought at that instant, must have had a secret life in which she tore the wings off flies.

"You will leave my room," she announced, "like young ladies and gentlemen. In single file, by rows. Mr. Alcott, you may lead the way."

Well, at least we were moving. But then, as the classroom emptied and I could hear the wild hollering echoing along the hallway, Mrs. Neville said, "Cory Mackenson? Step to my desk, please."

I did, under silent protest. Mrs. Neville offered me a smile from a mouth that looked like a red-rimmed string bag. "Now, aren't you glad you decided to apply yourself to your math?" she asked.

"Yes ma'am."

"If you'd studied as hard all year, you might've made the honor roll."

"Yes ma'am." Too bad I hadn't gotten a drink of Potion Number Ten back in the autumn, I was thinking.

The classroom was empty. I could hear the echoes fading. I smelled chalk dust, lunchroom chili, and pencil-sharpener shavings; the ghosts were already beginning to gather.

"You enjoy writing, don't you?" Mrs. Neville asked me, peering over her bifocals.

"I guess."

"You wrote the best essays in class and you made the highest grade in spelling. I was wondering if you were going to enter the contest this year."

"The contest?"

"The writing contest," she said. "You know. The Arts Council sponsors it every August."

I hadn't thought about it. The Arts Council, headed by Mr. Grover Dean and Mrs. Evelyn Prathmore, sponsored an essay and story-writing contest. The winners got a plaque and were expected to read their entries during a luncheon at the library. I shrugged. Stories about ghosts, cowboys, detectives, and monsters from outer space didn't seem much like contest-winning material; it was just something I did for me.

"You should consider it," Mrs. Neville continued. "You have a way with words."

I shrugged again. Having your teacher talk to you like a regular person is a disconcerting feeling.

"Have a good summer," Mrs. Neville said, and I realized suddenly that I was free.

My heart was a frog leaping out of murky water into clear sunlight. I said, "Thanks!" and I ran for the door. Before I got out, though, I looked back at Mrs. Neville. She sat at a desk with no papers on it that needed grading, no books holding lessons that needed to be taught. The only thing on her desk, besides her blotter and her pencil sharpener that would do no more chewing for a while, was a red apple Paula Erskine had brought her. I saw Mrs. Neville, framed in a spill of sunlight, reach for the apple and pick it up as if in slow motion. Then Mrs. Neville stared out at the room of empty desks, carved with the initials of generations who had passed through this place like a tide rolling into the future. Mrs. Neville suddenly looked awfully old.

"Have a good summer, Mrs. Neville!" I told her from the doorway.

"Good-bye," she said, and she smiled.

I ran out along the corridor, my arms unencumbered by books, my mind unencumbered by facts and figures, quotations and dates. I ran out into the golden sunlight, and my summer had begun.

I was still without a bike. It had been almost three weeks since Mom and I had gone to visit the Lady. I kept bugging Mom to call her, but Mom said for me to be patient, that I'd get the new bike when it arrived and not a minute before. Mom and Dad had a long talk about the Lady, as they sat on the porch in the blue twilight, and I guess I wasn't supposed to be listening but I heard Dad say, "I don't care what she dreams. I'm *not* goin'." Sometimes at night I awakened to hear my father crying out in his sleep, and then I'd hear Mom trying to calm him down. I'd hear him say something like ". . . in the lake . . ." or ". . . down in the dark . . ." and I knew what had gotten into his mind like a black leech. Dad had started pushing his plate away at dinner when it was still half full, which was in direct violation of his "clean your plate, Cory, because there are youngsters starvin' in India" speech. He'd started losing weight, and he'd had to pull the belt in tight on his milkman trousers. His face had begun changing, too; his cheekbones were getting sharper, his eyes sinking back in their sockets. He listened to a lot of baseball on the radio and watched the games on television, and as often as not he went to sleep in his easy chair with his mouth open. In his sleep, his face flinched.

I was getting scared for him.

I believe I understand what was gnawing at my father. It was not simply the fact that he'd seen a dead man. It was not the fact that the dead man had been murdered, because there had been murders—though, thank goodness, relatively few—in Zephyr before. I think the meanness of the act, the brutal cold-bloodedness of it, was what had eaten into my father's soul. Dad was smart about a lot of things; he was commonsense smart, and he knew right from wrong and he was a man of his word, but he was naive about the world in many ways. I don't think he'd ever believed that evil could exist in Zephyr. The idea that a fellow human being could be beaten and strangled, handcuffed to a wheel and denied a Christian burial in God's earth—and that this terrible thing had happened right in his own hometown where he'd been born and raised—had hurt something deep inside him. Broken something, maybe, that he couldn't fix by himself. Maybe it was also because the murdered man seemed to have no past, and that no one had responded to Sheriff Amory's inquiries.

"He had to be *somebody*," I'd heard Dad telling Mom one night, through the wall. "Didn't he have a wife, or children, or brothers or sisters? Didn't he have folks of his own? My God, Rebecca, he had to have a *name!* Who was he? And where did he come from?"

"That's for the sheriff to find out."

"J.T. *can't* find out anythin'! He's given it up!"

"I think you ought to go see the Lady, Tom."

"No."

"Why not? You saw the drawin'. You know it's the same tat-too. Why won't you at least go talk to her?"

"Because—" He paused, and I could tell he was searching in-side himself for an answer. "Because I don't believe in her kind of magic, that's why. It's false trickery. She must've read about that tattoo in the *Journal*."

"It wasn't described in such detail in the paper. You know that. And she said she heard voices and piano music, and she saw a pair of hands. Go talk to her, Tom. Please go."

"She doesn't have anythin' to tell me," Dad said firmly. "At least not anythin' I want to hear."

And that was where it stood, as my father's sleep was haunted by a drowned phantom with no name.

On this first day of summer, though, I wasn't thinking about any of that. I wasn't thinking about Old Moses, or Midnight Mona, or the man with the green-feathered hat. I was thinking of joining my friends in what had become our ritual of celebration.

I ran home from school. Rebel was waiting for me on the front porch. I told Mom I'd be back after a while, and then I ran into the woods behind our house with Rebel at my heels. The forest was green and glorious, a warm breeze stirring through the foliage and trees and the bright sun slanting down. I reached the forest trail and followed it deeper into the woods, and Rebel veered off to chase a squirrel up a tree before he came on. It took me about ten minutes to break through the forest and reach the wide green clearing that stood on a rolling hillside with Zephyr stretched out below. My friends, who'd come on their bikes, were already there with their dogs: Johnny Wilson with his big red

Chief, Ben Sears with Tumper, and Davy Ray Callan with his brown-and-white-spotted Buddy.

The wind was stronger up here. It whirled around and around in the clearing, a happy circle of summer air. "We made it!" Davy Ray shouted. "School's out!"

"School's out!" Ben yelled, and jumped around like a pure idiot with Tumper barking at his side.

Johnny just grinned, and he stood staring down at our hometown with the sun hot on his face.

"You ready?" Ben asked me.

"Ready," I told him, my heart starting to beat hard.

"Everybody ready?" Ben shouted.

We were.

"Let's go, then! Summer's started!" Ben began to run around the edges of the clearing in a wide circle, with Tumper loping along behind. I followed him, Rebel weaving in and out of my track. Johnny and Davy Ray started running behind me, their dogs racing back and forth across the clearing and tusseling with each other.

We ran faster and faster. The wind was first in our faces and then at our backs. We ran around the clearing on our sturdy young legs, the wind speaking through the pines and oaks that rimmed our playground. "Faster!" Johnny shouted, limping just a little on his clubfoot. "Gotta go faster!"

We kept going, fighting the wind and then flying before it. The dogs ran beside us, barking with the sheer happiness of movement. The sun sparkled on the Tecumseh River, the sky was clear azure, and summer's heat bloomed in our lungs.

It was time. Everyone knew it was time.

"Ben's goin' up first!" I shouted. "He's gettin' ready! He's gettin'—"

Ben gave a holler. Wings tore through the back of his shirt as they grew from his shoulder blades.

"His wings are gettin' bigger!" I said. "They're the same color as his hair, and they're lazy from not bein' used for so long, but now they're startin' to beat! Look at 'em! Just look!"

Ben's feet lifted off the earth, and his wings began to take him upward.

"Tumper's goin', too!" I said. "Wait for him, Ben!"

Tumper's wings unfurled. Yapping nervously, the dog ascended beneath his master's heels. "Come on, Tumper!" Ben cried out. "Let's go!"

"Davy Ray!" I said. "Do you feel it?"

He wanted to. He really did, but I could tell he wasn't ready. "Johnny!" I said. "You're about to go!"

Johnny's wings, when they exploded from his shoulder blades, were shimmering black. He went up with big red Chief flapping at his side. I looked up at Ben, who was already fifty feet above the earth and flying like a pudgy eagle. "Ben's leavin' you, Davy Ray! Look up there at him! Hey, Ben! Call Davy Ray!"

"Come on up, Davy Ray!" Ben shouted, and he turned a barrel roll. "The air's just fine!"

"I'm ready!" Davy Ray said, his teeth clenched. "I'm ready! Talk me up, Cory!"

"You can feel your wings startin' to grow, can't you? Yeah, I see 'em! They're gettin' ready to bust free! Here they come! They're loose!"

"I feel 'em! I feel 'em!" Davy Ray grinned, sweat on his face. His sleek auburn-colored wings began to flap, and he ascended with a swimming motion. I knew that Davy Ray was not afraid of flying; he never had been in the summers we'd been coming here. He was only afraid of that first leap of faith when you left the ground. "Buddy's comin' after you!" I shouted as the dog's brown-and-white-spotted wings caught the air. Buddy dog-paddled upward.

My own wings suddenly burst from my shoulder blades, unfurling like brown flags. They ripped through my shirt, hungry for wind. I felt the delirium of freedom lighten my bones. As I began to rise, I had a few seconds of panic akin to the summer's first jump into the cold waters of the public pool. My wings had been tight and dormant under my flesh since the end of August, and though they might have twitched every once in a while around Halloween, Thanksgiving, Christmas vacation, and Easter break, they had been asleep and only dreaming of this day. They felt heavy and ungainly, and I wondered—as I did every summer since our ritual had begun—how such things could read the air almost of their own accord. And then my wings filled up with wind and I felt their awesome muscular might. They gave a jerking motion, like the reaction after a sneeze. The second flap was more controlled and powerful; the third was as pretty as poetry. My wings began to beat in the current of air. "I'm doin' it!" I shouted as I rose after my friends and their dogs in the bright sky.

I heard a familiar barking, close behind. I looked back. Rebel's white wings had grown, and he was following me. I flapped upward, following the others who followed Ben. "Not so fast, Ben!" I cautioned, but he was soaring toward seventy feet. He deserved to fly, I thought, for what he had endured on the ground. Tumper and Buddy swooped around and around in a long lazy circle and Rebel barked to be allowed in the game. Chief, like his master, was more of a loner. Then Rebel swooped over toward me again and licked my face, and I put my arm around his neck and together we soared above the treetops.

Davy Ray had conquered his fears. He made a caw-caw-cawing sound and he put his head straight down with his arms rigid at his sides and he dove at the earth, laughing. His wings were smoothed back along his shoulders, his face contorted by the rush of air. "Pull up, Davy Ray!" I shouted as he streaked past me with Buddy in dogged pursuit. "Pull up!"

But Davy kept going down toward the green forest. When it seemed he was doomed to crash like a meteor, his wings suddenly spread out like a beautiful fan and he jackknifed his body upward. He could've chewed on pine needles if he'd wanted. Davy flew across the treetops, yelling with delight, but Buddy crashed through a few thin branches before he got himself straightened out again. The dog came up from the trees spitting and growling, leaving shell-shocked squirrels in his wake.

I kept rising toward Ben. Off by himself, Johnny was executing slow figure-eights. Rebel and Tumper began playing chase sixty feet above the ground. Ben grinned at me, his face and shirt damp with sweat, his shirttail hanging out. "Cory!" he said. "Watch this!" Then he closed his arms over his belly and pulled his knees up tightly and he whooped as he cannonballed down. As Davy had done, Ben opened his wings large to catch the wind when he wanted to slow his speed, but here something went wrong. One of his wings didn't open full. Ben yelped, knowing he was in trouble. He cartwheeled, his arms flailing. "I'm goin' dowwwnnnn!" Ben wailed on a wing and a prayer.

He slammed into the treetops, belly first.

"You okay?" Davy Ray asked him.

"You all right?" I asked.

Johnny stopped running, too, and Tumper ran over to his master and licked Ben's face. Ben sat up and showed us a skinned elbow. "Wow," he said. "That stung a little bit." Blood was showing.

"Well, you shouldn't have gone so fast!" Davy Ray told him. "Numb nuts!"

"I'm okay, really I am." Ben stood up. "We're not through flyin' yet, are we, Cory?"

He was ready to go again. I started running, my arms spread out at my sides. The others sped around me in all directions, their arms out, too, and the wind buffeting us. "Now Davy Ray's up to seventy feet," I said, "and Buddy's right there with him. Johnny's doin' a figure-eight at fifty feet. Come on, Ben! Get out of those trees!"

He came up, pine needles in his hair, his mouth split by a grin.

The first day of summer was always a wonderful time.

"This way, fellas!" Davy Ray shouted as he began flying toward Zephyr. I followed him. My wings knew the blue roads.

The sun was hot on our backs. The houses of Zephyr lay below us like toys on gum-stick streets. The cars looked like little

windups you might buy at the five and dime. We flew on over
the Tecumseh's sparkling brown snake, over the gargoyle bridge
and the old railroad trestle. I could see some fishermen in a row-
boat down there. If Old Moses decided to grab their bait, they
wouldn't be sitting so calmly waiting for a mudcat.

Our small shadows, and those of our dogs, moved across the
earth like secret writing. We flew over the dark brown, oblong
stain of Saxon's Lake. I didn't like it, even as I caught a warm current and zoomed up to seventy feet. I didn't like what was lying
in it like a seed in a rotten apple. Davy dove down and flew less
than ten feet over the lake's surface. I figured he'd better be careful; if his wings got wet, he was through flying until they dried
out. Then he ascended again, and all of us flew over the forest and
farmland that lay beyond Saxon's Lake like a patchwork quilt of
wild green and burnished brown.

"Where are we now, Cory?" Davy Ray asked.

I said, "We're almost to . . ."

Robbins Air Force Base, a huge flat clearing amid an ocean
of woods. I pointed out a silver jet fighter heading in for a landing. Beyond the base, and off limits to everybody including boys
with wings, was a testing ground where the fighter pilots shot at
dummy ground targets and bombers occasionally dropped a real
payload that rattled the windows of Zephyr. The airfield was the
boundary of our jaunt, and we turned around in the hot blue and
began flying back the way we'd come: over fields and forest, lake,
river, and rooftops.

With Rebel at my side, I circled above my house. The other
guys were swooping around their own houses, their dogs barking
happily. I realized how small my house was compared to the great
world that stretched off in all directions. From my height I could
see roads going off to the horizon, and cars and trucks on those
roads heading to destinations unknown. Wanderlust is part of
summer, too; I was feeling it, and wondering if I would ever travel
those roads, and if I did where I would be going. I wondered, as
well, what might happen if Mom or Dad suddenly walked out of

the house, saw my shadow and Rebel's on the yard, and looked up. I doubt if they ever knew their son could fly.

I made a circle of the chimneytops and turrets of the Thaxter mansion, at the top of Temple Street. Then I rejoined my friends, and we reached the clearing on tired wings.

We made a few circles, descending one after the other like graceful leaves. The ground was a jolt under my heels, and I kept running as my wings and body adjusted again to earth's grasp. Then we were all on the ground, running around the clearing with our dogs, first pushing the wind and then being pushed by it. Our wings folded up and returned to their hidden sheaths in our hollow shoulder blades; the dogs' wings slid down into the flesh and sealed over with a rippling of hair—white, brown, red, brown and white spotted. Our torn shirts mended themselves, and no mother would ever know what had burst through them. We were drenched with sweat, our faces and arms shining with it, and as we became earthbound again we ceased our running and dropped exhausted to the grass.

The dogs were upon us at once, licking our faces. Our ritual flight had ended for another summer.

We sat around for a while, talking once our hearts and minds had settled down. We talked about all the things we were going to do this summer; there were so many things, the days wouldn't be long enough. But we all decided we wanted to go camping, and that was for sure.

Then it was time to go home. "See you guys!" Ben said as he wheeled away on his bike with Tumper in pursuit. "Catch ya later!" Davy Ray told us as he departed on his bike and Buddy sprinted after a cottontail rabbit. "See you later!" Johnny said as he pedaled away with faithful Chief loping at his side. I waved. "Alligator!" I said.

I walked home, pausing to throw a few pine cones for Rebel to chase. He barked furiously at a snake hole he'd discovered, but I pulled him away from it before whatever was inside came sliding out. It was a mighty big snake hole.

At home, Mom looked at me aghast when I strolled into the kitchen. "You're drippin' wet!" she said. "What've you been *doin'?*"

I shrugged as I reached for the pitcher of cold lemonade. "Nothin' much," I answered.

2

Barbershop Talk

L ITTLE BIT OFF THE TOP and thin the sides out, Tom?"
"That'll do me, I believe."

"You got it, my friend."

This was how Mr. Perry Dollar, the owner of Dollar's Barbershop on Merchants Street, began every haircut. It never mattered how a fellow requested his hair cut; he always walked out with a little bit off the top and the sides thinned out. Of course, we're talking about a real haircut here, none of that "hair-styling" stuff. For one dollar and fifty cents, you got the treatment: wrapped to the neck under a crisp blue-striped barber towel, scissors-trimmed and clippers-raked, hot lather applied to the back of your neck and the fine hairs there scraped off with a freshly stropped straight razor, followed by a liberal dousing from one of the mystery bottles of Wildroot, Vitalis, or Brylcreem hair dressings. I say "mystery bottles" because every time I got my hair cut at Mr. Dollar's, those bottles, on a shelf above the barber chair, were exactly half full and never seemed to go up or down an inch. When the haircutting was done—"the scalping" was much the better term for it—and Mr. Dollar unpinned the barber towel from around your neck and swept the dead hairs out of your collar with a brush that felt like whiskers from a boar's snout, the adults got to reach into the peanut-brittle jar and the kids got their choice of lime, lemon, grape, or cherry suckers.

"Hot day," Mr. Dollar commented as he lifted up Dad's hair with a comb and snipped the ends with scissors.

"Sure is."

"Known it hotter, though. One hundred and three degrees this day in 1936."

"One hundred and *four* degrees this day in 1927!" said Mr. Owen Cathcoate, an aged specimen who was playing checkers with Mr. Gabriel "Jazzman" Jackson at the back of the barbershop, where the overhead fan kept the place the coolest. Mr. Cathcoate's wrinkled face was dotted with liver spots, like a map of some strange and foreign country. He had narrow-slit eyes and long-fingered hands, and his scraggly yellowish-white hair hung down around his shoulders, which must have been torture for Mr. Dollar to have to look at. Mr. Jackson was a big-bellied black man with iron-gray hair and a small, neat mustache, and he shined and repaired shoes for people who brought them in, his workshop being at the rear of Mr. Dollar's place. Mr. Jackson got his nickname because, as Dad told me, he could "blow butterflies and hornets out of that clarinet of his." The clarinet, in a well-seasoned black case, was never far from Mr. Jackson's side.

"Be a whole lot hotter 'fore July gets here," Mr. Jackson said as he pondered the pieces. He started to make a move and then thought better of it. "Owen, I do believe you're tryin' to put me between a rock and a hard place, ain't you?"

"I wouldn't dream of such a thing, Mr. Jackson."

"Oh, you sly old fox you!" the Jazzman said when he saw the simple but deadly trap Mr. Cathcoate had laid open for him. "Gonna skin me up and serve me for dinner, huh? Well, I'd be mighty tough to chew on!" He made a move that for the moment got him out of danger.

Mr. Dollar was short and stocky and had a face like a contented bulldog. His gray eyebrows stuck out everywhichway like wild weeds, and his hair was shaved to the sandy scalp. He could make the neatest parts of anybody I've ever seen. He knew all there was to know about the history of Zephyr. Because he had been the only barber in town for over twenty years, he had his finger on the roaring pulse of gossip and he could tell you everything that was going on, if you had an afternoon to sit and listen. He also had a nifty collection of tattered comic books, *Field & Stream*s, and *Sports Illustrated*s, and I had heard from Davy Ray that Mr. Dollar kept a box of *Stag, Confidential,* and *Argosy* magazines in the back for adults only.

"Cory?" Mr. Dollar said as he cut my father's hair. "You met the new boy yet?"

"No sir?" I didn't know there *was* a new boy.

"Came in here yesterday with his dad to get a haircut. Got good hair, but that cowlick about blunted my scissors." *Snip, snip,* they sang. "He just moved here last week."

"New family rentin' that house on the corner of Greenhowe and Shantuck?" Dad asked.

"Yeah, that's them. The Curliss family. Nice people. All of 'em got good hair."

"What's Mr. Curliss do?"

"Salesman," Mr. Dollar said. "Sells shirts for some company in Atlanta. The boy's a couple of years younger than Cory. I set him up on the horse and he didn't squirm a bit."

The horse was a carved golden palomino that had been salvaged from a doomed merry-go-round somewhere; now it was bolted to the floor next to the regular barber's chair. Only babies got their hair cut while sitting on the horse, even though there were times when I wished I might be able to sit on that horse again and put my feet in the stirrups while my hair was being snipped. Still, the fact that the Curliss boy—at nine or ten years of age, say—wanted to sit on the horse told me he must be a pansy.

"Mr. Curliss seems like a decent fella," Mr. Dollar went on, following the scissors across my father's scalp. "Quiet, though. Kinda timid for a salesman, I'd say. That's a hard row to hoe."

"I'll bet," Dad said.

"I got the impression Mr. Curliss has moved around quite a bit. He told me all the places he and the family have lived. I guess, bein' a salesman, you'd have to be prepared to go where the company says go."

"I couldn't do that," Dad said. "I've gotta have roots." Mr. Dollar nodded. He left that topic and wandered through others like a man through high grass, not seeing anything but the next step. "Yessir," he said. "If them Beatle boys came in here, they'd sure 'nuff leave lookin' like men 'stead of women." His eyebrows squeezed together as he wandered on in a new direction. "Communists say they're gonna bury us. Gotta stop 'em while we can, 'fore they get to our country. Send our boys to bust their tails in that place over there . . . y'know, where they grow all the bamboo."

"Vietnam," Dad supplied.

"Right. That's the place. Kill 'em there and we won't have to worry no more." Mr. Dollar's scissors were getting up to speed. A new thought was being born somewhere between Mr. Dollar's ears. "J.T. ever figure out who went down in Saxon's Lake, Tom?"

I watched my father's face. No expression registered there, but I knew this question must be stabbing him. "No, Perry. He never did."

"He was a federal man, is what I think," the Jazzman ventured. "Must've been lookin' for stills. I think the Blaylocks killed him."

"That's what Mr. Sculley believes, too," Dad said.

"The Blaylocks are bad news, that's the truth." Mr. Dollar switched on his clipper and worked on Dad's sideburns. "Wouldn't be the first man they've killed."

"Why do you say that?"

"Sim Sears used to buy whiskey from the youngest boy,

Donny. Oh—" Mr. Dollar looked at me. "I'm not talkin' out of school, am I?"

"It's all right," Dad told him. "Go ahead."

"Well, this is from Sim's mouth, so I guess he's come to grips with it. Anyway, Donny Blaylock used to sell moonshine to Sim, and Sim told me Donny and him got drunk up in the woods one night—the night that meteor fell up there near Union Town— and Donny told him things."

"Things?" Dad prodded. "What things?"

"Donny told Sim he'd killed a man," Mr. Dollar said. "Didn't tell him the why, the when, or the who. Just that he'd killed a man and he was glad of it."

"Does J.T. know about this?"

"Nope. And he won't hear it from me, either. I don't want to get J.T. killed. You ever see Biggun Blaylock?"

"No."

"Big as a moose and full of the devil. If I told J.T. what Sim had told me, he'd have to go out and find the Blaylocks. If he *did* find 'em, which I doubt he could, that bunch would hang him up by his heels and cut his throat open like a—" Again Mr. Dollar looked at me, sitting there, all eyes and ears, behind a Hawkman comic book. "Well, I kinda figure that'd be the last of our sheriff," Mr. Dollar finished.

"The Blaylocks don't own the county!" Dad said. "If they committed a murder, they ought to pay for it!"

"That's right, they should," Mr. Dollar agreed as he returned to his clipping. "Biggun came in here last November to pick up a pair of boots he was havin' resoled. Remember that, Jazzman?"

"Shore do. Fine, expensive boots. I was scared to death of gettin' a scuff on 'em."

"You know what Biggun said as he was payin' for his boots?" Mr. Dollar asked my father. "He said they were his stompin' boots, and anybody who got under 'em wouldn't be standin' up again. I figured that to mean he didn't want anybody messin' in his business. So who's gonna be fool enough to go lookin' to get killed by the Blaylocks?"

"That's what happened to that fella at the bottom of the lake," the Jazzman said. "He was messin' in the Blaylocks' business." *Bidness,* he pronounced it.

"I don't care if they brew up 'shine and sell it outta the back of their trucks," Mr. Dollar went on. "No harm done to *me.* I don't care if they fix the stock car races, because I'm not a gambler. I don't care what they do to them fallen angels at Grace Stafford's, because I'm a family man."

"Hold on," Dad said. "What about Grace Stafford's place?"

"Ain't her place. She just manages it. The Blaylocks own it, lock, stock, and hair curlers."

Dad grunted softly. "I didn't know that."

"Oh, yeah!" Mr. Dollar applied lather to the back of Dad's neck and worked a straight razor along the leather strop. "The Blaylocks are rakin' it in, that's for sure. Makin' a killin' off the Air Force fellas." With a steady hand, he began shaving my father's neck. "The Blaylocks are too much for J.T. to handle. It'd take Edgar Hoover himself to throw 'em in jail."

"Wyatt Earp could do it." Mr. Cathcoate spoke up now. "If he was still alive, I mean."

"I reckon he could at that, Owen." Mr. Dollar glanced at me, gauging my interest, and then back to the old man. "Hey, Owen! I don't think young Cory here knows about you and Wyatt Earp!" Mr. Dollar winked at me conspiratorially. "Tell him the tale, why don't you?"

Mr. Cathcoate didn't answer for a moment, but it was his turn and he didn't move any of the checkers pieces. "Naw," he replied at last. "I'll let it rest."

"Come on, Owen! Tell the boy! You want to hear it, don't you, Cory?" Before I could say yes or no, Mr. Dollar plowed on. "See there? He wants to hear it!"

"Long time gone," Mr. Cathcoate said quietly.

"Eighteen hundred and eighty-one, wasn't it? October twenty-sixth at Tombstone, Arizona? You were all of nine years old?"

"That's right." Mr. Cathcoate nodded. "I was nine years old."

"And tell the boy what you did on that day."

Mr. Cathcoate sat staring at the checkers board. "Go on, Owen," the Jazzman urged in a gentle voice. "You tell him."

"I . . . killed a man on that day," Mr. Cathcoate said. "And I saved the life of Wyatt Earp at the O.K. Corral."

"There you go, Cory!" Mr. Dollar grinned. "Bet you didn't know you were sittin' in here with a real live *gunfighter,* did you?" The way Mr. Dollar said that, though, made me think he didn't believe a word of it, and that he enjoyed goading Mr. Cathcoate about it.

Of course I'd heard about the O.K. Corral. Every boy with even a passing interest in cowboys and the Wild West knew that story, about the day the Earp brothers—Wyatt, Virgil, and Morgan—and cardsharp Doc Holliday faced down the rustling Clantons and McLowerys in the hot dust of Tombstone. "Is that for real, Mr. Cathcoate?" I asked.

"For real. I was lucky that day. I was just a kid, didn't know nothin' about guns. Almost shot my foot off."

"Tell him how you saved ol' Wyatt," Mr. Dollar urged as he blotted the last of the lather off the back of Dad's neck with a steaming towel.

Mr. Cathcoate frowned. I figured he didn't like remembering it, or else he was trying to put the details together again. A ninety-two-year-old man has to open a lot of locks to recall a day when he was nine years old. But I suppose that particular day was worth remembering.

Mr. Cathcoate finally said, "Wasn't supposed to be anybody on the street. Everybody knew the Earps, Doc Holliday, the McLowerys, and the Clantons were gonna spill blood. It had been a long time brewin'. But I was there, hidin' behind a shack. Little fool, me." He pushed his chair back from the checkers board, and he sat with his long-fingered hands twined together and the fan's breeze stirring his hair. "I heard all the shoutin', and all the guns goin' off. I heard bullets hittin' flesh. That's a sound you don't forget if you live to be a hundred and ninety-two." His slitted eyes stared at me, but I could tell he was looking toward the past, where dust clouds rose from the bloodstained earth and shadows aimed their six-guns. "A terrible lot of shootin'," he said. "A bullet went through the shack next to my head. I heard it whine. Then I got down low and I stayed there. Pretty soon a man came staggerin' past me and fell to his knees. It was Billy Clanton. He was all shot up, but he had a gun in his hand. He looked at me. Right at me. And then he coughed and blood spurted out of his mouth and nose and he fell on his face right next to me."

"Wow!" I said, my arms chillbumped.

"Oh, there's more!" Mr. Dollar announced. "Tell him, Owen!"

"A shadow fell on me," Mr. Cathcoate said, his voice raspy. "I looked up, and I saw Wyatt Earp. His face was covered with dust, and he seemed ten feet tall. He said, 'Run home, boy.' I can hear him say that, clear as a bell. But I was scared and I stayed where I was, and Wyatt Earp walked on around to the other side of the shed. The fight was over. Clantons and McLowerys were lyin' on the ground shot to pieces. Then it happened."

"What happened?" I asked when Mr. Cathcoate paused to breathe.

"The fella who'd been hidin' in an empty rain barrel raised up and took aim with his pistol at Wyatt Earp's back. I'd never seen him before. But he was right there, as close to me as you are. He took aim, and I heard him click the trigger back."

"This here's the good part," Mr. Dollar said. "Then what, Owen?"

"Then . . . I picked up Billy Clanton's pistol. Thing was as heavy as a cannon, and it had blood all over the grip. I could hardly hold it." Mr. Cathcoate was silent; his eyes closed. He went on: "Wasn't time to call out. Wasn't time to do a thing except what I did. I was just meanin' to scare the fella by firin' into the sky, and to get Mr. Earp's attention. But the gun went off. Just like that: *boom*." His eyes opened at the memory of the shot. "Knocked me down, 'bout busted my shoulder. I heard the bullet ricochet off a rock about six inches from my right foot. That bullet went straight through the fella's gunhand wrist. Blew the pistol out of his hand, broke his wrist open so the edge of a bone was stickin' out. He bled like a fountain. And as he was bleedin' to death I was sayin', 'I'm sorry, I'm sorry, I'm sorry.' 'Cause I didn't mean to kill anybody. I just meant to keep Mr. Earp from gettin' killed." He sighed, long and softly; it was like the sound of wind blowing dust over the graves on Boot Hill. "I was standin' over the body, holdin' Billy Clanton's gun. Doc Holliday came up to me, and he gave me a four-bit piece and he said, 'Go buy yourself a candy stick, kid.' That's how I got the name."

"What name?" I asked.

"The Candystick Kid," Mr. Cathcoate answered. "Mr. Earp came to my house to have dinner. My dad was a farmer. We didn't have much, but we fed Mr. Earp as best we could. He gave me Billy Clanton's gun and holster as a gift for savin' his life." Mr. Cathcoate shook his scraggly-maned head. "I should've thrown that damn gun down the well, like my momma wanted me to."

"Why?"

" 'Cause," he said, and here he seemed to get irritable and agitated, "I *liked* it too much, that's why! I started learnin' how to *use* it! Started likin' its smell, and its weight, and how it felt warm in my hand after it had just gone off, and how that bottle I was aimin' at flew all to pieces in a heartbeat, that's why." He scowled as if he'd just had a taste of bitter fruit. "Started shootin' birds out of the sky, and believin' I was a quick-draw artist. Then it started workin' on my mind, wonderin' how fast I could be against some other boy with a gun. I kept practicin', kept slappin' that leather and pullin' that hogleg out time and again. And when I was sixteen years old I went to Yuma in a stagecoach and I killed a gunslinger there name of Edward Bonteel, and that's when I put a foot in hell."

"Ol' Owen here got to be quite a name," Mr. Dollar said as he brushed the clipped hairs from Dad's shoulders. "The Candystick Kid, I mean. How many fellas did you send to meet their Maker, Owen?" Mr. Dollar looked at me and quickly winked.

"I killed fourteen men," Mr. Cathcoate said. There was no pride in his voice. "Fourteen men." He stared at the red and black squares of the checkerboard. "Youngest was nineteen. Oldest was forty-two. Maybe some of 'em deserved to die. Maybe that's not for me to say. I killed 'em, every one, in fair fights. But I was lookin' to kill 'em. I was lookin' to make a big name for myself, be a big man. The day I got shot by a younger, faster fella, I decided I was livin' on borrowed time. I cleared out."

"You got shot?" I asked. "Where'd it hit you?"

"Left side. But I aimed better. Shot that fella through the forehead, smack dab. My gunfightin' days were over, though. I headed east. Wound up here. That's my story'

"Still got that gun and holster, don't you, Candystick?" Mr. Dollar inquired.

Mr. Cathcoate didn't reply. He sat there, motionless. I thought he'd gone to sleep, though his heavy-lidded eyes were still open. Then, abruptly, he stood up from his chair and walked on stiffened legs to where Mr. Dollar was standing. He pushed his face toward Mr. Dollar's, and I saw his expression in the mirror; Mr. Cathcoate's age-spotted face was grim and thin-lipped, like a skull bound up with brown leather. Mr. Cathcoate's mouth split open in a smile, but it was not a happy smile. It was a terrible smile, and I saw Mr. Dollar shrink back from it.

"Perry," Mr. Cathcoate said, "I know you think I'm an old fool half out of my head. I accept the fact that you laugh at me when you think I'm not lookin'. But if I didn't have eyes in the back of my head, Perry, I wouldn't be alive right now."

"Uh . . . uh . . . why, no, Owen!" Mr. Dollar blubbered. "I'm not laughin' at you! Honest!"

"Now you're either lyin', or callin' me a liar," the old man said, and something about the soft way he said that made my bones grow cold.

"I'm . . . sorry if you think I'm—"

"Yes, I still have the gun and holster," Mr. Cathcoate inter-rupted him. "I kept 'em for old time's sake. Now, you understand this, Perry." He leaned in closer, and Mr. Dollar tried to smile but he only summoned up a weak grin. "You can call me Owen, or Mr. Cathcoate. You can call me Hey, you or Old Man. But you're not to call me by my gunfighter name. Not today, not tomorrow, not ever. Do we see eye to eye on that, Perry?"

"Owen, there's no call to be—"

"Do we see eye to eye?" Mr. Cathcoate repeated.

"Uh . . . yeah. We do. Sure." Mr. Dollar nodded. "Whatever you say, Owen."

"No, not whatever I say. Just this."

"Okay. No problem."

Mr. Cathcoate stared into Mr. Dollar's eyes for another few seconds, as if looking for the truth there. Then he said, "I'll be leavin' now," and he walked to the door.

"What about our game, Owen?" the Jazzman asked.

Mr. Cathcoate paused. "I don't want to play anymore," he said, and then he pushed through the door and out into the hot June afternoon. A wave of heat rolled in as the door settled shut. I stood up, went to the plate-glass window, and watched Mr. Cath-coate walking slowly up the sidewalk of Merchants Street, his hands in his pockets.

"Well, what do you think about that?" Mr. Dollar asked. "What do you suppose set him off?"

"He knows you don't believe none of that story," the Jazzman said as he began to put away the checkers pieces and the board.

"Is it true, or not?" Dad stood up from the chair. His ears had been lowered considerably, the back of his neck ruddy where it had been shaved and scrubbed.

" 'Course it's not true!" Mr. Dollar laughed with a snort. "Owen's crazy! Been out of his head for years!"

"It didn't happen like he said it did?" I kept watching Mr. Cathcoate move away up the sidewalk.

"No. He made the whole thing up."

"How do you know that for sure?" Dad asked.

"Come on, Tom! What would a Wild West gunfighter be doin' in Zephyr? And don't you think it'd be in the history books if a kid saved Wyatt Earp's life at the O.K. Corral? I went to the library and looked it up. Ain't no mention of any kid savin' Wyatt Earp's life, and in this book I found about gunfighters there's nobody called the Candystick Kid, either." Mr. Dollar brushed hair out of the chair with furious strokes. "Your turn, Cory. Get on up here."

I started to move away from the window, but I saw Mr. Cathcoate wave to someone. Vernon Thaxter, naked as innocence, was walking on the other side of Merchants Street. Vernon was walking fast, as if he had somewhere important to go, but he lifted his hand in greeting to Mr. Cathcoate.

The two crazy men passed each other, going their separate ways.

I didn't laugh. I wondered what it was that had made Mr. Cathcoate want to believe so badly that he'd been a gunfighter, just as Vernon Thaxter believed he really had somewhere to go.

I got up in the chair. Mr. Dollar pinned the barber towel around my neck, and he combed through my hair a few times as Dad sat down to read a *Sports Illustrated*.

"Little bit off the top and thin the sides out?" Mr. Dollar asked.

"Yes sir," I said. "That'd be fine."

The scissors sang, and little dead parts of me flew off.

3

A Boy and a Ball

I T WAS ON THE front porch when we got home from Mr. Dollar's.

Right there, on its kickstand.

A brand new bicycle.

"Gosh," I said as I got out of the pickup. That's all I could say. I walked up the porch steps in a trance, and I touched it.

It was not a dream. It was real, and it was beautiful.

Dad whistled in appreciation. He knew a good-looking bike when he saw it. "That's some piece of work, huh?"

"Yes sir." I still couldn't believe it. Here was something I had desired in my heart for a long, long time. It belonged to me now, and I felt like the king of the world.

In later years I would think that no woman's lips had ever been as red as that bike. No low-slung foreign sports car with wire wheels and purring engine would ever look as powerful or as capable as that bike. No chrome would ever gleam with such purity, like the silver moon on a summer's night. It had a big round headlight and a horn with a rubber bulb, and its frame looked as strong and solid as the biceps of Hercules. But it looked *fast,* too;

its handlebars sloped forward like an invitation to taste the wind, its black rubber pedals unscuffed by any foot before mine. Dad ran his fingers along the headlight, and then he picked the bike up with one hand. "Boy, it hardly weighs anything!" he marveled. "Lightest metal I've ever felt!" He put it down again, and it settled on its kickstand like an obedient but barely tamed animal.

I was on that seat in two seconds. I had a little trouble at first, because the way both the handlebars and the seat tilted forward I felt like my balance was off. My head was thrust over the front wheel, my back pressed down in a straight line in emulation of the bike's spine. I had the feeling of being on a machine that could easily get out of my control if I wasn't careful; there was something about it that both thrilled and scared me.

Mom came out of the house. The bike had arrived about an hour before, she told us. Mr. Lightfoot had brought it in the back of his truck. "He said the Lady wants you to ride easy on it until it gets used to you," she said. She looked at Dad, who was walking in a circle around the new bike. "He *can* keep it, can't he?"

"I don't like us acceptin' charity. You know that."

"It's not charity. It's a reward for a good deed."

Dad continued his circling. He stopped and prodded his shoe at the front tire. "This must've cost her an awful lot of money. It's a fine bike, that's for sure."

"Can I keep it, Dad?" I asked.

He stood there, his hands on his hips. He chewed on his bottom lip for a moment, and then he looked at Mom. "It's not charity?"

"No."

Dad's gaze found me. "Yeah," he said, and no word was ever more welcome. "It's yours."

"Thanks! Thanks a million times!"

"So now that you've got a new bike, what're you gonna name it?" Dad asked.

I hadn't thought about this yet. I shook my head, still trying to get used to the way it held my body forward like a spear.

"Might as well take it out for a spin, don't you think?" He slid an arm around Mom's waist, and he grinned at me.

"Yes sir," I said, but I got off to chop the kickstand up and guide it down the porch steps. It seemed an indignity to jar the bike before we'd gotten to know each other. Either that, or I feared waking it up just yet. I sat on the seat again, my feet on the ground.

"Go ahead," Dad told me. "Just don't burn up the street."

I nodded, but I didn't move. I swear I thought I felt the bike tremble, as if with anticipation. Maybe it was just me.

"Crank 'er up," Dad said.

This was the moment of truth. I took a breath, put one foot on a pedal, and pushed off with the other. Then both feet were on the pedals, and I aimed the bike toward the street. The wheels turned with hardly any noise, just a quiet *tick . . . tick . . . tick* like a bomb about to go off.

"Have fun!" my mother called as she opened the porch door.

I looked back and took a hand off the handlebars to wave, and the bike suddenly lurched out of my control and zigzagged wildly. I almost went down in my first crash, but I grasped hold again and the bike straightened out. The pedals were smooth as ice cream, the wheels spinning faster across the hot pavement. This was a bike, I realized, that could get away from you like a rocket. I tore away along the street, the wind hissing through my newly cut hair, and to tell the truth, I felt as if I was hanging on for dear life. I was used to an old, sluggish chain and sprocket that needed a lot of leg muscle, but this bike demanded a lighter touch. When I put on the brakes the first time, I almost flew off the seat. I spun it around in a wide circle and gave it more speed again, and I got going so fast so quickly, the back of my neck started sweating. I felt one pedal-push away from leaving the ground, but the front wheel responded to my grip on the handlebars seemingly even as I *thought* what direction I wanted to turn. Like a rocket, the bike sped me through the tree-shaded streets of my hometown, and as we carved the wind together I decided that would be its name.

"Rocket," I said, the word whirling away behind me in the slipstream. "That sound all right to you?"

It didn't throw me off. It didn't veer for the nearest tree. I took that as a yes.

I started getting bolder. I sideslipped and figure-eighted and curb-jumped, and Rocket obeyed me without hesitation. I leaned over those handlebars and pumped the pedals with all my strength and Rocket shot along Shantuck Street, the pools of shadow and sunlight opening up before me. I zipped up onto the sidewalk, where the tires barely registered the passing cracks. The air was hot in my lungs and cool on my face, and the houses and trees were whipping past in a sublime blur. At this instant I felt at one with Rocket, as if we were of the same skin and grease, and when I grinned, a bug flew into my teeth. I didn't care; I swallowed it because I was invincible.

And such ideas inevitably lead to what next occurred.

I hit a patch of broken sidewalk without slowing down or trying to miss it, and I felt Rocket shudder from fender to fender. A noise like a grunt ran through the frame. The jolt knocked one of my hands loose from the handlebars, and Rocket's front tire hit an edge of concrete and the bike bucked up and twisted like an angry stallion. My feet left the pedals and my butt left the seat, and as I went off into the air I thought of something Mom had said: *The Lady wants you to ride easy on it until it gets used to you.*

I didn't have much time to ponder it. In the next second I crashed into a hedge in somebody's yard and my breath left me in a *whoosh* and the green leaves took me down. I had nearly ripped a hole clear through the hedge. My arms and cheeks were scratched up some, but nothing seemed to be skinned up and bleeding. I got out of the hedge, shaking off leaves, and I saw Rocket lying on its side in the grass. Terror gripped me; if this new bike was busted up, Dad's spanking hand would be finding work. I knelt beside Rocket, checking the bike for damage. The front tire was scuffed and the fender crimped, but the chain was still on and the handlebars straight. The headlight was unbroken, the frame unbent. Rocket had been bruised but was amazingly healthy for such a nasty spill. I righted the bike, thanking whatever angel had been riding on my shoulder, and as I ran my fingers over the dented fender I saw the eye in the headlamp.

It was a golden orb with a dark pupil, and it stared at me with what might have been a brooding tolerance.

I blinked, startled.

The golden eye was gone. Now the headlight was just a plain bulb behind a circle of glass again.

I kept staring at the headlight. There was no eye in it. I rolled Rocket around, from sun to shadow and back again, but the image did not return.

I felt my head, searching for a lump. I found none.

It's crazy, the things a boy can imagine.

I got back on the seat and started pedaling along the sidewalk again. This time I took it slow and easy, and I hadn't gone twenty feet before I saw all the glass from a broken Yoo-Hoo bottle scattered across the sidewalk in front of me. I swerved Rocket over the curb and onto the street, missing the glass fragments and saving Rocket's tires. I hated to think what might have happened if I'd gone over that glass at high speed; a few scratches from a leafy hedge were mild compared to what could have been.

We had been very lucky, Rocket and me.

Davy Ray Callan lived nearby. I stopped at his house, but his mother said Davy Ray had gone to the ball field with Johnny Wilson to practice. Our Little League team—the Indians, for whom I played second base—had lost our first four games and we needed all the practice we could get. I thanked Mrs. Callan and I aimed Rocket toward the field.

It wasn't far. Davy Ray and Johnny were standing out in the sunshine and the red dust, pitching a ball back and forth. I rode Rocket onto the field and circled them, and their mouths dropped open at the sight of my new bike. Of course they had to touch it, too, had to sit on it and pedal it around a little. Next to Rocket, their bikes looked like dusty antiques. Still, this was Davy Ray's opinion of Rocket: "It don't handle so good, though, does it?" And Johnny's: "It sure is pretty, but the pedals are stiff." I realized they were not saying this simply to rain on my parade; they were good friends, and they rejoiced in my happiness. The fact of the matter is that they preferred their own bikes. Rocket had been made for me and me alone.

I rested Rocket on its kickstand and watched while Davy Ray threw high fly balls to Johnny. Yellow butterflies flew from the grass, and overhead the sky was blue and cloudless. I looked toward the brown-painted bleachers, under the signs advertising different Merchants Street stores, and I saw a figure sitting at the top.

"Hey, Davy!" I said. "Who's that?"

Davy glanced over and then lifted his glove to snare Johnny's return pitch. "I don't know. Just some kid, been sittin' there since we got here."

I watched the guy. He was hunkered forward, watching us, with one elbow on a knee and his chin propped on his palm. I turned away from Davy and walked toward the bleachers, and the kid at the top suddenly stood up as if he meant to run.

"What're you doin' up there?" I called to him.

He didn't answer. He just stood there, and I could tell he was trying to decide whether to take to his heels or not.

I got closer. I didn't recognize him; he had short-cropped dark brown hair with a wiry cowlick sticking up from the left side of his head, and he wore glasses that seemed too big for his face. He was maybe nine or ten years old, I figured, and he was a real beanpole, with gawky arms and legs. He wore blue jeans with patched knees and a white T-shirt, and the buttermilk pallor of his skin told me he didn't get outside very much. "What's your name?" I asked him as I reached the fence between the field and the bleachers.

He didn't reply.

"Can you *talk?*"

I saw him tremble. He looked as scared as a deer caught in a hunter's flashlight.

"I'm Cory Mackenson," I said. I stood there, waiting, with my fingers grasping the fence's mesh. "Don't you have a name?"

"Yeth," the boy answered.

I thought he'd said *Seth* at first, and then it dawned on me that he had a lisp. "What is it?"

"Nemo," he said.

"Nemo? Like Captain Nemo?"

"Huh?"

A student of Jules Verne he was not. "What's your last name?"

"Curlith," he said.

Curlith. It took me a few seconds to decipher it. Not Curlith, but Curliss. The new boy in town, the one who had a traveling salesman as a father. The boy who sat on the horse to get his hair cut at Mr. Dollar's. The pansy.

Nemo Curliss. Well, the name suited him. He looked like something a net might drag up from twenty thousand leagues. But my parents had taught me that everybody deserved respect, no matter if they were pansies or not, and to tell the truth, I was nothing to write home about in the physical looks department. "You're new in town," I offered.

He nodded.

"Mr. Dollar told me about you."

"He did?"

"Yeah. Said"—*you sat on the horse,* I almost told him—"you got a haircut."

"Uh-huh. 'Bout thaved me baldheaded," Nemo said, and he scratched the top of his scalp with a thin-fingered hand attached to a white, bony wrist.

"Heads up, Cory!" I heard Davy shout. I looked up. Johnny had put all his strength into a fly ball that not only overshot Davy's glove, but cleared the fence, banged against the second row of bleachers, and rolled down to the bottom.

"Little help!" Davy said, smacking his glove with his fist.

Nemo Curliss walked down from the top and picked up the

ball. He was the littlest runt I think I'd ever seen. My own arms were skinny, but his were all bones and veins. He looked at me, his dark brown eyes magnified owlish by his glasses. "Can I throw it back?" he asked.

I shrugged. "I don't care." I turned toward Davy, and maybe it was mean but I couldn't suppress a wicked smile. "Comin' at you, Davy."

"Oh, wow!" Davy started backing up in mock terror. "Don't scorch me, kid!"

Nemo walked up to the top bleacher again. He squinted toward the field. "You ready?" he yelled.

"I'm ready! Throw it, big hoss!" Davy answered.

"No, not you," Nemo corrected him. "That other guy out there." And then he reared back, swung his arm in a circle that was impossible for the eye to follow, and the ball left his hand in a white blur.

I heard the ball hiss as it rose into the sky, like a firecracker on a short fuse.

Davy cried out, "Hey!" and backpedaled to get it, but the ball was over him and gone. Beyond Davy, Johnny looked up at the falling sphere and took three steps forward. Then two steps back. One more step back, to where he'd been standing when the ball was thrown. Johnny lifted his hand and held his glove out in front of his face.

There was a sweet, solid *pop* as the ball kissed leather.

"Right in the *pocket!*" Davy shouted. "Man, did you see that thing fly?"

Out toward first base, Johnny removed his glove and wrang his catching hand, his fingers stinging with the impact.

I looked at Nemo, my mouth agape. I couldn't believe anybody as little and skinny as him could throw a baseball over the bleachers fence, much less half the width of the field and into an outstretched glove. What's more, Nemo didn't even act as if it had hurt his arm, and a heave like that would've left my shoulder sore for a week, even if I could've gotten that kind of distance out of it. It was a major league throw if I'd ever seen one. "Nemo!" I said. "Where'd you learn to throw a ball like that?"

He blinked at me behind his glasses. "Like what?" he asked.

"Come down here. Okay?"

"Why?" Nemo looked scared again. I had the feeling that he was well acquainted with the bad end of the stick. There are three things every town in the country has in common: a church, a secret, and a bully ready to tear the head off a skinny kid who couldn't fight his way out of a paper bag. I imagined that Nemo Curliss, in following his salesman daddy from town to town, had seen his share of those. I felt ashamed for my wicked smile. "It's all right," I said. "Just come on down."

"Man, what a throw!" Davy Ray Callan, having retrieved the ball from Johnny, jogged up to where Nemo was entering the field through the players' gate. "You really nailed it in there, kid! How *old* are you?"

"Nine," was the answer. "Almost nine and a half."

I could tell Davy was as puzzled as I was about Nemo's size; there should have been no way on earth for a runt like that to drill a baseball into a mitt as he had. "Go stand on second base, Johnny!" I shouted, and Johnny waved and ran over to take the position. "You want to throw some, Nemo?"

"I don't know. I'm thaposed to be gettin' home thoon."

"It won't take long. I'd kinda like to see what you can do. Davy, can he wear your glove?"

Davy took it off. The glove swallowed Nemo's left hand like a brown whale. "Why don't you stand on the pitcher's mound and throw Johnny a few?" I suggested.

Nemo looked at the pitcher's mound, at second base, and then at home plate. "I'll thand right there," he said, and he walked to the batter's box while Davy and I stood dumbfounded. From home plate to second base was quite a toss for guys our age, much less anybody nine-and-a-half years old. "You sure, Nemo?" I asked, and he said, "Thure."

Nemo took the ball out of the glove with what might have

been reverence. I watched his long fingers work around it, find a grip on the seams, and fasten themselves. "Ready?" he called.

"Yeah, I'm ready! Let 'er ri—"

Smack!

If we hadn't seen such a thing with our own eyes, none of us would ever have believed it. Nemo had wound up and pitched in a heartbeat, and if Johnny hadn't been extra quick, the ball would've caught him right in the center of his chest and knocked him flat. As it was, the sheer power of the pitch made Johnny stagger back off second base, dust smoking from the ball in his clenched glove. Johnny began to walk around in a circle, his face pinched with pain.

"You okay?" Davy shouted.

"Hurts a little," Johnny answered. Davy and I knew it must be bad for Johnny to admit it. "I can take another one." We were too far away to hear him say, under his breath, *"I hope."* He threw the ball back in a high arc to Nemo, who stepped forward six paces, watched the ball speed downward toward his face, and plucked it out of the air at the very last second. The kid knew what economy of movement was all about, but I swear he'd been an instant away from a smashed nose.

Nemo returned to the plate. He wiped dust off the tops of his brown loafers by rubbing them on the backs of his jeans legs. He started to wind up, and Johnny braced for the throw. Nemo unwound and put the ball back in his glove. "Throwin' ain't nothin'," he told us, as if all this attention embarrassed him. "Anybody with an arm can do it."

"Not like that!" Davy Ray said.

"You guyth think thith is a *big deal* or thomethin'?"

"It's fast," I said. "Real fast, Nemo. The pitcher on our team's not even as fast, and he's twice your size."

"Thith ith eathy thuff." Nemo looked out at Johnny. "Run for turd bayth!"

"What?"

"Run for turd bayth!" Nemo repeated. "Hold your glove any-where, just keep it open and where I can thee it!"

"Huh?"

"Run as fath as you can!" Nemo urged. "You don't have to look at me, jutht keep your glove open!"

"Go ahead, Johnny!" Davy called. "Do it!"

Johnny was a brave fellow. He showed it right then, as he started pounding the dirt between second and third bases. He didn't look toward home, but his head and shoulders were pulled in tight and his glove was down in front of his chest, the pocket open and facing Nemo Curliss.

Nemo pulled in a quick breath. He drew back, his white arm flashed, and the ball went like a bullet.

Johnny was going full out, his gaze fixed on third base. The ball popped into his glove when he was still a half-dozen steps from third, and the feel of it wedging solidly into the pocket was so startling that Johnny lost his balance and went down on the ground in a slide that boiled up yellow dust. When the dust began to clear, Johnny was sitting on third base staring at the ball in his glove. "Wow," he said, stunned. "Wow."

I had never in my life seen a baseball thrown with such amazing accuracy. Johnny hadn't even had to reach an inch for it; in fact, he hadn't even known the ball was coming until it hit him in the glove. "Nemo?" I said. "You ever pitched on a Little League team before?"

"Nope."

"But you've played ball before, haven't you?" Davy Ray asked.

"Nope." He frowned and pushed his glasses up with a finger because the bridge of his nose was getting slick with sweat. "My mom won't let me. Thays I might get hurt."

"You've *never* played ball on a team?"

"Well, I've got a ball and glove at home. Thometimeth I practith catchin' fly ballth. Thometimeth I thee how far I can throw. I thet up bottleth on a fence potht and knock 'em down. Thuff like that."

"Doesn't your dad want you to play ball?" I asked.

Nemo shrugged and scuffed the dust with the toe of his loafer. "He don't have much to thay about it."

I was struck with wonder. Standing before me, in the shape of a skinny little runt with thick glasses and a lisp, was a natural. "Will you pitch me a few?" I asked, and he said he would. I got Johnny's glove—which he gave up gladly from his sore hand—and I tossed the ball to Nemo. I ran to second base and planted myself. "Put it right here, Nemo!" I told him, and I extended my arm and held the mitt level with my shoulder. Nemo nodded, wound up, and let fly. I never had to move my hand. The ball smacked into the glove with a force that jangled the nerves all the way from my fingertips to my collarbone. When I threw it back, Nemo had to run forward and dart and weave to catch it. Then I backed up some more, out toward center field, where the weeds were sprouting. I lifted the mitt up over my head. "Right here, Nemo!"

Nemo crouched down, almost on his knees. His head was bent forward, as if he were trying to squeeze himself into a tight knot. He stayed that way for a few seconds, the sunlight glinting off his glasses, and then he exploded.

He flew up from his crouch like Superman bursting out of a phone booth. His throwing arm whipped back and then forward. If anybody's jaw had been caught by that flashing, bony elbow they'd have been spitting out a mouthful of broken teeth. The ball left Nemo's hand and it came at me like gangbusters.

It was a low ball, and it almost skimmed the dust between the batter's box and the pitcher's mound. But it was rising as it passed over the mound, and it seemed to be picking up speed, too. It was still rising as it zipped over second base. I heard Davy yelling at me, but I don't know what he was saying. My attention was riveted to that flying white sphere. I kept the glove up over my head, exactly where it had been when the ball was thrown, but I was prepared to duck to keep from getting plastered. The ball entered the outfield, and I could hear its hissing, full of steam and

menace. I didn't move my feet. I had time to swallow—*gulp*—
and then the ball was upon me.

It popped into the mitt's pocket, its impact strong enough to
make me step back a couple of paces. I closed my hand around the
ball, trapping it, and I could feel its heat throbbing like a pulse
through the cowhide.

"Cory!" Davy Ray was shouting, his hands up to bracket his
mouth. "Cory!"

I didn't know what Davy was hollering about, and I didn't
care. I was in a trance. Nemo Curliss had an unearthly arm. How
much of this had been a gift and how much he had trained himself to do, I didn't know, but one thing was clear: Nemo Curliss
possessed that rare combination of arm and eye that elevated him
above mere mortals. In other words, he was a humdinger.

"Cory!" This time it was Johnny yelling. "Look out!"

"What?" I called.

"Behind you!" Johnny screamed.

I heard a sound like scythes at work, slicing wheat. I turned
around, and there they were.

Gotha and Gordo Branlin, grinning astride their black bicycles, their peroxided yellow hair aflame with sunlight. They were
coming at me through the knee-high grass beyond the mowed
outfield, their legs pumping the pedals. Green grasshoppers
and black field crickets leaped for their lives under the grinding wheels. I wanted to run, but my legs were locked up. The
Branlins stopped with me between them, Gotha on my right and
Gordo on my left. Sweat glistened on their angular faces, their
eyes cutting into me. I heard a crow cawing somewhere, like the
devil's laughter.

Gotha, the oldest at fourteen, reached out and prodded the
baseball mitt with his index finger. "You playin' *ball,* Cory?" The
way he said it, it sounded dirty.

"He's playin' *with* his balls," Gordo snickered. He was thirteen, and just a shade smaller than Gotha. Neither one of them
were very big, but they were wiry and fast as whippets. Gordo

had a little scar between his eyebrows and another on his chin that said he was no stranger to either pain or bloodshed. He looked toward home plate, where Davy, Johnny, and Nemo stood. "Who the *fuck* is that?"

"New kid," I said. "His name's Nemo."

"Asshole?" Gotha stared at Nemo, too, and I could see the wolfishness in the Branlins' faces. They smelled sheep's blood. "Let's go see Asshole," he said to Gordo, and started pedaling. Gordo hit the bottom of my mitt with his hand and made the ball jump out. As I bent over to pick it up, he spat a wad into my hair. Then he pedaled away after his brother.

I knew what was going to happen. It was bad enough that Nemo was so small and skinny, but when the Branlins heard that lisp, it was going to be all she wrote. I held my breath as the Branlins approached Rocket. As they passed, Gotha kicked Rocket to the ground with supreme indifference. I swallowed my rage like a bitter seed, not knowing that it would bear fruit.

The Branlins pulled their black bikes to a halt, with the three boys between them. "You guys playin' a game?" Gotha asked, and he smiled like the snake in the Garden of Eden.

"Just throwin' the ball around some," Davy Ray told him.

"Hey, niggerblood," Gordo said to Johnny. "What're you lookin' at?"

Johnny shrugged and stared at the ground.

"You smell like shit, you know that?" Gordo taunted.

"We don't want any trouble," Davy said. "Okay?"

"Who said anythin' about trouble?" Gotha uncoiled from his bike and stood up. He rested the bike on its kickstand and leaned against it. "We didn't say anythin' about trouble. Gimme a cigarette."

Gordo reached into a back pocket and gave his brother a pack of Chesterfields. Gotha produced a matchbook that had Zephyr Hardware & Feeds across the front. He put a cigarette into his mouth and held the matchbook out to Nemo Curliss. "Light one."

Nemo took it. His hands were trembling. It took him three scrapes to make the match flare.

"Light my cigarette," Gotha ordered.

Nemo, who perhaps had seen many other Gothas and Gordos in many other towns, did as he was told. Gotha drew in smoke and exhaled it through flared nostrils. "Your name's Asshole, ain't it?"

"My . . . name ith . . . Nemo."

"*Ith?*" Gordo sprayed spittle. "*Ith?* What's the matter with your mouth, Asshole?"

I was picking up Rocket from the grass. Here I faced a decision. I could get on Rocket and ride away, leaving my friends and Nemo Curliss to their fates, or I could join them. I was no hero, that's for sure. My fighting ability was a fantasy. But I knew that if I rode away from that place and point in time, I would be forever disgraced. Not that I didn't want to, and not that every fiber of good sense wasn't telling me to haul ass.

But some good sense you listen to, and some good sense you can't live with.

I walked toward a beating, my heart pounding on its root.

"You look like a queer," Gordo said to Nemo Curliss. "Is that what you are?"

"Hey . . . listen, guys." Davy Ray managed a frail smile. "Why don't you guys—"

Gotha whirled on him, took two strides, planted a hand on Davy's chest, and shoved him hard, knocking him to the ground by hooking a sneakered foot around Davy's ankle. Davy grunted as he hit, dust pluming up around him. Gotha stood over him, smoking the Chesterfield. "You," he said. "Just. Shut. Up."

"I've gotta get home." Nemo started to walk away, but Gordo grabbed his arm and held him.

"C'mere," Gordo said. "You don't wanna go nowhere."

"Yeah, I do, 'cauth my mom thays I've gotta—"

Gordo howled with laughter, the sound startling birds out of the trees around the field. "Listen to him, Gotha! He's got shit in his mouth!"

"I think he's been suckin' too many cocks," was Gotha's opinion. "Is that right?" He aimed his hard stare at Nemo. "You been suckin' too many cocks?"

What made the Branlins the way they were was anybody's guess. Maybe the meanness had been born in them; maybe it had developed, like the pus around a wound that will not heal. In any case, the Branlins knew no law but their own, and this situation was rapidly spiraling into the danger zone.

Gordo shook Nemo. "That right? You like to suck cocks?"

"No." Nemo's voice was choked.

"Yes he does," Gotha said, his shadow heavy across Davy Ray. "He likes to suck big fat donkey cocks."

"No, I don't." Nemo's chest shook, and the first sob squeezed out.

"Oh, momma's little baby's gonna cry now!" Gordo said, grinning.

"I . . . wanna go . . . home . . ." Nemo began to sob, the tears flooding up behind his glasses.

There is nothing more cruel in this world than a young savage with a chip on his shoulder and anger in his soul. It is worse still when there is a yellow stripe down his back, as evidenced by the fact that the Branlins never went after boys their age or older.

I looked around. A car was passing the field, but its driver paid us no notice. We were on our own out here, under the scorching sun.

"Put the baby down, Gordo," Gotha said. His brother shoved Nemo to the ground. "Feed the baby, Gordo," Gotha said, and Gordo unzipped his blue jeans.

"Hey, come on!" Johnny protested. "Don't!"

Gordo, holding his exposed penis, stood over Nemo Curliss. "Shut up, niggerblood, if you don't want some rain in your face, too."

I couldn't take any more of this. I looked at the baseball in my hand. Nemo was crying. Gordo was waiting for the water to flow. I just couldn't take it.

I thought of Rocket being kicked over. I thought of the tears on Nemo's face. I threw the baseball at Gordo from about ten feet.

It didn't really have a lot on it, but it made a solid *thunk* as it hit his right shoulder. He wailed like a bobcat and staggered away from Nemo just as his fountain arced. The urine wet the front of his jeans and ran down his legs, but Gordo was grasping his shoulder and his face was all screwed up and he was yelling and sobbing at the same time. Gotha Branlin turned toward me, the cigarette clenched between his teeth and smoke whirling from his mouth. His cheeks flamed, and he propelled himself at me. Before I could think to dodge, he rammed me full force. The next thing I knew I was flat on my back with Gotha sitting on top of me, his weight crushing my chest. "I . . . can't . . . I can't . . . breathe . . ." I said.

"Good," he said, and he hit me in the face with his right fist.

The first two punches hurt. Real bad. The next two about knocked me cold, but I was squirming and yelling and trying to get away, and the scarlet blood was all over Gotha's knuckles. "Ohhhhh shit, my arm's broke!" Gordo moaned, on his knees in the grass.

A hand grabbed Gotha's peroxided hair. Gotha's head was jerked back, the cigarette fell from his mouth, and I saw Johnny standing over him. Then Davy Ray said, "Hold him!" and he smashed his fist into Gotha's nose.

The lump of flesh burst open. Blood streamed from Gotha's nostrils, and Gotha roared like a beast and got off me. He attacked Davy Ray, hammering at him with his fists. Johnny went after him, trying to grab Gotha's arms, but Gotha twisted around and swung a blow that crunched against the side of Johnny's head. Then Gordo was up again, his face a blotched rictus of pure rage, and he ran in kicking at Johnny's legs. Johnny went down, and I saw a fist bust him right in the eye. Davy Ray shouted, "You bastards!" and flung himself at Gotha, but the older boy grabbed him by the collar and swung him around like a laundry bag before throwing him to the ground. I was sitting up, blood in my mouth. Nemo was up and running for his life, but he tripped over his own tangled legs and fell headlong into the grass.

What followed in the next thirty seconds I don't like to think about. First Gotha and Gordo left Davy Ray crumpled up and crying, and then they pounced on Johnny and worked him over with brutal precision. When Johnny was gasping for air, the blood bubbling from his nostrils, the Branlins advanced on me again.

"You little piece o' shit," Gotha said, his nose dripping. He put his foot on my chest and slammed me down on my back again. Gordo, still holding his shoulder, said, "Lemme have him."

I was too dazed to fight back. Even if I hadn't been dazed, I couldn't have done very much against those two without a spiked mace and a broadsword and fifty more pounds on my bones.

"Stomp his ass, Gordo," Gotha urged.

Gordo grabbed the front of my shirt and started to haul me to my feet. My shirt ripped, and I remember thinking that Mom was going to tear me up.

"I'll kill you," somebody said.

Gotha laughed like a bark. "Put it down, kid."

"I'll kill you, I thwear I will!"

I blinked, spat blood, and looked at Nemo Curliss, who stood fifteen feet away. The baseball was in his hand, his skinny arm cocked back.

Now, this was an interesting situation. I'd been lucky in hitting Gordo's shoulder; in Nemo's hand, however, that hard round sphere was a lethal weapon. I had no doubt that Nemo could hit either one of the Branlins right between the eyes and knock their brains out. I had no doubt, either, that he *would*. Because I saw his eyes magnified behind those glasses. The fury trapped in them, like a distant conflagration, was terrible to behold. He was no longer crying or trembling. With that baseball in his grip, he was the master of the universe. I really think he was ready to kill somebody. Maybe it was the rage at being born a runt, of having a lisp, of attracting bullies like a weak calf makes a predator's mouth water. Maybe he was full to the gullet with being shoved and taunted. Whatever it was, it was there like a deadly resolve in his eyes.

Gordo let me go. Lip-ripped and shirt-ripped, I sat in the grass.

"Look at me shake," Gotha said silkily as he took a step toward Nemo.

Gordo fanned out a few paces from his brother. His penis was still hanging out of his jeans. I wondered if that would make a good target. "Throw it, chickenshit," Gordo said.

A Branlin was very close to death.

"Hey, you boys! Hey, there!"

The voice came across the field at us, from the road that ran along its edge. "Hey, you boys all right?"

I turned my head, my face as heavy as a bag of stones. Parked on the roadside was a mailman's truck. The mailman himself was walking toward us, a pith helmet shading his face. He wore shorts with black socks, and sweat stains darkened his blue shirt.

Like any animals, the Branlins knew the sound of the hinge on a cage's lid. Without a word to each other, they turned away from the carnage they had created and ran to their bikes. Gordo hurriedly pushed his penis back in and zipped up his fly, then he swung himself up in the seat. Gotha paused to kick Rocket over again; I suppose the temptation to ruin was just too great. Then he got on his bike and the two brothers started pedaling frantically back the way they'd come. "Wait a minute!" the mailman shouted, but the Branlins listened only to their inner demons. They raced across the field, dust swirling up behind them, and then they hit the trails they'd carved through the brushy grass and were gone into the patch of woods that stood beyond. Some ravens screamed in there: scavengers, welcoming their own.

It was all over but the cleaning up.

Mr. Gerald Hargison, our mailman who delivered my monthly issue of *Famous Monsters* magazine in a plain brown envelope, reached me and stopped when he saw my face. "Good God!" he said, which told me it was bad. *"Cory?"*

I nodded. My lower lip felt as big as a goosedown pillow, and my left eye was swelling up.

"You okay, boy?"

I didn't feel like twirling a Hula Hoop, that's for sure. But I could stand up, and all my teeth were still in their sockets. Davy Ray was all right, too, except his face was a mass of bruises and one of the Branlins had stepped on his fingers. Johnny Wilson, however, had been the hardest hit. Mr. Hargison, who had a fleshy, ruddy-cheeked face and smoked plastic-tipped cheroots when he was walking his route, winced as he helped Johnny sit up. Johnny's Cherokee hatchet of a nose was broken, no doubt about it. The blood was dark red and thick, and Johnny's swollen eyes couldn't hold a focus. "Boy?" Mr. Hargison said to him. "How many fingers am I holdin' up?" He held up three, right in front of Johnny's face.

"Six," Johnny said.

"I believe he's got a—"

And here was a word that never failed to frighten, giving images of brain-damaged drooling.

"—concussion. I'm gonna take him to Doc Parrish. Can you two get home?"

Us *two?* I saw Davy Ray, but where was Nemo? The ball was lying on the ground next to home plate. The boy with the perfect arm was gone.

"Those were the Branlin brothers, weren't they?" Mr. Hargison helped Johnny stand, and he took a handkerchief from his shorts pocket and held it against Johnny's nostrils. In no time, the white was spotted with blood. "Those fellas need their butts kicked."

"You're gonna be all right, Johnny," I told him, but Johnny didn't answer me and he walked rubber-legged as Mr. Hargison led him to the truck. Davy and I stood watching as Mr. Hargison got him in and then went around and started the engine. Johnny leaned back in the seat, his head lolling. He'd been hurt bad.

After Mr. Hargison had turned the mail truck around and

dropped down to rest. We got the ice cream salt, but on the way back, in the Jaybird's bulky old Ford, another test began.

"Jerome Claypool lives just down the road," he said. "He's a good ole fella. Want to drop by and say howdy?"

"We'd better get the ice cream salt to—"

"Yeah, Jerome's a good ole fella," the Jaybird said as he turned the Ford toward his friend's house.

Six miles later, he stopped in front of a ramshackle farmhouse that had a rotting sofa, a cast-off wringer, and a pile of moldering tires and rusted radiators in the front yard. I think we had crossed the line between Zephyr and Dogpatch by way of Tobacco Road somewhere a few miles back. Obviously, though, Jerome Claypool was a popular good ole fella, because there were four other cars parked in front of the place as well. "Come on, Cory," the Jaybird said as he opened his door. "We'll just go in a minute or two."

I could smell the stench of cheap cigars before we got to the porch. The Jaybird knocked on the door: *rap rap rapraprap*. "Who is it?" a cautious voice inquired from within. My grandfather replied, "Blood 'n Guts," which made me stare at him, thinking he'd lost whatever mind he had left. The door opened on noisy hinges, and a long-jawed face with dark, wrinkle-edged eyes peered out. Those eyes found me. "Who's *he?*"

"My grandboy," Jaybird said, and put his hand on my shoulder. "Name's Cory."

"Jesus, Jay!" the long-jawed face said with a scowl. "What're you bringin' a *kid* around here for?"

"No harm done. He won't say nothin'. Will you, Cory?" The hand tightened.

I didn't understand what was going on, but clearly this was not a place Grandmomma Sarah would have enjoyed visiting. I thought of Miss Grace's house out beyond Saxon's Lake, and the girl named Lainie who'd furled her wet pink tongue at me. "No sir," I told him, and the grip relaxed again. His secret—whatever it might be—was safe.

"Bodean won't like this," the man warned.

"Jerome, Bodean can stick his head up his ass for all I care. You gonna let me in or not?"

"You got the green?"

"Burnin' a hole," the Jaybird said, and touched his pocket.

I balked as he started pulling me over the threshold. "Grandmomma's waitin' for the ice cream sa—"

He looked at me, and I saw something of his true nature deep in his eyes, like the glare of a distant blast furnace. On his face there was a desperate hunger, inflamed by whatever was going on in that house. Ice cream salt was forgotten; ice cream itself was part of another world six miles away. "Come on!" he snapped.

I stood my ground. "I don't think we ought to—"

"You don't *think!*" he said, and whatever was pulling him into that house seized his face and made it mean. "You just do what I tell you, hear me?"

He gave me a hard yank and I went with him, my heart scorched. Mr. Claypool closed the door behind us and bolted it. Cigar smoke drifted in a room where no sunlight entered; the windows were all boarded up and a few measly electric lights were burning. We followed Mr. Claypool through a hallway to the rear of the house, and he opened another door. The windowless room we walked into was layered with smoke, too, and at its center was a round table where four men sat under a harsh light playing cards, poker chips in stacks before them and glasses of amber liquid near at hand. "Fuck that noise!" one of the men was saying, making my ears sting. "I ain't gonna be bluffed, no sir!"

"Five dollars to you, then, Mr. Cool," another one said. A red chip hit the pile at the table's center. A cigar tip glowed like a volcano in the maelstrom. "Raise you five," the third man said, the cigar wedged in the side of a scarlike mouth. "Come on, put up or shut—" I saw his small, piggish eyes dart at me, and the man slapped his cards facedown on the table. "*Hey!*" he shouted. "What's that kid doin' in here?"

Instantly I was the focus of attention. "Jaybird, have you gone fuckin' crazy?" one of the other men asked. "Get him out!"

"He's all right," my grandfather said. "He's family."

"Not *my* family." The man with the cigar leaned forward, his thick forearms braced on the table. His brown hair was cropped in a crew cut, and on the little finger of his right hand he wore a diamond ring. He took the cigar from his mouth, his eyes narrowed into slits. "You know the rules, Jaybird. Nobody comes in here without gettin' approved."

"He's all right. He's my grandson."

"I don't care if he's the fuckin' prince of England. You broke the rules."

"Now, there's no call to be ugly about it, is th—"

"You're *stupid!*" the man shouted, his mouth twisting as he spoke the word. A fine sheen of sweat glistened on his face, and his white shirt was damp. On the breast pocket, next to a tobacco stain, was a monogram: BB. *"Stupid!"* he repeated. "You want the law to come in and bust us up? Why don't you just give a map to that goddamned sheriff?"

"Cory won't say anythin'. He's a good boy."

"That so?" The small pig eyes returned to me. "You as stupid as your grandpap, boy?"

"No sir," I said.

He laughed. The sound of it reminded me of when Phillip Kenner threw up his oatmeal in school last April. The man's eyes were not happy, but his mouth was tickled. "Well, you're a smart little fella, ain't you?"

"He takes after me, Mr. Blaylock," the Jaybird said, and I realized the man who thought I was so smart was Bodean Blaylock himself, brother of Donny and Wade and son of the notorious Biggun. I recalled my grandfather's brash pronouncement at the door that Bodean could stick his head up his ass; right now, though, it was my grandpop who looked butt-faced.

"Like hell he does," Bodean told him, and when he laughed again he looked around at the other gamblers and they laughed, too, like good little Indians following the chief. Then Bodean stopped laughing. "Hit the road, Jaybird," he said. "We've got some high rollers comin' in here directly. Bunch of flyboys think they can make some money off me."

My grandfather cleared his throat nervously. His eyes were on the poker chips. "Uh . . . I was wonderin' . . . since I'm here and all, mind if I sit in for a few hands?"

"Take that kid and make dust," Bodean told him. "I'm runnin' a poker game, not a baby-sittin' service."

"Oh, Cory can wait outside," the Jaybird said. "He won't mind. Will you, boy?"

"Grandmomma's waitin' for the ice cream salt," I said.

Bodean Blaylock laughed again, and I saw the crimson flare in my grandfather's cheeks. "I don't care about no damned ice cream!" the Jaybird snapped, a fury and a torment in his eyes. "I don't care if she waits till midnight for it, I can do whatever I damn well please!"

"Better run on home, Jaybird," one of the other men taunted. "Go eat yourself some ice cream and stay out of trouble."

"*You shut up!*" he hollered. "*Here!*" He dug into his pocket, brought out a twenty-dollar bill, and slammed it on the table. "Am I in this game, or not?"

I almost choked. Twenty dollars to risk playing poker. That was an awful lot of money. Bodean Blaylock smoked his cigar in silence, and looked back and forth from the money to my granddaddy's face. "Twenty dollars," he said. "That'll hardly get you started."

"I've got more, don't you worry about it."

I realized the Jaybird must've raided the cash jar, or else he had a secret poker-playing fund hidden away from my grandmother. Surely she wouldn't approve of this, and surely the Jaybird had agreed to get the ice cream salt as a ruse to come here. Maybe he'd just planned on dropping by to see who was playing, but I could tell the fever had him and he was going to play come hell or high water. "Am I in, or not?"

"The kid can't stay."

"Cory, go sit in the car," he said. "I'll be there in a few minutes."

"But Grandmomma's waitin' for—"

"Go do like I said and do it right *now!*" the Jaybird yelled at me. Bodean stared at me through a haze of smoke. His expression said: *See what I can do to your granddaddy, little boy?*

I left the house. Before I got to the door, I could hear the sound of a new chair scraping up to the table. Then I walked out into the hot light and I put my hands in my pockets and kicked a pine cone across the road. I waited. Ten minutes went past. Then ten more. A car pulled up, and three young men got out, knocked on the front door, and were admitted by Mr. Claypool. The door closed again. Still my grandfather didn't emerge. I sat in the car for a while, but the heat was so bad my sweat drenched my shirt and I had to peel myself off the seat and get out again. I paced up and down in front of the house, and I paused to watch ants stripping a dead pigeon to the bones. Maybe an hour went past. At some point, though, I realized my grandfather was treating me like a little piece of nothing, and that was how he was treating Grandmomma Sarah, too. Anger started building in me, beginning in the belly like a dull, throbbing heat. I stared at the door, trying to will him to come out. The door remained closed.

The thought came to me, shocking in its decisiveness: *To hell with him.*

I got the box of ice cream salt, and I started walking.

The first two miles were all right. On the third, the heat began getting to me. Sweat was pouring down my face, and my scalp felt as if it were aflame. The road shimmered between its walls of pine forest, and only a couple of cars passed, but they were going in the wrong direction. The pavement started burning my feet through my shoes. I wanted to sit down in some shade and rest, but I did not because resting would be weakness; it would be saying to myself that I shouldn't have tried to walk six miles in hundred-degree heat and blazing sun, that I should have stayed at that house and waited for my grandfather to come out when he was good and ready. No. I had to keep going, and worry about my blisters later.

234 / Robert McCammon

I started thinking about the story I was going to write about this. In that story, a boy would be crossing a burning desert, a boxful of priceless crystals entrusted to his care. I looked up to watch hawks soaring in the thermals, and when my attention roamed from what I was doing I stepped in a pothole, twisted my ankle, and fell down and the box of ice cream salt burst open beneath me.

I almost cried.

Almost.

My ankle hurt, but I could still stand on it. What hurt me most was the ice cream salt glistening on the pavement. The bottom of the box had broken open. I scooped ice cream salt up in my hands, filled my pockets, and started limping on again.

I was not going to stop. I was not going to sit in the shade and cry, my pockets leaking salt. I was not going to let my grandfather beat me.

I was nearing the end of the third mile when a car's horn honked behind me. I looked around, expecting the Jaybird's Ford. It was, instead, a copper-colored Pontiac. The car slowed, and Dr. Curtis Parrish looked at me through the rolled-down passenger window. "Cory? You need a ride?"

"Yes sir," I said gratefully, and I climbed in. My feet were about burned to the nubs, my ankle swelling up. Dr. Parrish gave it the gas, and we rolled on. "I'm stayin' at my grandfolks'," I said. "About three miles up the road."

"I know where the Jaybird lives." Dr. Parrish picked up his medical bag, which was sitting between us, and put it onto the backseat. "Awful hot day. Where were you walkin' from?"

"I . . . uh . . ." Here was a crossroads of conscience, thrust upon me. "I . . . had to run an errand for my grandmother," I decided to say.

"Oh." He was quiet for a moment. Then: "What's that spillin' out of your pocket? Sand?"

"Salt," I said.

"Oh," he said, and he nodded as if this made sense to him.

"How's your daddy doin' these days? Things ease up at work for him?"

"Sir?"

"You know. His work. When Tom came to see me a few weeks ago, he said his workload was so tough he was havin' trouble sleepin'. I gave him some pills. You know, stress can be a mighty powerful thing. I told your dad he ought to take a vacation."

"Oh." This time I was the one who nodded, as if this made sense. "I think he's doin' better," I said. *I gave him some pills.* Dad hadn't said anything about his work being tough, or that he'd gone to see Dr. Parrish. *I gave him some pills.* I stared straight ahead, at the unfolding road. My father was still trying to escape the realm of troubled spirits. It occurred to me that he was hiding part of himself from Mom and me, just as the Jaybird hid his poker fever from my grandmother.

Dr. Parrish went with me to the front door of my grandparents' house. When Grandmomma Sarah answered his knock, Dr. Parrish said he'd found me walking on the side of the road. "Where's your granddaddy?" she asked me. I must've made a pained face, because after a few seconds of deliberation she answered her own question. "He's gotten himself into some mischief. Uh-huh. That's just what he's done."

"The box of salt busted open," I told her, and I showed a handful of it, my hair wet with sweat.

"We'll get us a new box. We'll save what's in your pockets for the Jaybird." I wasn't to know it for a while, but for the next week every meal the Jaybird sat down to eat would be so loaded with salt his mouth would pucker until it squawked. "Would you come in for a cold glass of lemonade, Dr. Parrish?"

"No, thank you. I've got to get back to the office." His face clouded over, a concern was working its way out of him. "Mrs. Mackenson, did you know Selma Neville?"

"Yes, I know her. Haven't seen her for a month or more, though."

"I just came from her house," Dr. Parrish said. "You know she'd been fightin' cancer for the last year."

"No, I surely didn't!"

"Well, she put up a good fight, but she passed on about two hours ago. She wanted to pass at home instead of a hospital."

"My Lord, I didn't know Selma was sick!"

"She didn't want a fuss. How she got through her last year teachin' I'll never know."

It hit me who they were talking about. Mrs. Neville. My Mrs. Neville. The teacher who'd said I should enter the short-story contest this year. *Good-bye*, she'd said as I'd left her room on the first day of summer. Not *see you next year* or *see you in September,* but a firm and final *good-bye*. She must've known she was dying, as she sat behind that desk in summer's light, and she had known that for her there would be no new class of grinning young monkeys in September.

"Thought you might like to know," Dr. Parrish said. He touched my shoulder with a hand that had two hours ago pulled a sheet over Mrs. Neville's face. "You take care now, Cory." He turned around and walked to his Pontiac, and my grandmother and I watched him drive away.

An hour later, the Jaybird came home. He wore the expression of a man whose last friend had kicked him in the rump and whose last Washington had snickered as it sailed off into another man's pocket. He tried to work up a show of anger at me, for "runnin' off and worryin' me half to death" but before he could get steamed up on that route Grandmomma Sarah derailed him by asking, very quietly, where the ice cream salt was. The Jaybird wound up sitting by himself on the porch in the fading light, moths whirling around him, his face long and haggard and his spirits as low as his flagging jimbob. I felt kind of sorry for him, actually, but the Jaybird was not the kind of man you felt sorry for. One word of regret from me would've made him sneer and swagger. The Jaybird never apologized; he was never wrong. That was why he had no true companions, and that was why he sat alone on that porch in the company of dumb gleaming wings that swirled around him like his ancient memories of pretty farmers' daughters.

One last incident marked my week with my grandparents. I had not slept well on Friday night. I dreamed of walking into my classroom, which was empty of everyone but Mrs. Neville, sitting behind her desk straightening papers. Golden light slanted across the floor, bars of it striping the blackboard. The flesh of Mrs. Neville's face had shriveled. Her eyes looked bright and large, like the eyes of a baby. She held her back rigid, and she watched me as I stood on the threshold between the hallway and classroom. "Cory?" she said. "Cory Mackenson?"

"Yes ma'am," I answered.

"Come closer," she said.

I did. I walked to her desk, and I saw that the red apple there on its edge had dried up.

"Summer's almost over," Mrs. Neville told me. I nodded. "You're older than you were before, aren't you?"

"I had a birthday," I said.

"That's nice." Her breath, though not unpleasant, smelled like flowers on the verge of decay. "I have seen many boys come and go," she said. "I've seen some grow up and set roots, and some grow up and move away. The years of a boy's life pass so fast, Cory." She smiled faintly. "Boys want to hurry up and be men, and then comes a day they wish they could be boys again. But I'll tell you a secret, Cory. Want to hear it?"

I nodded.

"No one," Mrs. Neville whispered, "ever grows up."

I frowned. What kind of secret was that? My dad and mom were grown-up, weren't they? So were Mr. Dollar, Chief Marchette, Dr. Parrish, Reverend Lovoy, the Lady, and everybody else over eighteen.

"They may look grown-up," she continued, "but it's a disguise. It's just the clay of time. Men and women are still children deep in their hearts. They still would like to jump and play, but that heavy clay won't let them. They'd like to shake off every chain the world's put on them, take off their watches and neckties and Sunday shoes and return naked to the swimming hole, if just for one day. They'd like to feel free, and know that there's a momma and daddy at home who'll take care of things and love them no matter what. Even behind the face of the meanest man in the world is a scared little boy trying to wedge himself into a corner where he can't be hurt." She put aside the papers and folded her hands on the desk. "I have seen plenty of boys grow into men, Cory, and I want to say one word to you. *Remember.*"

"Remember? Remember what?"

"Everything," she said. "And anything. Don't you go through a day without remembering something of it, and tucking that memory away like a treasure. Because it is. And memories are sweet doors, Cory. They're teachers and friends and disciplinarians. When you look at something, don't just look. *See* it. Really, really *see* it. See it so when you write it down, somebody else can see it, too. It's easy to walk through life deaf, dumb, and blind, Cory. Most everybody you know or ever meet will. They'll walk through a parade of wonders, and they'll never hear a peep of it. But you can live a thousand lifetimes if you want to. You can talk to people you'll never set eyes on, in lands you'll never visit." She nodded, watching my face. "And if you're good and you're lucky and you have something worth saying, then you might have the chance to live on long after—" She paused, measuring her words. "Long after," she finished.

"How's all this stuff supposed to happen?" I asked.

"First things first. Enter the short-story contest, like I told you."

"I'm not good enough."

"I'm not saying you are. Yet. Just do the best you can, and enter the contest. Will you do that?"

I shrugged. "I don't know what to write about."

"You will," Mrs. Neville said. "When you make yourself sit and look at a blank piece of paper long enough, you will. And don't think of it as writing. Just think of it as telling your friends a story. Will you at least try?"

"I'll think about it," I said.

"Don't think too hard," she cautioned me. "Sometimes thinking gets in the way of doing."

"Yes ma'am."

"Ah, well." Mrs. Neville pulled in a breath and let it slowly out. She looked around the classroom at the empty desks carved with initials. "I have done my best," she said quietly, "and that is all I can do. Oh, you little children, what years you have ahead." Her gaze returned to me. "Class dismissed," she said.

I woke up. It was not quite light yet. A rooster was crowing to herald the sun. The Jaybird's radio was on in their bedroom, tuned to a country station. The sound of a steel guitar, alone and searching over the dark miles of woods and meadows and roads, has always had the power to break my heart in two.

Mom and Dad came to pick me up that afternoon. I kissed Grandmomma Sarah good-bye, and I shook the Jaybird's hand. He put a little extra pressure into his grip. I squeezed back. We knew each other. Then I went out to the pickup truck with my folks, and I found they'd brought Rebel along, so I climbed into the truckbed and let my legs hang over the edge and Rebel nudged up close to me and blew dog breath in my face but it was fine with me.

Grandmomma Sarah and the Jaybird stood on their front porch and waved good-bye. I went home, where I belonged.

7

My Camping Trip

THERE IS NOTHING MORE frightening or exciting than a blank piece of paper. Frightening because you're on your own, leaving dark tracks across that snowy plain, and exciting because no one knows your destination but yourself, and even you can't say exactly where you'll end up. When I sat down at my typewriter to chop out that story for the Zephyr Arts Council Writing Contest, I was so scared it was all I could do to spell my name. Concocting a story for yourself and a story that you know strangers are going to read are two different animals; the first is a comfortable pony, the second a crazy bronco. You just have to hold tight, and go along for the ride.

The sheet of paper stared me in the face for quite a while. At last I decided to write about a boy who runs away from his small town to see the world. I got two pages done before it became clear my heart wasn't in it. I started on a tale about a boy who finds a magic lantern in a junkyard. That, too, went into the wastebasket. A story about a ghost car was going pretty well until it hit the wall of my imagination and burst into flames.

I sat there, staring at another fresh sheet of paper.

The cicadas were whirring in the trees outside. Rebel barked at something in the night. From far away I heard a car's engine growl. I thought of my dream about Mrs. Neville, and what she'd said: *Don't think of it as writing. Think of it as telling your friends a story.*

What if? I asked myself. What if I was to write about something that had really happened?

Like . . . Mr. Sculley and the tooth of Old Moses. No, no. Mr. Sculley wouldn't want people coming around to his place to see it. All right then, what about . . . the Lady and the Moon Man? No, I didn't know enough about them. What about . . .

. . . the dead man in the car at the bottom of Saxon's Lake?

What if I was to write a story about what had happened that morning? Write about the car going into the water, and Dad jumping in after it? Write about everything I'd felt and seen on that March morning before the sun? And what if . . . what if . . . I wrote about seeing the man in the green-feathered hat, standing there at the edge of the woods?

Now, this I could get fired-up about. I began with my father saying, "Cory? Wake up, son. It's time." Soon I was back in the milk truck with him, on our way through the silent early morning streets of Zephyr. We were talking about what I wanted to grow up to be, and then suddenly the car came out of the woods right in front of us, my dad twisted the milk truck's wheel, and the car went over the edge of the red rock cliff into Saxon's Lake. I remembered my father running toward the lake, and how my heart had clutched up as he'd leaped into the water and started swimming. I remembered watching the car starting to go down, bubbles bursting around its trunk. I remembered looking around at the woods across the road and seeing the figure standing there wearing a long overcoat that flapped in the wind and a hat with a green—

Wait.

No, that's not how it had been. I had stepped on the green feather, and found it on the bottom of my muddy shoe. But where else could a green feather come from but the band of a hat? Still and all, I was writing this as it had really been. I hadn't actually seen the green-feathered hat until the night of the flood. So I stuck to the facts, and wrote about the green feather as I'd found it. I left out the part about Miss Grace, Lainie, and the house of bad girls, figuring Mom wouldn't care to read about it. I read the story over and decided it wasn't as good as I could do, so I rewrote it. It was hard making talking sound like talking. Finally, though, after three times through my Royal, the story was ready. It was two pages long, double-spaced. My masterpiece.

When Dad, clad in his red-striped pajamas and his hair still damp from his shower, came in to say good night, I showed him the two sheets of paper.

"What's this?" He held the title up under my desk lamp. "'Before the Sun,'" he read, and he looked at me with a question in his eyes.

"It's a story for the writin' contest," I said. "I just wrote it."

"Oh. Can I read it?"

"Yes sir."

He began. I watched him. When he got to the part about the car coming out of the woods, a little muscle tensed in his jaw. He put out a hand to brace himself against the wall, and I knew he was reading about swimming out to the car. I saw his fingers slowly grip and relax, grip and relax. "Cory?" Mom called. "Go lock Rebel in for the night!" I started to go, but Dad said, "Wait just a minute," and then he returned to the last few paragraphs.

"Cory?" Mom called again, the TV on in the front room.

"We're talkin', Rebecca!" Dad told her, and he lowered the pages to his side. He stared at me, his face half in shadow.

"Is it okay?" I asked.

"This isn't what you usually write," he said quietly. "You usually write about ghosts, or cowboys, or spacemen. How come you to write somethin' like this?"

I shrugged. "I don't know. I just thought . . . I'd write somethin' true."

"So this is true? This part about you seein' somebody standin' in the woods?"

"Yes sir."

"Then how come you didn't tell me about it? How come you didn't tell Sheriff Amory?"

"I don't know. Maybe . . . I wasn't sure if I really saw somebody or not."

"But you're sure now? Almost six months after it happened, you're sure now? And you could've told the sheriff this, and you didn't?"

"I . . . guess that's right. I mean . . . I *thought* I saw somebody standin' there. He was wearin' a long overcoat, and he—"

"You're sure it was a man?" Dad asked. "You saw his face?"

"No sir, I didn't see his face."

Dad shook his head. His jaw muscle twitched again, and a pulse throbbed at his temple. "I wish to God," he said, "that we'd never driven along that road. I wish to God I'd never jumped in after that car. I wish to God that dead man at the bottom of the lake would leave me alone." He squeezed his eyes shut, and when he opened them again they were bleary and tortured. "Cory, I don't want you showin' this to anybody else. Hear me?"

"But . . . I was gonna enter it in the con—"

"No! God, no!" He clamped a hand to my shoulder. "Listen to me. All this happened six months ago. It's history now, and there's no need dredgin' it all up again."

"But it happened," I said. "It's real."

"It was a bad dream," my father answered. "A very bad dream. The sheriff never found anybody missin' from town. Nobody missin' from anywhere around here who had a tattoo like that. No wife or family ever turned up huntin' a lost husband and father. Don't you understand, Cory?"

"No sir," I said.

"That man at the bottom of Saxon's Lake never was," Dad said, his voice hurt and husky. "Nobody cared enough about him to even *miss* him. And when he died, beat up so bad he hardly looked like a man anymore, he didn't even get a proper burial. I was the last person on this earth to see him before he sank down forever. Do you know what that's done to me, Cory?"

I shook my head.

My father looked at the story again. He put the two pages back on my desk, next to the Royal typewriter. "I knew there was brutality in this world," he said, but he kept his eyes averted from mine. "Brutality is part of life, but . . . it's always somewhere else. Always in the next town. Remember when I was a fireman, and I went out when that car crashed and burned between here and Union Town?"

"Little Stevie Cauley's car," I said. "Midnight Mona."

"That's right. The tire tracks on the pavement said that another car forced Stevie Cauley off the road. Somebody deliberately wrecked him. The car's gas tank ruptured, and it blew sky high. That was brutality, too, and when I saw what was left of a livin', breathin' young man, I—" He flinched, perhaps recalling the sight of charred bones. "I couldn't understand how one human bein' could do that to another. I couldn't understand that kind of hate. I mean . . . what road do you take to get there? What is it that has to get inside you and twist your soul so much you can take a human life as easily as flickin' a fly?" His gaze found mine. "You know what your granddaddy used to call me when I was your age?"

"No sir."

"Yellowstreak. Because I didn't like to hunt. Because I didn't like to fight. Because I didn't like to do any of the things that you're supposed to like, if you're a boy. He forced me to play football. I wasn't any good at it, but I did it for him. He said, 'Boy, you'll never be any good in this life if you don't have the killer instinct.' That's what he said. 'Hit 'em hard, knock 'em down, show 'em who's tough.' The only thing is . . . I'm not tough. I never was. All I ever wanted was peace. That's all. Just peace." He walked to my window, and he stood there for a moment listening to the cicadas. "I guess," he said, "I've been pretendin' for a long time that I'm stronger than I am. That I could put that dead man in the car behind me and let him go. But I can't, Cory. He calls to me."

"He . . . *calls* to you?" I asked.

"Yes, he does." My father stood with his back to me. At his sides, his hands had curled into fists. "He says he wants me to know who he was. He wants me to know where his family is, and if there's anybody on this earth who mourns for him. He wants me to know who killed him, and why. He wants me to *remember* him, and he says that as long as whoever beat him and strangled him to death walks free, I will have no more peace for the rest of my life." Dad turned toward me. I thought he looked ten years older than when he'd taken the two pages of my story in his hand. "When I was your age, I wanted to believe I lived in a magic town," he said softly, "where nothin' bad could ever happen. I wanted to believe everyone was kind, and good, and just. I wanted to believe hard work was rewarded, and a man stood on his word. I wanted to believe a man was a Christian every day of the week, not just Sunday, and that the law was fair and the politicians wise and if you walked the straight path you found that peace you were searchin' for." He smiled; it was a difficult thing to look at. For an instant I thought I could see the boy in him, trapped in what Mrs. Neville's dream-shape had called the clay of time. "There never was such a place," my father said. "There never will be. But knowin' can't stop you from wishin' it was so, and every time I close my eyes to sleep, that dead man at the bottom of Saxon's Lake tells me I've been a damned fool."

I don't know why I said it, but I did: "Maybe the Lady can help you."

"How? Throw a few bones for me? Burn a candle and incense?"

"No sir. Just talk," I said.

He looked at the floor. He drew a deep breath and slowly freed it. Then he said, "I've gotta get some rest," and he walked to the door.

"Dad?"

He paused.

"Do you want me to tear the story up?"

He didn't answer, and I thought he wasn't going to. His gaze flickered back and forth from me to the two sheets of paper. "No," he said at last. "No, it's a good story. It's true, isn't it?"

"Yes sir."

"It's the best you can do?"

"Yes sir."

He looked around at the pictures of monsters taped on the walls, and his eyes came to me. "You're sure you wouldn't rather write about ghosts, or men from Mars?" he inquired with a hint of a smile.

"Not this time," I told him.

He nodded, chewing on his lower lip. "Go ahead, then. Enter it in the contest," he said, and he left me alone.

On the following morning, I put my story in a manila envelope and rode Rocket to the public library on Merchants Street, near the courthouse. In the library's cool, stately confines, where fans whispered at the ceiling and sunlight streamed through blinds at tall arched windows, I handed my contest entry—marked "Short Story" on the envelope in Crayola burnt umber—to Mrs. Evelyn Prathmore at the front desk. "And what little tale might we have here?" Mrs. Prathmore asked, smiling sweetly.

"It's about a murder," I said. Her smile fractured. "Who's judgin' the contest this year?"

"Myself, Mr. Grover Dean, Mr. Lyle Redmond from the English department at Adams Valley High School, Mayor Swope, our well-known published poet Mrs. Teresa Abercrombie, and Mr. James Connahaute, the copy editor at the *Journal*." She picked up my entry with two fingers, as if it were a smelly fish. "It's about a *murder*, you say?" She peered at me over the pearly rims of her eyeglasses.

"Yes ma'am."

"What's a nice, polite young man like you writin' about *mur-*

der for? Couldn't you write about a happier subject? Like . . . your dog, or your best friend, or—" She frowned, at her wit's end. "Somethin' that would enlighten and entertain?"

"No ma'am," I said. "I had to write about the man at the bottom of Saxon's Lake."

"Oh," Mrs. Prathmore looked at the manila envelope again. "I see. Do your parents know you're enterin' this in the contest, Cory?"

"Yes ma'am. My dad read it last night."

Mrs. Prathmore picked up a ball-point pen and wrote my name on the envelope. "What's your telephone number?" she asked, and when I told her she wrote that underneath my name. "All right, Cory," she said, and she summoned up a cool smile, "I'll see that this gets where it needs to go."

I thanked her, and I turned around and walked toward the front door. Before I got out, I glanced back at Mrs. Prathmore. She was bending the envelope's clasp back to unseal it, and when she saw me looking she stopped. I took this as a good sign, that she was eager to read my entry. I went on out into the sunlight, unchained Rocket from a park bench, and pedaled home.

No doubt about it, summer was on the wane.

The mornings seemed a shade cooler. The nights were hungry, and ate more daylight. The cicadas sounded tired, their whirring wings slowing to a dull buzz. From our front porch you could look almost due east and see a single Judas tree up in the forested hills; its leaves had turned crimson almost overnight, a shock amid all that green. And the worst—the very worst for those of us who loved the freedom of summer's days—was that the television and radio trumpeted back-to-school sales with depressing fervor.

Time was running out. So one evening at supper I broached the subject. Bit the bullet. Took the bull by the horns. Jumped in headfirst.

"Can I go campin' overnight with the guys?" was the question that brought silence to the table.

Mom looked at Dad. Dad looked at Mom. Neither of them

looked at me. "You said I could if I went to Granddaddy Jaybird's for a week," I reminded them.

Dad cleared his throat and swirled his fork in his mashed potatoes. "Well," he said, "I don't see why not. Sure. You guys can pitch a tent in the back and make a campfire."

"That's not what I mean. I mean campin' out. Like out in the woods."

"There are woods behind the house," he said. "That's woods enough."

"No sir," I said, and my heart was beating harder because for me this was really being daring. "I mean way out in the woods. Out where you can't see Zephyr or any lights. Like real campin'."

"Oh, my," Mom fretted.

Dad grunted and put his fork down. He folded his fingers together, and the thought lines deepened into grooves between his eyes. All this was, I knew from past experience, the first signs of the word "no" being born. "Way out in the woods," he repeated. "Like how far out?"

"I don't know. I thought we could hike somewhere, spend the night, and then come back in the mornin'. We'd take a compass, and sandwiches, and Kool-Aid, and we'd take knapsacks and stuff."

"And what would happen if one of you boys broke an ankle?" Mom asked. "Or got bitten by a rattlesnake? Or fell down in poison ivy, and Lord knows that's everywhere this summer." I hung on; she was working up to full speed. "What would happen if you got attacked by a bobcat? Lord, a hundred things could happen to you in the woods, and none of them good!"

"We'd be all right, Mom," I said. "We're not little kids anymore."

"You're not grown up enough to go wanderin' around out in the woods by yourselves, either! What if you got out there at night two miles from home and a storm blew up? What if it started lightnin' and thunderin'? What if you or one of the others got sick to your stomach? You know, you can't just find a phone and call home out there. Tell him it's a bad idea, Tom."

He made a face; the dirty jobs always fell to the father.

"Go on," Mom urged. "Tell him he can wait until he's thirteen."

"You said last year I could wait until I was twelve," I reminded her.

"Don't talk smart, now! Tom, tell him."

I awaited the firm, resolute "no." It came as a real surprise, then, when my dad asked, "Where would you get the compass?"

Mom looked at him in horror. I felt a spark of hope leap within me. "From Davy Ray's dad," I said. "He uses it when he goes huntin'."

"Compasses can break!" Mom insisted. "Can't they?" she asked Dad.

My father kept his attention on me, his expression solid and serious. "Goin' out on an overnight hike isn't any game for children. I know plenty of men who've gotten lost in the woods, and they'll tell you right off what it feels like to be without a bed or a bathroom, have to sleep on wet leaves and scratch skeeter bites all night. That sound like fun to you?"

"I'd like to go," I said.

"You talk to the other guys about this?"

"Yes sir. They all said they'd like to go, too, if their folks'll let 'em."

"Tom, he's too young!" Mom said. "Maybe next year!"

"No," my father answered, "he's not too young." My mother wore a stricken look; she started to speak again, but Dad put a finger to her lips. "I made a deal with him," he told her. "In this house, a man stands on his word." His gaze swung back to me again. "Call 'em. If their parents say all right, it's all right with us, too. But we'll talk about how far you can go, and when we expect you back, and if you're not back by the time we agree on, you'll have a tough time sittin' down for a week. Okay?"

"Okay!" I said, and I started to go for the phone but Dad said, "Hold on. Finish your supper first."

After this, events gained momentum. Ben's parents gave their approval. Davy Ray's folks said okay. Johnny, however, could not go with us, though he pleaded for my dad to talk to his. Dad did what he could, but the judgment was already passed. Because of Johnny's dizzy spells, his parents were afraid for him to be out in the woods overnight. Once again the Branlins had robbed him.

And so, on a sunny Friday afternoon, laden with knapsacks, sandwiches, canteens of water, mosquito repellent, snakebite kits, matches, flashlights, and county maps we'd gotten from the courthouse, Davy Ray, Ben, and I struck out from my house into the beckoning forest. All our good-byes had been said, our dogs locked up, our bicycles porched and chained. Davy carried his father's compass, and he wore a camouflage-print hunting cap. We all wore long pants, to guard our shins against thorns and snake fangs, and our winter boots. We were in it for the long haul, and we set our faces against the sun like pioneers entering the forest primeval. Before we reached the woods, though, my mother the constant worrier called from the back porch, "Cory! Have you got enough toilet paper?"

I said I did. Somehow, I couldn't imagine Daniel Boone's mother asking him that question.

We climbed the hill and crossed the clearing from where we had flown on the first day of summer. Beyond it the serious woods began, a green domain that might've given Tarzan pause. I looked back at Zephyr lying below us, and Ben stopped and then so did Davy Ray. Everything seemed so orderly: the streets, the roofs, the mowed lawns, the sidewalks, the flowerbeds. What we were about to enter was a wild entanglement, a dangerous realm that offered neither comfort nor safety; in other words, in that one moment I realized exactly what I'd gotten myself into.

"Well," Davy Ray said at last, "I guess we'd better get movin'."

"Yeah," Ben murmured. "Get movin'."

"Uh-huh," I said.

We stood there, the breeze on our faces and sweat on our necks. Behind us, the forest rustled. I thought of the hydra's heads, swaying and hissing, in *Jason and the Argonauts*.

"I'm goin'," Davy Ray said, and he started off. I turned away from Zephyr and followed him, because he was the guy with the compass. Ben hitched his knapsack's straps in a notch tighter, the tail of his shirt already beginning to wander out of his pants, and he said, "Hold up!" and came on as fast as he could.

The forest, which had been waiting a hundred years for three boys just like us, let us in and then closed its limbs and leaves at our backs. Now we had set foot in the wilderness, and we were on our own.

Pretty soon we were drenched with sweat. Going up and down wooded ridges in the heavy August heat was no easy task, and Ben started puffing and asking Davy Ray to slow down. "Snake hole!" Davy Ray shouted, pointing at an imaginary hole at Ben's feet, and that got Ben moving lickety-split again. We traveled through a green kingdom of sun and shadow, and we found honeysuckle boiling in sweet profusion and blackberries growing wild and of course we had to stop for a while and take a taste. Then we were on the march again, following the compass and the sun, masters of our destinies. Atop a hill we found a huge boulder to sit on, and we discovered what appeared to be Indian symbols carved into the stone. Alas, though, we weren't the first to make this find, because nearby was a Moon Pie wrapper and a broken 7-Up bottle. We went on, deeper into the forest, determined to find a place where no human foot had ever marked the dirt. We came to a dried-up streambed and followed it, the stones crunching under our boots. A dead possum, swarming with flies, snared our attention for a few minutes. Davy Ray threatened to pick up the possum's carcass and throw it at Ben, but I talked him out of such a grisly display and Ben shuddered with relief. Farther ahead, at a place where the trees thinned and white rocks jutted from the earth like dinosaur ribs, Davy Ray stopped and bent down. He came up holding a black arrowhead, almost perfectly formed, which he put in his pocket for Johnny's collection.

The sun was falling. We were sweaty and dusty, and gnats spun around our heads and darted at our eyeballs. I have never understood the attraction of gnats to eyeballs, but I believe it's the equivalent of moths to flames; in any case, we spent a lot of time digging the little dead things out of our watering orbs. But as the sun settled and the air cooled, the gnats went away. We began to wonder where we might find a place to spend the night, and it was right about then that the truth of the matter came clear.

There were no mothers and fathers around to make our suppers. There were no televisions, no radios, no bathtubs, no beds, and no lights, which we began to fully realize as the sky darkened to the east. How far we were from home we didn't know, but for the last two hours we'd seen no mark of civilization. "We'd better stop here," I told Davy Ray, and I indicated a clearing, but he said, "Ah, we can go on a little farther," and I knew his curiosity about what lay over the next ridge was pulling him onward. Ben and I kept up with him; as I've said before, he was the guy with the compass.

Our flashlights came out to spear through the gathering gloom. Something fluttered in front of my face and spun away: a bat on the prowl. Another something scuttled away through the underbrush at our approach, and Ben kept asking, "What was that? What was that?" but neither of us could answer. At last Davy Ray stopped walking, and he shone his flashlight around and announced, "We'll set up camp here." It was none too soon for Ben and me, because our legs were whipped. We shrugged the knapsacks off our aching shoulders and peed in the pine straw and then we set about finding wood for a fire. In this case we were lucky, because there were plenty of pine branches and pine cones lying about and those burned on half a match. So before long we had a sensible fire going, the firepit rimmed with stones as my dad had told me to do, and by its ruddy light we three frontiersmen ate the sandwiches our mothers had made.

The flames crackled. Ben discovered a pack of marshmallows his mom had put in his knapsack. We found sticks and began the joyful task of toasting. All around our circle was nothing but dark beyond the firelight's edge, and lightning bugs blinked in the trees. A breath of wind stirred the treetops, and way up there we could see the blaze of the Milky Way across the sky.

In this forest sanctuary our voices were quiet, respectful for where we were. We talked about our dismal Little League season, vowing that somehow we'd get Nemo Curliss on our team next year. We talked about the Branlins, and how somebody ought to clean their clocks for screwing up Johnny's summer. We talked about how far we must be from home; five or six miles, Davy Ray believed, while Ben said it must be more like ten or twelve. We wondered aloud what our folks were doing at that very same instant, and we all agreed they were probably worried sick about us but this experience would be good for them. We were growing up now, and it was high time they understood our childhood days were numbered.

In the distance an owl began to hoot. Davy Ray talked with great anticipation about Snowdown, who must even now be somewhere in the same woods sharing these sights and sounds, perhaps hearing the same owl. Ben talked about school getting ready to start soon, but we shushed him. We lay on our backs as the firelight dimmed, and stared up at the sky as we talked about Zephyr and the people who lived there. It was a magic town, we all agreed. And we were touched with magic, too, for having been born there.

Sometime after the flames had died and the embers glowed red, after the owl had gone to sleep and the soft warm breeze brought the fragrance of wild cherries into our campsite, we watched shooting stars streak incandescent blue and gold across the heavens. When the show had ended and we were all lying there thinking, Davy Ray said, "Hey, Cory. How about tellin' us a story?"

"Nah," I said. "I can't think of anythin'."

"Just make one up," Davy Ray urged. "Come on. Okay?"

"Yeah, but don't make it *too* scary," Ben said. "I don't wanna have bad dreams."

I thought for a while, and then I began. "Did you guys know they had a prison camp for Nazis around here? Dad told me all about it. Yeah, he said they had all these Nazis in this camp in the woods, and all of 'em were the worst killers you can think of. It was right near the Air Force base, only this is before it was an Air Force base."

"Is this for *real?*" Ben asked warily.

"Naw, dummy!" Davy Ray said. "He's makin' it up!"

"Maybe I am," I told him, "and maybe I'm not."

Davy Ray was silent.

"Anyway," I went on, "there was a fire in this prison camp, and some of the Nazis got out. And some of 'em were all burned up, like their faces were all messed up and stuff, but they got out, right in these woods, and—"

"You saw this on 'Thriller,' didn't you?" Davy Ray asked.

"No," I said. "It's what my dad told me. This happened a long time ago, before any of us were even born. So these Nazis got out into the woods right near here, and their leader—his name was Bruno—was a big guy with a scarred-up, burned face and he found a cave for everybody to live in. But there wasn't enough food for everybody, and so when some of them died the others cut up the bodies with knives and—"

"Oh, *gross!*" Ben said.

"And ate 'em, and Bruno always got the brains. He cracked open their skulls like walnuts, scooped out the brains with both hands, and threw 'em down his gullet."

"I'm gonna puke!" Davy Ray cried out, and made retching noises. Then he laughed and Ben laughed, too.

"After a long time—like two years—Bruno was the only one left, and he was bigger'n ever," I continued. "But his face never healed up from the fire. He had one eye on his forehead and the other eye hung down on his chin." This brought more gusts of laughter. "So after all that time in the cave, and eatin' the other Nazis up, Bruno was crazy. He was hungry, but he only wanted one thing to eat: brains."

"*Yech!*" Ben said.

"Brains was all he wanted," I told my audience of two. "He was seven feet tall and he weighed three hundred pounds, and he had a long knife that could slice the top of your head right off. Well, the police and the army were lookin' for him all this time but they never could find him. They found a forest ranger with the top of his head cut off and his brains gone. They found an old moonshiner dead and his brains gone, too, and they figured Bruno was gettin' closer and closer to Zephyr."

"Then they called in James Bond and Batman!" Davy Ray said.

"No!" I shook my head gravely. "There wasn't anybody to call in. There was just the policemen and the army soldiers, and every night Bruno walked through the forest carryin' his knife and a lantern, and his face was so ugly it could freeze people solid like Medusa and then *slash!* he cut somebody's head open and *splatter!* there were the brains down his throat."

"Oh, sure!" Ben grinned. "I'll bet ol' Bruno's still in these woods right now, eatin' people's brains for supper, huh?"

"Nope," I said, formulating the conclusion of my tale. "The police and the soldiers found him, and they shot him so many times he looked like Swiss cheese. But every so often, if you happen to be out in the woods on a real dark night, you can see Bruno's lantern movin' through the trees." I spoke this in an icy whisper, and neither Davy Ray nor Ben did any more laughing. "Yeah, you can see his lantern movin' as he wanders in search of somebody's brains to eat. He casts that light all around, and if you get close to it, you can see the shine of his knife, but don't look at his face!" I held up a warning finger. "No, don't you look at his face, 'cause it'll drive you crazy and it might just make you want to eat some *brains!*" I yelled the last word and jumped as I yelled it, and Ben hollered with fright but Davy Ray just laughed again.

"Hey, that's not funny!" Ben protested.

"You don't have to worry about ol' Bruno," Davy Ray told him. "You don't have any brains, so that lets you off the—"

Davy Ray stopped speaking, and he just sat there staring into the dark.

"What is it?" I asked him.

"Ahhhh, he's tryin' to scare us!" Ben scoffed. "Well, it ain't workin'!"

Davy Ray's face had gone white. I swear I saw his scalp ripple, and the hair stand up. He said, "Guh . . . guh . . . guh . . ." and he lifted his arm and pointed.

I turned around to look in the direction he indicated. I heard Ben make a choked gasp. My own hair jittered on my head, and my heart kaboomed.

A light was coming toward us, through the trees.

"Guh . . . guh . . . God a'mighty!" Davy Ray croaked.

We all three were struck with the kind of horror that makes you want to dig a hole, jump in, and pull the hole in after you. The light was moving slowly, but coming closer. And as it came closer it broke into two, and all of us got down on our quaking bellies in the pine straw. In another moment I could tell what it was: a car's headlights. The car looked like it was going to roll right over our hiding-place, and then it veered away and we watched its red taillights flare as the driver applied the brakes. The car kept going, following a winding trail that was only fifty yards or so from our campsite, and in a couple of minutes it had disappeared amid the trees.

"Did you guys see that?" Davy Ray whispered.

"'Course we saw it!" Ben whispered back. "We're right here, aren't we?"

"Wonder who was in that car, and why they're way out here?" Davy Ray looked at me. "You want to find out, Cory?"

"Probably moonshiners," I answered. My voice trembled. "I think we'd better leave 'em alone."

Davy Ray picked up his flashlight. His face was still pallid, but his eyes shone with excitement. "I'm gonna find out what's goin' on! You guys can stay here if you want to!" He stood up, flicked on the flashlight, and began to stealthily follow the car. He stopped when he realized we weren't with him. "It's okay," he said. "I won't think you guys are scared or anythin'."

"Good," Ben answered, "'cause I'm stickin' right here."

I stood up. If Davy Ray had enough courage to go, then so did I. Besides, I wanted to know who was driving a car way out here in the woods myself. "Come on!" he said. "But watch where you step!"

"I'm not stayin' here alone!" Ben hoisted himself to his feet. "You two are damn *crazy,* you know that?"

"Yeah." Davy Ray sounded proud about it. "Everybody stay low and no talkin'!"

We crept from tree to tree, following the trail that we hadn't even seen when we'd set up camp at nightfall. Davy Ray kept the flashlight's beam aimed at the ground, so it couldn't be spotted by anyone up ahead. The trail wound back and forth between the trees. The owl was hooting again, and lightning bugs blinked around us. We'd gone a couple of hundred yards more along the trail when Davy Ray suddenly stopped and whispered, "There it is!"

We could see the car ahead of us. It was sitting still, but its lights were on and the engine was rumbling. We crouched down in the pine straw, and I don't know about the others, but my heart was going a mile a minute. The car didn't move. Whoever was sitting behind the wheel didn't get out. "I've gotta pee!" Ben whispered urgently. Davy Ray told him to squeeze it.

After five or six minutes, we saw more lights coming through the woods from the opposite direction. It was another car, this one a black Cadillac, and it stopped, facing the first car. Davy Ray looked at me, his expression saying we'd really stumbled into something this time. I didn't particularly care what was going on; I just wanted to get away from what I figured was a meeting of moonshiners. Then the doors of the first car opened, and two people got out.

"Oh, man!" Davy Ray breathed.

Standing in the crossing of headlights were two men wearing ordinary clothes except until you got to their heads, which were covered by white masks. One of the men was medium-sized, the other was big and fat, with a belly that flopped over the waist of his jeans. The medium-sized man was smoking either a cigarette or cigar, it was hard to tell which, and he angled his masked head and blew smoke from the corner of his mouth. Then the Cadillac's doors opened, and I almost swallowed my heart when Bodean Blaylock slid out from behind the wheel. It was him, all right; I remembered his face from when he'd looked across the poker table at me, same to say he had my granddaddy and wasn't about to let him go. A slim man with slicked-back dark hair and a jutting slab of a chin got out of the passenger side; he was wearing tight black pants and a red shirt with cowboy spangles on the shoulders, and at first I thought it was Donny Blaylock but Donny didn't have a chin like that. This man opened the Cadillac's right rear door, and the whole car trembled as whoever was still inside started to climb out.

It was a mountain on two legs.

His gut was tremendous, straining the front of the red-checked shirt and overalls he wore. When he rose up to his full height, he was maybe six and a half feet tall. He was baldheaded except for a wisp of gray hair circling his acorn-shaped skull, and he had a trimmed gray beard that angled to a point below his chin. He breathed like a bellows, his face a ruddy mass of wrinkled flesh. "You boys goin' to a masquerade party?" he growled in a voice like a cement mixer, and he laughed *hut-hut-hut* like a big old engine starting to fire its plugs. Bodean laughed, and the other man laughed, too. The men wearing the masks shifted uneasily. "You fellas look like sacks of shit," the mountainous bulk said as he shambled forward. I swear his hands were the size of country hams, and his feet in their scuffed-up boots looked like they could stomp down small trees.

The masked man with the bulbous belly said, "We're incog . . . incog . . . We don't wanna be recognized."

"Shit, Dick!" the bearded monster said, and he guffawed again. "Have to be a blind fuckin' fool not to recognize your fat gut and ass!" Talk about the pot calling the kettle black, I thought.

"Awwww, you're not supposed to recognize us, Mr. Blaylock!" the man who'd been called Dick answered with a whine of petulance, and I realized with a double start that this man was Mr. Dick Moultry and the other was Biggun Blaylock, the fearsome head of the Blaylock clan himself.

Ben realized it, too. "Let's get outta here!" he whispered, but Davy Ray hissed. "Shut up!"

"Well," Biggun said, his hands on his massive hips, "I don't give a shit if you wear sackcloth and ashes. You bring the money?"

"Yes sir." Mr. Moultry reached into his pocket and brought out a wad of bills.

"Count it," Biggun ordered.

"Yes sir. Fifty . . . one hundred . . . hundred and fifty . . . two hundred . . ." He kept counting up to four hundred dollars. "Take the money, Wade," Biggun said, and the man in the spangled shirt walked forward to get it.

"Just a minute," the second masked man said. "Where's the merchandise?" He was talking in a low, gruff voice that sounded false, yet I knew that voice from somewhere.

"Bodean, get what the fella wants," Biggun told him, and Bodean took the Cadillac's keys from the ignition and walked back to the trunk. Biggun's gaze stayed fixed on the man with the false voice. I was glad it wasn't directed at me, because it looked so intense it could puddle iron. "It's fine, quality work," Biggun said. "Just what you boys asked for."

"It oughta be. We're payin' enough for it."

"You want a demonstration?" Biggun grinned, his mouth full of gleaming teeth. "If I were you, friend, I'd get rid of that cheroot."

The masked man took a final pull on it, then he turned and flicked it right where we were hiding. It fell into the pine straw about four feet in front of me, and I saw its chewed plastic tip. I knew who smoked cheroots with a tip like that. It was Mr. Hargison, our mailman.

Bodean had opened the trunk. Now he closed it again, and he approached the two masked men carrying a small wooden box in his arms. He carried it gently, as if it might hold a sleeping baby.

"I want to see it," Mr. Hargison said in a voice I'd never heard Mr. Hargison use.

"Show him what he's buyin'," Biggun told his son, and Bodean carefully released a latch and opened the box's top to reveal what lay within. None of us guys could see inside the box, but Mr. Moultry walked over to peer in and he gave a low whistle behind his mask.

"That suit you?" Biggun asked.

"It'll do just fine," Mr. Hargison said. "They won't know what hit 'em until they're tap-dancin' in hell."

"I threw in an extra." Biggun grinned again, and I thought he looked like Satan himself. "For good luck," he said. "Close it up, Bodean. Wade, take our money."

"Davy Ray!" Ben whispered. "Somethin's crawlin' on me!"

"Shut up, goofus!"

"I mean it! Somethin's on me!"

"You hear anythin'?" Mr. Moultry asked, and that question froze the marrow in my bones.

The men were silent. Mr. Hargison gripped the box with both hands, and Wade Blaylock had the fistful of money. Biggun's head slowly turned from side to side, his blast-furnace eyes searching the woods. *Hoot-hoot,* went the distant owl. Ben made a soft, terrified whining noise. I hugged the earth, my chin buried in pine straw, and near my face Mr. Hargison's cheroot smoldered.

"I don't hear nothin'," Wade Blaylock said, and he took the money to his father. Biggun counted it again, his tongue flicking back and forth across his lower lip, and then he shoved the cash into a pocket. "Okey-dokey," he said to the two masked men. "I reckon that concludes our bidness, gents. Next time you want a special order, you know how to find me." He started trudging back to get into the Cadillac again, and Bodean moved fast to open the door for him.

"Thank you kindly, Mr. Blaylock." Something about Mr. Moultry's voice made me think of a ratty dog trying to lick up to a mean master. "We sure do appreciate the—"

"*SPIIIIIDERS!*"

The world ceased its turning. The owl went dumb. The Milky Way flickered on the verge of extinction.

Ben hollered it again: "*Spiders!*" He started thrashing wildly amid the pine needles. "*They're all over me!*"

I couldn't draw a breath. Just couldn't do it. Davy Ray stared at Ben, his mouth hanging open as Ben writhed and yelled. The five men were frozen where they stood, all of them looking in our direction. My heart thundered. Three seconds passed like a lifetime, and then Biggun Blaylock's shout parted the night: "*Get 'em!*"

"Run!" Davy Ray hollered, scrambling to his feet. "Run for it!"

Wade and Bodean were coming after us, their shadows thrown large by the crossing of headlights. Davy Ray was already running back in the direction we'd come, and I said, "Run, Ben!" as I got up and fled. Ben squawked and struggled up, his hands madly plucking at his clothes. I looked over my shoulder and saw Wade about to reach Ben, but then Ben put on a burst of frantic speed and left Wade snatching at empty air. "Come back here, you little bastards!" Bodean yelled as he chased after Davy Ray and me. "Get 'em, damn it!" Biggun bellowed. "Don't let 'em get away!"

Davy Ray was fast, I'll say that for him. He left me behind pretty quick. The only trouble was, he had the flashlight. I couldn't see where I was going, and I could hear Bodean's breath rasping behind me. I dared to glance back again, but Ben had headed off in another direction with Wade at his heels. Whether Mr. Hargison and Mr. Moultry were coming after us, too, I didn't know. Bodean Blaylock was reaching for me, about to snag my collar. I ducked my head and changed directions on him, and he skidded in the pine straw. I kept going, through the dark wilderness. "Davy Ray!" I shouted, because I no longer could see his light. "Where are you?"

"Over here, Cory!" he called, but I couldn't tell where he was. Behind me, I heard Bodean crashing through the underbrush. I had to keep running, the sweat leaking from my face. "Cory! Davy Ray!" Ben shouted from somewhere off to the right. "Goddammit, bring 'em back here!" Biggun raged. I dreaded finding out what that monstrous mountain and his brood would do to us, because whatever had been going on back there was definitely something he'd wanted to keep a secret. I started to call for Ben, but as I opened my mouth my left foot slid on pine needles and suddenly I was rolling down an embankment like a sack of grain. I rolled into bushes and vines, and when I stopped I was so scared and dizzy I almost upchucked my toasted marshmallows. I lay there on my belly, my chin scraped raw by something I'd collided with, while I waited for a hand to winnow from the darkness and grab the back of my neck. I heard branches cracking; Bodean was nearby. I held my breath, fearing he could hear my heartbeat. To me it sounded like a drum corps all slamming an anvil with sledgehammers, and if Bodean couldn't detect it, he was surely as deaf as a post.

His voice drifted to me, from my left. "Might as well give up, kid. I know where you are."

He sounded convincing. I almost answered him, but I realized he was just as much in the dark as I was. I kept my mouth shut and my head low.

A few seconds later, Bodean shouted from a little farther away: "We're gonna find you! Oh yeah, don't you worry, we'll find every one of you sneakin' bastards!"

He was moving off. I waited a couple of minutes longer, listening to the Blaylocks calling to each other. Evidently, Davy Ray and Ben had both escaped and Biggun was furious about it. "You're gonna find those kids if it takes you all goddamn night!"

he roared at his sons, and they meekly answered "Yes sir." I figured I'd better get out while the getting was good, so I got up and crept away like a whipped pup.

I sure didn't know where I was going. I knew only that I needed to put as much distance between my skin and the Blaylocks as possible. I thought about doubling back and trying to find the other guys, but I was scared the Blaylocks would nab me. I just kept walking into the dark. If bobcats and rattlers were anywhere around, they couldn't possibly be worse than the two-legged beasts behind me. Maybe I walked for half an hour before I found a boulder to crouch on, and under the stars I realized my predicament: my knapsack, with all it contained, was back at the campsite, wherever that might be from here. I had no food, no water, no flashlight, no matches, and Davy Ray had the compass.

I had a crushing thought: Mom had been right. I should've waited until I was thirteen.

8

Chile Willow

I HAVE KNOWN LONG nights before. Like when I had strep throat and couldn't sleep and every minute seemed a torment. Or when Rebel had been sick with worms, and I stayed awake worrying as he coughed and whined. The night I spent huddled on that boulder, though, was an eternity of regret, fear, and discomfort all jammed into six hours. I knew one thing for sure: this was my last camping trip. I jumped at every imagined sound. I peered into the dark, seeing hulking shapes where there were only skinny pines. I would've tossed every issue of *National Geographic* on a bonfire for two peanut-butter sandwiches and a bottle of Green Spot. Sometime near dawn, the mosquitoes found me. They were so big I might've grabbed their legs and hitched a ride to Zephyr by air. I was miserable, from my red-blotched bites to my growling belly.

I had plenty of time, between slapping at skeeters and listening for the sounds of footsteps creeping up on me, to wonder what was in the box that Mr. Moultry and Mr. Hargison had paid four hundred dollars for. Man, that was a fortune of money! If the Blaylocks were involved, it had to be something wicked. What were Mr. Moultry and Mr. Hargison planning to do with the contents of that box? Something Mr. Hargison had said came back to me: *They won't know what hit 'em until they're tap-dancin' in hell.*

Whatever this was about, it was a bad enough business to be conducted late at night in the middle of the woods, and I had no doubt the Blaylocks would cut our throats—and maybe Mr. Moultry and Mr. Hargison would, too—to keep it a secret.

At last the sun began to rise, painting the sky pink and purple. I figured I'd better get moving again, in case the Blaylocks were somewhere close. Yesterday we'd been following the sun, and that had been afternoon, so I chose to head due east. I started off on aching legs, my heart hungry for home.

I figured I might be able to get to a high point and see Zephyr, or Saxon's Lake, or at least a road or a railroad track. On the hilltops, however, I could see only more woods. I did get a break, though, about two hours after dawn: a jet plane screamed overhead, and I saw its landing gears slide down. I changed course a few degrees, heading for what I hoped was the Air Force base. The woods, though, seemed to be thickening up rather than thinning. The sun was heating up, the ground rough underfoot, and soon I was wet with sweat. The gnats returned, with all their brothers, sisters, uncles, and cousins, and they swarmed around my head like a dark halo.

Soon I heard more jets shrieking, though I couldn't see them through the trees, and then I heard the dull *whump! whump! whump!* of explosions. I stopped, realizing I was near the bomb testing grounds. From the next ridge I could see dark plumes of smoke and dust rising into the sky to what I reasoned was the northeast. Which meant I was a long, arduous way from my front door.

My belly and the sun at its zenith told me it was high noon. I was supposed to have been home by now. My mother would start going crazy soon, and my dad would start warming up his whipping hand. What would hurt most would be admitting I wasn't as grown-up today as I thought I'd been yesterday.

I continued on, skirting the area where the bombs were

dropped. The last thing I needed was to be greeted by a few hundred pounds of high explosive. I pushed through tangles of thorns that bit my skin and tore my clothes, and I gritted my teeth and took what was coming to me. Little panics kept flaring up inside me, my mind seeing rattlesnakes in every shadow. If ever I wished I could really fly, now was the time.

And then, all of a sudden, I emerged from the pine woods into a green, leafy glade. Sunlight glittered off the rippling water of a small pond, and in that water a girl was swimming. She must've not been there long because only the ends of her long, golden hair were wet. She was as brown as a berry, the water glistening on her arms and shoulders as she stroked back and forth. I was about to call to her, and then she flipped over on her back and I saw she was naked.

Instantly my heart jumped and I stepped behind a tree, more afraid to startle her than anything else. Her legs kicked blissfully, the small buds of her breasts visible above the surface. She wore nothing to cover the area between her long, sleek thighs either, and I was ashamed to be looking but my eyes were spellbound. She turned and slid underwater. When she came up again, halfway across the pond, she swept her thick wet tresses back from her forehead and flipped over once more, gazing up at the blue sky as she floated.

Now, this was an interesting situation, I reasoned. Here I stood, hungry and thirsty, covered with mosquito bites and thorn welts, knowing my mother and father were calling up the sheriff and the fire chief by now, and twenty feet in front of me was a shimmering green pond with a naked blond girl floating in it. I hadn't gotten a good look at her face yet, but I could tell she was older than me, maybe fifteen or sixteen. She was long and lean, and she swam not with the splashy giddiness of a child but with an elegant, easy grace. I saw her clothes lying at the base of a tree on the other side of the pond, and a trail led off into the woods. The girl dove under, her legs kicking, then she resurfaced and slowly swam toward her clothes. She stopped, her feet finding the slippery bottom. Then she started wading in toward shore, and the moment of truth was thrust upon me.

"Wait!" I called out.

She spun around. Her face turned red and her hands flew up to cover her breasts, and then she ducked down in the water up to her throat. "Who's there? Who said that?"

"I did." I came out, sheepishly, from my hiding-place. "Sorry."

"Who are *you*? How long have you been standin' there?"

"Just a couple of minutes," I said. I followed it with a white lie. "I didn't see anythin'."

The girl was staring at me with open-mouthed indignation, her wet hair crimped around her shoulders. Her face was illuminated by a spill of sunlight through the trees, and I looked beyond her anger at a vision of beauty. Which surprised me, because the power of her beauty hit me so hard and suddenly. There are many things a boy considers beautiful: the shine of a bike's paint, the luster of a dog's pelt, the singing of a yo-yo as it loops the loop, the yellow harvest moon, the green grass of a meadow, and free hours at hand. The face of a girl, no matter how well-constructed, is usually not in that realm of appreciation. At that moment, though, I forgot about my hungry belly and my mosquito bites and my thorn stings. A girl with the most beautiful face I'd ever seen was staring at me, her eyes pale cornflower blue, and I had the feeling of waking up from a prolonged, lazy sleep into a new world I had never realized existed.

"I'm lost," I managed to say.

"Where'd you come from? Were you spyin' on me?"

"No. I . . . came from that way." I motioned in the direction behind me.

"You're tellin' a story!" she snapped. "Ain't nobody lives up in them hills!"

"Yeah," I said. "I know."

She remained hunkered down in the water, her arms around herself. I could tell that the anger was gradually leaving her, be-

cause the expression in her eyes was softening. "Lost," she repeated. "Where do you live?"

"Zephyr."

"Oh, now I know you're tellin' a story! Zephyr's all the way
on the other side of the valley!"

"I was campin' out last night," I told her. "Me and my friends.
Somethin' happened, and I got lost."

"What happened?"

I shrugged. "Some men got after us."

"Are you tellin' me the honest truth?"

"I am, I swear it."

"All the way from *Zephyr?* You must be worn out!"

"Kinda," I said.

"Turn around," she told me. "Don't you dare look till I say for
you to. All right?"

"All right," I agreed, and I turned my back to her. I heard her
getting out of the water, and in my mind I saw her naked from
head to toe. Clothes rustled. In a minute or two she said, "You can
turn around now." When I looked at her again, she was dressed in
a pink T-shirt, blue jeans, and sneakers. "What's your name?" she
asked, pushing her hair back from her forehead.

"Cory Mackenson."

"I'm Chile Willow," she said. "Come on with me, Cory."

Oh, she spoke my name so fine.

I followed her along the trail through the woods. She was
taller than me. She didn't walk like a little girl. She was sixteen,
I figured. Walking behind her, I inhaled her scent like the aroma
of dew on newly cut grass. I tried to step where she stepped. If I'd
had a tail, I would've wagged it. "I don't live too far," Chile Willow said, and I answered, "That's good."

On a dirt road stood a tarpaper shack with a chicken coop
next to it and a rust-eaten car hulk sitting on cinderblocks in the
weedy yard. The place was even worse than the run-down house
where Granddaddy Jaybird had lost his shirt playing poker. I had
already taken notice that Chile's jeans were patched and ragged,

and there were dime-sized holes in her T-shirt. The house she lived in made the poorest dwelling in Bruton look like a palace. She opened the screen door on squalling hinges and said into the gloom, "Momma? I found somebody!"

I entered the house after her. The front room smelled of harsh cigarette smoke and turnip greens. A woman was sitting in a rocking chair, knitting as she rocked. She stared at me with the same cornflower blue eyes as her beautiful daughter, from a face seamed with wrinkles and burned dry by hard work in the sun. "Throw him back," she said, and her needles never stopped.

"He's lost," Chile told her. "*Was* lost, I mean. Says he came from Zephyr."

"Zephyr," the woman said. Her eyes returned to me. She wore a dark blue shift with yellow needlework across the front, and she had on rubber flipflops. "You're a long way from home, boy." Her voice was low and husky, as if the sun had dried up her lungs, too. On a scarred little table near at hand was an ashtray full of cigarette butts, and half a cigarette still burning.

"Yes, ma'am. I sure would like to call my folks. Can I use your phone?"

"Ain't got no phone," she said. "This ain't Zephyr."

"Oh. Well . . . can somebody take me home?"

Chile's mother plucked the cigarette from the ashtray, took a long pull on it, and set it back down. When she spoke again, the smoke dribbled from her mouth. "Bill's took the truck off. Be back directly, I reckon."

I wanted to ask how long "directly" might be, but that would be impolite. "Can I have a glass of water?" I asked Chile.

"Sure thing. You ought to take off that shirt, too, it's wringin' wet. Go on, take it off." While Chile went back to the dismal little kitchen, I unbuttoned my shirt and peeled it away from my skin. "Done got yourself in some thorns, boy," Chile's mother said, her mouth leaking smoke again. "Chile, bring the iodine in here and doctor this boy." Chile answered, "Yes'm," and I folded my sweat-drenched shirt up and stood waiting for pleasure and pain.

Chile had to pump the water out of the kitchen faucet. Coming out, the water spat and gurgled. When it got to me, it was warm and tinged with brown and contained in a jelly glass with a picture of Fred Flintstone on it. I took a taste and smelled something foul. Then Chile Willow's face was near mine, and the sweetness of her breath was like new roses. She had a swab of cotton and a bottle of iodine. "This might hurt a little bit," she said.

"He can take it," her mother answered for me.

Chile went to work. I winced and drew in my breath as the stinging started and then deepened. As the pain progressed, I watched Chile's face. Her hair was drying, falling in golden waves over her shoulders. Chile got down on her knees before me, the red cotton swab leaving streaks of red across my flesh. My heart was beating harder. Her pale blue eyes met mine, and she smiled. "You're doin' just fine," she said. I smiled back, though I was hurting so bad I wanted to cry.

"How old are you, boy?" Chile's mother inquired.

"Twelve." Another white lie rolled out: "I'll be thirteen soon." I kept looking at Chile's eyes. "How old are *you?*" I asked her.

"Me? I'm an old lady. I'm sixteen."

"You go to the high school?"

"Went one year," she said. "That was enough for me."

"You don't go to *school?*" I was amazed at this fact. "Wow!"

"She goes to school," the mother said, her needles at work. "School of hard knocks, same as I did."

"Aw, Mom," Chile said; from her cupid's-bow mouth, two words could sound like music.

I forgot about the stinging. Pain was nothing to a man like me. As Chile's mother said, I could take it. I looked around the gloomy room, with its stained and battered sticks of furniture, and when I looked at Chile's face again, it was like seeing the sun after a long, stormy night. Though the iodine was cruel, her touch was gentle. I imagined she must like me, to be so gentle. I had seen her naked. In all my life I had seen no female naked but my mother. I had been in the presence of Chile Willow only a short time, but what is time when a heart speaks? My heart was speaking to Chile Willow in that moment, as she bathed my cuts and gave me a smile. My heart was saying *If you were my girlfriend I would give you a hundred lightning bugs in a green glass jar, so you could always see your way. I would give you a meadow full of wildflowers, where no two blooms would ever be alike. I would give you my bicycle, with its golden eye to protect you. I would write a story for you, and make you a princess who lived in a white marble castle. If you would only like me, I would give you magic. If you would only like me.*

If you would only—

"You're a brave little boy," Chile said.

From the rear of the house, a baby began crying.

"Oh, Lord," Chile's mother said, and she put aside her needles. "Bubba's woke up." She stood up and walked in the direction of the crying, her flipflops smacking the splintery floor.

"I'll feed him in a minute," Chile said.

"Naw, I'll do it. Bill's gonna be back soon, and if I was you, I'd put that ring back on. You know how crazy he gets."

"Uh-huh, do I ever." This was said under Chile's breath. Something in her eyes had darkened. She swabbed the last thorn scrape and capped the iodine bottle. "There you go. All done."

Chile's mother returned, holding an infant that wasn't a year old. I stood in the middle of the room, my skin screaming as Chile got off her knees and went back into the kitchen. When she came back, she was wearing a thin gold band on the third finger of her left hand. She took the baby from her mother and began to rock it and croon softly.

"He's a feisty thing," the older woman said. "Gonna be a handful, that's for sure." She went to a window and pulled aside a flimsy curtain. "Here comes Bill now. Gonna get your ride home, fella."

I heard the pickup truck clattering as it pulled up almost to the porch. A door opened and slammed. Then through the screen door came Bill, who was tall and slim and had a crew cut and was all of eighteen years old. He wore dirty jeans and a blue shirt with a grease stain on the front, and he had heavy-lidded brown eyes and was chewing on a match. "Who's *he?* " he asked, first thing.

"Boy needs a ride to Zephyr," Chile's mother told him. "Got hisself lost in the woods."

"I ain't gone take him to Zephyr!" Bill protested with a scowl. "It's hotter'n hell in that truck!"

"Where'd you go?" Chile asked, her arms full of baby.

"Fixed that engine for old man Walsh. And if you think that was fun, you got another think comin'." He glanced at her as he strode past toward the kitchen. I saw him look right through her, as if she wasn't even there, and Chile's eyes had deadened.

"You get any money?" the mother called after him.

"Yeah, I got some money! You think I'm stupid, I wouldn't get no money for a job like that?"

"Bubba needs some fresh milk!" Chile said.

I heard the faucet pumping slimy water. "Shit," Bill muttered.

"You gonna take this boy home to Zephyr, or not?" Chile's mother asked.

"Not," he answered.

"Here." Chile offered the baby to her mother. "I'll drive him, then."

"The hell you say!" Bill came back into the room, holding brown water in another Flintstones jelly glass. "You can't drive nowhere, you ain't got no license!"

"I keep tellin' you I ought to—"

"You don't need to do no drivin'," Bill said, and he looked right through her again. "Your place is in this house. Tell her, Mrs. Purcell."

"I ain't barkin' up nobody's tree," Chile's mother said, but she didn't take the infant. She sat down in her rocking chair, put the cigarette in her mouth, and gripped the knitting needles.

Bill drank down the brown water and made a face. "All right, then. Hell with it. I'll take him to that gas station over near the base. He can use the pay phone."

"That okay with you, Cory?" Chile asked me.

"I . . ." My head was still spinning, and the sight of that gold ring hurt my eyes. "I guess so."

"Well, you better take what I'm offerin' or I'll just kick your butt out the door," Bill warned.

"I don't have any money for the phone," I said.

"Boy, you're in damn sorry shape, ain't you?" Bill took the glass back to the kitchen. "You ain't gettin' none of my work money, that's for sure!"

Chile reached down into the pocket of her jeans. "I've got some money," she said, and her hand came out clutching a small red plastic purse in the shape of a heart. It was cracked and much-used, the kind of thing a little girl might buy at Woolworth's for ninety-nine cents. She popped it open. I saw a few coins inside it. "I just need a dime," I told her. She gave me a dime, one with Mercury's head on it, and I shoved it into my own pocket. She smiled at me, which was worth a fortune. "You'll get home all right."

"I know I will." I looked at the infant's face, and I saw he had her beautiful eyes of cornflower blue.

"Come on, if you're comin'," Bill said on his way past me to the door. He didn't spare a glance at his wife or baby. He went on out, the screen door slammed, and I heard the truck's engine snort.

I could not tear myself away from Chile Willow. In later years I would hear about the "chemistry" between two people, and what that meant; I would be told by my father about the "birds and the bees" but of course by then I would know all about it from my schoolmates. All I knew at that moment was a longing: to be older, taller, stronger, and handsome. To be able to kiss the lips of her lovely face, and crank back time so she didn't have Bill's baby in her arms. What I wanted to say to her, in that moment, was: *You should've waited for me.*

"Go on home where you belong, boy," Mrs. Purcell said. She was watching me intently, her needles paused, and I wondered if she knew what was in my head.

I would never set foot in this house again. I would never again see Chile Willow. I knew this, and I drank her in while I could.

Outside, Bill leaned on the horn. Bubba started crying again.

"Thank you," I told Chile, and I took my wet shirt and walked out into the sunlight. The truck was painted bilious green, its sides dented up, its body sagging to the left. A pair of red velvet dice dangled from the rearview mirror. I climbed into the passenger seat, a spring jabbing my butt. On the floorboard was a toolbox and coils of wires, and though the windows were rolled down, the interior smelled like sweat and a sickly sweet odor I later came to connect with miserable poverty. I looked at the house's doorway and saw Chile emerge into the light, cradling her baby. "Stop and get him some milk, Bill!" she called. I could see her mother standing behind her, in the musty gloom. It occurred to me that their faces were very much alike, though one had already been weathered by time and circumstance, probably a lot of disappointment and bitterness, too. I hoped Chile would be spared such a journey. I hoped she would never lock her smile away, and forget where she'd put the key.

"'Bye, now!" she said to me.

I waved. Bill pulled the pickup truck away from the house, and dust boiled up off the road between Chile Willow and me.

It was a mile or more until the pavement started. Bill drove in silence, and let me off at a gas station on the edge of the Air Force base. As I was getting out, he said, "Hey, boy! Better watch where you put your pecker." Then he drove away, and I stood alone on the hot concrete.

Pain was nothing to a man like me.

The gas station's owner showed me where the pay phone was. I started to put the Mercury-head dime into the slot, but I couldn't let go of it. It had come from Chile Willow's purse. I just couldn't. I asked the owner to let me borrow a dime, telling him my dad would pay him back. "I ain't no bank," he huffed, but he took a dime out of the cash register anyway. In another moment it was tinkling down into the pay phone. I dialed the number, and Mom picked up on the second ring.

My folks were there to pick me up in about half an hour. I expected the worst, but I got a rib-busting squeeze from my mother and my dad grinned and cuffed me on the back of my head and I knew I was in high cotton. On the drive home, I learned that Davy Ray and Ben had reached Zephyr together about seven this morning and Sheriff Amory knew the whole story, that two masked men had bought something in a wooden box from Biggun Blaylock and then the Blaylocks had chased us through the forest. "The men with the masks were Mr. Hargison and Mr. Moultry," I said. I felt bad about this, because I recalled that Mr. Hargison had saved our skins from the Branlins. Still and all, the sheriff needed to know.

We passed the Air Force base, its runways and barracks and buildings enclosed by a high mesh fence topped with barbed wire. We drove along the forest road, passing the turnoff to the house of bad girls. Dad slowed almost imperceptibly as we drove past Saxon's Lake, but he didn't look at it. The exact place where I'd seen the figure in the flapping coat was lost in summer growth. As soon as the lake was behind us, Dad picked up speed again.

I was lavished with attention when I got home. I got a big bowl of chocolate ice cream and all the Oreos I could eat. Dad called me "pal" and "partner" with just about every breath. Even Rebel almost licked my face off. I had been delivered from the wilderness, and I was okay.

Of course they wanted to hear about my adventure, and they pressed me to tell them more about the girl who had treated my thorn scrapes. I told them her name, that she was sixteen years old, and that she was as beautiful as Cinderella in that Walt Disney movie. "I do believe our pal's got himself a crush on her," Dad said to Mom, and he grinned. I said, "Awww, I don't have time for any old girl!"

But I fell asleep on the sofa with a dime in my hand.

Before the sun set on Saturday afternoon, Sheriff Amory dropped by. He had been to see Davy Ray and Ben; now it was my turn to be questioned. We sat on the front porch, Rebel sprawled beside my chair and occasionally lifting his head to lick my hand, while in the distance thunder grumbled amid the darkening clouds. He listened to my story about the wooden box, and when I came to the part about the masked men being Mr. Dick Moultry and Mr. Gerald Hargison, he said, "Why do you think it was them, Cory, if you couldn't see their faces?"

"'Cause Biggun Blaylock called the fat one Dick and I saw the cheroot Mr. Hargison threw away and that's what he smokes, the kind with the white plastic tip."

"I see." He nodded, his long-jawed face betraying no emotion. "You know, there are probably a lot of fellas around here who smoke cheroots like that. And just 'cause Biggun Blaylock called a man by his first name doesn't mean it was Dick Moultry."

"It was them," I said. "Both of them."

"Davy Ray and Ben told me they didn't know who the masked men were."

"Maybe they don't, sir, but I do."

"All right, then, I'll make sure I find out where Dick and Gerald were 'round about eleven last night. I asked Davy Ray and Ben if they could take me to where this thing happened, but they said they couldn't find it again. Could you?"

"No sir. It was near a trail, though."

"Uh-huh. Trouble is, there are an awful lot of old loggin' roads and trails cut through those hills. You didn't happen to see what was inside that box, did you?"

"No sir. Whatever it was, Mr. Hargison said it was gonna make some people tap-dance in hell."

Sheriff Amory's brow furrowed. His black eyes held a spark of renewed interest. "Now, why do you think he'd say somethin' like that?"

"I don't know. But Biggun Blaylock would. He said he threw an extra one into the box."

"An extra what?"

"I don't know that, either." I watched lightning flicker on the horizon from sky to earth. "Are you gonna find Biggun Blaylock and ask him?"

"Biggun Blaylock," the sheriff said, "is an invisible man. I hear about him, and I know the things he and his sons do, but I never see him. I think he's got a hideout somewhere in the woods, probably pretty close to where you boys were." He watched the lightning, too, and he wound the fingers of his big hands together and worked his knuckles. "If I could ever catch one of his sons at some mischief, maybe I could smoke Biggun out. But to tell you the truth, Cory, the sheriff's office in Zephyr is pretty much a one-man operation. I don't get a whole lot of money from the county. Heck," he said, and he smiled thinly, "I only got this job 'cause nobody else would have it. My wife's on me all the time to give it up, says I oughta go back into the house-paintin' business." He shrugged. "Well," he said, dismissing those thoughts, "a whole lot of people around here are scared of the Blaylocks. Especially of Biggun. I doubt I could deputize more than five or six men to help me comb the woods for him. And by the time we found him—if we ever did—he'd have known we were comin' long before we got there. See my problem, Cory?"

"Yes sir. The Blaylocks are bigger than the law."

"Not bigger than the law," he corrected me. "Just a whole lot meaner."

A storm was coming. The wind was in the trees. Rebel got up and sniffed the air.

Sheriff Amory stood up. "I'll be goin' now," he said. "Thanks for helpin' me." In the fading light he looked old and burdened, his shoulders slightly stooped. He called good-bye to Mom and Dad through the screen door, and Dad came out to see him off. "You take care of yourself, Cory," he told me, then he and Dad walked together to his car. I stayed on the porch, stroking Rebel, as Sheriff Amory and Dad talked a few minutes more. When the sheriff had driven off and Dad returned to the porch, it was he who appeared burdened. "Come on in, partner," he said, and held the door open for me. "It's gonna get bad out."

The wind roared that night. The rain pounded down, and the lightning was scrawled like the track of a mysterious finger over my hometown.

That was the night I first dreamed about the four black girls, all dressed up and with their shoes shined, who stood beneath a leafless tree calling my name again and again and again.

9

Summer Winds Up

AUGUST WAS DYING. So was summer. Schooldays, golden rule days; those lay ahead, on the gilded rim of autumn.

These things happened in the last days of summer: I learned that Sheriff Amory had indeed visited Mr. Hargison and Mr. Moultry. Their wives had told the sheriff that both men were home all night that particular night, that they hadn't even set one foot outside their front doors. The sheriff couldn't do anything else; after all, I hadn't seen the faces of the two men who'd accepted that wooden box from Biggun Blaylock.

The September issue of *Famous Monsters* came to my mailbox. On the envelope that bore my name there was a long green smear of snot.

Mom answered the telephone one morning, and said, "Cory! It's for you!"

I came to the phone. On the other end was Mrs. Evelyn Prathmore, who informed me that I had won third place in the short-story division of the Zephyr Art Council's Writing Contest. I was to be given a plaque with my name on it, she told me. Would I be prepared to read my story during a program at the library the second Saturday of September?

I was stunned. I stammered a yes. Instantly upon putting the telephone down, I was struck first with a surge of joy that almost lifted me out of my Hush Puppies and then a crush of terror that about slammed me to the floor. Read my story? *Aloud?* To a roomful of people I hardly knew?

Mom calmed me down. That was part of her job, and she was good at it. She told me I had plenty of time to practice, and she said I had made her so proud, she wanted to bust. She called Dad at the dairy, and he told me he'd bring me home two cold bottles of chocolate milk. When I called Johnny, Davy Ray, and Ben to tell them the news, they thought it was great, too, and they congratulated me, but all of them quickly pricked the boil of my nascent terror by reacting dolefully to the fact that I had to read my story aloud. What if your zipper breaks and it won't stay up? Davy Ray asked. What if you start shakin' so hard you can't even hold the paper? Ben asked. What if you open your mouth to talk and your voice goes and you can't even say a single word? Johnny asked.

Friends. They really know how to knock you off your pedestal, don't they?

Three days before school started, on a clear afternoon with fleecy clouds in the sky and a cool breeze blowing, we all rode our bikes to the ball field, our gloves laced to the handlebars. We took our positions around the diamond, which was cleated up and going to weed. On the scoreboard was the proof that our Little League team was not alone in agony; the men's team, the Quails, had suffered a five-to-zip loss from the Air Force base team, the High Flyers. We stood with pools of shadow around our ankles and threw a ball back and forth to each other as we talked with some sadness about the passing of summer. We were in our secret hearts excited about the beginning of school. There comes a time when freedom becomes . . . well, too free. We were ready to be regulated, so we could fly again next summer.

We threw fastballs and curves, fly balls and dust-kickers. Ben had the best wormburner you ever saw, and Johnny could make it fishtail an instant before it smacked into your glove. Too bad we were strikeout kings, each and every one. Well, there was always next season.

We'd been there maybe forty minutes or so, working up a sweat, when Davy Ray said, "Hey, look who's comin'!" We all looked. Walking through the weeds toward us was Nemo Curliss, his hands plunged deep into the pockets of his jeans. He was still a beanpole, his skin still buttermilk white. His mother ruled that roost, for sure.

"Hi!" I said to him. "Hey, Nemo!" Davy Ray called. "Come on and throw us a few!"

"Oh, great!" Johnny said, recalling his blistered hand. "Uh . . . why don't you throw some to Ben instead?"

Nemo shook his head, his face downcast. He continued walking across the field, passing Johnny and Ben, and he approached me at home plate. When he stopped and lifted his face, I saw he'd been crying. His eyes behind the thick glasses were red and swollen, the tear tracks glistening on his cheeks.

"What's wrong?" I asked. "Somebody been beatin' up on you?"

"No," he said. "I . . . I . . ."

Davy Ray came up, holding the baseball. "What is it? Nemo, you been cryin'?"

"I . . ." He squeezed out a small sob. He was trying to get control of himself, but it was more than he could manage. "I've gotta go," he said.

"Gotta go?" I frowned. "Go where, Nemo?"

"Away. Jutht . . ." He made a gesture with a skinny arm. "Jutht away."

Ben and Johnny arrived at home plate. We stood in a circle around Nemo as he sobbed and wiped his runny nose. Ben couldn't bear the sight, and he walked off a few paces and kicked a stone around. "I . . . went to your houth, to tell you, and your mom told me you were here," Nemo explained. "I wanted to let you know."

"Well, where do you have to go? Are you gonna go visit somebody?" I asked.

"No." Fresh tears ran down his face. It was a terrible sight to behold. "We've gotta move, Cory."

"*Move?* To where?"

"I don't know. Thomeblathe a long way from here."

"Gosh," Johnny said. "You hardly lived in Zephyr a whole summer!"

"We were hopin' you could play on our team next year!" Davy told him.

"Yeah," I said. "And we thought you were gonna go to our school."

"No." Nemo kept shaking his head, his puffy eyes full of torment. "No. No. I can't. We've gotta move. Gotta move tomorrow."

"*Tomorrow?* How come so fast?"

"Mom thez. Gotta move. Tho Dad can thell thome shirts."

The shirts. Ah yes, the shirts. Nobody wore tailored white shirts in Zephyr. I doubted that anybody wore tailored white shirts in any of the towns Mr. Curliss took his wife and son and his fabric swatches to. I doubted if anybody ever would.

"I can't . . ." Nemo stared at me, and the pain of his gaze made my heart hurt. "I can't . . . ever make no friendth," he said. "'Cauthe . . . we've alwath gotta move."

"I'm sorry, Nemo," I said. "Really I am. I wish you didn't have to move." On an impulse, I took the baseball out of my glove and held it out to him. "Here you go. You keep this, so you can remember your buddies here in Zephyr. Okay?"

Nemo hesitated. Then he reached out and wrapped the skinny fingers of his miracle pitching hand around the ball, and he accepted it. Here Johnny showed his true class; the baseball belonged to him, but he never said a word.

Nemo turned the baseball over and over between both hands,

and I saw the red-stitched seam reflected in his glasses. He stared at that baseball as if into the depths of a magic crystal. "I want to thtay here," he said softly. His nose was running, and he sniffled. "I want to thtay here, and go to thcool and have friendth." He looked at me. "I jutht want to be like everybody elth. I want to thtay here so *bad*."

"Maybe you can come back sometime," Johnny offered, but it was a measly crumb. "Maybe you can——"

"No," Nemo interrupted. "I'll never come back. Never. Never even for a thingle day." He turned his head, facing the house they would soon be leaving. A tear crawled down his face and hung quivering from his chin. "Mom thez Dadth gotta thell thirts tho we can have money. At night thometimeth thee hollerth at him and callth him lathee, and thee thez thee never thouda married him. And he thez, 'It'll be the nextht town. The nextht town, that'll be the lucky break.'" Nemo's face swung back to mine. It had changed in that instant. He was still crying, but there was rage in his eyes so powerful that I had to step back a pace to escape its heat. "Ith never gonna be the nextht town," he said. "We're gonna move and move and move, and my mom'th gonna alwath holler and my dad'th gonna alwath thay it'll be the nextht town. But it'll be a lie."

Nemo was silent, but the rage spoke. His fingers squeezed around the baseball, his knuckles whitening, his eyes fixed on nothing.

"We're gonna miss you, Nemo," I said.

"Yeah," Johnny said. "You're okay."

"You'll get up to the mound someday, Nemo," Davy Ray told him. "When you get there, you strike 'em all out. Hear?"

"Yeth," he answered, but there wasn't much conviction in his voice. "I with I didn't have to . . ." He faded off; there was no point in it, because he was a little boy and he had to go.

Nemo began walking home across the field, the baseball gripped in his hand. "So long!" I called to him, but he didn't respond. I imagined what life must be like for him: forbidden to play the game he was so naturally gifted at, shuttered away in a series of houses in a parade of towns, staying in one place only long enough to get picked on and beaten up but never long enough for guys to get to know who and what he was behind the pale skin, the lisp, and the thick glasses. I could never have stood such suffering.

Nemo screamed.

It came out of him with such force that the sound made us jump. The scream changed, became a wail that rose up and up, painful in its longing. And then Nemo spun around, his head and shoulders first and then his hips, and I saw his eyes were wide and enraged and his teeth were clenched. His throwing arm whipped around in a blur, his backbone popped like a whip, and he hurled that baseball almost straight up into the sky.

I saw it go up. I saw it keep going. I saw it become a dark dot. Then the sun took it.

Nemo was on his knees, the scream and the throw having drained all the strength out of him. He blinked, his glasses crooked on his face.

"Catch it!" Davy Ray said, squinting up. "Here it comes down!"

"Where?" Johnny asked, lifting his glove.

"Where is it?" I asked, stepping away from the others to try to find it in the glare.

Ben was looking up, too. His glove hung at his side. "That bugger," he said softly, "is *gone*."

We waited, searching the sky.

We waited, our gloves ready.

We waited.

I glanced at Nemo. He had gotten up, and was walking home. His stride was neither fast nor slow, just resigned. He knew what was waiting for him in the next town, and in the town after that. "Nemo!" I shouted after him. He just kept walking, and he did not look back.

We waited for the ball to come down.

After a while, we sat down in the red dirt. Our eyes scanned the sky as the fleecy clouds moved and the sun began to sink toward the west.

No one spoke. No one knew what to say.

In later days, Ben would speculate that the wind blew the ball into the river. Johnny would believe a flock of birds had hit it, and knocked it off course. Davy Ray would say something must've been wrong with the ball, that it had come to pieces way up there and we hadn't seen the skin and the innards plummet back to earth.

And me?

I just believed.

Twilight came upon us. At last I climbed on Rocket, the other guys got on their bikes, and we left the ball field and our summer dreams. Our faces now were turned toward autumn. I was going to have to tell somebody soon about the four black girls I saw in my sleep, the ones all dressed up and calling my name under a tree with no leaves. I was going to have to read my story about the man at the bottom of Saxon's Lake in front of a roomful of people. I was going to have to figure out what was in that wooden box Biggun Blaylock had sold in the dead of night for four hundred dollars.

I was going to have to help my father find peace.

We pedaled on, four buddies with the wind at our backs and all roads leading to the future.

Three

Burning Autumn

1

Green-Feathered Hat

"Cory?"

I pretended I didn't hear the ominous whisper.

"Cory?"

No. I wasn't going to look. At the front of the schoolroom, Mrs. Judith Harper—otherwise known as "Hairpie," "Harpy," and "Old Leatherlungs"—was demonstrating on the blackboard the division of fractions. Arithmetic was for me a walk into the Twilight Zone; this dividing fractions stuff was a mystifying fall into the Outer Limits.

"Cory?" she whispered again, behind me. "I've got a big ole green booger on my finger."

Oh my Lord, I thought. Not again!

"If you don't turn around and smile at me, I'm gone wipe it on the back of your neck."

It was the fourth day of class. I knew on the first day that it was going to be a long year, because some idiot had decreed the Demon a "gifted child" and had double-promoted her, and like the fickle finger of fate, Mrs. Harper had devised a seating chart—boy, girl, boy, girl, boy, girl—that put the Demon in the desk at my back.

And the worst part, the very worst, was that—as Davy Ray told me and laughed wickedly—she had a crush on me as big as the cheesy green moon.

"*Cory?*" Her voice demanded my attention.

I had to turn around. Last time I'd resisted, she'd smeared saliva on the back of my neck in the shape of a heart.

Brenda Sutley was grinning, her red hair oily and ratty and her wandering eyes shining with mischief. She held up her index finger, which had a dirt-grimed nail but no booger on it.

"Got'cha," she whispered.

"*Cory Jay Mackenson!*" Leatherlungs roared. "*Turn around this instant!*"

I did, almost giving myself whiplash. I heard the traitors around me giggling, knowing that the Harpy would not be satisfied with this display of respect. "Oh, I guess you know all about the division of fractions by now, don't you?" she inquired, her hands on hips as wide as a Patton tank. "Well, why don't you come up here and do some division for us, to show us how it's done?" She held the accursed yellow chalk out to me.

If I am ever on death row, the walk to the electric chair will be no more terrifying than that walk from my desk to the chalk in Mrs. Harper's hand and then, ultimately, to the blackboard. "All right," she said as I stood there shoulder-slumped and hang-doggy. "Write down these fractions." She rattled some off, and when I copied them my chalk broke and Nelson Bittner laughed and in two seconds I had a fellow sufferer up there with me.

Everybody knew by now: we weren't going to be able to defeat Mrs. Harper with a frontal attack. We weren't going to be able to storm her ramparts and yell victory over her scattered math books. It would have to be a slow, insidious war of snipers and booby traps, a painstaking probe to learn her weakness. All us kids had found out by now that all teachers had a sore spot; some went crazy over gum chewing, others insane over behind-the-back giggles, still others nuts over the repeated squeaking and scuffing of shoes on the linoleum. Machine-gun coughs, donkeylike snorts, a fusillade of throat clearing, spitballs stuck to the blackboard: all these were arsenals in the battle against Hitlerian teachers. Who knows? Maybe we could get the Demon to bring to class a dead, stinking animal in a shoebox, or get her to sneeze and blow ribbons of snot out of those talented nostrils of hers to make Mrs. Harper's hair uncurl.

"Wrong! Wrong! Wrong!" Leatherlungs bellowed at me as I finished my queasy attempt at fraction division. "Go sit down and pay attention, you blockhead!"

Between Leatherlungs and the Demon, I was really in for it.

After the three o'clock bell had rung and Davy Ray, Johnny, Ben, and I had jawed about the events of the day, I pedaled home on Rocket under a dark, glowering sky. I found Mom at home, cleaning the oven. "Cory!" she said when I walked into the kitchen intent on raiding the cookie jar. "Lady from the mayor's office called for you about ten minutes ago. Mayor Swope wants to see you."

"Mayor Swope?" I paused with my hand reaching for a Lorna Doone. "What for?"

"Didn't say what for, but she said it was important." Mom glanced out the window. "A storm's blowin' up. Your father'll drive you over to the courthouse, if you can wait an hour."

My curiosity was piqued. What would Mayor Swope want with *me?* I looked out the window as Mom continued her oven cleaning, and judged the gathering clouds. "I think I can get there before it starts rainin'," I said.

Mom pulled her head out of the oven, looked at the sky again, and frowned. "I don't know. It might start pourin' on you."

I shrugged. "I'll be all right."

She hesitated, her fretful nature gnawing at her. Ever since my camping trip, though, I could tell she'd been making a mighty effort to stop worrying so much about me. Even though I'd gotten lost, I'd proven I could survive in the face of hardship. Finally, she said, "Go on, then."

I took two Lorna Doones and headed for the porch.

"If it starts comin' down hard, you stay at the courthouse!" she called. "Hear?"

"I hear!" I told her, and I got on Rocket and pedaled as I crunched the Lorna Doones between my teeth. Not too far from the house, Rocket suddenly shuddered and I felt the handlebars jerk to the left. Ahead of me, the Branlins were pedaling side by side on their black bikes, but they were going in the same direction as me and didn't see me. Rocket wanted to turn to the left at the next intersection, and I followed Rocket's sage advice to take a detour.

Thunder was rumbling and it was starting to sprinkle a little as I reached the dark-stoned, gothic-styled courthouse at the end of Merchants Street. The drops were chilly; summer's warm rain was a thing of the past. I left Rocket chained to a fire hydrant and went into the courthouse, which smelled like a moldy basement. A sign on the wall said Mayor Swope's office was on the second floor, and I climbed the wide staircase, the high windows around me letting in murky, storm-blue light. At the top of the staircase, three carved gargoyles sat atop the black walnut banister, their scaly legs curled up and their claws folded across their chests. One wall was decorated with an old tattered Confederate flag and there were dusty display cases holding butternut uniforms riddled with moth holes. Above my head was a darkened glass cupola, reachable only by ladder, and through the cupola I heard thunder resonate as through a bell jar.

I walked along the long corridor, which had a floor of black and white linoleum squares. On either side were offices: License Bureau, County Tax Department, Probate Judge, Traffic Court, and the like. None of their lights were on. I saw a man with dark hair and a blue-paisley bow tie coming out of a pebbled-glass door marked Sanitation and Maintenance. He locked the door from a ring of jingling keys and looked at me. "Can I help you, young fella?" he asked.

"I'm supposed to see Mayor Swope," I said.

"His office is at the end of the corridor." He checked his

pocket watch. "Might be gone home by now, though. Most everybody leaves around three-thirty."

"Thank you," I told him, and I went on. I heard his keys jingling as he walked toward the stairs, and he whistled a tune I didn't know.

I passed the council's chambers and the recorder's office—both dark—and at the corridor's end I faced a big oak door with brass letters on it that said OFFICE OF THE MAYOR. I wasn't sure if I was supposed to knock or not, and there was no buzzer. I grappled with the question of etiquette here for a few seconds, as the thunder growled outside. Then I balled up my fist and knocked.

In a few seconds the door opened. A woman with horn-rimmed glasses and an iron-gray mountain of hair peered out. Her face was like a chunk of granite, all hard ridges and cliffs. Her eyebrows lifted in a question.

"I'm . . . here to see Mayor Swope," I said.

"Oh. You're Cory Mackenson."

"Yes ma'am."

"Come in." She opened the door wider, and I slipped in past her. As I did, I got a jolt of either violet-scented perfume or hair spray up my nostrils. I had entered a red-carpeted room which held a desk, a row of chairs, and a magazine rack. A map of Zephyr, brown at the edges, adorned one wall. On the desk there was an in tray and an out tray, a neat stack of papers, framed photographs of a baby being held between a smiling young woman and man, and a nameplate that said MRS. INEZ AXFORD and, underneath that in smaller letters, MAYOR'S SECRETARY.

"Just have a seat for a minute, please." Mrs. Axford walked across the room to another door. She rapped softly on it, and I heard Mayor Swope say in his mushmouth accent, "Yes?" from the other side. Mrs. Axford opened it. "The boy's here," she said.

"Thank you, Inez." I heard a chair creak. "I believe that finishes us up for the day. You can go on home if you like."

"Want me to send him in?"

"Two minutes and I'll be with him."

"Yes sir. Oh . . . did you sign that application for the new traffic lights?"

"Need to study that a little more, Inez. Get to it first thing in the mornin'."

"Yes sir. I'll be goin' on, then." She retreated from the mayor's domain and closed the door and said to me, "He'll be with you in two minutes." As I waited, Mrs. Axford locked her desk, got her sturdy brown purse, and straightened the photographs on her desk. She wedged her purse up under her arm, took a long look around the office to make sure everything was in its proper place, and then she walked out the door into the hallway without saying boot, shoot, or scoot to me.

I waited. Thunder boomed overhead and rolled through the courthouse. I heard the rain start—slowly at first, then building up to a hammering.

The door to the mayor's office opened, and Mayor Swope emerged. The sleeves of his blue shirt were rolled up, his initials in white on the breast pocket, his suspenders striped with red. "Cory!" he said, smiling. "Come in and let's have us a talk!"

I didn't know what to make of this. I knew who Mayor Swope was and all, but I'd never spoken to him. And here he was, smiling and motioning me into his office! The guys would believe this about as much as they believed I'd stuck a broomstick down Old Moses's throat!

"Come in, come in!" the mayor urged.

I walked into his office. Everything was fashioned of dark, glistening wood. The air smelled of sweet pipe tobacco. There was a desk in the office that seemed as big as the deck of an aircraft carrier. Shelves were full of thick, leatherbound books. They looked to me as if they had never been touched, because none had bookmarks in them. Two burly black leather chairs faced the desk over an expanse of Persian carpet. Windows afforded a view of Merchants Street, but right now the rain was streaming down them.

Mayor Swope, his gray hair combed back from a widow's

peak and his eyes dark blue and friendly, closed the door. He said, "Have a seat, Cory." I hesitated. "Doesn't matter which one." I took the one on his left. The leather pooted when I sat down in it. Mayor Swope settled himself in his own chair, which had scrolled armrests. On his flattop of a desk was a telephone, a leather-covered jar full of pens, a can of Field and Stream tobacco, and a pipe rack cradling four pipes. One of the pipes was white, and had a man's bearded face carved into it.

"Gettin' some rain out there, aren't we?" he asked, his fingers lacing together. He smiled again, and this close I saw his teeth were discolored.

"Yes sir."

"Well, the farmers need it. Just so we don't have another flood, huh?"

"Yes sir."

Mayor Swope cleared his throat. His fingers tapped. "Are your folks waitin' for you?" he asked.

"No sir. I came on my bike."

"Oh. Gosh, you're gonna have a wet ride home."

"I don't mind."

"Wouldn't be good," he said, "if you had an accident on the way. You know, with that rain comin' down so hard, a car could hit you, you could go down in a ditch and . . ." His smile had slipped. Now it crept back. "Well, it wouldn't be good."

"No sir."

"I suppose you're wonderin' why I wanted to see you?" I nodded.

"You know I was on the panel that judged the writin' contest? I enjoyed your story. Yessir, it deserved a prize." He picked up a briar pipe and popped open the can of tobacco. "It surely did. You're the youngest person ever to win a plaque in the contest." I watched his fingers as he began to fill the pipe's bowl with bits of tobacco. "I checked the records. You're the youngest by far. That ought to make you and your folks very proud."

"I guess so."

"Oh, you don't have to be so modest, Cory! I sure couldn't write like that when I was your age! No sir! I was good at math, but English wasn't my subject." He produced a pack of matches from his pocket, struck one, and touched it to the tobacco in his pipe. Blue smoke bloomed around his mouth. His eyes were on me. "You've got a keen imagination," he said. "That part in your story about seein' somebody standin' in the woods across the road. I liked that part. How'd you happen to come up with that?"

"It really—" *Happened*, I was going to say. But before I could, somebody knocked at the door. Mrs. Axford looked in. "Mayor Swope?" she said. "Lord, it's pourin' cats and dogs! I couldn't even get to my car, and I just had my hair fixed yesterday! Do you have an umbrella I might borrow?"

"I believe so, Inez. Look in that closet over there."

She opened a closet and rummaged around in it. "Should be one in the corner," Mayor Swope told her. "Smells awfully musty in here!" Mrs. Axford said. "I believe somethin's mildewed!"

"Yeah, gotta clean it out one of these days," he said.

Mrs. Axford came out of the closet clutching an umbrella. But her nose was wrinkled, and in her other hand she was clutching two articles of clothing that were white with mildew. "Look at these!" she said. "I believe mushrooms are growin' in here!"

My heart seized up.

Mrs. Axford was holding a mildew-blotched overcoat and a hat that appeared to have been run through a washer and wringer.

And in the band of that battered hat was a silver disc and a crumpled green feather.

"Whew! Just smell it!" Mrs. Axford made a face that might've stopped a clock. "What're you keepin' this stuff for?"

"That's my favorite hat. Was, at least. It got ruined the night of the flood, but I thought I could get it fixed. And I've had that raincoat for fifteen years."

"No wonder you won't let me clean out your closet! What else is in here?"

"Never you mind! Run on, now! Leroy's waitin' at home for you!"

"You want me to throw these in the garbage on my way out?"

"No, Lord no!" Mayor Swope said. "Just put 'em back in there and close the door!"

"I swear," Mrs. Axford said as she returned the items to the closet, "you men are worse about hangin' on to old clothes than little babies with their blankets." She closed the door with a firm *thunk*. "There. I can still smell that mildew, though."

"It's all right, Inez. You go on home, and be careful on the road."

"I will." She gave me a quick glance, and then she walked out of the office with the umbrella.

I don't think I had drawn a breath during that entire exchange. Now I pulled one in, and I shivered as the air burned my lungs.

"Now, Cory," Mayor Swope said, "Where were we? Oh yes: the man across the road. How'd you come up with that?"

"I . . . I . . ." The green-feathered hat was in a closet ten feet from me. Mayor Swope was the man who'd worn it that night when the floodwaters had raged in the streets of Bruton. "I . . . never said it was a man," I answered. "I just said . . . it was somebody standin' there."

"Well, that was a nice touch. I'll bet that was an excitin' mornin' for you, wasn't it?" He reached into another pocket, and when his hand came into view there was a small silver blade in it.

It was the knife I'd seen in his hand, that night when I was afraid he was going to sneak up behind my dad and stab him in the back for what he'd seen at Saxon's Lake.

"I wish I could write," Mayor Swope said. He turned the blade around. On its other end was a blunt little piece of metal, which he used to tamp the burning tobacco down in his pipe. "I've always liked mysteries."

"Me too," I managed to rasp.

He stood up, rain pelting the windows behind him. Lightning zigzagged over Zephyr, and the lights suddenly flickered. Thunder crashed. "Oh my," Mayor Swope said. "That was a little too close, wasn't it?"

"Yes sir." My hands were about to break the armrests of my chair.

"I want you," he said, "to wait right here for a minute. There's somethin' I want to show you, and I think it'll explain things." He crossed the room, the pipe clenched between his teeth and a scrawl of smoke behind him, and he went out into the area where Mrs. Axford's desk was. He left the door ajar, and I could hear him opening the drawer of a filing cabinet.

My gaze went to the closet.

The green feather was in there. So close. What if I was to pluck it from its hat and compare it to the green feather I'd found on the sole of my shoe? If the feathers matched, what then?

I had to move fast if I was going to move at all.

The filing cabinet's drawer closed. Another opened. "Just a minute!" Mayor Swope called to me. "It's not where it's supposed to be!"

I had to go. Right now.

I got up on rubbery legs and opened the closet. The reek of mildewed cloth hit me in the face like a damp slap. But the coat and the hat were there on the floor, nudged up into a corner. I heard the drawer slide shut. I grasped the feather and tugged at it. It wouldn't come loose.

Mayor Swope was coming back into the office. My heart was a cold stone in my throat. Thunder boomed and the rain slammed against the windows, and I grasped that green feather and jerked it and this time it tore loose from the hatband. It was mine.

"Cory? What're you doin' in—"

Lightning flared, so close you could hear the sizzle. The lights went out, and the next crack of thunder shook the windows.

I stood in the dark, the green feather in my hand and Mayor Swope in the doorway.

"Don't move, Cory," he said. "Say somethin'."

I didn't. I edged toward the wall and pressed my back against it.

"Cory? Come on, now. Let's don't play games." I heard him shut the door. A floorboard creaked, ever so quietly. He was moving. "Let's sit down and talk, Cory. There's somethin' very important you need to understand."

Outside, the clouds had gone almost black, and the room was a dungeon. I thought I could see his tall, thin shape gliding slowly toward me across the Persian carpet. I was going to have to get through him to the door.

"No need for this," Mayor Swope said, his voice trying to sound calm and reassuring. It had the same hollow ring as Mr. Hargison's false voice. "Cory?" I heard him release a long, resigned sigh. "You *know*, don't you?"

Darned right I knew.

"Where are you, son? Talk to me."

I didn't dare.

"How'd you find out?" he asked. "Just tell me that."

Lightning flickered and hissed. By its split-second glare I could see Mayor Swope, white as a zombie, standing at the center of the room with pipe smoke drifting around him like a wraith. Now my heart was really hammering; a spark of lightning had jumped off something metal clenched in his right hand.

"I'm sorry you found out, Cory," Mayor Swope said. "I didn't want you to get hurt."

I couldn't help it; in my panic, I blurted it out: "I wanna go home!"

"I can't let you do that," he said, and his shape began moving toward me through the electric-charged dark. "You understand, don't you?"

I understood. My legs responded first; they propelled me across the Persian carpet toward the way out, and my lungs snagged a breath and my hand gripped the green feather. I don't know how near I passed to him, but I got to the door unhindered and tried to twist the doorknob but my palm was slick with cold sweat. He must've heard the rattle, because he said, "Stop!" and I could sense him coming after me. Then the doorknob turned and the door opened and I shot through it as if from the barrel of a cannon. I collided with Mrs. Axford's desk, and I heard the photographs clatter as they fell.

"Cory!" he said, louder. "No!"

I caromed off the side of the desk, a human pinball in motion. I went into the row of chairs, striking my right knee on a hard edge. My lips let out a cry of pain, and as I tried to find the door into the hallway it seemed that the chairs had come to malevolent life and were blocking my way. A cold chill skittered up my spine as Mayor Swope's hand fell on my shoulder like a spider.

"*No!*" he said, and his fingers started to close.

I pulled loose. A chair was beside me, and I shoved it at Mayor Swope like a shield. He stumbled into it, and I heard him say "Oof!" as his legs got tangled up and he fell to the floor. Then I turned away from him, frantically searching for the door. At any second I expected a hand to seal itself around my ankle, and that hand to draw me to him like the tentacle of the glass-bowled monster of *Invaders from Mars*. Tears of terror were starting to burn my eyes. I blinked them away, and suddenly my hand found the cold knob of the door that led out. I twisted it, pushed through, and ran along the storm-darkened corridor, my footsteps ringing on the linoleum and thunder echoing through the halls of justice.

"Cory! Come back here!" he hollered as if he really thought I might. He was coming after me, and he was running, too. I had the mental picture of myself beaten to a pulp, my hand cuffed to Rocket, and Rocket tumbling down, down, down into the awful netherworld of Saxon's Lake.

I tripped over my own flying feet, fell, and skidded on my belly across the linoleum. My chin banged into the bottom of a wall, but I scrambled up and kept going, Mayor Swope's footsteps right behind me. "*Cory!*" he shouted, fury in his voice. It was surely the voice of a crazed killer. "*Stop where you are!*"

Like hell, I thought.

And then I saw dank gray light streaming through the cupola over the staircase and I started running down the stairs without even holding on to the railing, which was enough right there to cause my mother to go white-haired. Mayor Swope was puffing behind me, and his voice was losing its steam: "No, Cory! No!" I reached the bottom of the staircase, and I ran across the entrance lobby and out the front door into the chilly rain. The worst of the storm had already swept over Zephyr, and now squatted above the hills like a massive grayish-blue toad-frog. I got Rocket unlocked, but I left the chain hanging. I pedaled away from the courthouse just as Mayor Swope came through the door hollering at me to stop.

The last thing he hollered—and I thought this was strange, coming from a crazed killer—was "For God's sake, be careful!"

Rocket flew over the rain-pocked puddles, its golden eye picking out a path. The clouds were parting, shards of yellow sunlight breaking through. Dad had always told me that when it rained while the sun showed, the devil was beating his wife. Rocket dodged the splashing cars on Merchants Street and I hung on for the ride.

At home, Rocket skidded to a stop at the front porch steps and I ran inside, my hair plastered down with rain and my hand gripping the soggy green feather.

"Cory!" Mom called as the screen door slammed. "Cory Mackenson, come here!"

"Just a minute!" I ran into my room, and I searched the seven mystic drawers until I found the White Owl cigar box. I opened it, and there was the green feather I'd found on the bottom of my shoe.

"Come here this instant!" Mom shouted.

"Wait!" I placed the first green feather down on my desk, and the green feather I'd plucked from the mayor's hatband beside it.

"Cory! Come in here! I'm on the phone with Mayor Swope!"

Oh-oh.

My feeling of triumph cracked, collapsed, cascaded around my wet sneakers.

The first feather, the one that had come from the woods, was a deep emerald green. The one from the mayor's hatband was about three shades lighter. Not only that, but the hatband feather was at least twice as large as the Saxon's Lake feather.

They didn't match one iota.

"Cory! Come talk to the mayor before I get a switch after you!"

When I dared to walk into the kitchen, I saw that my mother's face was as red as a strangled beet. She said into the telephone, "No sir, I promise you Cory doesn't have a mental condition. No sir, he doesn't have panic attacks, either. Here he is right now, I'll put him on." She held the receiver out to me, and fixed me with a baleful glare. "Have you lost your *mind?* Take this phone and talk to the mayor!"

I took it. It was all I could do to utter one pitiable word: "Hello?"

"Cory!" Mayor Swope said. "I had to call to make sure you'd gotten home all right! I was scared to death you were gonna fall down those stairs in the dark and break your neck! When you ran out, I thought you were . . . like . . . havin' a fit or somethin'."

"No sir," I answered meekly. "I wasn't havin' a fit."

"Well, when the lights went out I figured you might be afraid of the dark. I didn't want you to hurt yourself, so I was tryin' to get you settled down. And I figured your mom and dad wouldn't want me to let you try gettin' home in that storm, either! If you'd gotten sideswiped by a car . . . well, thank the Lord it didn't happen."

"I . . . thought . . ." My throat choked up. I could feel my mother's burning eyes. "I thought . . . you were tryin' to . . . kill me," I said.

The mayor was silent for a few seconds, and I could imagine what he must be thinking. I was a pure number-one nut case. "*Kill* you? Whatever for?"

"Cory!" Mom said. "Are you crazy?"

"I'm sorry," I told the mayor. "My . . . imagination got away from me, I guess. But you said I knew somethin' about you, and you wondered how I'd found out, and—"

"No, not somethin' about *me*," Mayor Swope said. "Somethin' about your award."

"My *award?*"

"Your plaque. For winnin' third place in the short story contest. That's why I asked you to come see me. I was afraid somebody else on the awards panel had told you before I could."

"Told me what?"

"Well, I wanted to show it to you. I was bringin' your plaque in to show you when the lights went out and you went wild. See, the fella who engraves the plaques misspelled your name. He spelled Cory with an 'e.' I wanted you to see it before the ceremony so you wouldn't get your feelin's hurt. The fella's promised to do your plaque again, but he's got to do some softball awards first and he can't get to it for two weeks. Understand?"

Oh, what a bitter pill. What a bitter, bitter pill.

"Yes sir," I answered. I felt dazed, and my right knee was really starting to throb. "I do."

"Are you on . . . any medication?" the mayor asked me.

"No sir."

He grunted quietly. That grunt said, *You sure ought to be.*

"I'm sorry I acted a fool," I said. "I don't know what got into me." If he figured I was crazy now, I thought, just wait until he saw what I'd done to his hat. I decided to let him find that out for himself.

"Well," and the mayor gave a little laugh that told me he was finding some humor in this mess, "It's been a real interestin' afternoon, Cory."

"Yes sir. Uh . . . Mayor Swope?"

"Yes?"

"Uh . . . the plaque's okay as it is. Even with my name spelled wrong. You don't have to get it fixed." I figured this was penance of a sort; every time I looked at that plaque, I'd remember the day I shoved a chair at the mayor and knocked him down.

"Nonsense. We'll get it changed for you."

"I'd just as soon have it the way it is now," I told him, and I guess I sounded firm about it because Mayor Swope said, "All right, Cory, if that's what you really want."

He said he had to go get into a bathtub full of Epsom salts, and then he said he'd see me at the awards ceremony. When he hung up, I had to face my mother and explain to her why I'd thought Mayor Swope was going to kill me. Dad came in during this explanation, and though by all rights I should have been punished for my foolishness, my folks simply sent me to my room for an hour, which was where I was going to go anyhow.

In my room, I looked at the two mismatched green feathers. One bright, one sober. One small, one large. I picked up the Saxon's Lake feather and held it in the palm of my hand, and I found my magnifying glass and examined the feather's rills and ridges. Maybe Sherlock Holmes could've deduced something from it, but I was as confounded as Dr. Watson.

Mayor Swope had been the man in the green-feathered hat. His "knife" had been his pipe-cleaning tool. This feather in my hand had nothing to do with Mayor Swope's hat. Did it have anything to do with the figure I thought I'd seen standing at the edge of the woods, or the dead man at the bottom of the lake? One thing I knew for sure: there were no emerald-green birds in the woods around Zephyr. So where had that feather come from?

I put the mayor's feather aside, intending to return it to him though I knew deep down in my heart I never would, and I slid the Saxon's Lake feather back into the White Owl box which was deposited once more into one of the seven mystic drawers.

That night I dreamed again about the four black girls, all dressed up as if for church. I guessed the youngest was maybe ten or eleven, the other three around fourteen. Only this time they stood talking to each other under a green, leafy tree. Two of them were holding Bibles. I couldn't hear what was being said.

One of them laughed, and then the others laughed and the sound was like water rippling. Then there was a bright flash so intense I had to close my eyes, and I was standing at the center of thunder and a hot wind yanked at my clothes and hair. When I opened my eyes again, the four black girls were gone and the tree was stripped bare.

I woke up. There was sweat on my face, as if I had actually been kissed by that scorching breath. I heard Rebel barking in the dark from the backyard. I looked at the luminous dial of my alarm clock, seeing that it was almost two-thirty. Rebel barked on and on, like a machine, and his voice was igniting other dogs, so I figured since I was awake I'd go out and calm him down. I started out of my room, and I saw at once that a light was on in the den.

I could hear a scratching noise. I followed it to the den's threshold, and there I saw my father, wearing his pajamas sitting at his desk where he wrote out the checks for the bills. He gripped a pen in his hand, and under a pool of light he was writing or drawing something on a sheet of paper. His eyes looked feverish and sunken, and I saw that moisture glistened on his forehead just as it did on mine.

Rebel's barking broke. He started to howl.

Dad muttered, "Damn it," and stood up, being careful not to scrape his chair on the floor. I shrank back into a shadow; I'm not sure why I did this, but Dad looked like he didn't want to be disturbed. He walked to the back door, and I heard him go out to hush Rebel.

Rebel's howling ceased. Dad would be back in a minute or two.

I couldn't help it. I had to know what was so important for him to be up at two-thirty doing.

I walked into the den, and I looked at the sheet of paper.

On it, my father—who was by no means an artist—had drawn a half-dozen crude skulls with wings growing from their temples. There was a column of question marks, and the words

Saxon's Lake repeated five times. *The Lady* was written there, followed by another series of question marks. *Down in the dark* was there, the pen's point almost tearing through the paper. It was followed in capital letters by two desperate questions: WHO? WHY?

And then a progression that made me feel sick to my stomach:

I am.

I am afraid.

I am about to have a breakd

The back door opened.

I retreated to my shadow, and watched as Dad entered the den. He sat down again, and he stared at what he'd drawn and written.

I had never seen his face before. Not the face he wore now, at this quiet hour before the sun. It was the face of a frightened little boy, tortured beyond his understanding.

He opened a drawer and took out a coffee cup with Green Meadows Dairy stenciled on the side. He brought out a pack of matches. Then he folded the sheet of paper up, and began to tear it into small pieces. The fragments of it went into the coffee cup. When the paper was all torn up, Dad struck a match and dropped it into the cup, too.

There was a little smoke. He opened a window, and then there was none.

I slipped back to my room and lay down to think.

While I was dreaming of the four black girls in their Sunday dresses, what was my father being visited by? A mud-covered figure rising from the lake's murky depths, borne up by a fleet of moss-backed snapping turtles? A beaten and misshapen face, whispering *Come with me, come with me, down in the dark?* A handcuff on the wrist of a tattooed arm? Or the knowledge that it could be any man and every man who ends his life alone, forgotten, drifting down into oblivion?

I didn't know, and I was afraid to guess. But I knew this for sure: whoever had murdered that unknown man was killing my father, too.

At last sleep overtook me, and gentled me away from these tribulations. I rested, while around me my monsters kept their watch.

2

The Magic Box

T HE SATURDAY NIGHT OF the Zephyr Arts Council awards ceremony arrived. We all put on our Sunday clothes, jammed into the pickup truck, and headed for the library. My fright level, which had been hovering around eight on a scale of ten, now moved past nine. During the week, my so-called buddies had been telling me what might happen when I got up to read my story. If their predictions came true, I would break out in hives, pee in my pants, and lose my dinner from both ends in one simultaneous rush of shame and agony. Davy Ray had told me that to be safe I ought to put a cork in my butt. Ben had said I'd better be careful walking up to the podium in front of all those people, because that's when likely I'd have my accident. Johnny said he'd known a boy who got up to read something in front of people and he forgot how to read right then and there, had started babbling in what sounded like Greek or Zulu.

Well, I'd decided against the cork. But when I saw the lights on in the library and all the cars parked out front, I started regretting my decision. Mom put her arm around my shoulder. "You're gonna do just fine," she said.

"Yep," Dad said. He was wearing his father's face again, but he had dark hollows under his eyes and I'd heard Mom telling him he might need to start taking some Geritol. She knew something was wrong, of course, but she didn't know how deep the troubled current ran. "Just fine," he told me.

The library's meeting room was full of chairs, and at the front there was a table and the dreaded podium. Worse yet, there was a *microphone* at that podium! About forty people occupied the chairs, and Mayor Swope, Mrs. Prathmore, Mr. Grover Dean, and some of the other contest judges were moving around hobnobbing. I wanted to shrivel up and squeeze into a corner when Mayor Swope saw us and started walking over, but Dad placed his hand on my shoulder and I stood my ground.

"Hi there, Cory!" Mayor Swope smiled, but his eyes were wary. I figured he thought I might go crazy at any second. "You ready to read your story tonight?"

No sir, I wanted to say. "Yes sir," was what came out.

"Well, I think we're gonna have a good turnout." His attention went to my folks. "I suspect you two are awfully proud of your boy."

"We sure are," Mom said. "There's never been a writer in the family."

"He's surely got the imagination for it." Mayor Swope smiled again; it was a very tight smile. "By the way, Cory: I got my hat out of my closet to get it reshaped. You don't happen to know what became of the—"

"Luther!" a voice interrupted. "Just the man I need to see!"

Mr. Dollar, all dressed up in a dark blue suit and smelling of Aqua Velva, pushed up beside the mayor. I was never so relieved to see anyone in my life. "Yes, Perry?" Mayor Swope asked, turning away from me.

"Luther, you've gotta do somethin' about that danggoned *monkey!*" Mr. Dollar insisted. "That thing got on my roof last night and neither me nor Ellen could sleep a wink for all the racket it was makin'! The thing even did its business all over my car! I swear, there's gotta be a way to catch it!"

Ah, Lucifer. The monkey was still loose in the trees of Zephyr, and woe to the occupant of the house on whose roof Lucifer chose to squat. Because of the resulting furor and threatened lawsuits for property damage, Reverend Blessett had slinked out of town in mid-August and left no forwarding address.

"If you come up with a good idea, you let me know," Mayor Swope answered with a hint of irritation. "Short of askin' the Air Force boys to drop a bomb on the town, just about everythin's been tried."

"Maybe Doc Lezander can catch it, or we can pay somebody from a zoo to come in here and . . ." Mr. Dollar was still talking as Mayor Swope moved away, and Mr. Dollar followed him, prattling about the monkey. My folks and I took our seats, and I fidgeted as more people entered the room. Dr. Parrish came in with his wife, and lo and behold the Demon sashayed in with her fireplug mother and candlestick dad. I tried to shrink down in my chair, but she saw me and waved gleefully. Luckily there were no vacant chairs around us, or I'd have walked up to the podium with a booger on the back of my neck. Then my senses got another shock as Johnny Wilson and his parents came in. It wasn't two minutes later that Ben and his mother and dad entered, with Davy Ray and his folks close behind them. I was going to have to brave their leering mugs, but in truth I was glad to see them. As Ben had once told me, they were good old buddies.

It must be said that the people of Zephyr were supportive of their own. Either that, or there wasn't much good on television on Saturday nights. A closet was opened and more folding chairs brought out. The crowd hushed for a few seconds as Vernon Thaxter, wearing only the last shade of his summer tan, strode into the room with a big smile on his face. But people were used to Vernon by now, and they'd learned where to look and where not to. "That feller's still nekkid, Momma!" the Demon pointed out, but except for a few muffled chuckles and flushed faces, nobody made a scene. Vernon pulled a chair into a corner at the back of the room and sat there, contented as a cow. Bull, I mean.

By the time Mayor Swope and Mrs. Prathmore took a box full of plaques up to the table at the front, there were around seventy lovers of fine literature present. Mr. Grover Dean, a slender man of middle age who wore a neatly combed brown wig and round glasses with silver frames, went to the front, carrying a satchel, and he sat down at the table with the mayor and Mrs. Prathmore. He unzipped the satchel and slid out a stack of papers that I presumed were the winning entries in the three categories of short story, essay, and poetry.

Mayor Swope got up and tapped the microphone at the podium. He was greeted with a squeal of feedback and a noise like an elephant breaking wind, which brought a chorus of guffaws and made Mayor Swope motion for the man who operated the sound system. Everybody quietened at last, the microphone was adjusted, and the mayor cleared his throat and was about to speak when a ripple of whispers crossed the audience. I looked back toward the door, and my pounding heart leaped like a catfish. The Lady had just walked in.

She was dressed in violet, with a pillbox hat and gloves. There was a veil of fine netting over her face. She looked frail, her bluish-black arms and legs as thin as sticks. Supporting her with an ever-so-discreet hand to her elbow was Charles Damaronde, he of the massive shoulders and werewolf's eyebrows. Walking three steps behind the Lady was the Moon Man, carrying his cane and wearing a shiny black suit and a red necktie. He was hatless, his dark-and-light-divided face and forehead there for all to see.

I think you could've heard a pin drop. Or, more precisely, a booger fall from the Demon's nose. "Oh my," Mom whispered. Dad shifted nervously in his chair, and I believe he might've gotten up and walked out if he hadn't had to stay for me.

The Lady scanned the audience from behind her veil. All the chairs were taken. I got a quick glimpse of her green eyes—just a glint—but it was enough to make me think I smelled steamy earth and swamp flowers. Then, suddenly, Vernon Thaxter stood up and with a bow offered his chair to her. She said, "Thank you, sir," in her quavery voice and sat down, and Vernon remained standing at the back of the room while Charles Damaronde and the Moon Man stood on either side of the elegant Lady. A few people—not many, only five or six—got up not to offer their chairs but to stalk out. They weren't scared of her like Dad was; it was their indignation that black people had entered a room full of whites without asking permission. We all knew that, and the Lady did, too. It was the time we lived in.

"I guess we can get started," Mayor Swope began. He kept looking around at the crowd, then toward the Lady and the Moon Man, back to the crowd again. "I want to welcome you all to the awards ceremony of the 1964 Zephyr Arts Council Writing Contest. First off, I'd like to thank every one of the participants, without whom there could be no contest."

Well, it went on like that for a while. I might have drowsed off if I hadn't been so full of ants. Mayor Swope introduced all the judges and the Arts Council members, and then he introduced Mr. Quentin Farraday, from the Adams Valley *Journal,* who was there to take pictures and interview the winners. Finally, Mayor Swope sat down and Mrs. Prathmore took his place at the podium to call up the third-place winner in the essay division. An elderly woman named Delores Hightower shuffled up, took her essay from Mr. Dean, and read to the audience for fifteen minutes about the joys of an herb garden, then she was given her plaque and she sat down again. The first-place essay, by a beefy, gap-toothed man named George Eagers, concerned the time he had a flat tire near Tuscaloosa and the one and only Bear Bryant had stopped to ask him if he needed some help, thus proving the Bear's divinity.

The poetry division was next. Imagine my surprise when the Demon's mother stood up to read the second-place poem. This was part of it: "Rain, rain, go away,"/ said the sun, on a summer day./ "I have lots of shinin' to do yet,/ and those dark clouds make me get/ To cryin'." She read it with such emotion, I feared she was going to get to crying and rain on the whole room. The Demon and her father applauded so loud at the end of it, you'd have thought it was the Second Coming.

The first-place poem, by a little wrinkled old lady named Helen Trotter, was in essence a love letter, the first rhyme of which was: "He's always there to show he cares,/ whatever's right, that's what he dares," and the last rhyme: "Oh, how I love to see the smiling face/ Of our great state governor, George C. Wal-*lace*."

"Groan," Dad whispered. The Lady, Charles Damaronde, and the Moon Man were gracious enough to make no public comment.

"And now," Mrs. Prathmore announced, "we move into the short-story division."

I needed that cork. I needed it bad.

"This year we have the youngest winner ever on record since we began this contest in 1955. We had a little difficulty deciding if his entry was a short story or essay, since it's based on an actual event, but in the end we decided he showed enough flair and descriptive imagination to consider it a short story. Now, welcome if you will, our third-place winner, reading his story entitled 'Before the Sun': Cory Mackenson." Mrs. Prathmore led the applause. Dad said, "Go get 'em," to me, and somehow I stood up.

As I walked to the podium in a trance of terror, I heard Davy Ray giggling and then a soft *pop* as his dad cuffed him on the back of the neck. Mr. Dean gave me my story, and Mrs. Prathmore bent the microphone down so it could gather my voice. I looked out at that sea of faces; they all seemed to blur together, into a collective mass of eyes, noses, and mouths. I had a sudden fright: was my zipper up? Did I dare to look and see? I caught sight of the *Journal* photographer, his bulky camera poised. My heart was beating like the wings of a caged bird. Queasiness roiled in my belly, but I knew that if I threw up, I could never again face the light of day. Somebody coughed and somebody else cleared his throat. All eyes were on me, and in my hands the paper was shaking.

"Go ahead, Cory," Mrs. Prathmore urged.

I looked at the title, and I started to read it, but what felt like a spiny egg seemed to be lodged in my throat where the words were formed. Darkness lapped around the edges of my vision; was I about to pass out in front of all these people? Wouldn't that make a dandy front-page picture for the *Journal?* My eyes rolled back in my head, my body tumbling for the floor, my underpants white in the maw of my open zipper?

"Just take your time," Mrs. Prathmore said, and in her voice I heard her nerves starting to shred.

My eyes, which felt as if they were about to burst from my head, danced over the audience. I saw Davy Ray, Ben, and Johnny. None of them were grinning anymore; this was a bad sign. I saw Mr. George Eagers look at his wristwatch; another bad sign. I heard some malicious monster whisper, "He's *scared,* poor little boy!"

I saw the Lady rise to her feet at the back of the room. Behind her veil her gaze was cool and placid, like still green waters. She lifted her chin, and that movement spoke a single word: *Courage.*

I pulled in a breath. My lungs rattled like a freight train crossing a rickety bridge. I was here; this was my moment. I had to go on, for better or worse.

I said, "'Before the—'" My voice, thunderous through the microphone, shocked me silent again. Mrs. Prathmore placed her hand against my back, as if to steady me. "'—Sun,'" I went on. "By C-C-Cory Mackenson."

I started reading. I knew the words; I knew the story. My voice seemed to belong to someone else, but the story was part of me. As I continued on, from sentence to sentence, I was aware that the coughing and throat clearing had ceased. No one was whispering. I read the story as if traveling a trail through a familiar woods; I knew the way to go, and this was a comfort. I dared to glance up again at the audience, and when I did I felt it.

This was to be my first experience with it, and like any first experience, the feeling stays with you forever. What this was exactly I can't say, but it drove into my soul and made a home there. Everyone was watching me; everyone was *listening* to me.

The words coming out of my mouth—the words I'd conceived and given birth to—were making time null and void; they were bringing together a roomful of people into a journey of common sights, sounds, and thoughts; they were leaving me and traveling into the minds and memories of people who had never been at Saxon's Lake that chill, early morning in March. I could tell when I looked at them that those people were following me. And the greatest thing—the very greatest thing—is that they *wanted* to go where I led them.

All this, of course, I reasoned out much later. What struck me at the moment, beside getting to the end, was how quiet and still everybody had become. I had found the key to a time machine. I had discovered a current of power I'd never dreamed I possessed. I had found a magic box, and it was called a typewriter.

That voice coming out of me seemed to get stronger. It seemed to speak with expression and clarity rather than being a mumbled drone, which is how it had begun. I was amazed and elated. I actually—wonder of wonders—was enjoying reading aloud.

I reached the final sentence, and ran out of story.

For now.

My mother started applauding first. Then my dad, and the others in the room. I saw the Lady's violet-gloved hands clapping. The applause felt good; but it wasn't nearly as good as that feeling of leading people on a journey and them trusting you to know the way. Tomorrow I might want to be a milkman like Dad, or a jet pilot or a detective, but at that instant I wanted to be a writer more than anything on earth.

I accepted my plaque from Mayor Swope. When I sat down, people around me clapped me on the back, and I could tell by the way my mom and dad smiled that they were proud of me. I didn't mind that my name was misspelled on the plaque. I knew who I was.

The second-place winner, by Mr. Terrence Hosmer, was about a farmer trying to outsmart a flock of ravens after his corn crop. The first-place winner, by Mrs. Ada Yearby, concerned the midnight kneeling down of the animals at the birth of Jesus Christ. Then Mayor Swope thanked everyone for coming and said that we could all go home. On the way out, Davy Ray, Johnny, and Ben swarmed around me, and I believe I got more attention than even Mrs. Yearby. The Demon's mother waddled up to congratulate me, and she looked at my mother with her broad, mustached face and said, "You know, Brenda's birthday party is next Saturday and Brenda sure would like your boy to be there. You know, I wrote that poem for Brenda, 'cause she's a real sensitive child. Would your boy come to Brenda's birthday party? He don't have to bring no present or nothin'."

Mom looked at me for a cue. I saw the Demon, standing with her father across the room. The Demon waved at me and sniggered. Davy Ray elbowed me in the ribs; he didn't know how close he was to getting killed. I said, "Gee, Mrs. Sutley, I think I might have some chores to do at home on Saturday. Don't I, Mom?"

Mom, God love her, was quick. "Yes, you sure do! You've got to cut the grass and help your father paint the porch."

"Huh?" Dad said.

"It's got to be done," Mom told him. "Saturday's the only day we can all work on it together."

"And maybe I can get some guys to help," I offered, which made my buddies find wings on their feet.

"Well, if you wanna come to Brenda's party, she sure would like it. She's havin' her relatives over and all." Mrs. Sutley gave me a defeated smile. She knew. Then she returned to the Demon and said something to her and the Demon gave me that exact same smile. I felt like a heel on a dung-stained boot. But I couldn't encourage the Demon, I just couldn't! It was inhuman to ask me to. And oh brother, I could just imagine what the Demon's relatives must be like! That group would make the Munsters appear lovely.

We were almost out the door when a quiet voice spoke: "Tom? Tom Mackenson?"

My dad stopped and turned around.

He was in the presence of the Lady.

She was smaller than I remembered. She barely stood to my father's shoulders. But there was a strength in her that ten men couldn't have matched; you could see the force of life in her as you can see it in a weathered tree that has bent before the winds of countless storms. She had approached us without Mr. Damaronde or the Moon Man, who stood waiting at a distance.

"Hello again," Mom said. The Lady nodded at her. My dad wore the expression of a man trapped in a dark closet with a tarantula. His eyes were skittering around, searching for a way out, but he was too much of a gentleman to be rude to her.

"Tom Mackenson," she repeated. "You and your wife sure have raised a talented boy."

"I . . . we . . . we've done our best, thank you."

"And such a good *speaker*," the Lady went on. She smiled at me. "You've done well," she said.

"Thank you, ma'am."

"How's that bicycle doin'?"

"Fine. I named it 'Rocket.'"

"That's a nice name."

"Yes ma'am. And . . ." Tell her, I decided. "And it's got an eyeball in the headlight."

Her brows lifted, ever so slightly. "Is that a fact?"

"*Cory!*" Dad scolded. "Don't make up such things!"

"Seems to me," the Lady said, "a boy's bicycle needs to see where it's goin'. Needs to see whether there's a clear road or trouble ahead. Seems to me a boy's bicycle needs some horse in it, and some deer, and maybe even a touch of *rep*-tile. For cleverness, don't you know?"

"Yes ma'am," I agreed. She knew Rocket, all right.

"That was kind of you to give Cory a bike," Dad said to her. "I'm not one to accept charity, but—"

"Oh, it wasn't charity, Mr. Mackenson. It was repayment for a good deed. Mrs. Mackenson, is there anythin' at your house that Mr. Lightfoot needs to fix?"

"No, I think everythin's workin' just fine."

"Well," she said, and she stared at my father. "You never know when things are likely to suffer a breakdown."

"It was good to see you, Mrs. . . . uh . . . Lady." Dad took my mother's elbow. "We'd better be gettin' on home now."

"Mr. Mackenson, we have some matters to discuss," the Lady said as we all started moving away. "I believe you understand when I say they're matters of life and death?"

Dad stopped. I saw a muscle in his jaw work. He didn't want to turn back to her, but she was pulling at him. Maybe he felt her life force—her raw, primal power—heat up a notch, just as I did. He seemed to want to take another step away from her, but he just couldn't do it.

"Do you believe in Jesus Christ, Mr. Mackenson?" the Lady asked.

This question broke through his final barricade. He turned around to face her. "Yes, I do," he said solemnly.

"As do I. Jesus Christ was as perfect as a human bein' can be, yet he got mad and fought and wept and had days of feelin' like he couldn't go on another step. Like when the lepers and the sick folks almost trampled him down, all of 'em beggin' for miracles and doggin' him till he was about miracled out. What I'm sayin', Mr. Mackenson, is that even Jesus Christ needed help sometimes, and he wasn't too proud to ask for it."

"I don't need . . ." He let it go.

"You see," the Lady said, "I believe everybody has visions, now and again. I believe it's part of the human animal. We have these visions—these little snippets of the big quilt—but we can't figure out where they fit, or why. Most times they come in dreams, when you're sleepin'. Sometimes you can dream awake. Just about everybody has 'em, only they can't fathom the meanin'. See?"

"No," Dad said.

"Oh yes, you do." She raised a reedy finger. "Folks get all wrapped up in the sticky tape of this world, makes 'em blind, deaf, and dumb to what's goin' on in the other one."

"The other one? Other what?"

"The other world across the river," she answered. "Where that man at the bottom of Saxon's Lake is callin' to you from."

"I don't want to hear any more of this." But he didn't move.

"Callin' you," she repeated. "I'm hearin' him, too, and he's wreckin' my damn sleep, and I'm an old woman who needs some peace." She took a step closer to my father, and her eyes had him. "That man needs to tell who killed him before he can pass on. Oh, he's tryin', he's tryin' mighty hard, but he can't give us a name or a face. All he can give us are those little snippets of the big quilt. If you were to come see me, and let's us put our thinkin' caps on, maybe we could start sewin' those snippets together. Then you could get a good night's sleep again, so could I, and he could go on where he belongs. Better still: we could catch us a killer, if there's a killer here to be caught."

"I don't . . . believe in . . . that kind of non—"

"Believe it or don't believe it, that's your choice," the Lady interrupted. "But when that dead man comes callin' on you tonight—and he will—you won't have any choice but to hear him. And my advice to you, Mr. Mackenson, is that you ought to start listenin'."

Dad started to say something; his mouth opened, but his tongue couldn't jimmy the words out.

"Excuse me," I said to the Lady. "I wanted to ask you . . . if you've been . . . like . . . havin' any other dreams."

"Oh, most all the time," she said. "Trouble is, at my age, most all my dreams are reruns."

"Well . . . I was wonderin' if . . . you've been havin' any dreams about four girls."

"Four girls?" she asked.

"Yes ma'am. Four girls. You know. Dark, like you. And they're all dressed up, like it's a Sunday."

"No," she said. "I can't say that I have."

"I dream about 'em a lot. Not every night, but a lot. What do you suppose it means?"

"Snippet of a quilt," she said. "Could be somethin' you already know, but you don't know you know."

"Ma'am?"

"Might not be spirits talkin'," she explained. "Might just be your ownself, tryin' to figure somethin' out."

"Oh," I said. This must be why the Lady was picking up Dad's dreams but not mine; mine were not the ghosts of the past, but a shadow of the future.

"You'll have to come over to Bruton and see our new museum when it's done," the Lady said to Mom. "We've raised money to start buildin' onto the recreation center. Should be finished in a couple of months. Gonna have a nice exhibition room."

"I've heard about it," Mom said. "Good luck."

"Thank you. Well, I'll let you know when the openin' ceremony's gonna be. Remember what I've told you, Mr. Mackenson." She offered her violet-gloved hand, and my father took it. He might be fearful of the Lady, but he was first and foremost a gentleman. "You know where I live."

The Lady rejoined her husband and Mr. Damaronde, then they walked out into the warm, still night. We went out soon after them, and we saw them drive away in not the rhinestone Pontiac but a plain blue Chevrolet. The last of the attendees were talking on the sidewalk, and they took the time to tell me again how much they'd enjoyed my reading. "Keep up the good work!" Mr. Dollar said, and then I heard him brag to another man, "You know, I cut his hair. Yessir, I've been cuttin' that boy's hair for years!"

We drove home. I kept my plaque on my lap, clenched with both hands. "Mom?" I asked. "What kind of museum's gonna be in Bruton? They gonna have dinosaur bones and stuff?"

"Nope," my father told me. "It's gonna be a civil rights exhibit. I guess they'll have letters and papers and pictures, that kind of thing."

"Slave artifacts is what I hear," Mom said. "Like leg chains and brandin' irons, would be my guess. Lizbeth Sears told me she heard the Lady sold that big Pontiac and donated the money toward the buildin' costs."

"I'll bet whoever burned that cross in her front yard isn't exactly whistlin' 'Dixie' about this," Dad observed. "The Klan'll have somethin' to say, that's for sure."

"I think it's a good thing," Mom said. "I think they need to know where they've been to know where they're goin'."

"Yeah, I know where the Klan wishes they'd go, too." Dad slowed down and turned the pickup truck onto Hilltop Street. I caught a glimpse of the Thaxter mansion through the trees, its windows streaming with light. "She had a hard grip," Dad said, almost to himself. "The Lady, I mean." We knew who he was talking about. "Had a hard grip. And it was like she was lookin' right into me, and I couldn't stop her from seein' things that—" He seemed to realize we were still there, and he abruptly canceled that line of thought.

"I'll go with you," Mom offered, "if you want to go see her. I'll stay right by your side the whole time. She wants to help you. I wish you'd let her."

He was silent. We were nearing the house. "I'll think about it," he said, which was his way of saying he didn't want to hear any more talk about the Lady.

Dad might know where the Lady lived, and he might need her help to exorcise the spirit that called to him from the bottom of Saxon's Lake, but he wasn't ready yet. Whether he was ever going to be ready or not, I didn't know. It was up to him to take the first step, and nobody could make him do it. I had to concern myself with other problems for now: the dream of the four black girls, the Demon's crush on me, how I was going to survive Leatherlungs, and what I was going to write about next.

And the green feather. Always the green feather, its unanswered questions taunting me from one of the seven mystic drawers.

That night, Dad hung the plaque on a wall in my room for me, right over the magic box. It looked nice, up there between the pictures of a large fellow with bolts in his neck and a dark-caped individual with prominent teeth.

I had been charged with power and tasted life tonight. I had taken my own first step, however awkward, to wherever I was going. This feeling of sheer exhilaration might fade, might wane under the weight of days and diminish in the river of time; but on this night, this wonderful never-to-be-again night, it was alive.

3

Dinner with Vernon

To say the Demon pestered me in the following days about coming to her birthday party is like saying a cat has a fondness for the company of mice. Between the Demon's insistent whispering and Leatherlungs' window-shaking bellows, I was a bundle of nerves by Wednesday, and I still couldn't divide fractions.

On Wednesday night, just after supper, I was drying the dishes for Mom when I heard Dad say from the chair where he was reading the paper, "Car's stoppin' out front. We expectin' anybody?"

"Not that I know of," Mom answered.

The chair creaked as he stood up. He was going out to the porch. Before he went out the door, he gave a low whistle of appreciation. "Hey, you oughta come take a look at this!" he said, and then he went outside. We couldn't resist this invitation, of course. And there parked in front of our house was a long, sleek car with a paint job that gleamed like black satin. It had wire wheels and a shiny chrome grille and a windshield that seemed a mile wide. It was the longest and most beautiful car I'd ever seen, and it made our pickup truck look like a crusty old scab. The driver's door opened and a man in a dark suit got out. He came around the car and stepped onto our lawn, and he said, "Good evening" in an accent that didn't sound like he was from around here. He came on up the walk, into the porch light's circle, and we all saw he had white hair and a white mustache and his shoes were as shiny and black as the car's skin.

"Can I help you?" Dad asked.

"Mr. Thomas Mackenson?"

"Tom. That's me."

"Very good, sir." He stopped at the foot of the steps. "Mrs. Mackenson." He nodded at my mother, then he looked at me. "Master Cory?"

"Uh . . . I'm Cory, yes sir," I said.

"Ah. Excellent." He smiled, and he reached into the inside pocket of his coat and his hand came out holding an envelope. "If you please?" He offered the envelope to me.

I looked at Dad. He motioned for me to take it. I did, and the white-haired man waited with his hands clasped behind his back as I opened it. The envelope was sealed with a circle of red wax that had the letter T embossed in it. I slid from the envelope a small white card on which there were several lines of typed words.

"What's it say?" Mom leaned over my shoulder.

I read it aloud. "'Mr. Vernon Thaxter requests the pleasure of your company at dinner, on Saturday, September 19, 1964, at seven o'clock P.M. Dress optional.'"

"Casual wear recommended," the white-haired man clarified.

"Oh my," Mom said; her worry-bead words. Her brows came together.

"Uh . . . can I ask just who *you* are?" Dad inquired, taking the white card from me and scanning it.

"My name is Cyril Pritchard, Mr. Mackenson. I am in the employ of the Thaxter household. My wife and I have looked after Mr. Moorwood and young master Vernon for almost eight years."

"Oh. Are you . . . like . . . the butler or somethin'?"

"My wife and I serve as we're required, sir."

Dad grunted and frowned, his own mental worry-beads at work. "How come this was sent from Vernon and not from his father?"

"Because, sir, it's Vernon who wishes to have dinner with your son."

"And why is that? I don't recall Vernon ever meetin' my boy."

"Young master Vernon attended the Arts Council awards ceremony. He was very impressed with your son's command of the language. You know, he had aspirations of being a writer himself at one time."

"He wrote a book, didn't he?" Mom asked.

"Indeed he did. *The Moon My Mistress* was its title. Published in 1958 by Sonneilton Press in New York City."

"I took it out from the library," Mom admitted. "I have to say I wouldn't have bought it, not with that bloody meat cleaver on the front. You know, I always thought that was odd, because the book was more about life in that little town than the butcher who . . . well, you know."

"Yes, I do know," Mr. Pritchard said.

What I didn't know until later was that the butcher in Vernon's book had cut out a different intestine from a number of ladies every time the moon was full. Everybody in the fictional town raved over the butcher's steak-and-kidney pies, spicy Cajun sausages, and lady-finger meat-spread sandwiches.

"It wasn't bad, though, for a first novel," Mom said. "Why didn't he write another one?"

"The book unfortunately didn't sell, for whatever reason. Young master Vernon was . . . shall we say . . . disenchanted." His gaze returned to me. "What shall I tell young master Vernon in regards to the dinner invitation?"

"Hold your horses." Dad spoke up. "I hate to state the obvious, but Vernon's not . . . well, he's not in any mental shape to entertain guests up at that house, is he?"

Here Mr. Pritchard's stare went icy. "Young master Vernon is perfectly capable of entertaining a dinner guest, Mr. Mackenson. In response to your implied concern, your son would be safe with him."

"I didn't mean any offense. It's just that when somebody walks around naked all the time, you've got to believe he's not rowin' with both oars. I can't figure why Moorwood lets him go around like that."

"Young master Vernon has his own life. Mr. Thaxter has decided to let him do as he pleases."

"That's clear to see," Dad said. "You know, I haven't seen hide nor hair of Moorwood in . . . oh, I guess over three years. He was always a hermit, but doesn't he ever come up for air anymore?"

"Mr. Thaxter's business is taken care of. His rents are collected and his properties maintained. That was always his principal pleasure in life, and so it remains. Now: what may I tell young master Vernon, please?"

Vernon Thaxter had had a book published. A mystery, by the sound of it. A real book, by a real New York City publisher. I might never get the chance to talk to a real writer again, I thought. I didn't care if he was crazy, or walked around in his birthday suit. He had knowledge of a world far beyond Zephyr, and though this knowledge may have scorched him, I was interested in finding out his own experiences with the magic box. "I'd like to go," I said.

"That's a yes, I presume?" Mr. Pritchard asked my parents.

"I don't know, Tom," my mother said. "One of us ought to go, too. Just in case."

"I understand your hesitation, Mrs. Mackenson. I can only tell you that my wife and I know young master Vernon to be a gentle, intelligent, and sensitive man. He doesn't have any friends, not really. His father is and has always been very distant to him."

Again, the ice crept back into Mr. Pritchard's eyes. "Mr. Thaxter is a single-minded man. He never wanted young master Vernon to be a writer. In fact, up until quite recently he refused to allow the library to stock copies of *The Moon My Mistress*."

"What changed his mind?" Mom asked.

"Time and circumstances," Mr. Pritchard replied. "It became clear to Mr. Thaxter that young master Vernon did not have the aptitude for the business world. As I've said, young master Vernon is a sensitive man." The ice left him; he blinked, and even offered a shade of a smile. "Pardon me. I didn't mean to ramble on about concerns with which I'm sure you don't wish to be bothered. But young master Vernon is eager for an answer. May I tell him yes?"

"If one of us can go, too," Dad told him. "I've always wanted to see the inside of that house." He looked at Mom. "Is that all right with you?"

She thought about it for a minute. I watched for signs of a decision: the chewing of her lower lip usually brought forth a no, whereas a sigh and slight twitch of the right corner of her mouth was a yes being born. The sigh came out, then the twitch. "Yes," she said.

"Very good." Mr. Pritchard's smile was genuine. He seemed relieved that a positive decision had been reached. "I've been instructed to tell you that I'll pick you up here on Saturday evening at six-thirty. Is that suitable, sir?"

The question was directed to me. I said it would be fine.

"Until then." He gave us all a stiff-backed bow and walked to the black-satin-skinned car. The noise the engine made starting up was like hushed music. Then Mr. Pritchard drove away, and turned at the next intersection onto the upward curve of Temple Street.

"I hope everything'll be all right," Mom said as soon as we were back in the house. "I have to say, Vernon's book gave me the willies."

Dad sat down in his chair again and picked up the sports page where he'd left off. All the headlines were about Alabama and

Auburn football games, the religions of autumn. "Always wanted to see where ol' Moorwood lives. I guess this is as good an opportunity as I'll get. Anyhow, Cory'll have a chance to talk to Vernon about writin'."

"Lord, I hope you don't ever write anythin' as gruesome as that book was," Mom said to me. "It's strange, too, because all that gruesome stuff just seemed sewn in where it didn't have to be. It would've been a good book about a small town if all that murder hadn't been in there."

"Murders happen," Dad said. "As we all know."

"Yes, but shouldn't a book about *life* be good enough? And that bloody meat cleaver on the cover . . . well, I wouldn't have read it to begin with if Vernon's name hadn't been on it."

"All life isn't hearts and flowers." Dad put down his paper. "I wish it was, God knows I do. But life is just as much pain and mess as it is joy and order. Probably a lot more mess than order, too. I guess when you make yourself realize that, you"— he smiled faintly, with his sad eyes, and looked at me—"start growin' up." He began reading an article about the Auburn football team, then he put it aside again as another thought struck him. "I'll tell you what's strange, Rebecca. Have *you* seen Moorwood Thaxter in the last two or three years? Have you seen him just *once?* At the bank, or the barbershop, or anywhere around town?"

"No, I haven't. I probably wouldn't even know what he looks like, anyway."

"Slim old fella. Always wears a black suit and a black bow tie. I remember seein' Moorwood when I was a kid. He always looked dried up and old. After his wife died, he stopped comin' out of his house very often. But it seems like we would've seen him now and again, don't you think?"

"I've never seen Mr. Pritchard before. I guess they're all hermits."

"Except Vernon," I said. "Until the weather turns cold, I mean."

"Right as rain," Dad said. "But I think I might ask around to-morrow. Find out if anybody I know has seen Moorwood lately."

"Why?" Mom frowned. "What does it matter? You'll probably see him on Saturday night."

"Unless he's dead," came his answer. "Now, wouldn't that be somethin'? If Moorwood's been dead for two years or more, and everybody in Zephyr still jumps at the sound of his name because his dyin's been kept a secret?"

"And why would it be kept a secret? What would be the point?"

Dad shrugged, but I could tell he was thinking in overdrive. "Inheritance taxes, maybe. Greedy relatives. Legal mess. Could be a lot of things." A smile stole across his mouth, and his eyes sparkled. "Vernon would have to know it. Now, wouldn't that just be a hoot if a naked insane man owned most of this town and everybody did what he said to do because we thought it was Moorwood talkin'? Like the night the whole town turned out to keep Bruton from bein' washed away? I always thought that was peculiar. Moorwood was more interested in keepin' his money in a tight fist than givin' it away to Good Samaritans, even if they had to be threatened to be good."

"Maybe he had a change of heart," Mom suggested.

"Yeah. I suspect bein' dead can do that."

"You'll have your chance to find out on Saturday night," Mom said.

And so we would. Between now and then, however, I had to face the Demon and hear about how much fun her birthday party was going to be and how everybody else in the class would be there. Just as my father was asking around about sightings of Moorwood Thaxter, I asked my classmates at recess if they were going to the Demon's birthday party.

No one was. Most made comments that led me to believe they'd rather eat one of her dog dookey sandwiches than go to any party where they'd be at her booger-flicking, Munster-family mercy. I said I'd lie down in red-hot coals and kiss that baldheaded

Russian guy who beat his shoe on the table rather than go to the Demon's party and have to smell her stinking relatives.

But I didn't say this where she could hear me, of course. In fact, I was starting to feel more than a little sorry for her, because I couldn't find one single kid who was going to that party.

I don't know why I did it. Maybe because I thought of what it would feel like, to invite a classful of kids to your birthday party, offer to feed them ice cream and cake and they wouldn't even have to bring a present, and have every one of them say no. That is a hurtful word, and I figured the Demon would hear a lot of it in time to come. But I couldn't go to the party; that would be begging for trouble. On Thursday after school, I rode Rocket to the Woolworth's on Merchants Street, and I bought her a fifteen-cent birthday card with a puppy wearing a birthday hat on the front. Inside, under the doggerel poem, I wrote Happy Birthday from Your Classmates. Then I slid it into its pink envelope, and on Friday I got into the room before anybody else and put the envelope on the Demon's desk. I thanked God nobody saw me, either; I never would've lived it down.

The bell rang, and Leatherlungs took command. The Demon sat down behind me. I heard her open the envelope. Leatherlungs started hollering at a guy named Reggie Duffy because he was chewing grape bubble gum. This was part of the overall plan; we'd learned she despised the smell of grape bubble gum, and so almost every day somebody became a purple-mouthed martyr.

Behind me, I heard a faint *sniff.*

That was all. But it was a heart-aching sound, to think that fifteen cents could buy a happy tear.

At recess, on the dusty playground behind the school, the Demon fluttered from kid to kid showing them the card. Everybody had the good sense to pretend they already knew about it. Ladd Devine, a lanky kid with a red crew cut who was already showing signs of being a football star in his quick feet, loping passes, and general fondness for mayhem, began telling all the girls he'd bought the card when he heard they thought it was sweet. I didn't say anything. The Demon was already staring at Ladd with love in her eyes and a finger up her nose.

On Saturday evening, at the appointed time, Mr. Pritchard arrived at our house in the long black car. "Watch your manners!" Mom cautioned me, though it was meant for Dad, too. We weren't dressed up in suits; "casual wear" meant comfortable short-sleeved shirts and clean blue jeans. Dad and I climbed into the back of the car and the impression I had was of finding yourself in a cavern with walls of mink and leather. Mr. Pritchard sat divided from us by a pane of clear plastic. He drove us away from the house and took the turn up onto the heights of Temple Street, and we could hardly hear the engine or even feel a bump.

On Temple Street, amid huge spreading oaks and poplars, were the homes of the elite citizens of Zephyr. Mayor Swope's red brick house was there, on a circular driveway. Dad pointed out the white stone mansion of the man who was president of the bank. A little farther along the winding street stood the house of Mr. Sumpter Womack, who owned the Spinnin' Wheel, and directly across the way in a house with white columns lived Dr. Parrish. Then Temple Street ended at a gate of scrolled ironwork. Beyond the gate, a cobblestoned drive curved between rows of evergreens that stood as straight as soldiers at attention. The windows of the Thaxter mansion were ablaze with light, its slanted roofs topped with chimneys and bulbous onion-shaped turrets. Mr. Pritchard stopped to get out to open the gate, then he stopped again on the other side to close it. The car's tires made pillows out of the cobblestones. We followed the curve between the fragrant pines, and Mr. Pritchard pulled us to a halt under a large canvas awning striped with blue and gold. Beneath the awning, a stone-tiled entryway led to the massive front door. Before Dad could unlatch the car's door, Mr. Pritchard was there to do it for him. Then Mr. Pritchard, moving with the grace and silence of quicksilver, opened the mansion's front door for us, and we walked in.

Dad stopped. "Golly," was all he could say.

I shared his sense of awe. To describe the interior of the Thax-

ter mansion in the detail it deserves is impossible, but I was struck
by the vastness of it, the high ceilings with exposed beams and
chandeliers hanging down. Everything seemed to be shining and
gleaming and glinting, and our feet were cushioned by gardens of
Oriental weave. The air smelled of cedar and saddle soap. On the
walls pictures in gilded frames basked in pools of light. A huge
tapestry showing a medieval scene adorned one entire wall, and a
wide staircase swept up to the second floor like the sweet curve of
Chile Willow's shoulder. I saw textures of burled wood, burnished
leather, crushed velvet, and colored glass, and even the chandelier
bulbs were sparkling clean, not a cobweb between them.

A woman about the same age as Mr. Pritchard appeared from
a hallway. She wore a white uniform and had her snowy hair in
a bun clasped with silver pins. She had a round, pretty face and
clear blue eyes, and she said hello to us in the same accent as her
husband. Dad had told me it was British. "Young master Vernon's
with his trains," she told us. "He'd like you to join him there."

"Thank you, Gwendolyn," Mr. Pritchard said. "If you'll follow me, gentlemen?" He began walking into a corridot flanked
with more rooms, and we were quick to keep up. It was obvious
to us that you could put several houses the size of ours in this
mansion and still have room left over for a barn. Mr. Pritchard
stopped and opened a pair of tall doors and we heard the tinny
wail of a train whistle.

And there was Vernon, naked as the day he escaped the
womb. He was leaning over, examining something he held close
to his face, and we had quite a view of his rear end.

Mr. Pritchard cleared his throat. Vernon turned around, a locomotive in his hand, and he smiled so wide I thought his face
would split. "Oh, there you are!" he said. "Come on in!" We did.
The room had no furniture but a huge table on which toy trains
were chugging across a green landscape of miniature hills, forest,
and a tiny town. Vernon was attending to the locomotive's wheels
with a shaving brush. "Dust on the tracks," he explained. "If it
builds up, a whole train can crash."

I watched the train layout with pure amazement. Seven trains were in motion at the same time. Little switches were being thrown automatically, little signal lights blinking, little cars stopped at little railroad crossings. Sprinkled throughout the green forest were red-leafed Judas trees. The tiny town had matchbox houses and buildings painted to resemble brick and stone. At the terminus of the main street there was a gothic structure with a cupola: the courthouse where I'd fled from Mayor Swope. Roads snaked between the mounded hills. A bridge crossed a river of green-painted glass, and out beyond the town there was a large oblong black-painted mirror. Saxon's Lake, I realized. Vernon had even painted the shoreline red to represent the rocks there. I saw the baseball field, the swimming pool, the houses and streets of Bruton. Even a single rainbow-splashed house, at the end of what must be Jessamyn Street. I found Route Ten, which ran along the forest that opened up a space for Saxon's Lake. I was looking for a particular house. Yes, there it was, the size of my thumbnail: Miss Grace's house of bad girls. In the wooded hills to the west, between Zephyr and the off-map Union Town, there was a round scorch mark where some of the little trees had burned away. "Somethin' caught fire," I said.

"That's where the meteor fell," Vernon replied without even glancing at it. He blew on the locomotive's wheels, a naked Amazing Colossal Man. I found Hilltop Street, and our own house at the edge of the woods. Then I followed the stately curve of Temple Street, and right there stood the cardboard mansion my father and I were standing in.

"You're in here, Cory. Both of you are." Vernon motioned toward a shoebox beside his right hand, near a scatter of railroad cars, disconnected tracks, and wiring. On the shoebox's lid was written PEOPLE in black crayon. I lifted the lid and looked down at what must've been hundreds of tiny toy people, their flesh and hair meticulously painted. None of them wore any clothes.

One of the moving trains let out a high, birdlike whistle. Another was pulled by a steam engine, which puffed out circles of smoke the size of Cheerios. Dad walked around the gigantic, intricate layout, his mouth agape. "It's all here, isn't it?" he asked. "Poulter Hill's even got tombstones on it! Mr. Thaxter, how'd you *do* all this?"

He looked up from his work. "I'm not Mr. Thaxter," he said. "I'm Vernon."

"Oh. All right. Vernon, then. How'd you do all this?"

"Not overnight, that's for sure," Vernon answered, and he smiled again. From a distance his face was boyish; up close, though, you could see the crinkly lines around his eyes and two deeper lines bracketing his mouth. "I did it because I love Zephyr. Always have. Always will." He glanced at Mr. Pritchard, who'd been waiting by the door. "Thanks, Cyril. You can go now. Oh . . . wait. Does Mr. Mackenson understand?"

"Understand what?" Dad asked.

"Uh . . . young master Vernon wants to have dinner alone with your son. He wants you to eat in the kitchen."

"I don't get it. Why?"

Vernon kept staring at Mr. Pritchard. The older man said, "Because he invited your son to dinner. You came along, as I understand, as a chaperon. If you still have any . . . uh . . . reservations, let me tell you that the dining room is next to the kitchen. We'll be there eating our dinner while your son and young master Vernon are in the dining room. It's what he wants, Mr. Mackenson." This last sentence was spoken with an air of resignation.

Dad looked at me, and I shrugged. I could tell he didn't like this arrangement, and he was close to pulling up stakes.

"You're here," Vernon said. He put the locomotive down on a track, and it clickety-clicked out from under his hand. "Might as well stay."

"Might as well," I echoed to Dad.

"You'll enjoy the food. Gwendolyn's a fine cook," Mr. Pritchard added.

Dad folded his arms across his chest and watched the trains. "Okay," he said quietly. "I guess."

"Good!" Now Vernon truly beamed. "That's all, Cyril."

"Yes sir." Mr. Pritchard left, and the doors closed behind him.

"You're a milkman, aren't you?" Vernon asked.

"Yes, I am. I work for Green Meadows."

"My daddy owns Green Meadows." Vernon walked past me and around the table to check a connection of wires. "It's that way." He pointed off the table with one of his skinny arms in the direction of the dairy. "You know there's a new grocery store opening in Union Town next month? They're almost finished with that new shopping center there. Going to be what they call a supermarket. Going to have a whole big section of milk in—can you believe this?—plastic jugs."

"Plastic jugs?" Dad grunted. "I'll be."

"Everything's going plastic," Vernon said. He reached down and straightened a house. "That's what the future's going to be. Plastic, through and through."

"I . . . haven't seen your father for a good long while, Vernon. I talked to Mr. Dollar yesterday. Talked to Dr. Parrish and Mayor Swope today, too. Even went by the bank to talk to a few people. Nobody's seen your father for two or more years. Fella at the bank says Mr. Pritchard picks up the important papers and they come back signed by Moorwood."

"Yes, that's right. Cory, how do you like this bird's-eye view of Zephyr? Kind of makes you feel like you could fly right over the roofs, doesn't it?"

"Yes sir." I'd been thinking the exact same thing just a minute or so before.

"Oh, don't 'sir' me. Call me Vernon."

"Cory's been taught to respect his elders," Dad said.

Vernon looked at him with an expression of surprise and dismay. "Elders? But we're the same age."

Dad didn't speak for a few seconds. Then he said, "Oh" in a careful voice.

"Cory, come here and run the trains! Okay?" He was standing

next to a control box with dials and levers on it. "Express freight's coming through! Toot toot!"

I walked to the control box, which looked as complicated as dividing fractions. "What do I do?"

"Anything," Vernon said. "That's the fun of it."

Hesitantly, I started twisting dials and pushing levers. Some of the trains got faster, others slower. The steam engine was really puffing now. The signal lights blinked and the whistles blew.

"Is Moorwood still here, Vernon?" my father asked.

"Resting. He's upstairs, resting." Vernon's attention was fixed on the trains.

"Can I see him?"

"Nobody sees him when he's resting," Vernon explained.

"When is he *not* restin', then?"

"I don't know. He's always too tired to tell me."

"Vernon, would you look at me?" Vernon turned his head toward my dad, but his eyes kept cutting back to the trains. "Is Moorwood still alive?"

"Alive, alive-o," Vernon said. "Clams and mussels, alive, alive-o." He frowned, as if the question had finally registered. "Of *course* he's alive! Who do you think runs all this business stuff?"

"Maybe Mr. Pritchard does?"

"My daddy is upstairs resting," Vernon repeated with firm emphasis on the *resting*. "Are you a milkman or a member of the Inquisition?"

"Just a milkman," Dad said. "A curious milkman."

"And curiouser and curiouser you get. Pick up the speed, Cory! Number Six is running late!"

I kept twisting the dials. The trains were zipping around the bends and racing between the hills.

"I liked your story about the lake," Vernon said. "That's why I painted the lake black. It's got a dark secret deep inside, doesn't it?"

"Yes, si—Vernon," I corrected myself. I'd have to get used to being able to call a grown-up by his first name.

"I read about it in the *Journal*." Vernon reached out toward a hillside to straighten a crooked tree, and his shadow fell over the earth. Then, the task done, he stepped back and gazed down upon the town. "The killer had to know how deep Saxon's Lake is. So he has to be a local. Maybe he lives in one of those houses, right there in Zephyr. But, if I'm to understand the dead man was never identified and nobody's turned up missing since March, then he must not have been a local. So: what's the connection between a man who lives here and a man who lived somewhere far away?"

"The sheriff would like to know that, too."

"Sheriff Amory's a good man," Vernon said. "Just not a good sheriff. He'd be the first to admit it. He doesn't have the hound-dog instinct; he lets the birds fly when he's got his paws on them." Vernon scratched a place just below his navel, his head cocked to one side. Then he walked to a brass wallplate and flicked two switches. The room's lights went off; tiny lights in some of the toy houses came on. The trains followed their headlights around the tracks. "So early in the morning," he mused. "But if I was going to kill somebody, I'd have killed them early enough to dump them in the lake and be sure nobody was coming along Route Ten. Why'd the killer wait until almost dawn to do it?"

"I wish I knew," Dad said.

I kept playing with the levers, the dials illuminated before me.

"It must be somebody who doesn't get home delivery from Green Meadows," Vernon decided. "He didn't think about the milkmen's schedules, did he? You know what I believe?" Dad didn't answer. "I believe the killer's a night owl. I think dumping the body into the lake was the last thing he did before he went home and went to bed. I believe if you find a night owl who doesn't drink milk, you've got your killer."

"Doesn't drink milk? How do you figure that?"

"Milk helps you sleep," Vernon said. "The killer doesn't like to sleep, and if he works in the daytime, he'll drink his coffee black."

The only response Dad gave was a muffled grunt, whether in agreement or in sympathy I didn't know.

Mr. Pritchard returned to the darkened room to announce that dinner was being served. Then Vernon turned off the trains and said, "Come on with me, Cory," and I followed him as Dad went with the butler. We walked into a room with suits of armor standing in it, and there was a long table with two places set, one across from the other. Vernon told me to choose a seat, so I sat where I could see the knights. In a few minutes Gwendolyn entered, carrying a silver tray, and so began one of the strangest dinners of my life.

We had strawberry soup with vanilla wafers crumbled up in it. We had ravioli and chocolate cake on the same plate. We had lemon-lime Fizzies to drink, and Vernon put a whole Fizzie tablet in his mouth and I laughed when the green bubbles boiled out. We had hamburger patties and buttered popcorn, and dessert was a bowl of devil's food cake batter you ate with a spoon. As I ate these things, I did so with guilty pleasure; a kid's feast like this was the kind of thing that would've made my mother swoon. There wasn't a vegetable in sight, no carrots, no spinach, no brussels sprouts. I did get a whiff of what I thought to be beef stew from the kitchen, so I figured Dad was having a grown-up's meal. He probably had no idea what I was assaulting my stomach with. Vernon was a happy eater; he laughed and laughed and both of us wound up licking our batter bowls in a sugar-sopped delirium.

Vernon wanted to know all about me. What I liked to do, who my friends were, what books I liked to read, what movies I enjoyed. He'd seen *Invaders from Mars,* too; it was a linchpin between us. He said he used to have a great big trunk full of superhero comic books, but his daddy had made him throw them away. He said he used to have shelves of Hardy Boys mysteries, until his daddy had gotten mad at him one day and burned them in the fireplace. He said he used to have all the Doc Savage magazines and the Tarzan and John Carter of Mars books and the Shadow and Weird Tales and boxes of *Argosy* and *Boy's Life* magazines, but his daddy had said Vernon had gotten too old for those things and all of them, every one, had gone into the fire or the trash and burned to ashes or been covered in earth. He said he would give a million dollars if he could have them again and he said that if I had any of them I should hold on to them forever because they were magic.

And once you burn the magic things or cast them out in the garbage, Vernon said, you become a beggar for magic again.

"'I shall wear the bottoms of my trousers rolled,'" Vernon said.

"What?" I asked him. I'd never even seen Vernon wearing shorts before.

"I wrote a book once," he told me.

"I know. Mom's read it."

"Would you like to be a writer someday?"

"I guess," I said. "I mean . . . if I could be."

"Your story was good. I used to write stories. My daddy said it was fine for me to have a hobby like that, but never to forget that someday all this would be my responsibility."

"All what?" I asked.

"I don't know. He never would tell me."

"Oh." Somehow this made sense. "How come you didn't write another book?"

Vernon started to say something; his mouth opened, then closed again. He sat for a long moment staring at his hands, his fingers smeared with cake batter. His eyes had taken on a shiny glint. "I only had the one in me," he said at last. "I looked and I looked for another one. But it's not there. It wasn't there yesterday, it's not there today . . . and I don't think it'll be there tomorrow, either."

"How come?" I asked. "Can't you think of a story?"

"I'll tell you a story," he said.

I waited.

Vernon drew a long breath and let it go. His eyes were unfocused, as if he were struggling to stay awake but sleep was pulling him under. "There was a boy," he began, "who wrote a book about a town. A little town, about the size of Zephyr. Yes, very much like Zephyr. This boy wrote a book, and it took him four years to get everything exactly right. And while this boy was writing his book, his daddy . . ." He trailed off.

I waited.

"His . . . daddy . . ." Vernon frowned, trying to find his thoughts again. "Yes," he said. "His daddy told him he was nothing but a fool. His daddy said it night and day. You fool, you crazy fool. Spending your time writing a book, when you ought to know business. That's what I raised you for. Business. I didn't raise you to spend your time disappointing me and throwing your chances away, I raised you for business and your mother is looking at you from her grave because you disappointed her, too. Yes, you broke her heart when you failed college and that's why she took the pills that reason and that reason alone. Because you failed and all that money was wasted I should've just thrown it out the window let the niggers and the white trash have it." Vernon blinked; something about his face looked shattered. "'Negroes,' the boy said. We must be civilized. Do you see, Cory?"

"I . . . don't . . ."

"Chapter two," Vernon said. "Four years. The boy stood it for four years. And he wrote this book about the town, and the people in it who made it what it was. And maybe there wasn't a real plot to it, maybe there wasn't anything that grabbed you by the throat and tried to shake you until your bones rattled, but the book was about *life*. It was the flow and the voices, the little day-to-day things that make up the memory of living. It meandered like the river, and you never knew where you were going until you got there, but the journey was sweet and deep and left you wishing for more. It was alive in a way that the boy's life was not." He sat staring at nothing for a moment. I watched his chocolate-smeared fingers gripping at the table's edge. "He found a publisher," Vernon went on. "A real New York City publisher. You know, that's where the heart of things is. That's where they make the books by the hundreds of thousands, and each one is a child different and special and some walk tall and some are crippled, but they all go out into the world from there. And the boy got a call from New York City and they said they wanted to publish his book but would he consider some changes to make it even better than it was and the boy was so happy and proud he said yes he wanted it to be the very best it could be." Vernon's glassy eyes moved, finding pictures in the air.

"So," Vernon said in a quiet voice, "the boy packed his bags while his daddy told him he was a stupid fool that he'd come back to this house crawling and then we'd see who was right, wouldn't we? And the boy was a very naughty boy that day, he told his daddy he'd see him in the bad place first. He went from Zephyr to Birmingham on a bus and Birmingham to New York City on a train, and he walked into an office in a tall building to find out what was going to happen to his child."

Vernon lapsed into silence again. He picked up his batter bowl, trying to find something else to lick. "What happened?" I prodded.

"They told him." He smiled; it was a gaunt smile. "They said this is a business, like any other. We have charts and graphs, and we have numbers on the wall. We know that this year people want murder mysteries, and your town would make a wonderful setting for one. Murder mysteries, they said. Thrill people. We're having to compete with television now, they said. It's not like it used to be, when people had time to read. People want murder mysteries, and we have charts and graphs to prove it. They said if the boy would fit a murder mystery into the book—and it wouldn't be too difficult, they said, it wouldn't be too hard at all to do—then they would publish it with the boy's name right there on the cover. But they said they didn't like the title *Moon Town*. No, that wouldn't do. Can you write hard-boiled? they asked. They said they needed a hard-boiled writer this year."

"Did he do it?" I asked.

"Oh, yes." Vernon nodded. "Oh, he did it. Whatever they

wanted. Because it was so close, so close he could taste it. And he knew his daddy was watching over his shoulder. He did it." Vernon's smile was like a fresh wound in scar tissue. "But they were wrong. It was very, very hard to do. The boy got a room in a hotel, and he worked on it. That hotel . . . it was all he could afford. And as he worked on that rented typewriter in that mean little rented room, some of that hotel and some of that city got into him and made its way through his fingers into that book. Then one day he didn't know where he was anymore. He was lost, and there were no signs telling him which way to go. He heard people crying and saw people hurt, and something inside him closed up like a fist and all he wanted to do was get to that last page and get out of it. He heard his daddy laughing, late at night. Heard him say you fool, you little fool you should've stood your ground. Because his daddy was in him, and his daddy had come with him all that way from Zephyr to New York City."

Vernon's eyes squeezed shut for a few agonized seconds. Then they opened again, and I saw they were rimmed with red. "That boy. That stupid little foolish boy took their money, and he ran. Back to Zephyr, back to the clean hills, back where he could think. And then that book came out, with the boy's name on it, and he saw that cover and knew he had taken his child and he had dressed that beautiful child up like a prostitute and now only people who craved ugliness wanted her. They wanted to wallow in her, and use her up and throw her away because she was only one of a hundred thousand and she was crippled. And that boy . . . that boy had done it to her. That evil, greedy boy."

His voice cracked with a noise that startled me.

Vernon pressed his hand to his mouth. When he lowered his hand, a silver thread of saliva hung from his lower lip. "That boy," he whispered. "Found out very soon . . . that the book was a failure. Very soon. He called them. Anything, he said. I'll do anything to save it. And they said we have the charts and tables, and numbers on the wall. They said people were tired of murder mysteries. They said people wanted something different. Said they'd

like to see his next book, though. He had promise, they said. Just
come up with something different. You're a young man, they said.
You have lots of books in you." He wiped his mouth with the back
of his hand: a slow, labored movement. "His daddy was waiting.
His daddy grinned and grinned and kept on grinning. His daddy's face got as big as the sun and the boy was burned every time
he looked at it. His daddy said you're not fit to wear my shoes.
And I paid for those shoes. Yes I did. I paid for that shirt and
those pants. You're not fit to wear what good money buys you.
All you know is failure and failure and that's all you'll ever know
for the rest of your life, and he said if I died in my sleep tonight
it would be because you killed me with your failures. And that
boy stood at the foot of the stairs, and he was crying and he said
go on and die, then. I wish to God you would die, you . . . miserable . . . sonofabitch."

On that last terrible, hiss-breathed word I saw the tears jump
in his eyes as if he'd been speared. He made a soft moaning sound,
his face in torment like a Spanish painting I'd once seen of a naked
saint in *National Geographic*. A tear streaked down to his jaw, followed by a second that got caught in a smear of chocolate batter
in the corner of his mouth.

"Oh . . ." he whispered. "Oh . . . oh . . . no."

"Young master Vernon?" The voice was as soft as his, but spoken with firmness. Mr. Pritchard had come into the room. Vernon
didn't even look at him. I started to stand up, but Mr. Pritchard
said, "Master Cory? Please stay where you are for right now." I
stayed. Mr. Pritchard crossed the room and stood behind Vernon,
and he reached out and put a gentle hand on Vernon's thin shoulder. "Dinner's over, young master Vernon," he said.

The naked man didn't move or respond. His eyes were dull
and dead, nothing alive about him but the slow crawl of tears.

"It's time for bed, sir," Mr. Pritchard said.

Vernon spoke in a hollow, faraway voice: "Will I wake up?"

"I believe you will, sir." The hand patted his shoulder; it was a
fatherly touch. "You should say good night to your dinner guest."

Vernon looked at me. It was as if he'd never seen me before, as if I were a stranger in his house. But then his eyes came to life again and he sniffled and smiled in his boyish way. "Dust on the tracks," he said. "If it builds up, a train can crash." A frown passed over his features, but it was just a small storm and quickly gone. "Cory." The smile returned. "Thank you for having dinner with me tonight."

"Yes si—"

He held up a finger. "Vernon."

"Vernon," I repeated.

He stood up, and I did, too. Mr. Pritchard said to me, "Your father's waiting for you at the front door. You turn right and walk along the hallway, you'll come to it. I'll be outside to drive you home in a few minutes, if you'll just wait by the car." Mr. Pritchard grasped one of Vernon's elbows, and he guided Vernon to the door. Vernon walked like a very old man.

"I enjoyed my dinner!" I told him.

Vernon stopped and stared at me. His smile flickered off and on, like the sputtering of a broken neon sign. "I hope you keep writing, Cory. I hope everything good happens to you."

"Thank you, Vernon."

He nodded, satisfied that we had made a connection. He paused once more at the entrance to the dining room. "You know, Cory, sometimes I have the strangest dream. In it, I'm walking the streets in broad daylight and I don't have on any clothes." He laughed. "Not a stitch! Imagine that!"

I can't remember smiling.

Vernon let Mr. Pritchard lead him out. I looked around at the carnage of plates, and I felt sick.

The front door was easy to find. Dad was there; from the way he smiled, I could tell he had no inkling of what I'd witnessed. "You have a good talk?" I guess I mumbled something that satisfied him. "He treat you okay?" I just nodded. Dad was jovial and happy now that his belly was full of beef stew and Vernon hadn't hurt me. "Nice house, isn't it?" he asked as we walked to the long black car. "A house like this . . . there's no tellin' how much it cost."

I didn't know either. But I did know that it was more than any one human being ought to pay.

We waited to go home, and in a little while Mr. Pritchard walked out of the house to deliver us at our own front door.

4

The Wrath of Five Thunders

O N MONDAY MORNING I found the Demon had spurned me. She had eyes now only for Ladd Devine, and her fickle fingers left the back of my neck alone. It was the birthday card that had done it, and Ladd's unknowing declaration that he had sent it. Ladd was going to be a really good football player when he got to high school; between then and now, he would be getting plenty of practice running and dodging.

There was one last incident in the tale of the Demon's birthday. I asked her at recess, as she watched Ladd passing a football to Barney Gallaway, how her party had been. She looked at me as if I were one shade short of invisible. "Oh, we had fun," she said, her stare going back to the young football star. "My relatives came and ate ice cream and cake."

"Did you get any presents?"

"Uh-huh." She began to chew on a dirty fingernail, her hair stringy and oily and hanging in her face. "My momma and daddy gave me a nurse kit, my aunt Gretna gave me a pair of gloves she knitted, and my cousin Chile gave me a dried flower wreath to hang over my door for good luck."

"That's good," I said. "That's real—"

I had been about to move away. Now I stopped in my tracks.

"Chile?" I said. "What's her last name?"

"Purcell. Used to be, I mean. She got married to a fella and the stork brought 'em a little bitty baby." The Demon sighed. "Oh, ain't Ladd just the handsomest thing?"

God has a sense of humor that gets my goat sometimes.

September dwindled away, and one morning it was October. The hills were streaked with red and gold, as if some magician had painted the trees almost overnight. It was still hot in the afternoons, but the mornings began to whisper about sweaters. This was Indian summer, when you saw those purple-and-red-grained ears of corn in baskets in the grocery store and an occasional dead leaf chuckled along the sidewalk.

We had Show-and-Tell Day at our grade in school, which meant that everybody got to bring something important and tell why it was. I brought an issue of *Famous Monsters* to class, the sight of which would probably set Leatherlungs off like a Roman candle but would make me a hero of the oppressed. Davy Ray brought his "I Get Around" record, and the picture of an electric guitar he hoped to learn to play when his parents could afford lessons. Ben brought a Confederate dollar. Johnny brought his collection of arrowheads, all kept in separate drawers in a metal fishing-tackle box and protected by individual cotton balls.

They were a wonder to behold. Small and large, rough and smooth, light and dark: they beckoned the imagination on a journey into the time when the forest was unbroken, the only light was cast from tribal fires, and Zephyr existed only in a medicine man's fever. Johnny had been gathering the arrowheads ever since I'd known him, in the second grade. While the rest of us were running and playing without a moment's interest in that dusty crevice known as history, Johnny was searching the wooded trails and creekbeds for a sharp little sign of his heritage. He had collected over a hundred, lovingly cleaned them—but no shellac, that would be an insult to the hand that carved the flint—and tucked them away in the tackle box. I imagined he took them out at night, in his room, and over them he dreamed of what life was like in Adams Valley two hundred years ago. I wondered if he imagined there were four Indian buddies who had four dogs and four swift ponies, and that they lived in tepees in the same village and talked about life and school and stuff. I never asked him, but I think he probably did.

Before school began that morning of show-and-tell—which I had been dreading for several days because of what the Demon would offer up for appraisal—the guys and I met where we usually did, near the monkey bars on the dusty playground, our bikes chained to the fence along with dozens of others. We sat in the sun because the morning was cool and the sky was clear. "Open it," Ben said to Johnny. "Come on, let's see."

It didn't take much urging for Johnny to flip up the latch. He may have kept them protected like rare jewels, but he wasn't stingy about sharing their magic. "Found this one last Saturday," he said as he opened a wad of cotton and brought a pale gray arrowhead to the light. "You can tell whoever did this was in a hurry. See how the cuts are so rough and uneven? He wasn't takin' his time about it. He just wanted to make an arrowhead so he could go shoot somethin' to eat."

"Yeah, and from the size of it I'll bet all he got was a gopher," Davy Ray commented.

"Maybe he was a sorry shot," Ben said. "Maybe he knew he'd probably lose it."

"Could be," Johnny agreed. "Maybe he was a boy, and this was his first one."

"If I'd had to depend on makin' arrowheads to eat," I said, "I would've dried up and blown away mighty fast."

"You sure have got a lot of them." Ben's fingers might have been itching to explore in the tackle box, but he was respectful of Johnny's property. "Have you got a favorite one?"

"Yeah, I do. This is it." Johnny picked up a wad of cotton, opened it, and showed us which one.

It was black, smooth, and almost perfectly formed.

I recognized it.

It was the arrowhead Davy Ray had found in the deep woods on our camping trip.

"That's a beauty," Ben agreed. "Looks like it's been oiled, doesn't it?"

"I just cleaned it, that's all. It does shine, though." He rubbed the arrowhead between his brown fingers, and he placed it in Ben's pudgy hand. "Feel it," Johnny said. "You can hardly feel any cuts on it."

Ben passed it to Davy Ray, who passed it to me. The arrowhead had one small chip in it, but it seemed to melt into your hand. Rubbing it in your palm, it was hard to tell where arrowhead stopped and flesh began. "I wonder who made this one," I said.

"Yeah, I'd like to know, too. Whoever did it wasn't in any hurry. Whoever did it wanted to have a good arrowhead, one that would fly true, even if he lost it. Arrowheads were more than just the tips of arrows to Indians; they were like money, and they showed how much care you put into things. They showed how good of a hunter you were, whether you needed a lot of cheap old arrowheads to do the job, or if you had the time to make a few you could count on. I sure would like to know who made it."

This seemed important to Johnny. "I'll bet it was a chief," I offered.

"A *chief*? Really?" Ben's eyes got wide.

"He's fixin' to make up a story," Davy Ray told him. "Can't believe a thing he says from here on out."

"Sure it was a chief!" I said adamantly. "Yes, he was a chief and he was the youngest chief the tribe ever had! He was twenty years old and his father was a chief before him!"

"Oh, brother!" Davy Ray pulled his knees up to his chest, a knowing smile on his face. "Cory, if there's ever a biggest-liar-in-town contest, you'll win first prize for sure!"

Johnny smiled, too, but his eyes were keen with interest. "Go on, Cory. Let's hear about him. What was his name?"

"I don't know. It was . . . Runnin' Deer, I—"

"That's no good!" Ben said. "That's a girl Indian's name! Make his name . . . oh . . . a warrior's name. Like Heap Big Thundercloud!"

"Big Heap Do-Do!" Davy Ray cackled. "That's you, Ben!"

"His name was Chief Thunder," Johnny said, looking directly at me and ignoring the squabbling duo. "No. Chief *Five* Thunders. Because he was tall and dark and—"

"Cross-eyed," Davy Ray said.

"Had a clubfoot," Johnny finished, and Davy Ray shut up his giggling.

I paused, the arrowhead gleaming on my palm.

"Go ahead, Cory," Johnny urged in a quiet voice. "Tell us a story about him."

"Chief Five Thunders." I was thinking, weaving the story together, as my fingers squeezed and relaxed around the warm flint. "He was a Cherokee."

"Creek," Johnny corrected me.

"Creek, like I said. He was a Creek Indian, and his father was a chief but his father got killed when he was out huntin'. He went out huntin' for deer, and they found him where he'd fallen off a rock. He was dyin', but he told his son he'd seen Snowdown. Yes, he had. He'd seen Snowdown up close, close enough to see that white skin and those antlers that were as big as trees. He said as long as Snowdown lived in the woods, the world would keep goin'. But if anybody ever killed Snowdown, the world would end. Then he died, and Five Thunders was the new chief."

"I thought a chief had to fight to get to be chief," Davy Ray said.

"Well, sure he did!" I answered. "Everybody knows that. He had to fight a whole bunch of braves who thought they ought to be chief. But he liked peace better than he liked fightin'. It wasn't that he couldn't fight when he had to, it was just that he knew when to fight and when not to fight. But he had a temper, too. That's why they didn't call him just 'One Thunder' or 'Two Thunders.' He didn't get mad very much, but when he did—look out! It was like five thunders boomin' out all at the same time."

"The bell's about to ring," Johnny said. "What happened to him?"

"He . . . uh . . . he was the chief for a long, long time. Until he got to be sixty years old. Then he passed bein' chief to his son, Wise Fox." I glanced toward the entrance; kids were starting to go into the school. "But Five Thunders was the chief they remembered best, because he kept peace between his tribe and the other tribes, and when he died they took his best arrowheads and scattered them around the woods for people to find a hundred years later. Then they carved his name in a rock and they buried his body in the secret Indian burial ground."

"Oh, yeah?" Davy Ray grinned. "Where's that?"

"I don't know," I said. "It's a secret."

They groaned. The bell rang, summoning the kids in. I returned the arrowhead of Five Thunders to Johnny, who wrapped it in cotton and returned it to the tackle box. We stood up and started walking across the playground, puffs of dust rising behind our heels. "Maybe there really was somebody like Chief Five Thunders," Johnny said as we neared the door.

"Sure there was!" Ben spoke up. "Cory said so, didn't he?"

Davy Ray made a noise like the breaking of wind, but I knew he didn't mean it. He had a part to play in our group—the part of scoffer and agitator—and this he played very well. I knew what Davy Ray was inside; after all, it was he who had brought Five Thunders to life.

I heard Ladd Devine hollering, "Get away from me with those squirrel heads!" Some girl screamed and somebody shouted, "Oh, *gross!*" The Demon was in her element.

As I had predicted, the sight of cinematic monsters in her classroom enraged Leatherlungs. She threw a tantrum that made one of Five Thunders' outbreaks seem more like Half-a-Pipsqueak. Leatherlungs demanded to know if my parents knew what kind of garbage I was stuffing my mind with. Then she went into a tirade about how all decency and thoughtfulness in this world was going to ruin, just going to ruin, and why wasn't I interested in good reading instead of this monster trash? I just sat there and took it on the chin, like I was supposed to. Then the Demon opened up the shoebox she'd brought and stuck it in Leatherlungs' face and the sight of those four squirrel heads crawling with ants and their eyes poked out with a toothpick made Leatherlungs beat a hasty retreat to the teachers' lounge.

At last the three o'clock bell rang, and school was behind us for another day. We left Leatherlungs reduced to a raspy whisper. Out on the playground under the hot afternoon sun, clouds of dust stormed through the air as kids ran for freedom. As usual, Davy Ray was ragging Ben about something or other. Johnny put his tackle box on the ground as he unlocked his bike chain, and I knelt down to work the combination lock that secured Rocket.

It happened very fast. Such things always do.

They came out of the dust. I felt them before I saw them. The skin at the back of my neck drew tight.

"Four little pussies, all in a row," came the first taunt.

My head whipped around, because I knew that voice. Davy Ray and Ben ceased their wrangling. Johnny looked up, his eyes darkening with dread.

"There they are," Gotha Branlin said, with Gordo at his side. They wore their grins like open razors, their black bikes crouched behind them. "Ain't they sweet, Gordo?"

"Yeah, ain't they?"

"What's this?" With one quick movement, Gotha tore from my hand the magazine I'd brought for show-and-tell. It ripped along the staples, and on the cover Christopher Lee's Count Dracula hissed with impotent rage. "Look at this shit!" Gotha told his brother, and Gordo laughed at a picture of the sleek female robot from *Metropolis*. "I can see her fuckin' titties!" Gordo said. "Gimme it!" He grabbed the page, Gotha grabbed for it, and between their hands the picture dissolved as if consumed by acid. Gotha got most of it, though—the part showing a glimpse of metallic breasts—and it went down crumpled and dirty in his jeans pocket. Gordo squalled, "You shithole, give it here!" and he wrenched at the rest of the magazine while Gotha pulled at it, too. In another second the rest of the staples surrendered and pages of dark and glittering dreams, heroes and villains and fantastic visions, fluttered through the dust like bats in daylight. "You *ruined* it!" Gotha shrieked, and he shoved his brother so hard Gordo slammed to the ground on his back and a geyser of saliva shot from his mouth. Gordo sat up, his face swollen with rage and his eyes unspeakable, but Gotha cocked a fist back and stood over him like Godzilla over Ghidrah. "Come on and try it!" Gotha said. "Just come on!"

Gordo stayed where he was. His elbow was crushing a picture of King Kong fighting a wet-fleshed giant serpent. Even monsters had their collisions and death battles. Gordo's face was hard and bitter. Any other kid who'd taken so hard a blow would've sobbed at least once. I imagine a tear in the Branlin household was as rare as a dragon's tooth, and all those unshed tears and simmering rages had twisted Gotha and Gordo into what they were: two animals who could not escape their cages, no matter how hard they fought or how far away they roamed on those vulture bikes.

I might have felt sorry for them if they'd given you room to. But then Gotha said, "What's in here?" and he scooped the tackle box off the ground before Johnny could think to grab for it. Johnny made a choking sound as Gotha flipped the latch up and lifted the lid. The big rude hand went in and started plucking the wads of cotton open. "Hey, man!" he said to Gordo. "Look what squawboy's got! Arrowheads!"

"Why don't you leave us alone?" Davy Ray asked. "We're not botherin'—"

"*Shut your hole, dickhead!*" Gotha shouted at him, and Gordo got up grinning, their brotherly hate forgotten for the moment. Both of them started going through the collection of arrowheads, their fingers grasping and gripping; I would've hated to see what dinnertime at the Branlin household was like.

playing their harps to prancing sheep, had legs that looked about as sturdy as rain-soaked twigs. Davy Ray and I eased down into the sofa's cushiony grip. The sofa creaked ever so slightly, but my heart jumped in my throat.

"Now! Thinkin' cap on! Fingers flow like the waves! One, two, three, one, two, three." Miss Blue Glass started motioning up and down with her baton as the pudgy fingers of Ben's right hand tried to play the same five notes with some resemblance to rhythm. Soon enough, though, he was pounding those notes as if trying to crush fire ants. "Flow like the waves!" Miss Blue Glass said. "Softly, softly! One, two, three, one, two, three!"

Ben's playing was less wavy and more sludgy. "I can't do it!" he wailed, and he pulled his hand away from those frightful keys. "My fingers are gettin' all crossed up!"

"Sonia, give that boy a rest!" Miss Green Glass called from the rear of the house. "You're gonna wear his fingers to the bone!" Her voice was more trombone than flute.

"You just mind your own beeswax now, Katharina!" Miss Blue Glass retorted. "Ben's got to learn the proper technique!"

"Well, it's his first lesson, for pity's sake!" Miss Green Glass walked out of a hallway into the living room. She put her hands on her skinny hips and glowered at her sister from behind her own black-framed glasses. She was wearing all green, the shades varying from pale to forest. She made you feel a little seasick just looking at her. Her blondish-white hair was piled higher than Sonia's, and had a vague pyramidal shape about it. "Not everybody's a musical genius like you, you know!"

"Yes I do know, thank you very much!" Swirls of red had crept into Miss Blue Glass's ivory cheeks. "I'll thank you not to interrupt Ben's lesson!"

"His time's about over, anyway. Who's your next victim?"

"Winifred Osborne is my next *student,*" Miss Blue Glass said pointedly. "And if it wasn't for your magazine subscriptions, I wouldn't have to go back to teachin' piano to begin with!"

"Don't you blame my magazine subscriptions! It's your own

self at fault! I swear, if you buy another set of dinner plates, I'm gonna go straight out of my head! What're you buyin' all those dinner plates for when we don't ever have anybody to dinner?"

"Because they're pretty, that's why! I like pretty things! And I could ask you why you went out and bought a collection of First Lady thimbles when you can't even sew a stitch!"

"Because they're gonna grow in value, that's why! You wouldn't know an investment if it crawled up on one of those dumb dinner plates and begged you to eat it with a biscuit!"

I feared the Glass sisters were going to come to blows. The timbres of their voices sounded like a duel of slightly off-key musical instruments. Caught between them, Ben appeared about to leap from his skin. Then something went *crooaaakk* from the rear of the house. It was the kind of noise I would've imagined the tentacled Martian in the bowl could make. Miss Blue Glass jabbed the baton at her sister and snapped, "See there? You've upset him! Are you satisfied now?"

The door chimes rang. "It's probably the neighbors fussin' about your hollerin'!" Miss Green Glass predicted. "They can hear you all the way to Union Town!"

Johnny stood there when Miss Blue Glass opened the door. He was bundled up in a dark brown jacket over a black turtleneck. "I'm here to wait for Ben," he said.

"Lord have mercy! Is the whole world waitin' for Ben?" She made a face as if she'd bitten into a lemon, but she said, "He's still got five minutes! Come on in, then!" Johnny entered the house, and he saw our edgy faces and realized he had stepped into something that was not a pile of roses.

Crooaaakk! Crooaaakk! the thing in the back room squawked.

"Would you see to him if you aren't too busy?" Miss Blue Glass told her sister. "Since you've stirred him up, at least see to him!"

"I swear I'd move out of here if I could find a cardboard box worth livin' in!" Miss Green Glass groused, but she stalked into the hallway again and the ruckus was over at least for the moment.

"Lord, I'm worn out!" Miss Blue Glass picked up an old church bulletin and fanned herself with it. "Ben, get up and I'll show you what you can be playin' if you'll do your exercises like I've told you."

"Yes ma'am!" He jumped up.

Miss Blue Glass settled herself on the piano bench. Her hands with their long elegant fingers poised over the keyboard. She closed her eyes, getting in the mood I guess. "I used to teach this song to all my students when I was teachin' piano full-time," she said. "Ever heard of 'Beautiful Dreamer'?"

"No ma'am," Ben said. Davy Ray elbowed me in the ribs and rolled his eyes.

"This is it," Miss Blue Glass explained, and she began to play.

It wasn't the Beach Boys, but it was nice. The music swarmed out of that piano and filled up the room, and Miss Blue Glass swayed slightly from side to side on the bench as her fingers rippled across the keyboard. I have to say, it did sound pretty.

Then a terrible screech intruded. The hairs on the back of my neck stood up and strained at their roots. The noise felt like jagged glass hammered into your earhole.

"Skulls and bones! Hannah Furd! Skulls and bones! Cricket in Rinsin!"

Miss Blue Glass stopped playing. "Katharina! Feed him a cracker!"

"He's goin' crazy in here! He's beatin' at his cage!"

"Skulls and bones! Draggin me packin! Skulls and bones!"

I didn't know if those words were what the thing was screaming, but that's what it sounded like to me. Ben, Davy Ray, Johnny, and I looked at each other as if we'd walked into a nuthouse. *"Hannah Furd! Crooaaakk! Cricket in Rinsin!"*

"A cracker!" Miss Blue Glass yelled. "Do you know what a *cracker* is?"

"I'll crack your head in a minute!"

The screaming and screeching went on. Over this tumult, the door chimes rang again.

"It's that song, I'm tellin' you!" Miss Green Glass hollered. "He goes insane every time you play it!"

"*Crooaaakk! Draggin me packin! Hannah Furd! Hannah Furd!*"

I got up and opened the front door in prelude to running out. A middle-aged man and a little girl eight or nine years old stood on the porch. I recognized the man. Mr. Eugene Osborne was the cook at the Bright Star Cafe. "We're here for Winifred's piano less—" he began, before the caterwauling started up again. "*Skulls and bones! Crooaaakk! Cricket in Rinsin!*"

"What in the *world* is that racket?" Mr. Osborne asked, his hand on the little girl's shoulder. Her blue eyes were wide and puzzled. On Mr. Osborne's knuckles, I saw, were faded tattooed letters. A *U.S.* on the thumb, and on the following fingers *A, R, M,* and *Y.*

"That's my parrot, Mr. Osborne." Miss Blue Glass came up and shoved me aside. She was mighty strong to be so thin. "He's havin' a little trouble lately."

Miss Green Glass emerged from the hallway, carrying a bird-cage that contained the source of all that noise. It was a fairly large parrot, and it was fluttering at the bars and shaking like a tornado-spun leaf. "*Skulls and bones!*" it shrieked, showing a black tongue. "*Draggin me packin!*"

"You give him a cracker!" Miss Green Glass put the bird cage down on the piano bench, none too gently. "I'm not gettin' my fingers snapped off!"

"I fed *yours* all the time, and I sure risked my fingers!"

"I'm not feedin' that thing!"

"*Hannah Furd! Draggin me packin! Skulls and bones!*" The par-rot was a bright turquoise blue, not a speck of any other color on him except for the yellow of his beak. He attacked the bars, blue feathers flying.

"Well, then get him to the bedroom!" Miss Blue Glass said. "Put the night cloth over him and settle him down!"

"I'm a slave! I'm just a slave in my own home!" Miss Green

Glass wailed, but she picked up the birdcage by its handle again and left the living room.

"*Skulls and bones!*" the parrot shrieked in parting "*Cricket in Rinsin!*"

A door closed, and the noise was thankfully muffled.

"He has a little bitty problem," Miss Blue Glass said to Mr. Osborne with a nervous smile. "He doesn't seem to like one of my favorite songs. Please come in, come in! Ben, that finishes your lesson for this evenin'! Remember, now! Thinkin' cap on! Fingers flow like the waves!"

"Yes, ma'am." Then he said under his breath to me, "Let's get outta here!"

I started out, following Davy Ray. The parrot had quieted, perhaps calmed by its night cloth. And then I heard Mr. Osborne say, "First time I ever heard a parrot curse in German."

"I'm sorry, Mr. Osborne?" Miss Blue Glass lifted her penciled-on eyebrows.

I stopped at the door, and turned to listen. Johnny bumped into me.

"Curse in German," Mr. Osborne repeated. "Who taught him those words?"

"Well, I . . . have no idea what you're talkin' about, I'm sure!"

"I was a cook for the Big Red One in Europe. Got the chance to talk to a lot of prisoners, and believe me I know some foul words in German when I hear 'em. I just heard an earful."

"My . . . parrot said those things?" Her smile flickered off and on. "You're mistaken, of course!"

"Let's go!" Johnny told me. "The carnival's waitin'!"

"Wasn't just cursin', either," Mr. Osborne went on. "There were other German words in there, but they were all garbled up."

"My parrot is *American,*" Miss Blue Glass informed him with an upward tilt of her chin. "I have no earthly idea what you're talkin' about!"

"Well, okay, then." He shrugged. "Don't matter none to me."

"Boys! Will you close that door and stop lettin' all the heat out?"

"Come on, Cory!" Davy Ray called, already astride his bike. "We're late enough as it is!"

A door opened in the back. Miss Green Glass said from the hallway, "He's quiet now, thank the Lord! Just don't play that song again, whatever you do!"

"I've told you it's not that song, Katharina! I used to play it for him all the time and he loved it!"

"Well, he hates it now! Just don't play it!"

Their squawking was beginning to remind me of two squabbling old parrots, one blue and one green. "Close that door, if you please!" Miss Blue Glass yelled at me, and Johnny gave me a shove onto the porch to uproot my feet. He closed the door behind us, but we could still hear the Glass sisters clamoring like buzz saws. I pitied that poor little Osborne girl.

"Those two are loony!" Ben said as he got on his bike. "Man, that was even worse than *school!*"

"You must've done somethin' to make your mom awful mad at you," was Davy Ray's opinion. "Time's wastin'!" He gave a whoop and took off in the direction of the carnival, his bike's pedals flying.

I lagged behind the others, though they kept yelling for me to catch up. German curse words, I was thinking. How come Miss Sonia Glass's parrot knew German curse words? As far as I knew, neither of the sisters spoke anything but Southern English. I hadn't realized Mr. Osborne was in the Big Red One. That, I knew from my reading, was a very famous infantry division. Mr. Osborne had really been there, on the same war-torn earth as Sgt. Rock! Wow, I thought. Neato!

But how come the parrot knew German curse words?

Then the happy sounds of the carnival drifted to me along with the aromas of buttered popcorn and carameled apples. I left the German-cursing parrot behind, and sped up to catch my buddies.

We paid our dollars at the admission gate and threw ourselves into the carnival like famished beggars at a feast. The strings of lightbulbs gleamed over our heads like trapped stars. A lot of kids our age were there, along with their parents, and some older people and high school kids, too. Around us the rides grunted, clattered, and rattled. We bought our tickets and got on the Ferris wheel, and I made the mistake of sitting with Davy Ray. When we got to the very top and the wheel paused to allow riders on the bottommost gondola, he grinned and started rocking us back and forth and yelling that the bolts were about to come loose. "Stop it! Stop it!" I pleaded, my body freezing solid to offset his elasticity. At that height, I could see all across the carnival. My gaze fell on a garish sign with crude green jungle fronds and the red, dripping words FROM THE LOST WORLD.

I paid Davy Ray back in the haunted house. When the warty-nosed witch jumped out of the darkness at our clanking railcar, I grabbed the back of his neck and wailed to shame the scratchy recorded gibberings of ghost and goblin. "Quit it!" he said after he'd come down onto his seat again. Outside, he told me the haunted house was the dumbest thing he'd ever seen in his life and it wasn't even a bit scary. But he sure was walking funny, and he hustled himself off to the row of portable toilets.

We stuffed our faces with cotton candy, buttered popcorn, and glazed miniature doughnuts. We ate candied apples covered with peanuts. We packed away corn dogs and drank enough root beer to make our bellies slosh. Then Ben wanted to ride the Scrambler, with results that were not pretty. We got him into one of the portable toilets, and luckily his aim was good and his clothes were spared a Technicolor splatter.

Ben passed on entering the tent that displayed the big, wrinkled one-eyed face. Davy Ray almost chewed his way through the canvas in his hurry to get in there, but Johnny and I went with him against our better judgment.

In the gloomy confines, a dour-looking man with a nose as large as a dill pickle held court before a half-dozen other freak aficionados. He went on for a while about the sins of the flesh and the eye of the Lord. Then he drew back a small curtain and switched on a spotlight and there in a big glass bottle was a shriveled, pink and naked baby with two arms, two legs, and a Cyclops eye in the center of its domed forehead. I winced and Johnny shifted uncomfortably when the man picked up the formaldehyde-filled bottle, the Cyclops baby drifting in its dream. He started showing it to everybody up close. "This is the sin of the flesh, and here's the eye of God as punishment for that sin," he said. I had the feeling he might get along famously with Reverend Blessett. When the man paused in front of me, I saw that the eye was golden, like Rocket's. The baby's face was so wrinkled it might have been that of a tiny old man, about to open his toothless mouth and call for a sip of white lightning to ease his aches. "Notice, son, how the finger of God has wiped clean the means of sin," the man said, his baggy-drawered eyes glinting with a spark of evangelical fever. I saw what he meant: the baby had neither male nor female equipment. There was nothing but wrinkled pink skin down there. The man turned the bottle to show me the baby's back. The baby drifted against the glass, and I heard its shoulder make a soft wet noise of collision.

I saw the Cyclops baby's shoulder blades. They were thick, bony protrusions. Like the stumps of wings, I thought.

And I knew. I really did.

The Cyclops baby was somebody's angel, fallen to earth.

"Woe to the sinner," the man said as he moved on to Johnny and Davy Ray. "Woe to the sinner, under the eye of God."

"Ah, that was a *gyp!*" Davy Ray ranted when we were outside on the midway again. "I thought it was gonna be alive! I thought it could talk to you!"

"Didn't it?" I asked him, and he looked at me like I was halfway around the bend.

We went to a show where motorcycle drivers raced around and around a caged-in cylinder, the engines screaming right in front of our faces and the tires gripping disaster's edge. Then we went to the Indian pony show, under a large tent where palefaces who wouldn't know Geronimo from Sitting Bull jumped around in loincloths and feathers and tried to spur some spirit into horses one hay bale away from the glue factory. The finale came when a wagon with cowboys on it circled the tent with the pseudo-Indians in pursuit, and the cowboys shot off their blanks and the white redmen hollered and ran for their lives. Alabama history was never so boring, but at the end of the show Johnny gave a wan smile and said that one of the ponies, a little tawny thing with a swayed back, looked as if it really could gallop if it had half a field.

By this time Davy Ray was freak-hungry again, so we accompanied him to see a rail-skinny red-haired woman who could make electric bulbs light up by holding them in her mouth. Next was the Al Capone Death Car, the display of which showed bleeding bodies sprawled on a city sidewalk while leering gangsters raked the air with tommy-gun bullets. The actual car, which had a dummy behind the wheel and four dummies standing there gawking at it, was a piece of junk Mr. Sculley would've scorned. We hung in with Davy Ray, as he worked up to speed. The Gator Boy, the Human Caterpillar, and the Giraffe-Necked Woman lured him from behind their canvas folds.

And then we rounded a corner, and we caught that smell.

Just a hint of it, drifting down at the bottom below the reeks of hamburger grease and doughnut fat.

Lizardy, I thought.

"Ben's messed his pants!" Davy Ray said. He should talk.

"Did not!" Ben ought to know by now not to invoke this vicious cycle.

"There it is," Johnny said, and right in front of me was the huge red LOST with THE and WORLD on either side of it.

The trailer had steps that went up into a large, square boxcar-like opening. A dingy brown curtain was pulled across it. At the ticket booth, a man with greasy strands of dark hair combed flat across his bald skull was sitting on a stool, chewing on a toothpick and reading a Jughead comic book. His small, pale blue marbles of eyes flickered up and saw us, and he reached drowsily for a microphone. His voice rasped through a nearby speaker: "Come one, come all! See the beast from the lost world! Come one, come . . ." He lost interest in his spiel and returned to the cartoon balloons.

"Stinks around here," Davy Ray said. "Let's go!"

"Wait a minute," I told him. "Just a minute."

"Why?"

LOST filled up my vision. "I might want to see what this is."

"Don't waste your money on this!" Ben warned. "It'll be a big snake or somethin'!"

"Well, it can't be any dumber than the Death Car!"

They had to agree with that.

"Hey, there's a two-headed bull over yonder!" Davy Ray pointed to the painted canvas. "That's for me!" He started walking off, and Ben took two steps with him but stopped when he realized Johnny and I weren't following. Davy Ray glanced back, scowled, and stopped, too. "It'll be a *gyp!*" he said.

"Maybe," I answered. "But maybe it'll be—"

Something neat, I was about to say.

But there came the sound of a massive body shifting its weight. The trailer groaned. *Boom!* went the noise of bulk hitting wood. The entire trailer shivered, and the man behind the ticket booth reached down at his side and picked up something. Then he started banging on the trailer with a baseball bat studded with nails. I could see where countless nail points had scarred the huge red T of LOST.

Whatever was inside settled down. The trailer ceased its motions. The man put the baseball bat away, his face an expressionless blank.

"Whoa," Ben said quietly. "Mighty big critter in there."

My curiosity was raging. The swampy smell seemed to be keeping customers away, but I had to know. I approached the ticket seller.

"One?" He didn't even look up.

"What is it?" I asked.

"It's from the lost world," he answered. Still he stared at the comic book. His face was gaunt, his cheeks and forehead pitted with acne scars.

"Yes sir, but what *is* it?"

This time he did look up. I almost had to step back, because simmering in his eyes was a fierce anger that reminded me of Branlin fury. "If I told you that," he said, sucking noisily on his toothpick, "then it wouldn't be no surprise, would it?"

"Is it . . . like . . . a freak or somethin'?"

"You go in." He smiled coldly, showing little nubs of chewed-down teeth. "Then you tell me what you saw."

"Cory! Come on!" Davy Ray was standing behind me. "This is a gyp, I said!"

"Oh it is, is it?" The man slapped his comic book down. "What do you know, kid? You don't know nothin' but this little blister of a town, do you?"

"I know a gyp when I see it!" He caught himself. "Sir."

"Do you? Boy, you don't know your head from your ass! Get on out of here and quit botherin' me!"

"I sure will!" Davy Ray nodded. "You bet I will! Come on, Cory!" He stalked off, but I stayed. Davy Ray saw I wasn't coming, and he made a noise like a fart and went over to a concession stand near the two-headed bull.

"One," I told the man as I dug a quarter out of my jeans pocket.

"Fifty cents," he said.

"Everythin' else is a quarter!" Ben had come up beside me, with Johnny on my other side.

"This is fifty cents," the man repeated. "Thing's gotta eat. Thing's *always* gotta eat."

I slid the money in front of him. He put the two quarters into a tin can that sounded all but empty, then he tore a ticket and gave me half. "Go up through that curtain and wait for me. There's another curtain on the other side. Don't go through that one till I come up. Hear?" I said I did, and I climbed the steps. The lizardy, swampy odor was terrible, and under that was the sickly-sweet smell of rotting fruit. Before I reached that curtain, I was debating the wisdom of my curiosity. But I pushed through it, and I stood in near darkness. "I'll go, too," I heard Johnny say behind me. Then I waited. I reached out and felt a rough burlap curtain between me and whatever else was in the trailer.

Something rumbled, like a distant freight train.

"Move on in some," the ticket man said, speaking to me as he came up the steps, herding Johnny and Ben. When he pushed the first curtain open, I saw he was holding the nail-studded baseball bat. I gave the other guys room to stand between the curtains. Ben pinched his nostrils shut and said, "That smells *sick!*"

"Likes ripe fruit," the man explained. "Sometimes it goes over."

"What is this thing?" Johnny asked. "And what's the lost world?"

"The lost world is lost! Just like it says. What's lost is no more and can never be again. That get through your skull?"

None of us liked his attitude. Johnny probably could've punched his lights out. But Johnny said, "Yes sir."

"Hey, I'm comin' up!" It was Davy Ray. "Where's everybody?"

The man moved onto the stairs to block his way. "Fifty cents or forget it."

Of course this caused an outburst. I peered through the curtain to watch Davy Ray wrangle with the man. Davy Ray was chewing on a Zero candy bar, the white kind with chocolate nougat in the center. "If you don't shut up," the man warned, "I'm gonna charge you seventy-five cents! Pay up or take a walk!"

Two quarters changed possession. Davy Ray squeezed in with us, and then the man entered muttering sourly. He said to me, "You, boy! Go on through!"

I pushed aside the rough burlap. As I entered, the smell almost knocked me out. The guys filed in behind me, then Mr.

Attitude. Four oil lamps, hanging from ceiling hooks, afforded the only light and it was murky at best. In front of me was what appeared to be a big hogpen, enclosed by iron bars the thickness of pythons. Something lay in that pen that was so huge it made my legs go wobbly. I heard Ben gasp behind me. Johnny gave a low whistle. In the pen were piles of rotting, moldy fruit rinds. The fetid decay lay in a soup of greenish-brown mud and, to be delicate here, the mud was adorned with dozens of brown chunks as long as my father's arm and twice as thick. A dark cloud of flies whirled above the pen like a miniature tornado. The smell of all this at close range was bad enough to knock the stripes off a skunk. Little wonder Mr. Attitude's tin can was empty.

"Step up there and take a look!" he said. "Go on, you paid for it!"

"I'm gonna puke!" Ben wailed, and he had to turn and run out.

"I ain't givin' no refunds!" Mr. Attitude hollered after him.

Maybe it was the man's brawling voice. Maybe it was the way we all smelled to that thing in the pen. But suddenly it started heaving itself up from its mud bed, and the huge bulk just kept getting bigger as more of it shucked free from the liquidy mess. The thing, gave a single snort that rumbled like a hundred bassoons. Then it lumbered over toward the far side of the trailer, its wet gray flesh glistening with mud and filth, a universe of flies crawling on its hide. With a shriek of shocks and stressed timbers, the entire trailer suddenly began tilting to that side, and all three of us yowled and hollered with the conviction of fear we'd never felt in the haunted house.

"Hold still, you shithead!" Mr. Attitude stood up on a wooden platform. "I said hold still 'fore you throw us over!" He lifted that baseball bat and brought it savagely down.

The sound of that bat smacking flesh made my stomach lurch. I almost lost my carnival feast, but I clenched my teeth together. Mr. Attitude kept hitting the beast: a second time, a third, and a fourth. The creature made no noise, but with the fourth blow it staggered away from the trailer's wall toward the center of the pen again and the trailer righted itself.

"And stay there, ya dumb shit!" Mr. Attitude yelled.

"Are you tryin' to *kill* it, mister?" Davy Ray asked.

"That sonofabitch don't feel no pain! He's got skin like fuckin' armor plate! Hey, don't you be tellin' me my business or I'll throw you outta here on your ass!"

I didn't know if the creature could feel pain or not. All I knew was that I was looking at a big slab of wrinkled gray flesh with dots of blood welling up out of it.

The thing was half the height of an elephant and about as big as our pickup truck. As the thick muscles of its haunches quivered, flies rose lazily into the air. In the murky lamplight, as the creature stood motionless in its mudhole with its stumpy legs mired in rotten fruit rinds and its own excrement, I could see the stubs of three horns rising up from a neckplate of bone covered with leathery gray flesh.

I almost fell down, but I feared what might be on that floor.

"This here's an old thing," Mr. Attitude said. "You know how some turtles can live for two hundred, three hundred years? Well, this thing's so old he makes them turtles look like teenagers. Older'n Methuselah's pecker," he said, and laughed as if this was funny.

"Where'd you find him?" I heard my voice ask, my mind too stunned to connect.

"Bought him for seven hundred dollars, cash on the barrel. Fella had him on the circuit in Louisiana, down in Cajun land. Before that, guy out in Texas was showin' him. Before the Texan, fella in Montana trucked him around. I guess that was in the twenties. Yeah, he's been around some."

Davy Ray said, in a quiet and uneasy voice, "He's bleedin'." He held half of the Zero candy bar down at his side, his appetite vanished.

"Yeah, so what? Gotta smack him some to make him pay attention. Hell, he's got a brain 'bout the size of a walnut, anyhow."

"Where'd he come from?" I asked. "I mean . . . who found him first?"

"It was a long time ago. I don't remember what that Cajun fucker told me. Somethin' about . . . some professor found him. Either in the Amazon jungle or the Belgian Congo, I forget which. Up on some plateau nobody can get to or find again. His name was . . . Professor Chandler . . . no . . ." He frowned. "Callander . . . no, that ain't it." He snapped his fingers. "Professor Challenger! He's the one found it and brung it back! Know what it is? It's a tri . . . a tri—"

"—ceratops," I finished for him. I knew my dinosaurs, and that's no lie.

"Yeah, a tricereytopalis," Mr. Attitude said. "That's just what it is."

"Somebody cut his horns off," Johnny said. He, too, had recognized it, and he walked past me and clamped his hands to the iron bars. "Who cut his horns off, mister?"

"Me, myself, and I. Had to. You shoulda seen them fuckers. Like spears they were. He kept bustin' through the trailer's walls with 'em. Tore right through sheet metal. My chain saw broke all to pieces 'fore I was even half through, had to use a fuckin' ax. He just laid there. That's what he does, just lays there and eats and shits." Mr. Attitude kicked at a white-molded watermelon rind that had somehow been shoved out of the mudhole. "Know how much it costs to keep that old fucker in *fruit* this time of year? Man, that was the dumbest seven hundred dollars I *ever* spent!"

Davy Ray stepped up to the bars beside Johnny. "How come he only eats fruit?"

"Oh, he can eat most anythin'. Once carnival season's over, I feed him garbage and tree bark." Mr. Attitude grinned. "Fruit makes him smell better, y'see."

The triceratops's small black eyes slowly blinked. His massive head moved from one side to the other, searching for a thought. The pen was hardly large enough for him to turn around in. Then he exhaled a long breath and eased down into the mud again, and he stared at nothing with tendrils of blood creeping down his flank.

"Awful tight in there, ain't it?" Davy Ray asked. "I mean . . . don't you ever let him out?"

"Hell, no! How would I get him back in again, genius?" He leaned over the iron bars, which came to his waist when he was standing on the wooden platform. "Hey, shithead!" he yelled. "Why don't you *do* somethin' to earn your fuckin' keep? Why don't you learn to balance a ball on your snout, or jump through a hoop? Thought I could fuckin' *train* you to do some tricks! How come you don't do nothin' but sit there lookin' stupid?" Mr. Attitude's face contorted, and its anger was ugly. "Hey, I'm talkin' to you!" He smacked the beast's back with the baseball bat once and then again, the nails drawing blood. The triceratops's watery eyes closed in what might have been mute suffering. Mr. Attitude lifted the bat for a third blow, his nubby teeth clenched.

"Don't do that, mister," Davy Ray said.

And something in his voice meant it.

The bat paused in its descent. "What'd you say, boy?"

"I said . . . don't do that. Please," he added. "It's not right."

"Might not be right," Mr. Attitude agreed, "but it *is* fun." And he whacked the triceratops across the back a third time with all his strength.

I saw Davy Ray's hand clench as he mashed the remaining half of the Zero candy bar.

"I've had enough," Johnny said. He turned away from the pen and walked past me and out of the trailer.

"Let's go, Davy Ray," I told him.

"It's not right," Davy Ray repeated. Mr. Attitude had stopped beating the beast, and the nails were slicked with red. "Somethin' like this shouldn't be caged up in a mudhole."

"You had your fifty cents' worth," the man said. He sounded drained, sweat glistening on his forehead. I guess it was hard work, whacking those nails in and pulling them out. The act of violence seemed to have sapped some of his anger. "Go on home, country boys," he said.

Davy Ray didn't budge. His eyes reminded me of smoldering coals. "Mister, don't you know what you've *got?*"

"Yep. One big fuckin' headache. You wanna buy him? Hell, I'll cut you a deal! Get your daddy to bring me five hundred dollars, I'll sure as shit unload him in your front yard and he can sleep in your fuckin' bed with you."

Davy Ray was not suckered by this spiel. "It's not right," he said, "to hate somethin' just for bein' alive."

"What do *you* know?" Mr. Attitude sneered. "You don't know shit about *nothin'*, kid! You live twenty more years and see what I seen of this stinkin' world and then you come tell me what to do and what not to do!"

Then Davy Ray did a strange thing. He threw the mashed-up Zero candy bar into the mud right under the triceratops's beaky snout. It made a little *plop* as it went into the liquid. The triceratops just sat there, its eyes heavy-lidded.

"Hey! Don't you be throwin' nothin' in that pen, boy! Both of you just *git!*"

I was on my way out.

I heard a great gobbling sound and looked around to see the triceratops opening its mouth and scooping up the Zero and the surrounding mud like a living bulldozer. The beast chewed a few times and then he tilted his head back to let all the muck slide down his throat.

"Go on!" Mr. Attitude told us. "I'm shuttin' down for the—"

The trailer trembled. The triceratops was standing up, dripping like an ancient swamp oak. I swear his rust-colored tongue, which was as big as a dinner plate, emerged to lick his gray, mud-caked mouth. His head with its three hacked-off horn stumps tilted toward Davy Ray, and he began lumbering forward.

It was like watching a tank build up to speed. And then he lowered his head to collide with the iron bars, and the thick plate of bone made a noise like the popping together of two giants' football helmets. The triceratops stepped back three paces and with a snorting grunt he crashed his head against the iron bars again.

"Hey! Hey!" Mr. Attitude was yelling.

The triceratops shoved forward, his feet or paws or whatever they were sliding in the mud. His strength was awesome; muscles rippled beneath the elephantine flesh, and flies fled the quake. The iron bars groaned and began to bend outward, bolts making a squealing noise as they came loose.

"Hey, quit it! *Quit!*" Mr. Attitude started beating the triceratops again, and droplets of blood flew from the nails. The beast paid no attention, but kept bending the bars in his effort, I realized, to get to Davy Ray. "You sonofabitch! You stupid old fucker!" the man hollered as the baseball bat rose and fell. He looked at us, his eyes wild. "Get out! You've drivin' him crazy!"

I grabbed Davy Ray's arm and pulled at him. He came with me, and we heard more bolts breaking loose behind us. The trailer started rocking like a demonic cradle; the triceratops, it seemed to me, was throwing a fit. We got down the steps, and saw Johnny standing upwind while Ben—a perfect picture of misery—was sitting on an up-turned soft-drink case with his face buried in his hands.

"He was tryin' to get out," Davy Ray said as we watched the trailer shake, rattle, and roll. "Did you see that?"

"Yeah, I did. He went crazy."

"Bet he never had a candy bar before," he said. "Not in his whole life. He likes Zeros as much as I do, huh? Boy, I've got a whole boxful at home he'd like to get into, I'll bet!"

I wasn't sure the taste of a candy bar had done it, but I said, "I think you're right."

The trailer's rocking subsided. In a few minutes Mr. Attitude came out. His clothes and face were splattered with gobbets of mud and dookey. Both Davy Ray and I started shaking trying to hold in our belly laughs. Mr. Attitude drew the curtain, pulled a door shut, and locked it with a chain and padlock. Then he looked at us and exploded. *"Get outta here, I said! Go on, before I—"* He came at us, waving the nail-studded baseball bat, and we let our laughter go and ran.

The carnival was closing for the night, the midway's crowd dwindling, the rides shutting down and the freak-show barkers hanging up their superlatives. The lights began to go off, one by one.

We walked to where we'd left our bikes. The air had gotten frosty. Winter was on the march.

Ben, his load somewhat lightened, had returned to the land of the living and was chattering happily. Johnny didn't say much, but he did mention how neat the motorcycle riders were. I said I could build a haunted house that would scare the pickles out of people, if I had a mind to. Davy Ray, however, said nothing.

Until we got to our bikes. Then Davy Ray said, "I wouldn't like to live that way."

"What way?" Ben asked.

"In that pen. You know. Like the thing from the lost world."

Ben shrugged. "Ahhhhh, he's probably used to it by now."

"Bein' used to somethin'," Davy Ray answered, "is not the same as likin' it. Numb nuts."

"Hey, don't get mad at *me!*"

"I ain't mad at anybody." Davy Ray sat on his bike, his hands clenching the grips. "It's just . . . I sure would hate to live that way. Could hardly move. Sure couldn't see the sun. And every day would be just like the day before, even if you lived a million days. I can't stand the thought of that. Can you, Cory?"

"It would be pretty awful," I agreed.

"That man'll kill it real soon, the way he's beatin' it. Then he can go dump it on a garbage pile and be done with it." Davy Ray looked up at the sickle moon, his breath white. "Thing wasn't *real*, anyhow. That man was a low-down liar. It was a deformed rhinoceros, that's all it was. So, see? It *was* a gyp, like I told you." And he started pedaling away before I could argue with him.

That was our visit to the Brandywine Carnival.

Early Saturday morning, sometime around three, the civil defense siren atop the courthouse began yowling. Dad got dressed so fast he put his underwear on backward, and he took the pickup to go find out what was happening. I thought the Russians were bombing us, myself. When Dad returned near four o'clock, he told us what he'd learned.

One of the carnival's attractions had escaped. Broken right out of its trailer and left it in kindling. The man who owned it had been sleeping in another trailer. I later heard Dad tell Mom it was a trailer occupied by a red-haired woman who did strange things with lightbulbs. Anyway, this thing had gotten loose and rampaged down the midway like a Patton tank, tearing through tents like they were heaps of autumn leaves. This thing had evidently run right down Merchants Street and smashed into several stores, then had turned a number of parked cars into Mr. Sculley's fodder. Had to have done ten thousand dollars' worth of damage, Dad said Mayor Swope had told him. And they hadn't caught the thing yet. It had gotten into the woods and headed for the hills while everybody was still jumping into their boots. Except Mr. Wynn Gillie had seen it when it had crashed its head through the bedroom wall of his house, and Mr. Gillie and his wife were now being treated for shock at the hospital in Union Town.

The beast from the lost world was free, and the carnival left without him.

I let it wait until Sunday evening. Then I called the Callan house from Johnny's, and we used the telephone in the back room while his folks were watching TV. Davy Ray's little brother Andy answered. I asked to speak to Mr. Callan.

"What can I do for you, Cory?" he asked.

"I was callin' for my dad," I told him. "We're gonna be takin' Rebel's pen down this week, and we were wonderin' if you might have . . . oh, a chain cutter we could use?"

"Well, you'll probably need wire cutters for that job. There's a difference."

"There's some chain needs to be cut, too," I said.

"Okay, then. No problem. I'll have Davy Ray bring it over tomorrow afternoon, if that'll suit you. You know, I bought that chain cutter a few years ago but I never use it. Down in the basement in a box somewhere."

"Davy Ray'll probably know where it is," I said.

Mr. Attitude had slinked away, most likely because a seven-hundred-dollar loss was cheaper than a ten-thousand-dollar vacation in jail. Many mighty hunters went out on the trail of the beast from the lost world, but they returned with dookey on their boots and their egos busted.

I have a picture in my mind.

I see the park after the carnival has packed up and gone. It is clear again, except for a few scatters of sawdust, crushed Dixie cups, and ticket stubs the cleanup crew has left like a dog marking its territory.

But this year the wind blows Zero wrappers before it, and they make a sound like giggling as they pass.

Four

Winter's Cold Truth

A Solitary Traveler—Faith—Snippets of the Quilt—
Mr. Moultry's Castle—Sixteen Drops of Blood—
The Stranger Among Us

1

A Solitary Traveler

Y OUR FATHER'S LOST his job," Mom said.

I had just walked in from school, with Thanksgiving four days behind us. This news hit me like a blow to the belly. Mom's face was grim, her eyes already seeing days of hardship ahead. She knew the red-ink realities of her baking business; Big Paul's Pantry had an immense section of pies and cakes as well as milk in disposable plastic jugs.

"They told him when he went in," she continued. "They gave him two weeks' pay and a bonus, and they said they couldn't afford him anymore."

"Where is he?" I dropped my books on the nearest flat surface.

"Gone somewhere, about an hour ago. He sat around most of the day, couldn't eat a bite of lunch or hardly talk. Tried to sleep some, but he couldn't. I believe he's about wrecked, Cory."

"Do you know where he's gone?"

"No. He just said he was goin' somewhere to think."

"Okay. I'm gonna try to find him."

"Where're you goin'?"

"Saxon's Lake, first," I told her, and I walked out to Rocket.

She followed me to the porch. "Cory, you be care—" She stopped herself. It was time to admit that I was on my way to being a man. "I hope you find him," she offered.

I rode away, under a low gray sky threatening sleet.

It was a good haul out there from my house. The wind was blowing against me. As I pedaled on Route Ten, my head thrust forward over the handlebars, I looked cautiously from side to side at the wind-stripped woods. The beast from the lost world was still at large. That in itself wasn't a fearful thing, since I doubted the triceratops wanted to have much to do with the entrapping mudhole of civilization. What made me cautious was the fact that two days before Thanksgiving Marty Barklee, who brought the newspapers in from Birmingham before the sun, had been driving along this very road when a massive bulk had come out of the woods and slammed into his car so hard that its tires left the pavement. I'd seen Mr. Barklee's car. The passenger side was crushed in as if kicked by a giant steel boot, the window smashed all to pieces. Mr. Barklee had said the monster had literally hit and run. I believed the triceratops had staked out his claim in these dense and swampy woods around Saxon's Lake, and any vehicles on Route Ten were in jeopardy because the triceratops thought they were rival dinosaurs. Whether he would think Rocket was worth a snort and charge, I didn't know. I just knew to keep pedaling and looking. Evidently, Mr. Attitude had not realized that instead of a big gray lump that sat snoozing in the mud, he owned a Patton tank that could outrun a car. Freedom will sure speed your legs, that's for sure. And for all its age and size, the triceratops was at heart a boy.

Other than having Davy Ray show up at my front door with a chain cutter, I never let on what I suspected. Johnny didn't either, and we never told Ben because sometimes Ben had a runaway mouth. Davy Ray didn't speak a word about it other than to remark he hoped they just let the creature live out its days in peace. I was never exactly sure, but it seemed like the kind of thing

Davy Ray might have done. How was he to know the triceratops was going to do ten thousand dollars' worth of damage? Well, glass could be replaced and metal hammered out. Mr. Wynn Gillie and his wife moved to Florida like they'd been wanting to do for five or six years. Before Mr. Gillie left, Mr. Dollar told him the swamps of Florida were full of dinosaurs, that they came to your back door begging for table scraps. Mr. Gillie turned paste-white and started shaking until "Jazzman" Jackson told him Mr. Dollar was only pulling his leg.

As I turned the curve that would take me past Saxon's Lake, I saw Dad's pickup truck parked over near the red rock cliff. I coasted, trying to figure out what I was going to say. Suddenly I had run out of words. This was not going to be like feeding the magic box; this was real life, and it was going to be very, very hard.

I didn't see him anywhere around the truck as I eased Rocket onto the kickstand. And then I did see him: a small figure, sitting on a granite boulder halfway around the lake. He was staring out across the black, wind-rippled water. As I watched him, I saw him lift a bottle to his lips and drink deeply. Then he lowered the bottle, and sat there staring.

I began walking to him through a morass of reeds and stickerbushes. The red mud squished under my shoes, and I saw my father's footprints in it. He had come this way many times before, because he'd trampled down a narrow trail through the worst of the undergrowth. In doing this he had unconsciously continued his work as a father, by making the path just a little easier for the son.

When I got nearer, he saw me coming. He didn't wave. He lowered his head, and I knew he, too, had run out of words.

I stood ten feet away from him on the boulder, which at one time had been part of the lip of Saxon's Quarry. He sat with his head bowed and his eyes closed, and beside him was a plastic jug half-full of grape juice. I realized he had gone shopping at Big Paul's Pantry.

The wind shrilled around me and made the trees' bare branches clatter. "You all right?" I asked.

"No," he said.

"Mom told me."

"Figured."

I dug my hands into the pockets of my fleece-lined denim jacket, and I gazed out over the dark, dark water. Dad didn't say anything for a long time, and neither did I. Then he cleared his throat. "Want some grape juice?"

"No sir."

"Got plenty left."

"No sir, I'm not thirsty."

He lifted his face to me. In the hard, cold light he looked terribly old. I thought I could see his skull beneath the thin flesh, and this sight frightened me. It was like looking at someone you loved very much, slowly dying. His emotions had already been balanced on the raw edge. I remembered his desperately scribbled questions in the middle of the night, and his unspoken fears that he was about to suffer a breakdown. I saw all too clearly that my father—not a mythic hero, not a superman, but just a good man—was a solitary traveler in the wilderness of anguish.

"I did everythin' they asked me to," he said. "Worked a double route. Picked up the slack when it needed pickin' up. Got there early and stayed late doin' stock work. I did whatever they wanted." He looked up, trying to find the sun, but the clouds were plates of iron. "They said, 'Tom, you have to understand how it is.' They said, 'We've got to cut to the bone to keep Green Meadows afloat.' And you know what else they said, Cory?"

"No sir."

"They said home milk delivery is as dead as the dinosaurs. They said there's no room for it in all those shelves of plastic jugs. They said the future is gonna be easy come and easy go, and that's what people want." He laced his fingers together, a muscle in his gaunt jaw working. "That's not what *I* want."

"We'll be all right," I said.

"Oh, yeah." He nodded. "Yes, we will be. I'll find somethin' else. I went by the hardware store before I came here and wrote up an application. Mr. Vandercamp Junior might need a truck driver. Heck, I'd work behind a cash register. But I really did think that in three more years I'd be an assistant foreman on the loadin' dock. I really did. Dumb, huh?"

"You didn't know."

"I *never* know," he said. "That's my trouble."

The water rippled as the wind swept across it, kicking up little wavelets. In the woods beyond, unseen crows cawed. "It's cold, Dad," I said. "We ought to go home."

"I can't wait for your granddad to find out about this." He was talking about the Jaybird. "Won't he have a fine old laugh?"

"Mom and me won't be laughin'," I said. "Neither will anybody else."

He picked up the grape juice jug and took another long swig. "Went by Big Paul's Pantry, too. I walked in there and saw all that milk. A white sea of it." He looked at me again. His lips were blue. "I want things to stay the way they are. I don't want a gum-chewin' girl who doesn't know my name to take my money and not even smile when I ask her how she's doin'. I don't want supermarkets open until eight o'clock at night and full of lights that hurt your eyes. Families ought to be home together at eight o'clock at night, not out at the supermarket buyin' stuff that the big banners hangin' from the ceilin' say you ought to buy. I mean . . . if it goes so far, even in the little ways, we can't ever go back. And someday somebody'll say, 'Oh, it's so fine we can go to the supermarket after dark and we can pick and choose from shelves of stuff we've never even heard of before, but whatever happened to those milkmen, or those fellas used to sell watermelons out of the back of their trucks, or that woman who sold fresh vegetables right out of her garden and smiled like the sun when you said good mornin'?' Somebody'll say, 'Oh, they sell all those things at the supermarket now, and you don't have to go hither and yon to buy what you need, it's all under one roof. And why don't they do that to everythin'? Just put a whole town's stores under one roof so the rain won't fall on you and you won't get cold. Wouldn't that be a jim-dandy idea?'" My father worked his knuckles for a moment. "And then you'll have stores and roads and houses, but you won't have towns anymore. Not the way they are now. And you'll walk into one of those stores under one roof and you'll ask for somethin' and the gum-chewin' girl'll say no, we don't have that. We don't have that, and we can't get it for you because they don't make that anymore. That's not what people want, you see. People only want what the big banners hangin' from the ceilin' tell them to want. We only have those things, and they're made by machines a thousand a minute. But they're perfect, she'll say. Not an imperfection in the lot. And when you use it up or get tired of it or when the banners change, you can just throw it away because it's made to be thrown away. Now! she'll say, How many of these perfect things do you need today, and please hurry because there's a line behind you."

He was silent. I heard his knuckles crack.

"It's just one supermarket," I said.

"The first one," he replied.

He narrowed his eyes, and for maybe a minute he stared out at the lake as the wind scrawled patterns across its surface.

"I hear you," he said softly.

I knew who he was talking to. "Dad? Can we go home?"

"You go on. I'm gonna sit here and listen to my friend."

I heard the wind and the crows, but I knew my father heard another voice. "What's he sayin', Dad?"

"He's sayin' the same thing he always says. He's sayin' he's not gonna let me alone until I come with him, down in the dark."

Tears came to my eyes. I blinked them away. "You're not gonna go, are you?"

"No, son," he said. "Not today."

I almost told him about Dr. Lezander. My mouth opened, but my brain posed a question: What would I tell my father? That

Dr. Lezander didn't like milk and was a night owl, and Vernon Thaxter believed those were the qualities of a killer? What came out of my mouth was: "The Lady knows things, Dad. She can help us if we ask her."

"The Lady," he repeated. His voice sounded thick. "She pulled a good one on Biggun Blaylock, didn't she?"

"Yes sir, she did. She could help us if we go see her."

"Maybe so. Maybe not." He frowned, as if the thought of asking the Lady's help caused him deep pain. It was surely no worse than the pain already lodged and festering. "I'll tell you what," he said as the frown went away. "I'll ask my friend what he thinks."

I was scared for him. Very, very scared. "Please come home soon," I told him.

"I will." He nodded. "Soon."

I left him there, sitting on the boulder under the low gray clouds. When I made my way to Rocket, I looked back and saw him standing on the boulder's edge. His attention was fixed on the water below him, as if he were searching for the trace of a car in those terrible depths. I started to call to him, to warn him away from the edge, but then he walked back to where he'd been and sat down again.

Not today, he'd said. I had to believe him.

I pedaled home the way I'd come, and I had way too much on my mind to even give a thought to the beast from the lost world.

The following days were gray and cold, the hills around Zephyr brown as the grass on Poulter Hill. We entered December, the jolly month. Dad was around some days when I got home from school, and some days he was not. Mom, who suddenly appeared strained and tired beyond her years, said he was out looking for work. I hoped he wasn't back on that boulder, contemplating the future in a mirror of black glass.

The mothers of my friends were supportive. They started bringing over covered dishes, baskets of biscuits, homemade canned goods, and such. Mr. Callan promised to bring us some venison from his first kill of the season. Mom insisted on baking everyone cakes in return. Dad ate the food, but I could tell it was killing him to take such obvious charity. Evidently the hardware store didn't need a truck driver, nor did it need another man behind the cash register. Often at night I heard Dad up and about, rambling around the house. It started being that he slept much of the day, until eleven or so, and remained awake until after four in the morning. It was a night owl's hours.

One Saturday afternoon Mom asked me to ride to the Woolworth's on Merchants Street and pick her up a box of cake pans. I started out, Rocket easy beneath me. I went to the store, bought the cake pans, and started back.

I stopped in front of the Bright Star Cafe.

Mr. Eugene Osborne worked in there. Mr. Eugene Osborne had been in the Big Red One infantry division. And Mr. Eugene Osborne knew German curse words when he heard them.

This had been nagging at me, like a small little demon's voice at the back of my head, since the night we'd gone to the Brandywine Carnival. How could a parrot know German curse words if its owner spoke no German? And something else I remembered Mr. Osborne saying: *Wasn't just cursin', either. There were other German words in there, but they were all garbled up.*

How could such a thing be?

I left Rocket outside and walked into the Bright Star.

It wasn't much of a place, just a few tables and booths and a counter where people could sit on stools and jaw with the two waitresses, old Mrs. Madeline Huckabee and younger Carrie French. I have to say that Miss French got most of the attention, because she was blond and pretty and Mrs. Huckabee resembled two miles of bad road. But Mrs. Huckabee had been a waitress at the Bright Star long before I was born, and she ruled the cafe with an iron glance. The Bright Star was by no means very active this time of day, but a few people were inside drinking coffee, most of them elderly retired men. Mr. Cathcoate was among them, sitting in a booth reading a newspaper. The television above the counter was on. And sitting at the counter grinning at Miss French was none other than whale-sized Mr. Dick Moultry.

He saw me, and his grin vanished like a ghost at dawn.

"Hi, there!" Miss French said, offering me a sunny smile as I approached the counter. If it weren't for her buck teeth, she might have been as lovely as Chile Willow. "What can I do for you?"

"Is Mr. Osborne here?"

"Sure is."

"Can I talk to him, please?"

"Hold on a minute." She went to the window between the counter and the kitchen. I noticed Mr. Moultry's huge belly pressing against the counter's edge as he leaned forward to get a look at her legs. "Eugene? Somebody wants to talk to you!"

"Who?" I heard him ask.

"Who?" she asked me. Miss French didn't move in my circles, and I didn't come into the Bright Star enough to warrant recognition.

"Cory Mackenson."

"Oh, are you Tom's boy?" she inquired, and I nodded. "Tom's boy!" she told Mr. Osborne.

My dad, like the Beach Boys, got around. I felt Mr. Moultry watching me. He took a loud slurp of coffee, trying to get my attention, but I didn't favor him with it.

Mr. Osborne walked through a swinging door. He was wearing an apron and a white cap, and he wiped his hands on a cloth. "Afternoon," he said. "What can I do for you?"

Mr. Moultry was leaning forward, all ears and belly. I said, "Can we sit down? Over there, maybe?" I motioned toward a back booth.

"Guess so. Lead the way."

When we'd gotten situated, with my back to Mr. Moultry, I said, "I was at Miss Glass's house when you brought Winifred in for her piano lesson."

"I remember that."

"You remember the parrot? You said it was cursin' in German."

"If I know German, it was. And I do."

"Do you remember what else the parrot was sayin'?"

Mr. Osborne leaned back in the booth. He cocked his head to one side, his hand with its U.S. ARMY tattoo on the fingers toying with a fork from the place setting. "What's all this about, if you don't mind me askin'?"

"Nothin' special." I shrugged. "It just got my curiosity up, that's all."

"Your curiosity, huh?" He smiled faintly. "You came in here to ask me what a parrot said?"

"Yes sir."

"That was almost three weeks ago. How come you didn't want to know before now?"

"I guess I had other things on my mind." I *had* wanted to know, of course, but with the escape of the beast from the lost world and Dad's losing his job, I hadn't given it the highest priority.

"I don't rightly remember what it said, except for the spicy words I couldn't repeat to you without Tom's permission."

"I didn't know my dad came in here."

"Sometimes he does. He came in to fill out an application."

"Oh. Gosh," I said. "I didn't know my dad could *cook*."

"Dishwasher," Mr. Osborne said, watching me carefully. I think I flinched a little. "Actually, Mrs. Huckabee does all the hirin'. Runs this place like boot camp, she does."

I nodded, trying not to meet his steady gaze.

"That parrot," he said, and his smile widened. "That blue parrot. Cursed a blue streak. Not surprisin', though, is it? Since he belonged to Miss Blue Glass, I mean."

"I guess not." I hadn't known any adults called her Miss Blue Glass.

"What's this about, Cory? Really."

"I want to be a writer," I answered, though I don't know why. "Stuff like this is interestin' to me."

"A *writer?* Like writin' stories and all?"

"Yes sir."

"Seems like that would be a hard row to hoe." He put his elbows on the table. "Is this . . . like . . . research for a story or somethin'?"

"Yes sir." I saw a ray of light. "Yes sir, it sure is!"

"You're not writin' a story about Miss Blue Glass, are you?"

"I'm writin' . . . a story about a parrot," I said. "That speaks German."

"Are you, now? Well, how about that! When I was your age, I wanted to be a detective or a soldier. I got my wish on one count." He looked at his tattooed fingers. "I think I might've been better off bein' a detective," he said with a quiet sigh that spoke volumes about what real-life soldiering was as opposed to playing out scenes from *Combat* in the woods.

"Can you remember what else that parrot said, Mr. Osborne?"

He grunted, but his smile was still friendly. "If you've got to have determination to be a writer, you're well on your way. Is knowin' all this so important to you?"

"Yes sir. It's real important."

Mr. Osborne paused, thinking it over. Then he said, "It was all jumbled up, really. Didn't make a whole lot of sense."

"I'd just like to know."

"Let's see, then. Got to crank my mind back some. I'll tell you a secret." He leaned forward a little. "When you work with Mrs. Huckabee, you hear a lot of blue language." I looked around for her, but she was either in the kitchen or the rest room. "I remember the parrot sayin' somethin' about—" He closed his eyes, bringing it back. "Who knows?"

"Can't you remember?" I prodded.

"No, that's it." His eyes opened. "'Who knows?' That's what the parrot was sayin' when it wasn't spoutin' off the curses."

"Who knows what?" I asked.

"Search me. Just 'Who knows?' is all I could get out of it. That, and what I thought sounded like a name."

"A *name?* What was it?"

"Hannaford, I think it was. At least it sounded like it was close to that."

Hannah Furd, I thought.

"I could be wrong, though. I only heard the name once. But I'm not wrong about the cursin' believe you me!"

"Do you remember somethin' Miss Green . . . uh . . . Miss Katharina Glass said about the parrot goin' crazy when that song was played?" I tried to think of the name of it. "'Beautiful Dream'?"

"'Dreamer,'" he corrected me. "Oh, yeah. That's the song Miss Blue Glass taught *me.*"

"Taught *you?*"

"That's right. I always wanted to play a musical instrument. I took lessons from Miss Blue Glass . . . oh, I guess it was four years ago when she was teachin' full-time. She had a lot of older students, and she taught us all that song. Now that you mention it, I don't recall that parrot screamin' around back then like he did that night. Funny, huh?"

"Strange." It was my turn to correct him.

"Yeah. Well, I'd best get back to work." He'd seen Mrs. Huckabee emerge from the rest room, and she was dragon enough to scare a soldier. "Does that help you any?"

"I think so," I said. "I'm not sure yet."

Mr. Osborne stood up. "Hey, how about puttin' me in that story?"

"What story?"

He looked at me oddly again. "The story you're writin' about the blue parrot."

"Oh, that story! Yes sir, I sure will!"

"Say somethin' nice about me," he requested, and he started toward the kitchen door again. Some man in a brown uniform was on television, raising a ruckus.

"Hey, Eugene!" Mr. Moultry hollered. "Get a load of this jackass!"

"Mr. Osborne?" I asked, and he gave me his attention before he looked at the television set. "Do you think Miss Blue Glass would mind playin' that song again, with the parrot in the room? And maybe you could listen to it and see what it was sayin'?"

"I think that'd be kinda difficult," he said.

"Sir?"

"Miss Blue Glass took that parrot to Dr. Lezander a couple of weeks ago. It had a brain fever or somethin' birds get. That's what the doc told her. Anyhow, the parrot kicked the bucket. What is it, Dick?"

"Lookit this guy!" Mr. Moultry said, motioning to the man snarling on the television screen. "Name's Lincoln Rockwell! Sonofagun's the head of the American Nazi Party, if you can believe that garbage!"

"American Nazis?" I saw the back of Mr. Osborne's neck redden. "You mean I helped beat their butts over in Europe, and now they're right here in the U.S. of A.?"

"Says they're gonna take over the country!" Mr. Moultry told him. "Listen to him go on, it'll split your ribs!"

"If I could get hold of him, I'd split his ugly *head!*"

I was on my way out, my mind heavy with thoughts. Then I heard Mr. Moultry—whom ex-Sheriff Amory had said was a member of the Ku Klux Klan—laugh and say, "Well, that's one thing he's got right! I say ship all the niggers back to Africa! I sure as blazes wouldn't want one in my *house,* like a certain somebody invites that Lightfoot nigger right into their front door!"

I had caught this remark, and I knew who it was aimed at. I stopped and looked at him. Mr. Moultry was grinning and talking to Mr. Osborne, the man on the television screen going on about "racial purity," but Mr. Moultry was watching me from the corner of his eye. "Yeah, my house is my castle! I sure as blazes wouldn't stink my castle up by askin' a nigger to come in and make hisself at home! Would you, Eugene?"

"Lincoln Rockwell, huh?" Mr. Osborne said. "That's a hell of a name for a Nazi."

"Seems like some people would know better than to be friends with niggers, don't it, Eugene?" Mr. Moultry plowed on, baiting me.

At last what was being said got through to Mr. Osborne. He regarded Dick Moultry as one might look at rancid cheese. "A man named Ernie Graverson saved my life in Europe, Dick. He was blacker'n the ace of spades."

"Oh . . . listen . . . I didn't mean no . . ." Mr. Moultry's grin was pathetic. "Well," he said as he struggled for his dignity, "there's always one or two gonna have the brains of a white man instead of a gorilla."

"I think," Mr. Osborne said, clamping that U.S. ARMY hand on Mr. Moultry's shoulder and putting some muscle into his grip, "you'd better shut your mouth, Dick."

Mr. Moultry didn't make another peep.

I left the Bright Star, and the brown-uniformed man who was being interviewed on television. I pedaled Rocket home, the cake pans in Rocket's basket. But all the way I was puzzling over the blue parrot—the recently deceased blue parrot, that is—who spoke German.

When I got home, Dad was sleeping in his chair. The Alabama game on the radio had ended before I went to the Woolworth's, and now the radio was tuned to a country music station. I delivered the cake pans to Mom and then watched my father sleep. He was curled up, his arms gripped across his chest. Trying to hold himself together, I thought. He made a soft husking noise, his mouth on the verge of a snore. Something passed through his mind that made him flinch. His eyes came open, red-rimmed, and he seemed to stare right at me for a couple of seconds before his eyes closed again.

I didn't like the way his face looked in sleep. It looked sad and starved, though our food was plentiful. It looked defeated. There was honor in being a dishwasher, of course. I'm not saying there's not, because every labor has its share of honor and necessity. But I couldn't help thinking that he must be on despair's front porch, to have to walk into the Bright Star Cafe and apply to be a dishwasher when assistant foreman of the dairy's loading dock had been so very close. His face suddenly twisted in the grip of a daymare, his mouth letting loose a quiet groan. Even in sleep, he couldn't escape for long.

I walked into my room, shut the door, and I opened one of the seven mystic drawers. I brought out the White Owl cigar box, lifted its lid, and looked at the feather under my desk lamp.

Yes, I decided, my heartbeat quickening. Yes.

It could be a parrot's feather.

But it was emerald green. Miss Blue Glass's German-cursing parrot had been turquoise, not a speck of any other color on it except for the yellow of its beak.

Too bad Miss Green Glass hadn't been the one with the parrot, I thought. That way it would've been emerald green for—

—sure, I thought. And suddenly I felt as if I'd just leaped off a red rock cliff.

Something Miss Blue Glass had said when Miss Green Glass refused to feed the parrot a cracker for fear of losing her fingers.

Three words.

I.

Fed.

Yours.

Your what? Parrot?

Had both Glass sisters, who lived their lives in a strange agreement of mimicry and competition, each owned a parrot? Had there been a second parrot—this one emerald green and missing a feather—somewhere else in that house, as silent as the first was raucous?

A phone call would tell me.

I gripped the feather in my palm. My heart was pounding as I left my room, headed for the telephone. I didn't know the number, of course; I'd have to look it up in the slim directory.

Before I could get to the Glass number, the phone rang.

I said, "I'll get it!" and picked it up.

I would remember for the rest of my life the voice that spoke.

"Cory, this is Mrs. Callan. Let me speak to your mother, please."

The voice was tight and scared. Instantly I knew something was terribly wrong. "Mom!" I shouted. "Mom, it's Mrs. Callan!"

"Don't wake your father!" Mom scolded when she came to the phone, but a grunt and rustle told me it was too late. "Hello, Diane. How are——" She stopped. I saw her smile break. *"What?"* she whispered. "Oh . . . my Jesus . . ."

"What is it? What is it?" I asked. Dad came in, bleary-eyed.

"Yes, we will," Mom was saying. "Of course. Yes. As soon as we can. Oh, Diane, I'm so sorry!" When she returned the receiver to its cradle, her eyes were full of tears and her face bleached with shock. She looked at Dad, and then at me. "Davy Ray's been shot," she said. My hand opened, and the green feather drifted away.

Within five minutes we were in the pickup truck, headed to the hospital in Union Town. I sat between my folks, my mind fogged with what Mom had told me. Davy Ray and his father had gone hunting today. Davy Ray had been excited about being with his dad, out in the winter-touched woods on the trail of deer. They had been coming down a hill, Mrs. Callan had said. Just an ordinary hill. But Davy Ray had stepped into a gopher hole hidden under dead leaves and fallen forward, and as he'd fallen his rifle had gotten caught up beneath him, aimed at his lungs and heart. The rifle had gone off on the impact of body and earth. Mr. Callan, not a man in the best physical shape, had picked up his son in his arms and run a mile through the woods with him back to their truck.

Davy Ray had gone into emergency surgery, Mom said. The damage was very bad.

The hospital was a building of red stone and glass. I thought it looked small to be such an important place. We went in through the emergency entrance, where a nurse with silver hair told us where to go. In a waiting room with stark white walls, we found

Davy Ray's parents. Mr. Callan was wearing camouflage-print hunting clothes with blood all over the front, a sight that knocked the breath out of me. He had daubed olive green greasepaint on his cheeks and across the bridge of his nose. It was smeared, and looked like the most horrible bruise. I guess he was in too much shock to even wash his face; what was soap and water compared to flesh and blood? He still had forest dirt crusted under his fingernails. He was frozen in the instant of disaster. Mrs. Callan and Mom hugged each other, and Mrs. Callan began to cry. Dad stood with Mr. Callan at a window. Davy Ray's little brother Andy wasn't there, probably dropped off at a relative's or neighbor's house. He was much too young to understand what a knife was doing inside Davy Ray.

I sat down and tried to find something to read. My eyes couldn't focus on the magazine pages. "So fast," I heard Mr. Callan say. "It happened so fast." Mom sat with Mrs. Callan and they held hands. A bell bonged somewhere in the hospital's halls, and a voice over a loudspeaker called for Dr. Scofield. A man in a blue sweater looked into the waiting room, and everybody gave him their rapt attention but he said, "Any of you folks the Russells?" He went away, searching for some other suffering family.

The minister from the Union Town Presbyterian Church, where the Callans belonged, entered and asked us all to link hands and pray. I held one of Mr. Callan's hands; it was damp with nervous moisture. I knew the power of prayer, but I was through being selfish. I wanted Davy Ray to be all right, of course, and that's what I prayed for with all my heart, but I would never dream of wishing Rebel's death-in-life on a force of nature like Davy Ray.

Johnny Wilson and his mother and father showed up. Johnny's father, a stoic like his son, spoke quietly to Mr. Callan but showed no emotion. Mrs. Wilson and my mom sat on either side of Mrs. Callan, who couldn't do much but stare at the floor and say, "He's a good boy, he's such a good boy," over and over again, as if preparing herself to argue with God for Davy Ray's life.

Johnny and I didn't know what to say to each other. This was the worst thing either of us had ever been through. Ben and his parents came in a few minutes after the Wilsons, and then some of Davy Ray's relatives. The Presbyterian minister took Mr. and Mrs. Callan away with him, for more intimate prayer, I presumed, and Ben, Johnny, and I stood out in the hallway talking about what had happened. "He's gonna be okay," Ben said. "My dad says this is a real good hospital."

"My dad says Davy Ray was lucky it didn't kill him right off," Johnny said. "He says he knew a boy who shot himself in the stomach, and he didn't last but a couple of hours."

I checked my Timex. Davy Ray had been in the operating room for four hours. "He'll make it," I told the others. "He's strong. He'll make it."

Another hour crept slowly past. Night had fallen, and with it a cold mist. Mr. Callan had washed the greasepaint from his face, scrubbed the dirt from beneath his fingernails, and accepted the loan of a green hospital shirt. "That's my last huntin' trip," he said to my father. "I swear to Jesus it is. When Davy Ray gets out of this, we're strippin' the gun rack clear to the wood." He put his hand to his face and choked back a sob. Dad put his arm around Mr. Callan's shoulder. "Know what he said to me today, Tom? Wasn't ten minutes before it happened. He said, 'If we see it, we won't shoot at it, will we? We're just out huntin' deer, aren't we? We won't shoot it if we see it.' You know what he was talkin' about?"

Dad shook his head.

"The thing that ran away from the carnival. Now, what do you think got that in his mind?"

"I don't know," Dad said.

It hurt me to hear these things.

A doctor with short-cropped gray hair and wire-rimmed glasses came in. Instantly the Callans were on their feet. "May I speak with both of you outside, please?" he asked. Mom gripped Dad's hand. I knew, as well, that this was not good news.

When they returned, Mr. Callan told everyone Davy Ray was out of the operating room. Davy Ray's condition was guarded, and the night would tell the tale. He thanked everyone for coming and showing their support, and he said we all ought to go home and get some sleep.

Ben and his parents stayed until ten, and then they left. The Wilsons went home a half-hour later. Gradually, the relatives thinned out. The Presbyterian minister said he would stay as long as they wanted him there. Mrs. Callan grasped my mother's hand, and asked her not to go just yet. So we waited in that room with the stark white walls as the mist turned to rain, the rain stopped, fog drifted across the windows, and mist returned.

Past midnight, Mr. Callan went to get a cup of coffee from a machine down the hall. He returned a few minutes later with the gray-haired doctor. "Diane!" he said excitedly. "Diane, he's come to!"

They rushed out, their hands linked.

Ten minutes passed. Then, after what seemed an eternity, Mr. Callan walked back into the waiting room. I have seen cigarette burns with more life than his eyes possessed. "Cory?" he said softly. "Davy Ray wants to see you."

I was afraid.

"Go on, Cory," my father urged. "It's all right."

I stood up, and I followed Mr. Callan.

The doctor was standing outside Davy Ray's room, talking to their minister. They made a grim picture. Mr. Callan opened the door, and I walked in. Mrs. Callan was in there, sitting in a chair beside a bed enveloped by a filmy oxygen tent. Plastic tubing snaked up from the figure that lay under a pale blue sheet and connected with bags full of blood and clear liquid. A machine showed a green dot, blipping slowly on a round black screen. Mrs. Callan saw me and leaned over toward the head under that tent. "Davy Ray? He's here."

I heard the sound of labored breathing, and I smelled Clorox and Pine Sol. Rain began to tap against the window. Mrs. Callan said, "Cory, sit here," and she stood up. I went to her. Mrs. Callan picked up one of Davy Ray's hands; it was as white as Italian marble. "I'll be right here, Davy Ray." She summoned up a smile with a mighty effort, and then she lowered his hand to the bed once more and moved away.

I stood next to the bed, looking through the oxygen tent at my friend's face.

He was very pale, with dark purplish hollows under his eyes. Somebody had combed his hair, though. The comb had been wet. He was all covered up, so I saw no indication of the wound that had brought him here. Tubes came out of his nostrils, and his lips were gray. His face looked waxen, and his eyes were staring right at me.

"It's me," I said. "Cory."

He swallowed thickly. Maybe the green blip had picked up a little, or maybe it was my imagination.

"You took a fall," I said, and instantly thought that was the stupidest thing ever uttered.

He didn't answer. He couldn't speak, I thought. "Ben and Johnny were here," I offered.

Davy Ray breathed. The breath became a word: *"Ben."* One side of his mouth hitched up. "Numb nuts."

"Yeah," I said, and I tried to smile. I wasn't as strong as Mrs. Callan. "Do you remember much about what happened?"

He nodded. His eyes were feverishly bright. "Tell you," he said, his voice crushed. "Have to tell you."

"All right," I said, and I sat down.

He smiled. "Saw him."

"You did?" I leaned forward conspiratorially. I caught a whiff of something that smelled bloody, but I didn't show it. "You saw the thing from the lost world?"

"No. Better." His smile went away as he swallowed painfully, then came back. "Saw Snowdown," he said.

"Snowdown," I whispered. The great white stag with antlers like oak trees. Yes, I decided. If anyone deserved to see Snowdown, it would be Davy Ray.

"Saw him. That's why I fell down. Wasn't watchin'. Oh, Cory," he said. "He's so pretty."

"I'll bet he is," I said.

"He's *bigger* than they say! And he's a whole lot *whiter,* too!"

"I'll bet," I said, "he's the most beautiful stag there ever was."

"Right there," Davy Ray whispered. "He was right there in front of me. And when I started to tell my dad, Snowdown leaped. He just leaped, and he was gone. Then I fell down, 'cause I wasn't watchin'. But it wasn't Snowdown's fault I fell, Cory. Wasn't anybody's fault. Just happened."

"You're gonna be fine," I said. I watched a bloody bubble of saliva grow at the corner of his mouth.

"I sure am glad I saw Snowdown," Davy Ray said. "I wouldn't have missed it. For nothin'."

He was silent, but for the soft wet rattling of his breath. The machine *blip . . . blip . . . blipped.* "I guess I'd better go," I said, and I started to stand up.

His marble-white hand grasped my own.

"Tell me a story," he whispered.

I paused. Davy Ray watched me, his eyes needful. I settled back down again. He kept hold of my hand, and I didn't try to pull loose. He felt cold.

"All right," I said. I would have to put this together as I went, like the tale of Chief Five Thunders. "There was a boy."

"Yeah," Davy Ray agreed, "gotta be a boy."

"This boy could just think of it, and he could go to other planets. This boy could get the red sand of Mars on his sneakers, or he could skate on Pluto. He could ride his bike on Saturn's rings, and he could fight dinosaurs on Venus."

"Could he go to the sun, Cory?"

"Oh, sure he could. He could go to the sun every day, if he wanted to. That's where he went when he needed a good suntan. He just put on his sunglasses and went there, then he came back brown as a berry."

"Must've gotten awful hot, though," Davy Ray said.

"He took a fan with him," I said. "And this boy was friends with all the kings and queens of the planets, and he visited all their castles. He visited the red sand castle of King Ludwig of Mars, and the cloud castle of King Nicholas of Jupiter. He helped stop King Zanthas of Saturn and King Damon of Neptune from fightin', when they got into a war over who owned a comet. He went to the fire castle of King Burl of Mercury, and on Venus he helped King Swane build a castle in the tall blue trees. On Uranus King Farron asked him to stay all year, and be an admiral in the ice fleet navy. Oh, all the royalty knew about this boy. They knew there'd never be another boy just exactly like him, even if all the stars and planets burned out and were struck to light again a million times. Because he was the only one on the whole earth who could walk on the planets, and he was the only one whose name was written in their invitation books."

"Hey, Cory?"

"Yes?"

His voice was getting drowsy. "I'd kinda like to see a cloud castle, wouldn't you?"

"I sure would," I said.

"Gosh." He wasn't looking at me anymore. He was looking somewhere else, like a solitary traveler about to wish himself to a fabled land. "I never was afraid of flyin', was I?"

"Not a bit."

"I'm awful tired, Cory." He frowned, the red saliva beginning to thread down his chin. "I don't like bein' so tired."

"You oughta rest, then," I said. "I'll come see you tomorrow."

His frown vanished. A smile sneaked across his mouth. "Not if I go to the sun tonight. Then I'll have me a suntan and you'll be stuck here shiverin'."

"Cory?" It was Mrs. Callan. "Cory, the doctor needs to get in here with him."

"Yes ma'am." I stood up. Davy Ray's cold hand clung to

mine for a few seconds, and then it fell away. "I'll see you," I said through the oxygen tent. "Okay?"

"Good-bye, Cory," Davy Ray said.

"Good—" I stopped myself. I was thinking of Mrs. Neville, on the first day of summer. "I'll see you," I told him, and I walked past his mother to the door. A sob welled up in my throat before I got out, but I clenched it down. As Chile Willow's mother had said, I could take it.

There was nothing more we could do. We drove home, along misty Route Sixteen, where Midnight Mona arrowed in search of love. We didn't say much; at a time like this, words were empty vessels. At home, the green feather lay on the floor where it had drifted; it went back to its cigar box.

On Sunday morning I awakened with a start. Tears were in my eyes, the sunlight lying in stripes across the floor. My father was standing in the doorway, wearing the same clothes he'd had on all day yesterday.

"Cory?" he said.

Traveling, traveling: to see Kings Ludwig, Nicholas, Zanthas, Damon, Farron, Burl, and Swane. Traveling, traveling: to castles of red sand, hewn of blue trees, formed of fire, shaped of sculpted clouds. Traveling, traveling, with planets and stars beyond and invitation books open to a single name. The solitary traveler has left this world. He will not pass this way again.

2

Faith

I THOUGHT I HAD known Death.

I had walked with it, ever since I could remember sitting in front of the television set, or hunkered down with a box of buttered popcorn before the Lyric's silver screen. How many hundreds of cowboys and Indians had I witnessed fall, arrow-pierced or gut-shot, into the swirling wagon train dust? How many dozens of detectives and policemen, laid low by the criminal bullet and coughing out their minutes? How many armies, mangled by shells and burp guns, and how many monster victims screaming as they're chewed?

I thought I had known Death, in Rebel's flat, blank stare. In the last good-bye of Mrs. Neville. In the rush and gurgle of air as a car with a man at the wheel sank into cold depths.

I was wrong.

Because Death cannot be known. It cannot be befriended. If Death were a boy, he would be a lonely figure, standing at the playground's edge while the air rippled with other children's laughter. If Death were a boy, he would walk alone. He would speak in a whisper and his eyes would be haunted by knowledge no human can bear.

This was what tore at me in the quiet hours: *We come from darkness, and to darkness we must return.*

I remembered Dr. Lezander saying that as I'd sat on his porch with him facing the golden hills. I didn't want to believe it. I didn't want to think that Davy Ray was in a place where he could see no light, not even the candle that burned for him at the Presbyterian church. I didn't want to think of Davy Ray confined, closed away from the sun, unable to somehow breathe and laugh even if doing so was only shadow play. In the days that followed the death of Davy Ray, I realized what fiction I had been a witness to. The cowboys and Indians, the detectives and policemen, the armies and the monster victims, would all rise again, at the dimming of the stage lights. They would go home, to wait for a casting call. But Davy Ray was dead forever, and I could not stand the thought of him in darkness.

It got to where I couldn't sleep. My room was too dark. It got to where I wasn't sure what I'd seen, the night a blurred figure spoke to Rebel. Because if Davy Ray was in darkness, so, too, was Carl Bellwood. Rebel was. And all the sleepers on Poulter Hill and all the generations whose bones lay beneath the twisted roots of Zephyr's trees: they, too, had returned to darkness.

I remembered Davy Ray's funeral. How thick the red earth was, on the edges of the grave. How thick, how heavy. There was no door down there when the minister was finished and the people gone and the dirt shoveled in by Bruton men. There was only dark, and its weight made something crack inside me.

I didn't know where heaven was anymore. I wasn't sure if God had any sense, or plan or reason, or if maybe He, too, was in the dark. I wasn't sure of anything anymore: not life, not afterlife, not God, not goodness. And I anguished over these things as the Christmas decorations went up on Merchants Street.

Christmas was still two weeks away, but Zephyr struggled for a festive air. The death of Davy Ray had drowned everybody's joy. It was talked about at Mr. Dollar's, at the Bright Star Cafe, at the courthouse, and everywhere in between. He was so young, they said. Such a tragic accident, they said. But that's life, they said; whether we like it or not, that's life.

Hearing these things didn't help me. Of course my folks tried to talk to me about it, saying that Davy Ray's suffering was over and that he'd gone to a better place.

But I just couldn't believe them. What place would ever be better than Zephyr?

"Heaven," Mom told me as we sat together before the crackling fire. "Davy Ray's gone to heaven, and you have to believe that."

"Because why?" I asked her, and she looked as if I'd just slapped her face.

I waited for an answer. I hoped for one, but it came in a word that left me unsatisfied, and that word was "faith."

They took me to see Reverend Lovoy. We sat in his office at church, and he gave me a lemon candy from a bowl on his desk. "Cory," he said, "you believe in Jesus, don't you?"

"Yes sir."

"And you believe that Jesus was sent from God to die for the sins of man?"

"Yes sir."

"Then you also believe Jesus was crucified, dead and buried, and on the third day He arose from the grave?"

"Yes sir." Here I frowned. "But Jesus was Jesus. Davy Ray was just a regular boy."

"I know that, Cory, but Jesus came to earth to show us that there's more to this existence than we understand. He showed us that if we believe in Him, and follow His will and way, we, too, have a place with God in heaven. You see?"

I thought about this for a minute as Reverend Lovoy sat back in his chair and watched me. "Is heaven better than Zephyr?" I asked him.

"A million times better," he said.

"Do they have comic books there?"

"Well . . ." He smiled. "We don't really know what heaven will be. We just know it'll be wonderful."

"Because why?" I asked.

"Because," he answered, "we must have faith." He offered the bowl to me. "Would you like another candy?"

I couldn't picture heaven. How could a place be any good at all if it didn't have the things there you enjoyed doing? If there were no comic books, no monster movies, no bikes, and no country roads to ride them on? No swimming pools, no ice cream, no summer, or barbecue on the Fourth of July? No thunderstorms, and front porches on which to sit and watch them coming? Heaven sounded to me like a library that only held books about one certain subject, yet you had to spend eternity and eternity and eternity reading them. What was heaven without typewriter paper and a magic box?

Heaven would be hell, that's what.

These days were not all bleak. The Christmas lights, red and green, glowed on Merchants Street. Lamps shaped like the head of Santa Claus burned on the street corners, and silver tinsel hung from the stoplights. Dad got a new job. He began working three days a week as a stock clerk at Big Paul's Pantry.

One day Leatherlungs called me a blockhead six times. She told me to come up to the blackboard and show the class what I knew about prime numbers.

I told her I wasn't coming.

"Cory Mackenson, you get up here right now!" she roared.

"No, ma'am," I said. Behind me the Demon laughed gleefully, sensing a new assault in the war on Mrs. Harper.

"Get. Up. Here. This. *Minute!*" Leatherlungs' face bloomed red.

I shook my head. "No."

She was on me. She moved a lot faster than I ever would've thought. She grabbed two handfuls of my sweater and wrenched me up out of my desk so hard my knee hit and sent a shiver of pain through my leg, and by the time that pain got to my head it was sheer white-hot anger.

With Davy Ray and darkness and a meaningless word called faith lodged in my mind like thorns, I swung at her.

I hit her right in the face. I couldn't have aimed any better. Her glasses flew off, and she gave a croaking cry of surprise. The anger fled from me just that fast, but Leatherlungs hollered, *"Don't you hit me, don't you dare!"* and she grabbed my hair and started jerking my head. The rest of my classmates sat in stunned amazement; this was too much, even for them. I had stepped into a mythic realm, though I didn't know it yet. Leatherlungs slung me, I crashed into Sally Meachum's desk and about knocked her over, and then Leatherlungs was hauling me out the door on the way to the principal's office, raging every step.

Inevitably, the phone call brought both Mom and Dad. They were, to say the least, appalled at my behavior. I was suspended from school for three days, and the principal—a small, birdlike man named, fittingly, Mr. Cardinale—said that before I could return to class, I would have to write an apology to Mrs. Harper and have both my parents sign it.

I looked at him, with my parents right there in his office, and I told him I could be suspended for three months for all I cared. I told him I wasn't writing her any apology, that I was tired of being called a blockhead, and I was sick of math and sick of everybody.

Dad came up off his chair. "Cory!" he said. "What's wrong with you?"

"Never in the history of this school has a student struck a teacher!" Mr. Cardinale piped up. "Never! This boy needs a whippin' to remember, is what I think."

"I'm sorry to have to say it," Dad told him, "but I agree with you."

I tried to explain to them on the way home, but they wouldn't hear it. Dad said there was no excuse for what I'd done, and Mom said she'd never been so ashamed. So I just stopped trying, and I sat sullenly in the pickup with Rocket riding in the truckbed. The whipping was delivered by my father's hand. It was swift, but it was painful. I did not know that the day before, Dad had been ragged by his boss at Big Paul's Pantry about messing up the count on boxes of Christmas candy. I did not know that Dad's boss was eight years younger than he, that he drove a red Thunderbird, and that he called my father Tommy.

I bore the whipping in silence, but in my room I pressed my face into the pillow.

Mom came in. She said she couldn't understand the way I was acting. She said she knew I was still torn up about Davy Ray, but that Davy Ray was in heaven and life was for the living. She said I would have to write the apology whether I wanted to or not, and the sooner I did it the better. I lifted my face from the pillow, and I told her Dad could whip me every day from now until kingdom come, but I wasn't writing any apology.

"Then I believe you'd better stay in here and think about it, young man," she said. "I believe you'll think better on an empty stomach, too."

I didn't answer. There was no need. Mom left, and I heard my folks talking about me, what was wrong with me and why I was being so disrespectful. I heard the clatter of dinner plates and I smelled chicken frying. I just turned over and went to sleep.

A dream of the four black girls, the flash of light, and a soundless blast awakened me. I had knocked my alarm clock off the bedside table again, but this time my parents didn't come in. The clock was still working; it was almost two in the morning. I got up and looked out the window. A crescent moon appeared sharp enough to hang a hat on. Beyond the window's cold glass the night was still and the stars blazing. I wasn't going to write any apology; maybe this was the Jaybird showing up in me, but I was damned if I'd give the satisfaction to Leatherlungs.

I needed to talk to somebody who understood me. Somebody like Davy Ray.

My fleece-lined jacket hung in the closet near the front door. I didn't want to go out that way, because Dad might be awake. I put on a pair of corduroy jeans, two sweaters, and a pair of gloves.

Then I eased the window up. It squeaked once, a hair-raising sound, but I waited for a minute and heard no footsteps. Then I finished the job and slid out the window into the bitter air.

I closed the window behind me, but for a thin slice I could get my fingers hooked into. I got on Rocket, and rode away under the sharp-fanged moon.

The stoplights blinked yellow as I pedaled through the silent streets. My breath billowed out like a white octopus before me. I saw a few lights in houses: bathroom bulbs left on to ease the sleepy stumbling. My nose and ears got cold mighty fast; it was a night not fit for dog or Vernon Thaxter. On my way to Poulter Hill, I took a left turn and pedaled about a quarter mile more than I had to, because I wanted to see something. I coasted slowly past the house that sat on three acres and had a horse barn.

A light burned in an upstairs room. It looked too bright to be a bathroom bulb. Dr. Lezander was up, listening to the foreign countries.

A curious thought occurred to me. Maybe Dr. Lezander was a night owl because he feared the darkness. Maybe he sat up there in that room under the light, listening to voices from around the world, to reassure himself that he was not alone, even as the clock ticked through the lonely hours.

I turned Rocket away from Dr. Lezander's house. I had not pursued the mystery of the green feather any more since Davy Ray had died. A phone call to Miss Blue Glass was too much effort in this time of death and doubt. It was all I could do to fend off my own gathering darkness, much less think of what lay in the mud at the lightless bottom of Saxon's Lake. I didn't want to think that Dr. Lezander had anything to do with that. If he had, then what in this world was real and true anymore?

I reached Poulter Hill. The wrought-iron gates were locked, but since the stone wall around the cemetery was only two feet high, getting in was no feat of magic. I left Rocket to wait there, and I walked up the hill among the moon-splashed tombstones. As Poulter Hill stood on the invisible line between worlds, so, too, did it stand between Zephyr and Bruton. The white dead people lay on one side, the black dead people on the other. It made sense that people who could not eat in the same cafe, swim in the same public pool, or shop in the same stores would not be happy being dead and buried within sight of each other. Which made me want to ask Reverend Lovoy sometime if the Lady and the Moon Man would be going to the same heaven as Davy Ray. If black people occupied the same heaven as white people, what was the point of eating in different cafes here on earth? If black people and white people walked in heaven together, did that mean we were smarter or more stupid than God because on earth we shunned each other? Of course, if we all returned to darkness, there was no God and no heaven, anyway. How Little Stevie Cauley had managed to drive Midnight Mona through a crack of that darkness was another mystery, because I had seen him clear as I now saw the city of stones rising up around me.

There were so many of them. So many. I remember hearing this somewhere: when an old man dies, a library burns down. I recalled Davy Ray's obituary in the Adams Valley *Journal*. They said he had died in a hunting accident. They said who his mother and father were, that he had a younger brother named Andy and that he was a member of the Union Town Presbyterian Church. They said his funeral would be at ten-thirty in the morning. What they had left out stunned me. They hadn't said one word about the way the corners of his eyes crinkled up when he laughed, or how he would set his mouth to one side in preparation for a verbal jab at Ben. There had been no mention of the shine in his eyes when he saw a forest trail he hadn't explored before, or how he chewed his bottom lip when he was about to pitch a fastball. They had written down the cut-and-dried of it, but they had not mentioned the real Davy Ray. I wondered about this as I walked amid the graves. How many stories were here, buried and forgotten? How many old burned libraries, how many young ones that had been building their volumes year by year? And all those stories, lost. I wished there was a place you could go, and sit in a room like a movie theater and look through a catalogue of a zillion names and then you could press a button and a face would appear on the screen to tell you about the life that had been. It would be a living memorial to the generations who had gone on before, and you could hear their voices though those voices had been stilled for a hundred years. It seemed to me, as I walked in the presence of all those stilled voices that would never be heard again, that we were a wasteful breed. We had thrown away the past, and our future was impoverished for it.

I came to Davy Ray's grave. The headstone hadn't arrived yet, but a flat stone marker was set into the bare earth. He was neither at the bottom of the hill nor at the top; he occupied the middle ground. I sat down beside the marker, taking care not to trample on the slight mound that rain would settle and spring would sprout. I looked out into the darkness, under the cold, sharp moon. In the sunlight, I knew, there was a panoramic view of Zephyr and the hills from here. You could see the gargoyle bridge, and the Tecumseh River. You could see the railroad track as it wound its way through those hills, and the trestle as it crossed the river on its passage through Zephyr to the larger towns. It was a nice view, if you had eyes to see it. I somehow doubted that Davy Ray cared much whether he had a view of the hills and river or if his grave overlooked a swamp bowl. Such things might be important to the grievers, but not so much to the leavers.

"Gosh," I said, and my breath drifted out. "I sure am mixed up."

Had I expected Davy Ray to answer? No, I had not. Thus I was not disappointed at the silence.

"I don't know if you're in darkness or heaven," I said. "I don't know what would be so great about heaven if you can't get in a little trouble there. It sounds like church to me. Church is fine for an hour on Sunday, but I wouldn't want to live there. And I wouldn't want darkness, either. Just nothin' and nothin' and more nothin'. Everythin' you ever thought or did or believed just gone, like a ripple in a pond that nobody sees." I pulled my knees up to my chest, and locked my arms around them. "No voice to speak, no eyes to see, no ears, nothin' at all. Then what are we born for, Davy Ray?"

This question, as well, elicited a burst of silence.

"And I can't figure this faith thing out," I went on. "Mom says I ought to have it. Reverend Lovoy says I've *got* to have it. But what if there's nothin' to have faith in, Davy Ray? What if faith is just like talkin' on a telephone when there's nobody on the other end, but you don't know nobody's there until you ask 'em a question and they don't answer? Wouldn't it make you go kind of crazy, to think you spent all that time jawin' to thin air?"

I was doing some jawing to empty air myself, I realized. But I was comforted, knowing Davy Ray was lying beside me. I shifted over to a place where the brown grass was unmarked by shovels and I reclined on my back. I stared up at the awesome stars. "Look at that," I said. "Just look at that sky. Looks like the Demon blew her nose on black velvet, huh?" I smiled, thinking Davy Ray would've gotten a kick out of that. "Not really," I said. "Can you see that sky from where you are?"

Silence and more silence.

I folded my arms across my chest. It didn't seem so cold, with my back against the earth. My head was next to Davy Ray's. "I got whipped today," I confided. "Dad really blistered me. Maybe I deserved it. But Leatherlungs deserves to get whipped, too, doesn't she? How come nobody listens to kids, even when they've got somethin' to say?" I sighed, and my breath rose toward Capricorn. "I can't write that apology, Davy Ray. I just can't, and nobody's gonna make me. Maybe I was wrong, but I was only half wrong, and they want me to say I was whole wrong. I can't write it. What am I gonna do?"

I heard it then.

Not Davy Ray's voice, chiding me.

But a train's whistle, off in the distance.

The freight was coming through.

I sat up. Off in the hills I could see the headlight like a moving star as the train wound toward Zephyr. I watched it coming.

The freight would slow down as it approached the Tecumseh trestle. It always did. It would slow down even more as it crossed the trestle, its heavy wheels making the old structure moan and clatter.

As it came off the trestle, it would be slow enough to catch if someone had a mind to.

The moment wouldn't last very long. The freight would pick up speed, and by the time it had reached the far side of Zephyr it would be running fast again.

"I can't write any apology, Davy Ray," I said quietly. "Not tomorrow, not the day after that. Not ever. I guess I can't ever go back to school, huh?"

Davy Ray offered neither opinion nor advice. I was on my own.

"What if I was to go away for a while? Not long. Maybe two or three days. What if I was to show 'em I'd rather run away than write an apology? Then maybe they'd listen to me, don't you think?" I watched the moving star come nearer. The whistle blew again, maybe warning a deer off the track. I heard it say *Corrrrryyyyyyyyyy*.

I stood up. I could make it to the trestle if I ran to Rocket. But I had to go right this minute. Fifteen more seconds and I would face one more day of anger and disappointment from my parents. One more day of being a boy closed up in a room with an unwritten apology staring me in the face. The freight that was about to pass through always returned again. I reached into my pocket, and found two quarters left over from some purchase of popcorn or candy bar at the Lyric last winter when things were good.

"I'm goin', Davy Ray!" I said. "I'm goin'!"

I started running through the graveyard. As I reached Rocket and swung up onto the saddle, I feared I was already too late. I pedaled like mad for the trestle, the breath blooming around my face. I heard the moan and clatter as I pulled alongside the gravel-edged tracks; the freight was crossing, and I could yet meet it.

And then there it was, the headlight blazing. The huge engine came off the trestle and passed me, going a little faster than I could walk. Then the boxcars began going past: Southern Railroad cars, *bump ka thud, bump ka thud, bump ka thud* on the ties. Already the train was starting to pick up speed. I got off Rocket and put the kickstand down. I ran my fingers along the handlebar. For a second I saw the headlamp's golden eye, luminous with the moon. "I'll be back!" I promised.

All the boxcars were closed up, it seemed. But then here came one toward the end of the freight that had a door partway open. I thought of railroad bulls bashing heads and throwing freeloaders face-first into steam-scalded space, but I shook the thought away. I ran alongside the boxcar with the open door. A ladder was close at hand. I reached up, hooked four gloved fingers around a metal rung, got my thumb wedged there, too, and then I grabbed hold with the other hand and lifted my feet off the gravel.

I swung myself toward the boxcar's open door. I was amazed that I had such dexterity. I guess when you hear a few tons of steel wheels grinding underneath you, you can become an acrobat real quick. I went through that opening into the boxcar, my fingers released the iron rungs, and I hit a wooden floor sparsely covered with hay. The sound of my entrance was not gentle; it echoed in the boxcar, which was sealed shut on the other side. I sat up, hay all over the front of my outermost sweater.

The boxcar rumbled and shook. It was clearly not made for passengers.

But someone was indeed along for the ride.

"Hey, Princey!" a voice said. "A little bird just flew in!"

I jumped up. That voice had sounded like a combination of rocks in a cement mixer and a bullfrog's lament. It had come from the dark before me.

"Yes, I see him," another man answered. This voice was as

smooth as black silk and had the lilt of a foreign accent. "I think he almost broke his wings, Franklin."

I was in the company of boxcar-riding tramps who would slit my throat for the quarters in my pocket. I turned to jump through the doorway, but Zephyr was speeding past.

"I wouldn't, young man," the foreign-accented voice cautioned. "It would not be pretty."

I paused on the edge, my heart pounding.

"We ain't gonna bite ya!" the froggish cement-mixer voice said. "Are we, Princey?"

"Speak for yourself, please."

"Ah, he's just kiddin'! Princey's always kiddin', ain't ya?"

"Yes," the black silk voice said with a sigh, "I'm always kidding."

A match flared beside my face. I jumped again, and turned to see who stood there.

A nightmare visage peered at me, so close I could smell his musty breath.

The man would've made a railroad tie look like Charles Atlas. He was emaciated, his black eyes submerged in shadow pools and the cheekbones thrust against the flesh of his face. And what flesh! I had seen summer-baked creekbeds that held more moisture. Every inch of his face was cracked and wrinkled, and the cracks drew his mouth back from his yellow teeth and continued up like a weird cap over the hairless dome of his scalp. His long, skinny fingers, exposed by the matchlight, were likewise shriveled, as was the hand on which they were fixed. His throat was a dried mass of cracks. He wore a dusty white costume of some kind, but where shirt and pants met I couldn't tell. He looked like a stick in a bag of dirty rags.

I was frozen with terror, waiting for the blade to slice my neck.

The wrinkled man's other hand rose like an adder's head. I tensed.

He was holding a package with a few Fig Newtons in it.

"Well, well!" the foreign man said with obvious surprise. "Ahmet likes you! Take a Fig Newton, he doesn't speak."

"I . . . don't think I . . ."

The match went out. I could smell Ahmet next to me, an odor so dry it threatened to crisp the hairs in my nostrils. He breathed like the rustle of dead leaves.

A second match was struck. Ahmet had a black streak across his pointed chin. He still held the Fig Newtons, and now he nodded at me. When he did so, I thought I heard his flesh creak.

He was grinning like warmed-over Death. Baked and crusted Death, to be more exact. I slid a trembling hand into the package and accepted a Fig Newton. This seemed to appease Ahmet. He shambled over toward the boxcar's other side, and he knelt down and touched the match to three candle stubs stuck with wax to the bottom of an upturned bucket.

The light grew. And as it grew, it showed me things I wished I didn't have to look at.

"There," the foreign man said from where he sat with his shoulder against a pile of burlap sacks. "Now we see eye to eye."

I wished we'd been back to back with five miles between us.

If this man had ever seen the sun, the Lady was my grandmother. His skin was so pallid, he made the moon appear as dark as Don Ho. He was a young man, younger at least than my father, and he had fine blond hair combed back from a high forehead. A touch of silver glinted at his temples. He was wearing a dark suit, a white shirt, and a necktie. Only I could tell right off that his suit had seen better days from the patches around the shoulders, the cuffs of his shirt were frayed, and brown blotches marred his tie. Still, there was an elegance about this man; even sitting down, he commanded your attention with a stare that had a trace of well-bred haughtiness in it. His wingtips were scuffed. At first I thought he was wearing white socks, but then I realized those were his ankles. His eyes bothered me, though; in the candlelight, the pupils gleamed scarlet.

But this man, and Ahmet the dried-up one, looked like Troy

Donahue and Yul Brynner compared to the third monstrosity in that boxcar.

He was standing up in a corner. His head, which was strangely shovel-shaped, almost brushed the ceiling. The man must have been over seven feet tall. His shoulders looked as wide as some of the wings on the planes at Robbins Air Force Base. His body appeared bulky and lumpy and altogether not right. He was wearing a loose brown jacket and gray trousers with patches on the knees. The trousers looked as if they had gotten drenched and shrunken while he was still in them. The size of the man's shoes astounded me; to call them clodhoppers is like calling an atomic bomb a pregnant grenade. They were more like earthmovers.

"Hi dere," he said as his shoes slammed on the timbers and he came toward me. "I'm Franklin."

He was grinning. I wished he hadn't been. His grin made Mr. Sardonicus look unhappy. What was worse than his grin was a scar that sliced across his Neanderthal forehead and had been stitched together, it seemed, by a cross-eyed medical student with a severe case of hiccups. His huge face looked flattened, his shiny black hair all but painted on his skull. In the candlelight, he appeared as if something he'd recently eaten hadn't agreed with him. The misfortunate oaf was a sickly, grayish hue. And lo and behold! There from each side of the man's bull-thick neck protruded a small rusted screw.

"You want some wadda?" he asked, and he held up a dented canteen. In his hand, it seemed the size of a clamshell.

"Uh . . . no sir. No thank you. Sir."

"Wadda washes down da Fig Newton," he said. "Udderwise get stuck in da troat."

"I'm okay. Really." I cleared my throat. "See?"

"Hokay. Dass fine, den." He returned to his corner, where he stood like a grotesque statue.

"Franklin's a happy sort," Princey explained. "Ahmet's the quiet one."

"What are *you?*" I asked.

"I'm the ambitious type," he said. "What type are you?"

"Scared." I heard the rush of wind behind me. The freight train was speeding now, leaving Zephyr sleeping in peace.

"Sit down if you like," Princey offered. "It's not too clean in here, but neither is it a dungeon."

I looked longingly out the door. We must've been going . . .

". . . sixty miles an hour," Princey said. "Sixty-four, it feels to me. I'm a good judge of the wind."

I sat down, keeping my distance from all three of them.

"So." He slid his hands into the pockets of his coat. "Favor us with your destination, Cory."

"I guess I . . . wait a minute. Did I tell you my name?"

"You must have, I'm sure."

"I don't remember."

Franklin laughed. It sounded like a backed-up drain being Roto-Rootered. "Haw! Haw! Haw! Dere he goes again! Princey's got da best sense'a yuma!"

"I don't think I told you my name," I said.

"Well, don't be stubborn," Princey answered. "Everybody has a name. What's yours?"

"Co—" I stopped. Were these three insane, or was I? "Cory Mackenson. I'm from Zephyr."

"Going to . . . ?" he prompted.

"Where does the train go?" I asked.

"From here?" He smiled slightly. "To everywhere."

I glanced over at Ahmet. He was squatting on his haunches, watching me intently over the flickering candles. He wore sandals on his shriveled feet, his toenails two inches long. "Kinda cold to be wearin' sandals, isn't it?"

"Ahmet doesn't mind," Princey said. "That's his footwear of choice. He's Egyptian."

"*Egyptian?* How'd he get all the way here?"

"It was a long, dusty trail," he assured me.

"Who *are* you people? You look kinda—"

"Familiar if you're a devotee of the sweet science. Boxing, that is," Princey said, shoveling words in my mouth. "Ever heard of Franklin Fitzgerald? Otherwise known as Big Philly Frank?"

"No sir."

"Then why did you say you had?"

"I . . . *did* I?"

"Meet Franklin Fitzgerald." He motioned to the monster in the corner.

"Hello," I said.

"Pleased ta meet ya," Franklin replied.

"I'm Princey Von Kulic. That's Ahmet Too-Hard-to-Pronounce."

"Hee hee hee," Franklin giggled behind a massive hand with scarred knuckles.

"You're not American, are you?" I asked Princey.

"Citizen of the world, at your service."

"Where're you from, then?"

"I am from a nation that is neither here nor there. It is an unnation, if you will." He smiled again. "Unnation. I like that. My country has been ransacked by foreign invaders so many times, we give green stamps for raping and pillaging. It's easier to make a buck here, what can I say?"

"So you're a boxer, too?"

"Me?" He grimaced as if he had a bad taste in his mouth.

"Oh, no! I'm the brains behind Franklin's brawn. I'm his manager. Ahmet's his trainer. We all get along famously, except when we're trying to kill each other."

"Haw haw!" Franklin rumbled.

"We are currently between opponents," Princey said with a slight shrug. "Bound from the last place we were to the next place we will be. And such, I fear, is our existence."

I had decided that no matter how fearsome this trio appeared, they really meant me no harm. "Does Mr. Fitzgerald do a lot of fightin'?" I asked.

"Franklin will take on anyone, anywhere, at any time. Un-a place called Vietnam. Civil strifes broke out in the cities like skirmishes in an undeclared war. A vague sense of foreboding was spreading across the land, as we neared the plastic, disposable, commercial age. The world was changing; Zephyr was changing, too, and there was no going back to the world that used to be.

But: tonight was Christmas Eve and tomorrow was Christmas, and for now we had peace on earth.

It lasted about ten minutes.

We heard the shrieking of a jet plane over Zephyr. This in itself wasn't unusual, since we often heard jets at night either taking off from or landing at Robbins. But we knew the sound of those planes as we knew the freight train's whistle, and this plane . . .

"Sounds awfully low, doesn't it?" Mom asked.

Dad said it sounded to him like it was skimming the rooftops. He got up to go to the porch, and suddenly we heard a noise like somebody whacking a barrel with a fifty-pound mallet. The sound echoed over Zephyr, and in another moment dogs started barking from Temple Street to Bruton and the roving bands of carolers were forced to give up the holy ghost. We stood out on the porch, listening to the commotion. I thought at first that the jet had crashed, but then I heard it again. It circled Zephyr a couple of times, its wingtip lights blinking, and then it veered toward Robbins Air Force Base and sped away.

The dogs kept barking and howling. People were coming out of their houses to see what was going on. "Somethin's up," Dad said. "I think I'll give Jack a call."

Sheriff Marchette had stepped ably into the job J. T. Amory had vacated. Of course, with the Blaylocks behind bars, Zephyr's crime wave was over. The most serious task that lay before Sheriff Marchette was finding the beast from the lost world, which had attacked the Trailways bus one day and gave it such a hard knock with its sawed-off horns that the driver and all eight of the passengers were admitted to the Union Town hospital with whiplash.

Dad reached Mrs. Marchette, but the sheriff had already grabbed his hat and run out, summoned away from Christmas Eve dinner by a phone call. Mrs. Marchette told Dad what her husband had told her, and with a stunned expression Dad relayed the news.

"A bomb," he said. "A bomb fell."

"*What?*" Mom was already fearing Russian invasion. "*Where?*"

"On Dick Moultry's house," Dad said. "Mrs. Moultry told Jack it went right through the roof, the livin' room floor, and into the basement."

"My Lord! Didn't the whole house blow up?"

"No. The bomb's just sittin' in there." Dad returned the receiver to its cradle. "Just sittin' in there with Dick."

"With *Dick?*"

"That's right. Mrs. Moultry gave Dick a new workshop bench for Christmas. He was in the basement puttin' it together. Now he's trapped down there with a live bomb."

It wasn't very long before the civil defense siren began wailing. Dad got a phone call from Mayor Swope, asking him if he would meet with a group of volunteers at the courthouse and help spread the word from door to door that both Zephyr and Bruton had to be immediately evacuated.

"On Christmas *Eve?*" Dad said. "Evacuate the whole *town?*"

"That's right, Tom." Mayor Swope sounded at his rope's end. "Do you know a bomb fell out of a jet plane right into—"

"Dick Moultry's house, yeah I've heard. It fell out of a jet plane?"

"Right again. And we've gotta get these people out of here in case that damn thing blows."

"Well, why don't you call the air base? Surely they'll come get it."

"I just got off the phone with 'em. Their public relations spokesman, I mean. I told him one of his jets lost a bomb over our town, and you know what he said? He said I must've been in the

Christmas rum cake! He said no such thing happened, that none of their pilots were so careless as to accidentally hit a safety lever and drop a bomb on civilians. He said even *if* such a thing happened, their bomb deactivation team was not on duty on Christmas Eve, and *if* such a thing happened, he'd hope the civilians in that town upon which a bomb did *not* drop ought to have sense enough to evacuate because the bomb that did *not* fall from a jet plane could blow most of that town into toothpicks! Now, how about *that?*"

"He's got to know you're tellin' the truth, Luther. He'll send somebody to keep the bomb from explodin'."

"Maybe so, but *when?* Tomorrow afternoon? Do you want to go to sleep tonight with that thing tickin'? I can't risk it, Tom. We've got to get everybody out!"

Dad asked Mayor Swope to come pick him up. Then he hung up the phone and told Mom she and I ought to take the truck and get to Grand Austin and Nana Alice's for the night. He'd come join us when the work was done. Mom started to beg him to come with us; she wanted to, as much as rain wants to follow clouds. But she saw that he had decided what was right, and she would have to learn to deal with it. She said, "Go get your pajamas, Cory. Get your toothbrush and a pair of fresh socks and underwear. We're goin' to Grand Austin's."

"Dad, is Zephyr gonna blow up?" I asked.

"No. We're movin' everybody out just for safety's sake. The Air Force boys'll send somebody to get that thing real soon, I'm sure of it."

"You'll be careful?" Mom asked him.

"You know it. Merry Christmas." He smiled.

She couldn't help but return it. "You crazy thing, you!" she said, and she kissed him.

Mom and I got some clothes packed. The civil defense siren wailed for almost fifteen minutes, a sound so spine-chilling it even silenced the dogs. Already people were getting the message, and they were driving away to spend the night with relatives, friends in other towns, or at the Union Pines Motel in Union Town. Mayor Swope came by to pick up Dad. Then Mom and I were ready to go. Before we walked out the door, the phone rang and it was Ben wanting to tell me they were going to Birmingham to spend the night with his aunt and uncle. "Ain't it somethin'?" he said excitedly. "Know what I heard? Mr. Moultry's got two busted legs and a broke back and the bomb's lyin' right on top of him! This is really neat, huh?"

I had to agree it was. We'd never experienced a Christmas Eve quite like it.

"Gotta go! Talk to you later! Oh, yeah . . . Merry Christmas!"

"Merry Christmas, Ben!"

He hung up. Mom collared me, and we were on our way to Grand Austin and Nana Alice's house. I'd never seen so many cars on Route Ten before. Heaven help us all if the beast from the lost world decided to attack right about now; there'd be a bomb behind us, cars and trucks tumped over like tenpins, and people flying through the air without wings.

We left Zephyr behind, all lit up for Christmas.

The rest of this story I found out later, since I wasn't there.

Curiosity got the best of Dad. He had to see the bomb. So, as Zephyr and Bruton gradually emptied out, he left the group of volunteers he was riding with and walked a half-dozen blocks to where Mr. Moultry lived. Mr. Moultry's house was a small wooden structure painted pale blue with white shutters. Light was streaming upward through the splintered roof. The sheriff's car was parked out front, its bubble light spinning around. Dad climbed up onto the porch, which had been knocked crooked by the impact. The front door was ajar, the walls riddled with cracks. The bomb's velocity had shoved the house off its foundations. Dad went inside, and he couldn't miss the huge hole in the sagging floor because it had swallowed half the room. A few Christmas tree decorations were scattered about, and a little silver star lay balanced on the hole's ragged edge. The tree itself was missing.

He peered down. Boards and beams were tangled up like a plateful of macaroni. Plaster dust was the Parmesan cheese. There was the meatball of the bomb: its iron-gray tail fins protruded from the debris, its nose plowed right into the basement's dirt floor.

"Get me outta here! Ohhhhh, my legs! Get me to the hospital! Ohhhhh, I'm dyin'!"

"You're not dyin', Dick. Just don't try to move."

Mr. Moultry was lying amid wreckage with a carpenter's workbench on top of him, and atop that a beam as big around as a sturdy oak. It had split, and Dad figured it had been a support for the living room's floor. Lying across the beam that crisscrossed Mr. Moultry was the Christmas tree, its balls and bulbs shattered. The bomb wasn't on top of Mr. Moultry, but it had dug itself in about four feet from his head. Sheriff Marchette knelt nearby, deliberating the mess.

"Jack? It's Tom Mackenson!"

"Tom?" Sheriff Marchette looked up, his face streaked with plaster dust. "You ought to get outta here, man!"

"I wanted to come see it. Not as big as I thought it would be."

"It's plenty big enough," the sheriff said. "If this thing blows, it'll take the house and leave a crater where the whole block used to be."

"*Ohhhhh!*" Mr. Moultry groaned. His shirt had been torn open by the falling timbers, and his massive gut wobbled this way and that. "I said I'm dyin', damn it!"

"He hurt bad?" Dad asked.

"Can't get in there close enough to tell. Says he thinks his legs are broken. Maybe a busted rib or two, the way he's wheezin'."

"He always breathes like that," Dad said.

"Well, the ambulance ought to be here soon." Sheriff Marchette checked his wristwatch. "I called 'em directly I got here. I don't know what's keepin' 'em."

"What'd you tell 'em? That a fella got hit by a fallin' bomb?"

"Yes," the sheriff said.

"In that case, I think Dick's in for a long wait."

"Get me outta here!" Mr. Moultry tried to push some of the dusty tangle of lumber off him, but he winced and couldn't do it. He turned his head and looked at the bomb, sweat glistening on his suety cheeks. "Get *that* outta here! Jesus Christ, help me!"

"Where's Mrs. Moultry?" Dad asked.

"Huh!" Mr. Moultry's plaster-white face sneered. "She took off runnin' and left me here, that's what she did! Wouldn't even lift a finger to help me!"

"That's not quite right. She *did* call me, didn't she?" the sheriff pointed out.

"Well, what the hell are *you* good for? Ohhhhhh, my legs! They're broke plumb in two, I'm tellin' ya!"

"Can I come down?" Dad asked.

"Rather you didn't. Rather you got on out of here like any sane man should. But come on if you want to. Be careful, though. The stairs collapsed, so I set up a stepladder."

Dad eased himself down the ladder. He stood appraising the pile of timbers, beams, and Christmas tree on top of Mr. Moultry. "We can probably move that big one," he said. "I'll grab one end if you grab the other."

They cleared the tree aside and did the job, moving the oak-sized beam though their backs promised a rendezvous with deep-heating rub. Mr. Moultry, however, was still in a heap of trouble. "We can dig him out, take him to your car, and get him to the hospital," Dad suggested. "That ambulance isn't comin'."

The sheriff knelt down beside Mr. Moultry. "Hey, Dick. You weighed yourself lately?"

"Weighed myself? Hell, no! Why should I?"

"What did you weigh the last time you had a physical?"

"One hundred and sixty pounds."

"When?" Sheriff Marchette asked. "In the third grade? How much do you weigh right *now,* Dick?"

Mr. Moultry scowled and muttered. Then he said, "A little bit over two hundred."

"Try again."

"Aw, shit! I weigh two hundred and ninety pounds! Does that satisfy you, you sadist you?"

"Maybe got two broken legs. Broken ribs. Possible internal injuries. And he weighs two hundred and ninety pounds. Think we can get him up that ladder, Tom?"

"No way," my father said.

"My thoughts right on the button. He's stuck in here until somebody can bring a hoist."

"What do you mean?" Mr. Moultry squawked. "I gotta stay here?" He looked fearfully at the bomb again. "Well, for God's sake get that damn thing away from me, then!"

"I'd do that for you, Dick," the sheriff said. "I really would, but I'd have to touch it. And what if the thing's primed to go off and all it needs is a finger's touch? You think I want to be responsible for blowin' you up? Not to mention myself and Tom? No, sir!"

"Mayor Swope told me he talked to somebody at Robbins," Dad said to the sheriff. "Said the fella didn't believe—"

"Yeah, Luther came by here before he and his family hit the trail. He told me all about what that sumbitch said. Maybe the pilot was too scared to let anybody know how bad he messed up. Probably staggered out of a Christmas party and climbed right into the cockpit. All I know for sure is, nobody's comin' from Robbins to get this thing anytime soon."

"What am *I* supposed to do?" Mr. Moultry asked. "Just lie here and suffer?"

"I can go upstairs and fetch you a pilla, if you like," Sheriff Marchette offered.

"Dick? Dick, you okay?" The voice, tentative and afraid, was coming from upstairs.

"Oh, I'm just dandy!" Mr. Moultry hollered. "I'm just tickled pink"—*pank,* he pronounced it—"to be layin' down here with two busted legs and a bomb next to my melon! God a'mighty! I don't know who you are up there, but you're a bigger idiot than the fool who dropped that damn bomb in the first . . . *oh*. It's you."

"Hi there, Dick," Mr. Gerald Hargison said sheepishly. "How're you doin'?"

"I could just dance!" Mr. Moultry's face was getting splotched with crimson. "Shit!"

Mr. Hargison stood at the edge of the hole and peered down. "That's the bomb right there, is it?"

"No, it's a big goose turd!" Mr. Moultry raged. "'Course it's the bomb!"

While Mr. Moultry thrashed to get free again and only succeeded in raising a storm of plaster dust and causing himself considerable pain, Dad looked around the basement. Over in one corner was a desk, and above it a wall plaque that read A MAN'S HOME IS HIS CASTLE. Next to it was a poster of a bug-eyed black minstrel tap-dancing, and underneath it the hand-lettered sign THE WHITE MAN'S BURDEN. Dad wandered over to the desk, the top of which was six inches deep in untidy papers. He slid open the upper drawer and was hit in the face by the enormous mammary glands of a woman on a *Juggs* magazine cover. Underneath the magazine was a hodgepodge of Gem clips, pencils, rubber bands, and the like. An overexposed Kodak picture came to hand. It showed Dick Moultry wearing a white robe and cradling in one arm a rifle while the other embraced a peaked white cap and hood. Mr. Moultry was smiling broadly, proud of his accomplishments.

"Hey, get outta there!" Mr. Moultry swiveled his head around. "It ain't enough I'm layin' here dyin', you've gotta ransack my house, too?"

Dad closed the drawer on the picture and walked back to Sheriff Marchette. Above them, Mr. Hargison nervously scuffed his soles on the warped floor. "Listen, Dick, I just wanted to come by and see about you. Make sure you weren't . . . you know, dead and all."

"No, I'm not dead *yet*. Much as my wife wishes that bomb had clunked me right on the brainpan."

"We're headin' out of town," Mr. Hargison explained. "Uh . . . we probably won't be back until day after Christmas. Probably get back near ten o'clock in the mornin'. Hear me, Dick? Ten o'clock in the mornin'."

"Yeah, I hear you! I don't care what time you get back!"

"Well, we'll get back near ten o'clock. In the mornin', day after Christmas. Thought you might want to know, so you could set your watch."

"Set my *watch?* Are you—" He stopped. "Oh. Yeah. Okay, I'll do that." He grinned, his face sweating as he looked up at the sheriff. "Gerald and me are supposed to help a friend clean out his garage day after Christmas. That's why he's tellin' me what time he'll be back."

"Is that so?" the sheriff asked. "What friend might that be, Dick?"

"Oh . . . fella lives in Union Town. You wouldn't know him."

"I know a lot of people in Union Town. What's your friend's name?"

"Joe," Mr. Hargison said, at the exact second Mr. Moultry said, "Sam."

"Joe Sam," Mr. Moultry explained, still sweatily grinning. "Joe Sam Jones."

"I don't think you're gonna be helping any Joe Sam Jones clean out his garage the day after Christmas, Dick. I think you'll be in a nice secure hospital room, don't you?"

"Hey, Dick, I'm headin' off!" Mr. Hargison announced. "Don't you worry, you're gonna be just fine." And with that last word the toe of his left shoe nudged the silver Christmas tree star that lay balanced on the hole's ragged edge. Dad watched the little star fall as if in graceful slow motion, like a magnified snowflake drifting down.

It hit one of the bomb's iron-gray tail fins, and exploded in a shower of painted glass.

In the seconds of silence that followed, all four of the men heard it.

The bomb made a hissing sound, like a serpent that had been awakened in its nest. The hissing faded, and from the bomb's guts there came a slow, ominous ticking: not like the ticking of an alarm clock, but rather the ticking of a hot engine building up to a boil.

"Oh . . . shit," Sheriff Marchette whispered.

"Jesus save me!" Mr. Moultry gasped. His face, which had been flushed crimson a few moments before, now became as white as a wax dummy.

"The thing's switched on," Dad said, his voice choked.

Mr. Hargison's speech was by far the most eloquent. He spoke with his legs, which propelled him across the warped floor, out onto the crooked porch and to his car at the curb as if he'd been boomed from a cannon. The car sped away like the Road Runner: one second there, the next not.

"Oh God, oh God!" Tears had sprung to Mr. Moultry's eyes. "Don't let me die!"

"Tom? I believe it's time." Sheriff Marchette was speaking softly, as if the weight of words passing through the air might be enough to cause concussion. "To vamoose, don't you?"

"You can't leave me! You can't! You're the *sheriff!*"

"I can't do anythin' more for you, Dick. I swear I wish I could, but I can't. Seems to me you need magic or a miracle right about now, and I think the well's run dry."

"Don't leave me! Get me out of this, Jack! I'll pay you whatever you want!"

"I'm sorry. Climb on up, Tom."

Dad didn't have to be told a second time. He scaled that ladder like Lucifer up a tree. At the top, he said, "I'll steady the ladder for you, Jack! Come on!"

The bomb ticked. And ticked. And ticked.

"I can't help you, Dick," Sheriff Marchette said, and he climbed the ladder.

"No! Listen! I'll do anythin'! Get me out, okay? I won't mind if it hurts! Okay?"

Dad and Sheriff Marchette were on their way to the door.

"Please!" Mr. Moultry shouted. His voice cracked, and a sob came out. He fought against his trap, but the pain made him cry harder. *"You can't leave me to die! It's not human!"*

He was still shouting and sobbing as Dad and the sheriff left the house. Both their faces were drawn and tight. "Great job this turned out to be," Sheriff Marchette said. "Jesus." They reached the sheriff's car. "You need a ride somewhere, Tom?"

"Yeah." He frowned. "No." And he leaned against the car. "I don't know."

"Now, don't look like that! There's not a thing can be done for him, and you know it!"

"Maybe somebody ought to wait around, in case the bomb squad shows up."

"Fine." The sheriff glanced up and down the deserted street. "Are you volunteerin'?"

"No."

"Me, neither! And they're not gonna show up anytime soon, Tom. I think that bomb's gonna explode and we'll lose this whole block, and I don't know about you, but I'm gettin' out while I've still got my skin." He walked around to the driver's door.

"Jack, wait a minute," Dad said.

"Ain't got a minute. Come on, if you're comin'."

Dad got into the car with him, and Sheriff Marchette started the engine. "Where to?"

"Listen to me, Jack. You said it yourself: Dick needs magic or a miracle, right? So who's the one person around here who might be able to give it to him?"

"Reverend Blessett's left town."

"No, not him! *Her.*"

Sheriff Marchette paused with his hand on the gearshift.

"Anybody who can turn a bag of shotgun shells into a bag of garden snakes might be able to take care of a bomb, don't you think?"

"No, I don't! I don't think the Lady had a thing to do with

that. I think Biggun Blaylock was so blasted out of his mind on his own rotgut whiskey that he thought he was fillin' that ammo bag full of cartridges when all the time he was shovelin' the snakes in!"

"Oh, come on! You saw those snakes the same as I did! There were *hundreds* of 'em! How long would it have taken Biggun to find 'em all?"

"I don't believe in that voodoo stuff," Sheriff Marchette said. "Not one bit."

Dad said the first thing that came to mind, and saying it left a shocked taste in his mouth: "We can't be afraid to ask her for help, Jack. She's all we've got."

"Damn," the sheriff muttered. "Damn and double-damn." He looked at the Moultry house, light rising from its broken roof. "She might be gone by now."

"She might be. She might not be. Can't we at least drive over there and find out?"

Many houses in Bruton were dark, their owners having obeyed the siren and fled the impending blast. Her rainbow-hued dwelling, however, was all lit up. Tiny sparkling lights blinked in the windows.

"I'll wait right here," Sheriff Marchette said. Dad nodded and got out. He took a deep breath of Christmas Eve air and made his legs move. They carried him to the front door. He took the door's knocker, a little silver hand, and did something he never dreamed he would've done in a million years: he announced to the Lady that he had come to call.

He waited, hoping she would answer.

He waited, watching the doorknob.

He waited.

Fifteen minutes after my father took the silver hand, there was a noise on the street where Dick Moultry lived. It was a rumble and a clatter, a clanking and a clinking, and it caused the dogs to bark in its wake. The rust-splotched, suspension-sagging pickup truck stopped at the curb in front of the Moultry house, and a long, skinny black man got out of the driver's door. On that door was stenciled, not very neatly: LIGHTFOOT'S FIX-IT.

He moved so slowly it seemed that movement might be a painful process. He wore freshly washed overalls and a gray cap that allowed his gray hair to boil out from beneath it. In supreme slow motion, he walked to the truck's bed and strapped on his tool belt, which held several different kinds of hammers, screwdrivers, and arcane-looking wrenches. In a slow extension of time he picked up his toolbox, an old metal fascination filled with drawers that held every kind of nut and bolt under the workman's sun. Then, as if moving under the burden of the ages, Mr. Marcus Lightfoot walked to Dick Moultry's crooked entrance. He knocked at the door, even though it stood wide open: One . . . two . . .

Eternities passed. Civilizations thrived and crumbled. Stars were born in brawny violence and died doddering in the cold vault of the cosmos.

. . . three.

"Thank God!" Mr. Moultry shouted, his voice worn to a frazzle. "I knew you wouldn't let me die, Jack! Oh, God have mer—" He stopped shouting in mid-praise, because he was looking up through the hole in the living room's floor, and instead of help from heaven he saw the black face of what he considered a devil of the earth.

"Lawdy, lawdy," Mr. Lightfoot said. His eyes had found the bomb, his ear the ticking of its detonation mechanism. "You sure in a big pile'a mess."

"Have you come to watch me get blown up, you black savage?" Mr. Moultry snarled.

"Nossuh. Come ta keep you from gettin' blowed."

"*You?* Help *me?* Hah!" He pulled in a breath and roared through his ravaged throat: "*Jack! Somebody help me! Anybody white!*"

"Mr. Moultry, suh?" Mr. Lightfoot waited for the other man's lungs to give out. "That there bumb might not care for such a' noise."

Mr. Moultry, his face the color of ketchup and the sweat standing up in beads, began fighting his condition. He thrashed and clawed at the pile of debris; he grasped at his own shirt in a fit of rage and ripped the rest of it away; he gripped at the very air but found no handholds there. And then the pain crashed over him like one wrestler bodyslamming another and Mr. Moultry was left gasping and breathless but still with two broken legs and a bomb ticking next to his head.

"I believe," Mr. Lightfoot said, and he yawned at the lateness of the hour, "I'd best come on down."

It might have been New Year's Eve before Mr. Lightfoot reached the bottom of the stepladder, the tools in his belt jingling together. He grasped his toolbox and started toward Mr. Moultry, but the poster of the bug-eyed minstrel on the wall caught his attention. He stared at it as the seconds and the bomb ticked.

"Heh-heh," Mr. Lightfoot said, and shook his head. "Heh heh."

"What're you laughin' at, you crazy jigaboo?"

"Thass a white man," he said. "All painted up and lookin' the fool."

At last Mr. Lightfoot pulled himself away from the picture of Al Jolson and went to the bomb. He cleared away some nail-studded timbers and roof shingles and sat down on the red dirt, a process that was like watching a snail cross a football field. He drew the toolbox close to his side, like a trusted companion. Then he took a pair of wire-rimmed spectacles from the breast pocket of his shirt, blew on the lenses, and wiped them on his sleeve, all at excruciating slowness.

"What have I done to deserve this?" Mr. Moultry croaked.

Mr. Lightfoot got his spectacles on. "Now," he said. "I can." He leaned closer to the bomb, and as he frowned the small lines deepened between his eyes. "See what's what."

He took a hammer with a miniature head from his belt. He licked his thumb and—slowly, slowly—marked the hammer's head with his spit. Then he tapped the bomb's side so lightly it hardly made a noise.

"Don't hit it! Oh Jeeeeesus! You'll blow us both to hell!"

"Ain't," Mr. Lightfoot replied as he made small tappings up and down the bomb's side, "plannin' on it." He pressed his ear against the bomb's iron skin. "Uh-huh," he said. "I   hears   you   talkin'." As Mr. Moultry agonized in terrified silence, Mr. Lightfoot's fingers were at work, moving across the bomb as one might stroke a small dog. "Uh-huh." His fingers stopped on a thin seam. "Thass   the way   ta   your heart, ain't it?" He located four screws just below the tail fins, and he lifted the proper screwdriver from its place on his belt like a glacier melting.

"You came here to kill me, didn't you?" Mr. Moultry groaned. He received a punch of insight. "*She* sent you, didn't she? She sent you to kill me!"

"Got," Mr. Lightfoot said as he made the first turn of the first screw, "half   that   right."

Eons later, the final screw fell into Mr. Lightfoot's palm. Mr. Lightfoot had started humming "Frosty, the Snowman," in his somnolent way. Sometime between the removal of the second and third screws, the sound of the detonation mechanism had changed from a tick to a rasp. Mr. Moultry, lying in a stew of sweat, his eyes glassy and his head thrashing back and forth with dementia, had lost five pounds.

Mr. Lightfoot took from his toolbox a small blue jar. He opened it and with the tip of his index finger withdrew some greasy gunk the color of eel's skin. He spat into it, and smeared the gunk onto the seam that circled the bomb. Then he took hold of the tail fins and tried to give them a counterclockwise turn. They resisted. He tried it in the clockwise direction, but that, too, was fruitless.

"Listen here!" Mr. Lightfoot's voice was stern, his brow furrowed with disapproval. "Don't   you   gimme no   sass!" With the miniature hammer he clunked the screw holes, and Mr. Moultry lost another few ounces as his pants suddenly got wet. Then Mr. Lightfoot gripped the tail fins with both hands and pulled.

Slowly, with a thin high *skrreeeeek* of resistance, the bomb's tail section began to slide out. It was hard work, and Mr. Lightfoot had to pause to stretch his cramping fingers. Then he went back to it, with the determination of a sloth gripping a tree branch. At last the tail section came free, and exposed were electronic circuits, a jungle of different-colored wires, and shiny black plastic cylinders that resembled the backs of roaches.

"Hoooowheeee!" Mr. Lightfoot breathed, enchanted. "Ain't it pretty?"

"Killin' me . . ." Mr. Moultry moaned. "Killin' me dead . . ."

The rasping was louder. Mr. Lightfoot used a metal probe to touch a small red box from which the noise emanated. Then he used his finger, and he whistled as he drew the finger back. "Oh-oh," he said. "Gettin' kinda warm."

Mr. Moultry began to blubber, his nose running and the tears trickling from his swollen eyes.

Mr. Lightfoot's fingers were at work again, tracing the wires to their points of origin. The smell of heat rose into the air, which shimmered over the red box. Mr. Lightfoot scratched his chin. "Y'know," he said, "I believe we gots us a problem here."

Mr. Moultry trembled on the edge of coma.

"See, I"—Mr. Lightfoot tapped his chin, his eyes narrowed with concentration—"fix things. I don't break 'em." He drew in a long breath and slowly released it. "Gone have ta do a little breakin', seems ta me." He nodded. "Yessuh. Sure do hate ta break somethin' so pretty." He chose another, larger hammer. "Gone have ta do it." He cracked the hammer down on the red box. Its plastic skin split from one end to the other. Mr. Moultry's teeth gripped his tongue. Mr. Lightfoot removed the two plastic sections and regarded the smaller workings and wires within. "Jus' mysteries in mysteries," he said. He put his hand down into the toolbox and it came out holding a little wire cutter that still had its ninety-nine-cent price sticker on it. "Now, listen good," he told the bomb, "don't you burp in my face, hear?"

"Ohhhhh God, oh Jeeeesus above, oh I'm comin' to heaven, I'm comin'," Mr. Moultry gasped.

"You get there," Mr. Lightfoot said with a faint smile, "you tell St. Peter he's got a fix-it-man on the way." He reached the cutter toward two wires—one black, the other white—that crisscrossed at the heart of the machine.

"*Wait,*" Mr. Moultry whispered. "Wait . . ."

Mr. Lightfoot paused.

"Gotta get it off my soul," Mr. Moultry said, his eyes as bugged as the minstrel's. "Gotta get light, so I can fly to heaven. Listen to me . . ."

"Listenin'," Mr. Lightfoot told him as the bomb spoke on.

"Gerald and me . . . we . . . it was Gerald did the most of it, really . . . I didn't wanna have nothin' to do with it . . . but . . . it's set to go off at . . . ten in the mornin' . . . day after Christmas. Hear me? Ten in the mornin'. It's a box . . . full of dynamite . . . and an alarm clock timer. We paid Biggun Blaylock, and he . . . he got it for us." Mr. Moultry swallowed, perhaps feeling hell's fire under his buns. "It's set to blow up that civil rights museum. We . . . it was all Gerald's idea, really . . . decided to do it when we first heard the Lady was plannin' on buildin' it. Listen to me, Lightfoot!"

"Listenin'," he said slowly and calmly.

"Gerald planted it, somewhere around that museum. Could be in the recreation center. I don't know where it is, I swear to God . . . but it's over there right now, and it's gonna go off at ten in the mornin', day after Christmas."

"That right?" Mr. Lightfoot asked.

"Yes! It's the truth, and God take me to heaven 'cause I've freed my soul!"

"Uh-huh." Mr. Lightfoot reached out. He gripped the black wire with the cutter and *snip*, the black wire was parted. The bomb, however, would not be silenced so easily.

"Do you hear me, Lightfoot? That box of dynamite is over there right this minute!"

Mr. Lightfoot eased the cutter's blades around the white wire. A muscle clenched in his jaw, and sweat sparkled on his cheeks like diamond dust. He said, "No, it ain't."

"Ain't what?"

"Over there. Not no more. Done found it. Gone cut this wire now." His hand trembled. "Might blow if I've cut the wrong wire first."

"God have mercy," Mr. Moultry whined. "Oh Jesus I swear I'll be a good boy every day of my life if you just let me live!"

"I'm cuttin'," Mr. Lightfoot said.

Mr. Moultry squeezed his eyes shut. The cutter went *snip*.

KA-BOOOMMMMM!

In that tremendous roar of destruction and fire, Mr. Moultry screamed.

When his screaming wound down, he heard not the harps of the angels nor the devils singing "For He's a Jolly Good Fellow." He heard: "Heh heh heh   heh."

Mr. Moultry's eyes flew open.

Mr. Lightfoot was grinning. He blew a little flicker of blue flame from the snipped end of the white wire. The bomb was tamed and mute. Mr. Lightfoot spoke in a voice made hoarse by the tremendous yell he'd just yelled into Mr. Moultry's ear. "Beggin'   your pardon,   suh," he said. "Jus'   couldn't   pass   it   up."

Mr. Moultry seemed to deflate, as if he'd been punctured. With a slow hissing sound, he fainted dead away.

5

Sixteen Drops of Blood

I'M BACK.

The time bomb box full of dynamite—with an extra stick thrown in from the gracious hand of Biggun Blaylock—had indeed been found, not long after I had informed the Lady who my dream visitors were. I must've remembered that picture and kept it in the back of my head, and then after the cross-burning and my witnessing Mr. Hargison and Mr. Moultry buy the box from Biggun Blaylock, I must've known subconsciously what the box was. That's why I'd taken to knocking my alarm clock off my bedside table. The only hitch in this theory is that I'd never seen pictures of the girls who'd died at the 16th Street Baptist Church until at the museum. I don't think. Maybe they were in the *Life* magazine. Mom had thrown it out, though, so I can't say for sure.

The Lady put it together as soon as I'd told her. She organized everyone at the reception to start looking for a wooden box either in the recreation center, the civil rights museum, or in the vicinity outside. Nobody could find it, and we tore that place up searching. Then the Lady recalled that Mr. Hargison was a postman. Right outside the center, on the corner of Buckhart Street, was a mailbox. Charles Damaronde held Gavin by his heels as he slid into the mailbox, and we heard his muffled voice say, "Here it is!" He couldn't bring it up, though, because it was too heavy. Sheriff Marchette was called, and he came with Zephyr's postmaster, Mr. Conrad Oatman, who brought the mailbox key. In that box was enough dynamite to blow up the recreation center, the civil rights museum, and two or three houses across the street. Evidently, four hundred dollars was enough to buy a mighty big bang.

Mr. Hargison, knowing what times the mail was picked up and that the mailbox would not be opened again until sometime on the afternoon of December 26th, had set the alarm clock timer for ten on the dot. Sheriff Marchette said the bomb had been constructed by a professional, because you could adjust the timer to either twelve, twenty-four, or forty-eight hours. He told the Lady that he didn't want Mr Hargison or Mr. Moultry to know the bomb had been found yet, not until the innards were dusted for fingerprints. Mom and I had told Dad when we'd gotten home from the recreation center, and I have to say that both he and Sheriff Marchette did a good job of not spilling the beans when they were at Dick Moultry's house and Mr. Hargison walked in. Mr. Moultry's confession turned out to be the icing on the cake, since the time bomb yielded five prints that perfectly matched Mr. Hargison's. So those two were taken off pretty soon to visit the Federal Bureau of Investigation office in Birmingham, and needless to say their names were ticked off the roster of the residents of my hometown.

The civil rights museum had its grand opening. I had no more dreams of the four black girls. But if I ever wanted to see them again, I knew where to go.

The falling of the bomb from a jet plane and the finding of a Ku Klux Klan bomb in a mailbox outside the civil rights museum kept Zephyr buzzing in the days following Christmas. Ben, Johnny, and I debated whether Mr. Lightfoot had ever been really afraid of the bomb or not. Ben said he had been, while Johnny and I took the position that Mr. Lightfoot was like Nemo Curliss; instead of baseball, though, Mr. Lightfoot's natural affinity was to anything mechanical, even a bomb, so when he stared those wires down he knew exactly what he was doing every second. Ben, incidentally, had had an interesting experience in Birmingham. He and his mom and dad had stayed with Ben's uncle Miles, who worked at a downtown bank. Miles had given Ben a tour of the vault, and all Ben could talk about was the smell of money, how green it was and how pretty. He said Miles had actually let him hold a pack of fifty one-hundred-dollar bills, and Ben's fingers were still tingling. Ben announced that he didn't know what he was going to do in this life, but as far as possible it was going to involve lots and lots of money. Johnny and I just laughed at him. We missed Davy Ray, because we knew what his comment would've been.

Johnny had asked for and received two Christmas presents. One was a policeman's kit, complete with honorary badge, fingerprint powder, handcuffs, burglar dust that got on the shoes of burglars and only showed up under ultraviolet light, and a policeman's handbook. The other was a wooden display case with little shelves in it, to show his arrowhead collection. He filled it up except for one shelf, which was reserved for a certain smooth black arrowhead if Chief Five Thunders ever decided to give it up again.

A question remained about Mr. Lightfoot and the bomb. Mom voiced it two nights after Christmas, as a cold rain fell on Zephyr.

"Tom?" she said. We were all sitting in the front room, with the fireplace blazing. You couldn't have pried *The Golden Apples of the Sun* out of my hands with a crowbar. "What made Mr. Lightfoot go to Dick Moultry's house, anyway? I wouldn't have thought that was somethin' he might've volunteered to do."

Dad didn't answer.

Just as parents have sixth senses about their children, so, too, do children about their parents. I lowered my book. Dad continued to read the newspaper.

"Tom? Do you know what made Mr. Lightfoot do it?"

He cleared his throat. "Kind of," he said quietly.

"Well, what was it?"

"I guess . . . I had somethin' to do with it."

"*You* did? How?"

He lowered the paper, realizing there was no way out but the truth. "I . . . asked the Lady for help."

Mom sat in stunned silence. Rain struck the windows and the fireplace log popped, and still she didn't budge.

"I figured she was the only chance Dick had. After what she did with Biggun Blaylock's ammo bag . . . I thought she could help him. And I was right, it appears. She called Marcus Lightfoot while I was there at her house."

"Her *house?* I can't believe this! You went to the Lady's house?"

"Not just to it. Inside it. I sat down in her chair. I drank a cup of her coffee." He shrugged. "I suppose I was expectin' shrunken heads on the walls and black widow spiders in every corner. I didn't know she was *religious*."

"To the Lady's house," Mom said. "I just can't believe it! And after all this time when you were so afraid of her!"

"I wasn't afraid of her," Dad corrected Mom. "I was just . . . a little skittish, that's all."

"And she said she'd help Dick Moultry? Even when she knew he'd had a hand in settin' that time bomb?"

"Well . . . it wasn't quite that simple," my father admitted.

"Oh?" Mom waited. When Dad offered no more information, Mom said, "I'd like to hear it."

"She made me promise to come back. She said she could look at me and tell I was bein' eaten up alive. She said it showed in your face and in Cory's, too. She said we were all livin' under the strain of that dead man at the bottom of Saxon's Lake." Dad put the newspaper down and watched the fire. "And you know what?

She's right. I promised to go back to see her tomorrow evenin'
at seven o'clock. I was gonna tell you, eventually. Or maybe I
wasn't, I don't know."

"Pride, pride," Mom scolded him. "You mean to tell me you
did for Dick Moultry what you wouldn't do for *me?*"

"No. It's just that I wasn't ready. Dick needed help. I found
it for him. And now I'm ready to find it for myself and both of
you, too."

Mom got up from her chair. She stood behind my father, and
she put her hands on his shoulders and leaned her chin against his
head. I watched their shadows merge. He reached up and put his
arm around her neck. They stayed that way for a moment, heart-
close, as the fire cracked and sizzled.

It was time to go see the Lady.

When we arrived at her house at ten minutes before seven
o'clock, Mr. Damaronde answered the door. Dad had no qualms
about crossing the threshold; his fear of the Lady was gone. The
Moon Man came out, clad in his robe and slippers, and offered us
some pretzels. Mrs. Damaronde put on a pot of coffee—the New
Orleans kind with chicory, she said—and we waited in the front
room until the Lady was ready to see us.

I was keeping my suspicions about Dr. Lezander to myself.
I still couldn't let my heart believe that Dr. Lezander, who had
always been so kind and gentle to Rebel, might be a murderer. I
had the connection of the two parrots, but there was nothing to
connect Dr. Lezander with the dead man except a green feather,
and that was just my theory. So he didn't like milk and he was a
night owl; did that make him a killer? Before I told my parents, I
would need something more solid to go on.

We didn't have to wait very long. Mr. Damaronde asked us
to come back with him, and he led us not to the Lady's bedroom
but to another room across the hallway. In it, the Lady was sitting
in a high-backed chair behind a folding card table. She wore not
a voodoo robe or a wizard's cap, but just a plain dark gray dress
with a lapel pin in the shape of a dancing harlequin. On the floor

of what was obviously her consultation room was a rug of woven reeds, and a crooked tree grew from a big clay pot in the corner. The walls were painted beige and unadorned. Mr. Damaronde closed the door and the Lady said, "Sit down, Tom."

Dad obeyed. I could tell he was nervous, because I could hear his throat click when he swallowed. He flinched a little when the Lady reached down beside her chair and brought up a doctor's bag. She placed it on the table and unzipped it.

"Is this gonna hurt?" Dad asked.

"It might. Depends."

"On what?"

"How deep we have to cut to get at the truth," she answered. She reached into the bag and brought out something wrapped up in blue cloth. Then a silver filigreed box came out, followed by a deck of cards. She brought out a sheet of typing paper. In the overhead light I saw the Nifty watermark; it was the same brand of paper I used. Last out of the bag was a pill bottle containing three polished river pebbles: one ebony, one reddish-brown, one white with gray bands. She said, "Open your right hand," and when Dad did she unscrewed the pill bottle's cap and shook the river pebbles into his palm. "Work those in your hand awhile," she directed.

Dad gave a nervous smile as he did as she asked. "Did these come from Old Moses's stomach or somethin'?"

"No. They're just old pebbles I found. Keep workin' 'em, they'll calm you down."

"Oh," Dad said, rolling the worry-pebbles around and around in his palm.

Mom and I stood to one side, to give the Lady plenty of room to do what she was going to do. Whatever that might be. I don't know what I expected. Maybe one of those torchlit ceremonies with people dancing around in circles and hollering. But it wasn't like that at all. The Lady began to shuffle the cards, and the way she did it I suspected she might have given lessons to Maverick. "Tell me about your dreams, Tom," she said as the cards made a rhythmic *whirring* noise between her supple fingers.

Dad glanced uneasily at us. "Do you want them to go?" the Lady asked, but he shook his head. "I dream," he began, "about watchin' the car go into Saxon's Lake. Then I'm in the water with it, and I'm lookin' through the window at the dead man. His face . . . all smashed up. The handcuff on his wrist. The piano wire around his throat. And as the car's goin' down and the water starts floodin' in he—" Dad had to pause a minute. The pebbles clicked together in his palm. "He looks at me and he grins. That awful, smashed face grins. And when he speaks it's like . . . mud gurglin'."

"What does he say?"

"He says . . . 'Come with me, down in the dark.'" Dad's face was a study in pain, and it hurt me to look at it. "That's what he says. 'Come with me, down in the dark.' And he reaches for me, with his hand that isn't shackled. He reaches for me, and I pull back because I'm terrified he's gonna touch me. Then it ends."

"You have other recurrin' dreams?"

"A few. Not as strong as that one, though. Sometimes I think I hear piano music. Sometimes I think I hear somebody hollerin', but it sounds like gibberish. Occasionally I see a pair of hands holdin' that wire, and what looks like a thick wooden baton wrapped up with black tape. There are faces in there that are all blurred up, as if I'm lookin' at 'em through blood or my eyes can hardly hold a focus. But I don't have those nearly as much as the one about the man in the car."

"Did Rebecca tell you that I'm pickin' up some of those snippets, too?" She continued to shuffle the cards. It was a hypnotic, soothing sound. "I hear bits of piano music, the hollerin', and I see the wire and the crackerknocker. I've seen the tattoo, but not the rest of him." She smiled faintly. "You and me are plugged into the same socket, Tom, but you're gettin' more juice than I am. Can you beat that?"

"I thought you were supposed to be the mystic," Dad said.

"I am. Supposed to be. But everybody's got the dream-eyes, Tom. Everybody sees snippets of some quilt or another. You're real close to this one. Closer than I am. That's why."

Dad worked the river pebbles. The Lady shuffled her cards and waited.

"At first," he said, "I was havin' those dreams right when I went to bed. Then later on . . . they started comin' on me when I wasn't even asleep. Durin' the day. I just have a flash of that car, and that man's face, and I hear him callin'. He says the same thing, over and over: 'Come with me, down in the dark.' I hear that mud-gurglin' voice, and I've . . . I've come close to goin' to pieces over it, because I can't shake it. I can't get any rest. It's like I'm up all night, too scared to let myself sleep for fear of . . ." He trailed off.

"Yes?" the Lady prodded.

"For fear of . . . listenin' to that dead man, and doin' what he wants me to do."

"And what might that be, Tom?"

"I think he wants me to kill myself," Dad said.

The card shuffling ceased. Mom's hand found mine and clenched it hard.

"I think he . . . wants me to come to that lake and drown myself in it. I think he wants me to come with him, down in the dark."

The Lady watched him intently, her emerald eyes gathering light. "Why would he want you to do that, Tom?"

"I don't know. Maybe he wants company." He tried for a smile, but his mouth wouldn't work.

"I want you to think very, very carefully. Are those the exact words?"

"Yeah. 'Come with me, down in the dark.' He says it kinda gurgly, because I guess his jaw's busted or there's blood or water or mud in his mouth, but . . . yeah, that's it."

"Nothin' else? Does he call you by name?"

"No. That's all."

"You know, that's funny, don't you think?" the Lady asked.

Dad grunted. "I wish I knew what was so funny about it!"

"This: If the dead man has a chance to speak to you—to give

you a message—then why does he waste it on askin' you to commit suicide? Why doesn't he tell you who killed him?"

Dad blinked. Now the clickings of the pebbles stopped. "I . . . never thought about that."

"Think about it, then. The dead man has a voice, however torn up it is. Why doesn't he tell you the name of his killer?"

"I can't say. Seems he would if he could."

"He could." The Lady nodded. "If he was speakin' to *you,* that is."

"I'm not followin' you."

"Maybe," she said, "there are three plugs in that socket."

Realization crawled over Dad's face. Over mine and Mom's, too.

"The dead man isn't speakin' to you, Tom," the Lady said. "He's speakin' to his killer."

"You . . . mean I'm . . ."

"Pickin' up the killer's dreams, like I'm pickin' up yours. Oh, mercy! You've got some *strong* dream-eyes, Tom!"

"He doesn't . . . want me to . . . *kill* myself because I couldn't get him out?"

"No," the Lady said. "Of that I'm sure."

Dad pressed his free hand to his mouth. Tears blurred his eyes, and I heard Mom sob beside me at the sight. He leaned his head forward. A single tear dropped to the table.

"Cuttin' deep," the Lady said, and she put a hand on his forearm. "It's a good hurt, though, isn't it? Like cuttin' away a cancer."

"Yes." His voice cracked. "Yes."

"You want to go outside and walk around a bit, you go right ahead."

Dad's shoulders trembled. But the burden was leaving him, ton by ton. He drew a deep, gasping breath, like the breath of someone whose head has just broken the surface of dark water. "I'm all right," he said, but he didn't lift his face up just yet. "Give me a minute."

"All the minutes you need, take 'em."

At last he looked up. He was still the man he'd been a moment before; his face was still lined, his chin a little saggy. But in his eyes he was a boy again, and he was free.

"You interested in tryin' to find out who that killer might be?" the Lady asked.

Dad nodded.

"I've got my own host of friends across the river. You get to be my age, you've got more of 'em on that side than this. They see things, and sometimes they tell me. But they like to play games with me. They like to throw me a riddle or two. So they never come right out and answer any question directly; it's always a sly answer, but it's always the truth. You want to involve them in this matter?" It sounded like a question she was used to asking.

"I guess I do."

"Either do or not, no damn guessin' about it."

After the least bit of hesitation, my father said, "I do."

The Lady opened the silver filigreed box and shook six small bones out on the table. "Put down the pebbles," she said. "Pick up those in your right hand."

Dad looked distastefully at what lay before him. "Do I have to?"

The Lady paused. Then she sighed and said, "Naw. It's a mood-setter, is all." She used the edge of her hand to sweep the bones back into the silver box. She closed it and set it aside. Then she reached into the doctor's bag again. This time her hand came out with a small bottle of clear liquid and a plastic bag full of cotton swabs. She set these between them and opened the bottle. "You'll have to put the pebbles down, though. Hold out your index finger."

"Why?"

"Because I said so."

He did it. The Lady opened the bottle and upturned it over one of the cotton swabs. Then she dabbed the tip of Dad's index finger. "Alcohol," she explained. "Get it from Dr. Parrish." She

spread the Nifty typing paper down on the table. Then she un-
wrapped the object in the blue cloth. It was a stick with two
needles driven through one end. "Keep your finger still," she told
him as she picked up the needled stick.

"What're you gonna do? You're not gonna jab me with those,
are—"

The needles came down fast and rather roughly into the tip
of Dad's finger. "Ouch!" he said. I, too, had winced, my index
finger stinging with phantom pain. Instantly blood began to well
up from the needle holes. "Keep your blood off that paper," the
Lady told him. Working quickly, she dabbed alcohol on the index
finger of her own right hand and with her left she whacked the
needles down. Her blood was drawn, too. She said, "Ask your
question. Not aloud, but in your mind. Ask it clearly. Ask it like
you expect an answer. Go ahead."

"All right," Dad said after a few seconds. "What now?"

"What was the date that car went into Saxon's Lake?"

"March sixteenth."

"Squeeze eight drops of blood on the center of the paper.
Don't be stingy. Eight drops. Not one more and not one less."

Dad squeezed his finger, and the blood began dripping. The
Lady added eight drops of her own red blood to the white paper.
Dad said, "Good thing it didn't happen on the thirty-first."

"Take the paper in your left hand and crumple it up with the
blood inside it," the Lady instructed him, ignoring his witticism.
Dad did as she said. "Hold it and repeat the question aloud."

"Who killed that man at the bottom of Saxon's Lake?"

"Hold it tight," the Lady told him, and she pressed another
cotton swab to her bleeding finger.

"Are your friends here right this minute?" Dad asked, his left
fist around the crumpled-up paper.

"We'll soon find out, won't we?" She held out her left palm.
"Give it to me." When it was lodged there, she said sternly to the
air, "Don't ya'll show me up to be a fool, now. This is an important question, and it deserves an answer. Not no riddle, neither.

An answer we can figure out. Ya'll gone help us, or not?" She waited perhaps fifteen more seconds. Then she placed the crumpled paper in the middle of the table. "Open it," she said.

Dad took it. As he began to uncrumple it, my heart was slamming. If *Dr. Lezander* was scrawled there in blood, I was going to split my skin.

When the paper was open, Mom and I peered over his shoulder. There was a great big blotch of blood in the middle of the paper and other blotches all around it. I couldn't see a name in that mess to save my life. Then the Lady took a pencil from her bag and studied the paper for a moment, after which she began to play connect-the-blotches.

"I don't see a thing," Dad said.

"Have faith," she told him. I watched the pencil's tip at work, moving between the blood. I watched a long, curvy line swing out and in.

And suddenly I realized I was looking at a 3.

The pencil's tip kept moving. Curving again. Out and in, out and in.

A second 3. And then the pencil's tip ran out of blood blotches to connect.

"That's it," the Lady said. She frowned. "Two threes."

"That's sure not a name, is it?" Dad asked.

"They've riddled me again, is what they've done. I swear, I wish they'd make somethin' *easy* every once in a while!" She thunked the pencil down in disgust. "Well, that's all there's gonna be."

"That's *it?*" Dad sucked at his wounded finger. "You're sure you did this right?"

Words cannot describe the look she gave him. "Two threes," she said. "That's the answer. Three three. Maybe thirty-three. If we can figure out what that means, we'll have the killer's name."

"I can't think of anybody who has three letters in their first and last name. Or maybe it's an address?"

"I don't know. All I know is what I'm lookin' at: three three."

She slid the paper toward him; it was his to keep for his pain and trouble. "That's all I can do for you. Sorry there's nothin' more."

"I am, too," Dad said, and he took the paper and stood up.

Then the Lady removed her professional face and became sociable. She said she smelled the fresh coffee, and that there was chocolate roulage made by Mrs. Pearl from the Bake Shoppe. Dad, who had been eating like a bird before we came to the Lady's, ate two whopping pieces of roulage and washed them down with two cups of hot black chicory coffee. He and the Moon Man talked about that day the Blaylocks had been routed at the Trailways bus stop, and Dad laughed at the memory of Biggun running from a bag full of garden snakes.

My father was well and truly returned. Maybe even better than he was before.

"Thank you," Dad said to the Lady as we stood at the door ready to leave. Mom took her hand and kissed her ebony cheek. The Lady regarded me with her shining emerald eyes. "You still gone be a writer?" she asked me.

"I don't know," I said.

"Seems to me a writer gets to hold a lot of keys," she said. "Gets to visit a lot of worlds and live in a lot of skins. Seems to me a writer has a chance to live forever, if he's good and if he's lucky. Would you like that, Cory? Would you like to live forever?"

I thought about it. Forever, like heaven, was an awfully long time. "No ma'am," I decided. "I think I might get tired."

"Well," she said, and she placed a hand on my shoulder, "it seems to me a writer's voice is a forever thing. Even if a boy and a man are not." She leaned her face closer to mine. I could feel the heat of her life, like the sun glowing from her bones. "You're gonna be kissed by a lot of girls," she said. "Gonna kiss a lot of girls, too. But remember this." She kissed me, very lightly, on the forehead. "Remember when you do all that kissin' of girls and women in all the summers left ahead of you that you were first kissed"—her ancient, beautiful face smiled—"by a lady."

When we got home, Dad sat down with the telephone book

and scanned the names, looking for the address "thirty-three." There were two residents and a business: Phillip Caldwell at 33 Ridgeton Street, J. E. Grayson at 33 Deerman Street, and the Crafts Barn at 33 Merchants Street. Dad said Mr. Grayson went to our church, and that he was nearing ninety. He believed Phillip Caldwell was a salesman at the Western Auto in Union Town. The Crafts Barn, Mom knew, was run by a blue-haired woman named Edna Hathaway. She seriously doubted if Mrs. Hathaway, who went around supported by a walker, had had anything to do with the incident at Saxon's Lake. Dad decided Mr. Caldwell's house was worth a visit, and he planned to go early in the morning before Mr. Caldwell left for work.

A mystery could always get me out of bed. I was up bright-eyed by the time the clock showed seven, and Dad said I could go with him but I wasn't to say a word while he was talking to Mr. Caldwell.

On the drive over, Dad said he hoped I understood he might have to tell Mr. Caldwell a white lie. I feigned shock and dismay at this, but my own count of white lies had been on the heavy side lately so I couldn't really be disappointed in him. Anyway, it was for the right cause.

Mr. Caldwell's red brick house, four blocks past the gas station, was small and unremarkable. We left the pickup truck at the curb and I followed Dad to the front door. He pressed the buzzer and we waited. The door was opened by a middle-aged woman with jowly cheeks and sleepy eyes. She was still wearing her quilted pink robe. "Is Mr. Caldwell at home, please?" Dad asked.

"Phillip!" she called into the house. "Philllleeeeup!" She had a voice like a buzz saw at high pitch.

In another moment a gray-haired man wearing a bow tie, brown slacks, and a rust-colored sweater came to the door. "Yes?"

"Hi, I'm Tom Mackenson." Dad offered his hand. Mr. Caldwell shook it. "Aren't you the fella who works at the Western Auto in Union Town? Rick Spanner's brother-in-law?"

"That's right. Do you know Rick?"

"Used to work with him at Green Meadows. How's he doin'?"

"Better, now that he found a job. Had to move to Birmingham, though. I pity him, I wouldn't care for the big city myself."

"Me neither. Well, the reason I dropped by so early and all is . . . I lost my job at the dairy, too." Dad smiled tightly. "I'm workin' at Big Paul's Pantry now."

"Been there. Big ol' place."

"Yes, it is. A little too big for me. I was just wonderin' . . . uh . . . if . . . uh . . ." Even a white lie stuck in his craw. "If there were any jobs to be had at the Western Auto."

"No, not that I know of. We hired a new fella last month." He frowned. "How come you just didn't go by there and ask?"

Dad shrugged. "Thought I might save myself the gas, I suppose."

"You ought to go by and fill out an application. You never know what'll come up. The manager's name is Mr. Addison."

"Thank you, I might do that."

Mr. Caldwell nodded. Dad didn't retreat from the door. "Anythin' else I can do for you?"

Dad's eyes were searching the man's face. Mr. Caldwell lifted his eyebrows, waiting. "No," Dad said, and I heard in his voice that his answer had not been found. "I don't think so. Thanks anyway."

"All right. You come on by and fill out an application, Mr. Addison'll keep it on file."

"Okay, I'll remember that."

Back in the truck, Dad started the engine and said, "I believe that was a strikeout, don't you?"

"Yes sir." I had been trying to figure out what the numbers 3 and 3 might have to do with Dr. Lezander, but I, too, was coming up empty.

So was the truck. "Uh-oh!" Dad glanced at the gas gauge. "I'd better stop in and filllleeeeeup! Don't you think?" He smiled, and I returned it.

At the station, Mr. Hiram White shambled out of his cathedral of engine belts and radiators and started pumping the gas in. "Pretty day," Mr. White commented, looking up at the blue sky. It had gotten cold again, though; January was champing at its bit like an eager horse.

"Yes, it is," Dad agreed, leaning against the truck.

"Ain't gone be no gunplay today, is there?"

"I don't think so."

Mr. White grinned. "I swear, that was more excitin' than television!"

"I'm just thankful nobody got killed."

"Good thing the bus didn't come in while all that shootin' was goin' on, there would've been some dead bodies to sweep up."

"Right as rain."

"You heard about the bus gettin' hit by that monster out on Route Ten, didn't you?"

"Sure did." Dad checked his watch.

"'Bout knocked it off its wheels. You know Cornelius McGraw, been drivin' ol' thirty-three for eight years?"

"I don't know him personally."

"Well, he told me that monster was as big as a bulldozer. Said it ran like a deer, too. Said he tried to swerve, but it hit 'em broadside and he said the whole bus 'bout shook itself to pieces. Had to retire the bus is what they had to do."

"Is that right?"

"Sure is." Mr. White finished the job and pulled the nozzle from the truck's gas port. He wiped the end with a cloth so no drop of gas would mar the pickup's paint. "New bus has the route, but Corny's still drivin' it. Still number thirty-three, too, so things don't change so much, do they?"

"I don't know about that," Dad said, and paid him.

"Ya'll take care, now!" Mr. White told us as we drove away.

We were halfway home when Dad said, "I guess I'd better check the phone book again. Maybe I missed somethin'." He glanced at me, then back to the unwinding street. "I was wrong about the Lady, Cory. She's not evil, is she?"

"No sir."

"I'm glad I went. I feel lighter now, knowin' that man isn't callin' for me. I feel sorry for whoever he *is* callin', though. Poor devil must have a hell of a time sleepin', if he sleeps at all."

He's a night owl, I thought. It was time. "Dad?" I said. "I think I know who—"

"God have mercy!" Dad suddenly shouted, and he hit the brake so hard the pickup slewed around and went up onto somebody's lawn. The engine shuddered and died. "Did you hear what Mr. White said?" Dad's voice quavered with excitement. "Thirty-three! Ol' thirty-three, he said!"

"Sir?"

"The Trailways bus, Cory! It's number thirty-three! I was standin' right there listenin' to him, and I hardly heard it! You think that could be what those numbers mean?"

I was honored that he was asking my opinion, but I had to say, "I don't know."

"Well, the killer couldn't be Cornelius McGraw. He doesn't even live around here. But what would the bus have to do with whoever killed that man in Saxon's Lake?" He started puzzling it over, his hands clenched hard around the steering wheel. Then a woman holding a broom came out on her porch and started hollering at us to move the truck before she called the sheriff, so we had to go.

We returned to the gas station. Mr. White emerged again. "Sure went through that tank in a hurry, didn't ya?" he asked. Dad wasn't interested in filling up anything but his curiosity, though. When was number thirty-three due back in again? he asked Mr. White, and Mr. White said the next day around noon.

Dad said he'd be there.

Maybe he was wrong, he told Mom that night at dinner, but he was going to be at that gas station waiting for the bus at noon. It wasn't Cornelius McGraw he would be there to see, but he would be watching to find out who the bus brought to Zephyr or who it took away.

I was there with him as noon approached. Mr. White was driving us crazy talking about how hard it was to find good GoJo to clean the grease off your hands anymore. Then Dad said, "Here it comes, Cory," and he walked from cold shadow into crisp sunlight to meet it.

The Trailways bus, with number 33 on the plate above its windshield, swept on past without even slowing, though Mr. McGraw honked the horn and Mr. White waved.

Dad watched it go. But he turned to Mr. White again, and I saw by the set of his jaw that now my father was a man with a mission. "Bus come back through day after tomorrow, Hiram?"

"Sure does. Twelve noon, same as always."

Dad lifted a finger and tapped it against his lips, his eyes narrowed. I knew what he was thinking. How was he going to meet the bus on the days he had to work at Big Paul's Pantry?

"Hiram," he said at last, "you need any help around here?"

"Well . . . I don't know if I—"

"I'll take a dollar an hour," Dad said. "I'll pump the gas, I'll clean the garage, I'll do whatever you ask me to do. You want me to work overtime, that's fine. A dollar an hour. How about it?"

Mr. White grunted and stared at the cluttered garage. "I reckon I do need some stuff inventoried. Brake shoes, gaskets, radiator hoses, and such. And I could use another strong back." This from Quasimodo of the Belts. He stuck out his hand. "Got a job, if you want it. Startin' six in the mornin', if that's all right?"

"I'll be here," Dad said, grasping Mr. White's hand.

My father was nothing if not resourceful.

The bus passed through once more without even a hiss of brakes. But it was due again, twelve noon, same as always, and my dad would be there.

New Year's Eve came, and we watched on television the festivities in Times Square. At the stroke of midnight, someone shot off fireworks over Zephyr, the church bells rang, and horns honked.

It had become 1965. On New Year's Day we ate black-eyed peas to bring us silver, and collard greens to bring us gold, and we watched football games until our south ends were sore. Dad sat in his chair with a notepad on his lap, and though he hollered for his teams he was scribbling 33 . . . 33 . . . 33 into an interlocking mosaic of numbers with his ball-point pen. Mom chided him to put down that pen and relax, and he did for a little while but soon his fingers found it again. I could tell by the way she looked at him that she was getting worried about him once more; ol' number thirty-three was becoming as much an obsession as the bad dream had ever been. He was still having that dream, of course, but he knew the dead man was not calling him and that made a big difference. I suppose, though, that in my father's case it took one obsession to break another.

Ben, Johnny, and I and the rest of the childish generation returned to school. In my class, I discovered we had a new teacher. Her name was Miss Fontaine, and she was as young and pretty as spring. Beyond the windows, though, winter was starting to rage.

Every other day, near noon, my father would step outside the gas station's office into chilly wind or blowing sleet or cold pale sun. He would watch the Trailways bus—ol' number thirty-three with Cornelius McGraw at the wheel—as it approached, his heart beginning to pound.

But it didn't stop. Not once. It always kept going, bound for somewhere else.

Then Dad would return to the office, where he was likely to be playing dominoes with Mr. White, and he would sit down in a creaky chair and wait for the next move.

6

The Stranger Among Us

J ANUARY ADVANCED, cold as the tomb.

At eleven o'clock on the morning of Saturday, the six-teenth, I said good-bye to Mom and left home on Rocket to meet Ben and Johnny at the Lyric. The sky was plated with clouds, the threat of freezing rain in the air. I was bundled up like an Eskimo, but I'd soon be shedding my coat and gloves. The movie for today was called *Hell Is for Heroes,* the poster of which showed the sweat-ing faces of American soldiers crouched down behind machine gun and bazooka, awaiting the enemy attack. To accompany this carnage, there would be a program of Daffy Duck cartoons and the next chapter of *Fighting Men of Mars.* The last chapter had ended with the Fighting Men about to be crushed by a falling boulder at the bottom of a Martian mine shaft. I'd already plotted out their escape; they would scramble into a previously hidden tunnel at the very last second, thus escaping a flattening fate.

On my way to the theater, I myself took a fateful turn.

I pedaled to Dr. Lezander's house.

I hadn't seen him at church since Christmas Eve. Since I'd called him "Birdman," and looked him in his eyes of stone. I was beginning to wonder if he and Mrs. Lezander hadn't flown the coop. Several times I'd started to tell Dad my suspicions, but he had thirty-three on his mind and I had nothing but a green feather and two dead parrots. I stopped Rocket at the bottom of the driveway and sat there watching the house. It was dark. Empty? I wondered. Had the doctor and his wife cleared out in the dead of night, alerted by whatever it was I might know? I kept watch; there was no sign of light or life. The heroes and the fighting men could wait. I had to find out, and I began to pedal Rocket up the driveway to the house. I went around back. The PLEASE LEASH YOUR PETS sign was still up. I eased Rocket down on the kickstand and peered into the nearest window.

Dark upon dark. At first I saw only shapes of furniture, but as my eyes grew used to the gloom I was able to make out the twelve ceramic birds perched atop the piano. It was the den where the birdcages were. Dr. Lezander's office was below, closer to hell. I couldn't help but see Mrs. Lezander sitting at that piano, playing "Beautiful Dreamer" over and over again as the green and the blue parrots flapped wildly in their cages and shouted curses came up through the air vent. But why were the curses in German?

Lights hit me. My heart hammered; I felt like a prisoner in a jailbreak movie, caught by the roaming circle. I twisted around, and there were a car's headlights as the car pulled up to the back porch. It was a late-model steel-gray Buick with a chrome radiator that resembled a grinning mouthful of silver teeth; the doctor's work was well paid. I made a move toward Rocket, but it was too late to get the kickstand up before I heard a voice say "Who is that?" Mrs. Lezander got out, her bulk made bearish in a brown overcoat. She must've recognized my bike, because my collar was turned up. "Cory?"

I was caught. Easy, I thought. Just take it easy. "Yes ma'am," I answered. "It's me."

"This is providential," she said. "Will you help me, please?" She went around to the passenger side and opened the door. "I've got some groceries."

Rocket might have whispered to me in that second. Rocket might have said in a silken, urgent voice *Get away, Cory. Get away while you still can. I'll take you, if you'll just hang on.*

"Help me, please?" Mrs. Lezander hefted the first of a half-dozen burdened paper bags. On all of them, printed in red letters, was Big Paul's Pantry.

"I'm goin' to the movies," I said.

"It'll just take a minute."

What could be done to me in broad daylight? I took the bag. Mrs. Lezander, a second bag under one arm, slid her key into the back door's lock. A gust of wind blew around us, and I saw the folds of her overcoat move and I knew she had been the figure I saw standing at the edge of the woods.

"Go on," she said, "the door's open."

With Mrs. Lezander hulking at my back and a boulder of fear in my throat, I walked across the threshold as if into a mine shaft.

"Ten points," Mr. White said as he plunked down another domino.

"And ten," Dad said, his own domino going down at the end of the L-shaped pattern.

"I swear I didn't think you had that one!" Mr. White shook his head. "Tricky fella, ain't you?"

"I try my best."

There was a tapping sound. Mr. White peered out the window. The clouds had darkened, the gas station's light splashed across the concrete. Little flecks of sleet were striking the glass. Dad took the opportunity for a glance at the clock on the wall, which showed twelve minutes before noon. "All right, where was I?" Mr. White rubbed his chin and pondered his dominoes like a hunchbacked sphinx. "Here we go!" he said, and reached for one. "Just mark down fifteen points in my fa—"

Something hissed.

Dad turned his head to the left.

The Trailways bus was pulling in.

"—vor," Mr. White finished. "How do, how do! Look who's early this fine day!"

Dad was already on his feet. He walked past the cash register and the shelves of oil and gasoline additives toward the door. "Must've caught a tailwind!" Mr. White said. "Probably caught sight of that monster out on Route Ten, and Corny gave it the lead foot!"

Dad walked out into the cold. The bus pulled to a halt beneath the yellow TRAILWAYS BUS sign. The doors folded outward with a breath of hydraulics. "Watch your step, gents!" Dad heard the driver say.

Two men were getting off. Sleet hit Dad in the face and the wind whirled around him, but he stood his ground. One of the men looked to be in his sixties, the other half those years. The older man, who wore a tweed overcoat and a brown hat, carried a suitcase. The younger, dressed in blue jeans and a beige jacket, carried a duffel bag. "Enjoy your stay, Mr. Steiner!" Corny McGraw said, and the older man lifted a gloved hand and waggled the fingers. Hiram White, who'd come out of the office behind Dad, said, "Howdy" to the two men, and then he looked up the steps at Mr. McGraw. "Hey, Corny! You want some hot coffee?"

"No, I'm gettin' on down the road, Hiram. My sister Jenny had her baby this mornin', and as soon as I finish my route I can go see her. Third young'un, but first boy. Bring you a cigar next time 'round."

"I'll get a match ready. You be careful, Uncle Corny!"

"Ta-ta, ya'll," he said. The doors closed, the bus pulled away, and the two strangers stood facing my father.

The older one, Mr. Steiner, had a wrinkled face but a chin like a slab of granite. He was wearing glasses, flecks of sleet on the lenses. "Sir? Pardon me," he said with a foreign accent. "Is there a hotel?"

"Boardin'house will do," the younger one said; he had thinning blond hair and a flat midwestern brogue.

"No hotel in town," Dad said. "No boardin'house, either. We don't get a lot of visitors here."

"Oh my." Mr. Steiner frowned. "Where's the nearest hotel, then?"

"There's a motel in Union Town. The Union Pines. It's—" He stopped, his arm rising to point the way. "You fellas need a ride?"

"That would be very nice, thank you. Mr. . . . ?"

"Tom Mackenson." He shook the gloved hand. The man's grip jammed his knuckles.

"Jacob Steiner," the older man said. "This is my friend, Lee Hannaford."

"Pleased to meet the both of you," Dad said.

The sixth bag was the heaviest. It was full of dog-food cans. "That goes downstairs," Mrs. Lezander said as she put other canned goods into the cupboard. "Just set it on the counter, I'll take it myself."

"Yes ma'am."

The lights were on in the kitchen. Mrs. Lezander had shed her overcoat, and beneath it she wore a somber gray dress. She took a jar of Folger's instant coffee out of the fourth sack and opened it with a slight wrist-twist. "May I ask," she said, her broad back to me, "why you were looking in the window?"

"I . . . uh . . ." Think fast! I told myself. "I thought I'd drop by because . . . uh . . ."

Mrs. Lezander turned around and watched me, her eyes flat and impassive.

"Because . . . I wanted to ask Dr. Lezander if he . . . like . . . needed some help in the afternoons. I thought maybe I could clean up downstairs, or sweep, or—" I shrugged. "Whatever."

A hand grasped my shoulder from behind.

I almost cried out. I came very close to it. As it was, I felt my face freeze as the blood left it.

Dr. Lezander said, "An ambitious young man. Isn't that right, Veronica?"

"Yes, Frans." She turned away from me and continued putting the groceries up.

He released me. I looked at him. He obviously had just awakened; his eyes were sleep-swollen, the hairs had come out in a grizzle around his neatly trimmed chin beard, and he was wearing a red silk robe over pajamas. He yawned and stifled it with the same hand that had just been on my shoulder. "Coffee, please, dearest," he said. "The blacker the better."

She began to spoon coffee into a cup that had the picture of a collie on it. Then, that task done, she turned on the hot water faucet.

"I heard East Berlin this morning around four," he told her. "A wonderful orchestra was playing Wagner."

Mrs. Lezander filled the collie cup full of steaming water and stirred it. She handed the ebony coffee to her husband, who first inhaled its aroma. "Ahhhhhh, yes!" he said. "This should do the trick!" He took a little slurpy sip. "Good and strong!" he said, satisfied.

"I'd better be goin' now." I edged toward the back door. "Ben Sears and Johnny Wilson are waitin' for me at the Lyric."

"I thought you wanted to ask me about an afternoon job."

"Well . . . I'd better go."

"Oh, nonsense." He reached out again, and his hand found my shoulder. He had iron in his fingers. "I'd be pleased and happy to have you come by and help in the afternoons, Cory. As a matter of truth, I've been looking for a young apprentice."

"Really?" I didn't know what else to say.

"Really." He smiled with his mouth. His eyes were careful. "You're a smart young man, aren't you?"

"Sir?"

"A smart young man. Oh, don't be so modest! You pursue things, don't you? You grip a fact and shake it like a . . . like a terrier." His mouth smiled again, and the silver tooth sparkled. He took a longer sip of coffee.

"I don't know what you mean." I heard my voice tremble, the slightest bit.

"I admire that quality in you, Cory. The terrier determination to get to the root of things. That's a fine quality for a boy to have."

"His bicycle's outside, Frans," Mrs. Lezander said as she put away packs of Rice-A-Roni, the San Francisco treat.

"Bring it in, will you?"

"I've gotta go," I said, and now the fear had started choking me.

"Non"—he answered, smiling—"sense. If we have a freezing rain—and it certainly looks grim out there today—you don't want that fine bicycle of yours to be covered with ice, do you?"

"I . . . really have to—"

"I'll bring it in," Mrs. Lezander said, and she went outside. I watched, Dr. Lezander's hand on my shoulder, as the woman pushed Rocket across the threshold and into the den.

"Very good," Dr. Lezander said. He drank some more coffee. "Better safe than sorry, yes?"

Mrs. Lezander returned, sucking her left thumb. She brought it from her mouth to show blood on it. "Look at this, Frans. I cut myself on his bicycle." She said it with an almost clinical detachment. The thumb returned to her mouth. There was blood on her lower lip.

"While you're here, Cory, it seems to me you should see what your job would entail. Don't you agree?"

"Ben and Johnny . . . they're gonna miss me," I said.

"Yes, they will, I'm sure. But they'll go in and sit down and watch the film, won't they? They'll probably think"—he shrugged—"that something happened. Like things do to boys." His fingers began to knead my shoulder. "What film is it?"

"*Hell Is for Heroes*. It's an army picture."

"Oh, an *army* picture. I expect it's the conquering American heroes destroying the wretched German dogs, isn't it?"

"Frans," Mrs. Lezander said quietly.

A look passed between them, as hard and sharp as a dagger.

Dr. Lezander's attention returned to me. "Let's go downstairs, Cory. All right?"

"My mom's gonna be worried," I tried, but I knew it was no good.

"But she believes you're at the *film,* doesn't she?" His eyebrows lifted. "Now, let's go downstairs and see what I'm prepared to pay you twenty dollars a week to do."

My breath was stolen. "Twenty *dollars?*"

"Yes. Twenty dollars a week for an able and understanding apprentice seems like a bargain to me. Shall we go?" His hand guided me toward the steps that led down. It was a powerful hand, and it would not be denied. I had to go. Dr. Lezander flicked a switch that turned on the light over the stairs and flooded light below me. As I descended, I heard the rustle of his red silk robe and the shuffle of his slippers on the stairs. I heard him slurp his coffee. It was a greedy sound, and I was afraid.

My father had not taken Jacob Steiner and Lee Hannaford directly to the Union Pines Motel. On the way, jammed in the pickup truck with the wipers knocking away sleet, he'd asked them if they wanted some lunch. Both men had said yes, and that was how they'd wound up walking into the Bright Star Cafe.

"How about a booth in the back?" Dad asked Carrie French, and she guided them to one and left them with luncheon menu cards.

Mr. Steiner took off his gloves and overcoat. He was wearing a tweed suit and a pale gray vest. He hung his overcoat and his hat on a rack. His hair was as white and thick as a bristle brush. As Mr. Steiner slid into the booth and Dad sat down, too, the younger man peeled off his jacket. He was wearing a blue-checked shirt with the sleeves rolled up past his muscular biceps. And on the right bicep . . . there it was.

Dad said, "Oh my God."

"What is it?" Mr. Hannaford asked. "I'm not supposed to take my jacket off in here?"

"No, it's all right." A sheen of sweat had broken out on my father's forehead. Mr. Hannaford sat down beside Mr. Steiner. "I mean . . . that tattoo . . ."

"You got a problem with it, friend?" The younger man's slate-colored eyes had narrowed into dangerous slits.

"Lee?" Mr. Steiner cautioned. "No, no." It was like telling a bad dog to sit.

"No problem," Dad said. "It's just that . . ." He was having trouble breathing, and the room wanted to spin. "I've seen your tattoo before."

The two men were silent. Mr. Steiner spoke first. "May I ask where, Mr. Mackenson?"

"Before I tell you, I want to know where you've come from and why you're here." Dad pulled his gaze away from the faint outline of a skull with wings swept back from its temples.

"I wouldn't," Mr. Hannaford warned Mr. Steiner. "We don't know this guy."

"True. We don't know anyone here, do we?" Mr. Steiner glanced around, and Dad saw his hawklike eyes take in the scene. A dozen or so people were having lunch and shooting the breeze. Carrie French was fending off the good-natured flirting of a couple of farmers. The television was tuned to a basketball game. "How can we trust you, Mr. Mackenson?"

"What's not to trust?" Something about this man—the way he carried himself, the way his eyes were darting this way and that, sizing things up—made Dad ask the next question. "Are you a policeman?"

"By profession, no. But in a sense, yes."

"What profession are you in, then?"

"I am . . . in the field of historical research," Mr. Steiner answered.

Carrie French came over on her long, pretty legs, her order pad ready. "Help you today?"

"Got any griddle cakes?" Mr. Hannaford plucked a pack of Luckies out of his breast pocket.

"Beg pardon?"

"Griddle cakes! Do you have 'em here or not?"

"I think," Mr. Steiner said patiently as the younger man lit a cigarette, "that they're called pancakes in this part of the country."

"We're not servin' breakfast now." Carrie offered an uncertain smile. "Sorry."

"Just gimme a burger, then." He spouted smoke through his pinched nostrils. "Jesus!"

"Is the chicken noodle soup fresh?" Mr. Steiner asked, examining the menu card.

"Canned, but it's still good."

"I will not eat canned chicken noodle soup, my dear." He gazed at her sternly over the rims of his glasses. "I, too, will have a hamburger. *Very* well done, if you please." *Pliss*, he pronounced it.

Dad ordered the beef stew and a cup of coffee. Carrie paused. "Ya'll aren't from around here, are you?" she asked the two strangers.

"I'm from Indiana," Mr. Hannaford said. "He's from—"

"Warsaw, Poland, originally. And I can speak for myself, thank you."

"Both of you sure are a long way from home," Dad said when Carrie had gone.

"I live in Chicago now," Mr. Steiner explained.

"Still a long way from Zephyr." Dad's eyes kept ticking back to the tattoo. It looked as if the younger man had tried to bleach it out of his skin. "Does that tattoo mean somethin'?"

Lee Hannaford let smoke dribble from the corner of his mouth. "It means," he said, "that I don't like people askin' me my business."

Dad nodded. The first smolderings of anger were reddening his cheeks. "Is that so?"

"Yeah, it's so."

"Gentlemen, please," Mr. Steiner said.

"What would you say to this, hotshot?" Dad propped his elbows on the table and leaned his face closer to the younger man's. "What would you say if I told you that ten months ago I saw a tattoo just like yours on the arm of a dead man?"

Mr. Hannaford didn't respond. His face was emotionless, his eyes cold. He drew cigarette smoke in and blew it out. "Did he have blond hair?" he asked. "Kinda the same color as mine?"

"Yes."

"About the same build, too?"

"I think so, yes."

"Uh-huh." Mr. Hannaford leaned his chiseled face toward my father's. When he spoke, the words left smoke trails. "I'd say you saw my brother."

". . . and these cages must be kept scrupulously clean," Dr. Lezander was saying as he pointed them out. They were empty right now. "As well as the floor. If you come in three times a week, I expect the floor to be scrubbed three times a week. You'll be expected to water and feed all the animals in the kennel, as well as exercise them." I followed along behind him as he showed me from room to room in the basement. Every once in a while I would glance up and see an air vent overhead. "I order my hay in bales. You'd be expected to help unload the truck, cut the baling wire, and spread out hay for the horse stalls. I can attest that cutting baling wire is not an easy endeavor. It's tough enough to string a piano with. Plus your job will include whatever errands I need you to run." He turned to face me. "Twenty dollars a week for three afternoons, say from four until six. Does that sound fair?"

"Gosh." I couldn't believe this. Dr. Lezander was offering me a fortune.

"If you come in on Saturdays, I'll pay you an extra five dollars for . . . say, two until four." He smiled, again with just his mouth. He drank his coffee and set the collie cup down atop an empty wire-mesh cage. "Cory?" he said softly. "I do have two requests before I give you this job."

I waited to hear them.

"One: that your parents don't know how much I'm paying you. I think they should believe I'm paying you perhaps ten dollars a week. The reason I say this is that . . . well, I know your father's working at the gas station now. I saw him the last time I pulled in. I know your mother's struggling in her baking business. Wouldn't it be better for you if they didn't know how much money you were coming home with?"

"You think I ought to keep such a thing from them?" I asked, bewildered.

"It would be your decision, of course. But I believe both your mother and father might be . . . anxious to share your good fortune, if they were to know. And there are so *many* things a boy could buy with twenty-five dollars a week. The only problem is, you'd have to be discreet about those purchases. You couldn't spend it all in one place. I might even have to drive you to Union Town or Birmingham to spend some of that money. But couldn't you think of a few things you might like to have that your parents can't buy you?"

I thought. And then I answered: "No sir, I can't."

He laughed, as if this tickled him. "You will, though. With all that money in your pocket, you will."

I didn't answer. I didn't like what Dr. Lezander thought I would keep from my mother and father.

"Secondly." He folded his arms across his chest, and I saw his tongue probe the inside of his cheek. "There is the matter of Miss Sonia Glass."

"Sir?" My heart, which had settled down some, now speeded up again.

"Miss Sonia Glass," he repeated. "She brought her parrot to me. It died of a brain fever. Right here." He touched the wire-mesh cage. "Poor, poor creature. Now, it happens that Veronica and Miss Glass are in the same Sunday school class. Miss Glass, it seems, was terribly upset and puzzled by questions you asked her, Cory. She said you were very curious about a particular song, and why her parrot had . . . reacted strangely to that song." He smiled thinly. "Miss Glass told Veronica she thought you knew a secret, and might either Veronica or I know what it was? And there was some odd little thing as well, about you being in the possession of a green feather from Miss Katharina Glass's dead parrot. Miss Sonia said she couldn't believe her eyes when she saw it." He began working the knuckles of his right hand as he stared at the floor. "Are these things true, Cory?"

I swallowed hard. If I said they weren't, he'd know I was lying anyway. "Yes sir."

He closed his eyes. A pained expression stole over his face, there and then gone. "And where did you find that green feather, Cory?"

"I . . . found it . . ." Here was the moment of truth. I sensed something in that room coiled up like a snake and ready to strike. Though the overhead light was bright and harsh, the tile-floored room seemed to seethe with shadows. Dr. Lezander, I suddenly realized, had positioned himself between me and the stairs. He waited, his eyes closed. If I made a run for it, Mrs. Lezander would snare me even if I got past the doctor. Again, the choice was stolen from me. "I found it at Saxon's Lake," I said, braving the fates. "At the edge of the woods. Before the sun, when that car went down with a dead man handcuffed to the wheel."

With his eyes closed, Dr. Lezander smiled. It was a terrible sight. The flesh on his face looked tight and damp, his bald head shining under the light. Then he began to laugh: a slow leak of a laugh, bubbling from his silver-toothed mouth. His eyes opened, and they speared me. For a few seconds he had two faces: the lower one wore a silver-glinting smile; the upper one was pure fury. "Well, well," he said, and he shook his head as if he'd just heard the most amazing joke. "What are we going to do about *this?*"

"Have you ever seen this man before, Mr. Mackenson?"

Mr. Steiner had removed his wallet. He had taken a laminated card from it, and now he slid the card before my father as they sat at the back booth in the Bright Star Cafe.

It was a grainy black and white photograph. It showed a man wearing a white knee-length coat, waving and smiling to someone off the frame. He had dark hair that swept back like a skull-cap, and he had a square jaw and a cleft in his chin. Behind him was the hood of a gleaming car that looked like an antique, like from the thirties or forties. Dad studied the face for a moment; he paid close attention to the eyes and the white scar of a smile. For all his studying, however, it remained the face of a stranger.

"No," he said as he slid the picture back across the wood. "Never."

"He'll probably look different now." Mr. Steiner studied the picture, too, as if looking into the face of an old enemy. "He might have had some plastic surgery. The easiest way to change appearance is to grow a beard and shave your head. That way even your own mother wouldn't recognize you." *Mudder,* he'd said.

"I don't know that face. Sorry. Who is he?"

"His name is Gunther Down in the Dark."

"What?" Dad almost chewed on his heart.

"Gunther Down in the Dark," Mr. Steiner repeated. He spelled the last name, and then he pronounced it again: "Dahni-naderke."

Dad sat back in the booth, his mouth open. He gripped the table's edge to keep from being spun off the entire world. "My God," he whispered. "My God. 'Come with me . . . Dahni-naderke.'"

"Excuse me?" Mr. Steiner asked.

"Who is he?" Dad's voice was thick.

Lee Hannaford answered. "He's the man who killed Jeff, if my brother's body is lyin' at the bottom of that damned lake." Dad had told them the story of that morning last March. Mr. Hannaford looked mean enough to snap the head off a cobra. He hadn't eaten much of his hamburger, but he'd almost swallowed three Luckies. "My brother—my stupid-assed brother—must've been blackmailin' him, by what we can figure out. Jeff left a diary hidden in his apartment, back in Fort Wayne. It was in code, written in German. I found the diary in May, when I quit my job in California and came lookin' for him. It took us until a couple of weeks ago to figure the code out."

"It was based on Wagner's *Ring of the Nibelung*," Mr. Steiner said. "Very, very intricate."

"Yeah, he always was nuts about that code shit." Mr. Hannaford stabbed out another cigarette butt in his ketchupy plate. "Even as a kid. He was always doin' secret writin' and shit. So we pieced it together from the diary. He was blackmailin' Gunther Dahninaderke, first five hundred dollars a month, then eight hundred, then a thousand. It was down in the book that Dahninaderke lived in Zephyr, Alabama. Under a false name, I mean. Jeff and those scumbags helped him come up with a new identity, after he got in touch with 'em. But Jeff must've decided he wanted a payoff for his trouble. In the diary, he said he was gonna make a big score, get his stuff out of the apartment and move to Florida. He said he was drivin' down to Zephyr from Fort Wayne on the thirteenth of March. And that was the last entry." He shook his head. "My brother was fuckin' *crazy* to get involved in this. Well, I was crazy for gettin' involved in it, too."

"Involved in what?" Dad asked. "I don't understand."

"Do you know the term 'neo-Nazi'?" Mr. Steiner asked.

"I know what a Nazi is, if that's what you're askin'?"

"Neo-Nazi. A new Nazi. Lee and his brother were members of an American Nazi organization that operated in Indiana, Illinois, and Michigan. The symbol of that organization is the tattoo on Lee's arm. Lee and Jeff were initiated at the same time, but Lee left the group after a year and went to California."

"Damn straight." A match flared, and a Lucky burned. "I wanted to get as far away from those bastards as I could. They kill people who decide Hitler didn't shit roses."

"But your brother stayed with 'em?"

"Hell, yes. He even got to be some kind of storm-trooper leader or somethin'. Jesus, can you believe it? We were all-Americans on our high school football team!"

"I still don't know who this Gunther Dahninaderke fella is," Dad said.

Mr. Steiner laced his fingers together atop the table. "This is where I come in. Lee took the diary to be deciphered by the Department of Languages at Indiana University. A friend of mine there teaches German. When he got as far as deciphering Dahninaderke's name from that code, he sent the diary directly to me at Northwestern in Chicago. I took over the project from there in September. Perhaps I should explain that I am the director of the languages department. I am also a professor of history. And last but not least, I am a hunter of Nazi war criminals."

"Say again?" Dad asked.

"Nazi war criminals," Mr. Steiner repeated. "I have helped track down three of them in the last seven years. Bittrich in Madrid, Savelshagen in Albany, New York, and Geist in Allentown, Pennsylvania. When I saw the name Dahninaderke, I knew I was getting closer to the fourth."

"A war criminal? What did he do?"

"Dr. Gunther Dahninaderke was the directing physician at Esterwegen concentration camp in Holland. He and his wife Kara determined who was fit to work and who was ready to be gassed." Mr. Steiner flashed a quick and chilling smile. "It was they, you see, who decided on a sunny morning that I was still fit to live but my wife was not."

"I'm sorry," Dad said.

"That's all right. I knocked his front tooth out and spent a year at hard labor. But it made me hard, and it kept me alive."

"You . . . knocked his front tooth . . ."

"Right out of his head. Oh, those two were quite a pair." Mr. Steiner's face crinkled with the memory of pain. "We called his wife the Birdlady, because she had a set of twelve birds made from clay mixed with the ash of human bones. And Dr. Dahninaderke, who was originally a veterinarian from Rotterdam, had a very intriguing habit."

Dad couldn't speak. He forced it out with an effort. "What was it?"

"As the prisoners passed him on their way to the gas chamber, he made up names for them." Mr. Steiner's eyes were hooded, lost in visions of a horrible past. "Comical names, they were. I'll always remember what he called my Veronica, my beautiful Veronica with the long golden hair. He called her 'Sunbeam.' He said, 'Crawl right in, Sunbeam! Crawl right in!' And she was so sick she had to crawl through her own . . ." Tears welled up behind his glasses. He took them quickly off with the manner of a man who rigidly controlled his emotions. "Forgive me," he said. "Sometimes I forget myself."

"You okay?" Lee Hannaford asked my father. "You look awful white."

"Let me . . . let me see that picture again."

Mr. Steiner slid it in front of him.

Dad took a long breath. "Oh no," he said. "Oh please, no."

Mr. Steiner had heard it in Dad's voice: "You know him now."

"I do. I know where he lives. It's not far from here. Not very far at all. But . . . he's so *nice*."

"I know Dr. Dahninaderke's true nature," Mr. Steiner said. "And the true nature of his wife. You saw it when you looked at the face of Jeff Hannaford. Dr. Dahninaderke and Kara probably tortured him to find out who else knew where he was, or maybe they got the information about the diary out of him, and they beat him to death when he wouldn't tell them where it was or who else knew about it. When you looked at the face of Jeff Hannaford, you saw the twisted soul of Dr. Gunther Dahninaderke. I pray to God you don't have to look upon such a sight again."

Dad stood up and fumbled for his wallet, but Mr. Steiner

put money on the table. "I'll take you to him," Dad said, and he started for the door.

"Such a bright young man," Dr. Lezander said, standing between me and the way out. "There's that terrier determination, isn't it? Finding that green feather and then pursuing it to the end? I admire that, Cory, I truly do."

"Dr. Lezander?" I felt as if my chest were constricted by iron bands. "I sure would like to go home."

He took two steps toward me. I retreated as many.

He stopped, aware of his power over me. "I want that green feather. Do you know why?"

I shook my head.

"Because your having it upsets Miss Sonia. It's a reminder of the past, and she doesn't like that. The past should be put behind us, Cory. The world should go on, and leave the things of the past alone, don't you agree?"

"I don't—"

"But no, just like that green feather, the past has to turn up again and again and again. It has to be plowed up and spread out for everyone to see. The past has to be put on exhibit, and everyone who struggled to keep from drowning in that sludge has to pay the price over and over. It's not fair, Cory, it's not right. Do you see?"

I didn't. Somewhere along the line, his train had derailed.

"We were honorable," Dr. Lezander said, his eyes feverish. "We had *honor*. We had pride. And look at the world now, Cory! Look what it's become! We knew the destination, but they wouldn't let us take the world there. And now you see what you see. Chaos and vulgarity on all sides. Gross interbreedings and couplings that even animals wouldn't abide. You know, I had my chance to be a physician to human beings. I did. Many times. And do you know that I would rather kneel in the mud and attend to a swine than save a human life? Because that's what I think of the human race! That's what I think of the liars who turned their backs on us and sullied our honor! That's what I . . . that's what I . . . what I *think!*" He picked up the collie cup and flung it to the floor, and it hit the tiles near my right foot and shattered to pieces with a noise like a gunshot.

Silence.

In another moment, Mrs. Lezander called from upstairs: "Frans? What broke, Frans?"

His brain, I thought.

"We're talking," Dr. Lezander said to her. "Just talking, only that."

I heard her footsteps, heavy on the floor, as she moved away. Then a scraping sound above us.

And a few seconds later, the piano being played.

The tune was "Beautiful Dreamer." Mrs. Lezander was actually a very talented pianist. She had the hands for it, I recalled Miss Blue Glass saying. I wondered if she also had the hands that were strong enough to wrap hay-baling wire around a man's throat and strangle him to death. Or had Dr. Lezander done that as Mrs. Lezander had played that same tune in the den above and the parrots had squawked and screamed with the memory of brutal violence?

"Twenty-five dollars a week," Dr. Lezander said. "But you must bring me the green feather, and you must never, *never* talk to Miss Sonia Glass about this again. The past is dead. It should stay buried, where it belongs. Do you agree, Cory?"

I nodded. Anything to get out of there.

"Good boy. When can you bring me the feather? Tomorrow afternoon?"

"Yes sir."

"That's very, very good. When you bring it, I'll destroy it so Miss Sonia Glass won't think of the past anymore, and it won't hurt her. When you bring it, I'll give you your first week's money. Is that agreeable?"

"Yes sir." Anything, anything.

"All right, then." He moved aside from the stairs. "After you, *mein herr.*"

I started up.

The front doorbell rang. "Beautiful Dreamer" abruptly stopped. I heard the scrape again: the piano bench being pushed back. At the top of the stairs, Dr. Lezander put his hand on my shoulder again and held me. "Wait," he whispered.

We heard the front door opening.

"Tom!" Mrs. Lezander said. "What may I do for—"

"*Dad!*" I shouted. "*Help—*" Dr. Lezander's hand clamped over my mouth, and I heard him give a muffled cry of anguish that it had all come to this end.

"Cory! Get outta my way, you—!" Dad started into the house, with Mr. Steiner and Lee Hannaford behind him. He shoved the big woman aside, but in the next instant Mrs. Lezander bellowed, "*Nein!*" and slammed a forearm across the side of his face. He fell backward into Mr. Steiner, blood trickling from a gashed eyebrow. Only Mr. Steiner could understand the things Mrs. Lezander shouted to her husband: "Gunther, run! Take the boy and run!" As she was shouting, Mr. Hannaford grabbed her around her throat from behind and with all his weight and strength he wrestled her to the floor. She got up on one knee and fought back, but suddenly Mr. Steiner was on her, too, trying to pin her flailing arms. A coffee table and lamp crashed over. Mr. Steiner, his hat flown off and his lower lip burst open by one of her fists, yelled, "It's over, Kara! It's over, it's over!"

But it was not over for her husband.

At her warning cry, he had picked me up with one arm and scooped the car keys off the kitchen counter where his wife had left them. As I thrashed to get free, he dragged me out the back door into the falling sleet, the wind whipping his red silk robe. He lost a slipper, but he didn't slow down. He flung me into the Buick, slammed the door almost on my leg, and came close to sitting on my head when he leaped behind the wheel. He jammed the key into the ignition, turned it, and the engine roared to life. As he put the gears into reverse and the Buick's tires laid rubber on the driveway, I sat up in time to see Dad run out the back door into the glare of the headlights.

"Dad!" I reached for the door handle on my side. An elbow crashed into my shoulder and paralyzed me with pain, and when the hand gripped the back of my head and flung me down onto the floorboard like an old sack I lay there dazed and hurting. Dr. Gunther Dahninaderke, the murderer—whom I still knew as Dr. Frans Lezander, the murderer—crunched the gearshift into first and the Buick's engine screamed as the car tore away.

Behind us, my father was already running back through the house to get to the pickup. He jumped over the struggling bodies of Mr. Steiner, Mr. Hannaford, and Kara Dahninaderke. The woman was still fighting, but Mr. Hannaford was using his fists on her horsey face and the results were not on the side of beauty.

Dr. Lezander was racing through the streets of Zephyr, the Buick's tires shrieking at every turn. I started to crawl up from the floorboard, but Dr. Lezander shouted, "Stay there! Don't you move, you little bastard!" and he slapped me in the face and I slid back down again. We must've passed the Lyric; I wondered how much hell a hero could stand. We roared onto the gargoyle bridge, and when the steering wheel slipped out of Dr. Lezander's frantic hands for an instant, the Buick sideswiped the left side of the bridge and sent sparks and pieces of chrome flying into the air, the car's frame moaning with the impact. Then he seized control again and, his teeth gritted, he aimed us onto Route Ten.

I saw light leap from the rearview mirror and stab Dr. Lezander in the eyes. He shouted a curse in German that was louder than the Buick's wail, and I could just imagine what the parrots had had to endure that night. But I knew whose lights those were, ricocheting off the mirror. I knew who was behind us, right on the Buick's tail, pushing that old pickup truck to its point of explosion. I knew.

I reached up and grabbed the bottom of the steering wheel, jerking the car to the right. It went off the road onto loose gravel, the tires slipping. Dr. Lezander gave me another Germanic oath, hollered at the velocity and volume of a howitzer shell to the skull, and pounded my fingers loose with his fist. With that same fist, he knocked me in the forehead so hard I saw purple stars and that was the end of my heroics.

"Leave me alone!" Dr. Lezander screamed to the pickup truck whose headlights filled the rearview mirror. *"Can't you leave me alone?"* He fought the wheel around Route Ten's snaky curves, the force of gravity trying its best to rip the tires off. I pulled myself up on the seat again, my head still ringing, and Dr. Lezander yelled, "You little shit!" and grabbed the back of my coat, but he had to use two hands on the wheel so he released me.

I looked back at my father's pickup, twenty feet of sleet and air between Dad's front bumper and Dr. Lezander's rear bumper. We hurtled out of the series of tight curves, and I held on to the seat as Dr. Lezander accelerated, widening the distance between vehicles. I heard a *pop* and twisted my head in time to see Dr. Lezander reaching into the glove compartment, which he'd knocked open with a blow of his fist. His hand emerged gripping a snub-nosed .38 pistol. He threw that arm back, almost cuffing me in the head with the gun's barrel before I ducked, and he fired twice without aiming. The rear windshield exploded, the glass fragments flying toward Dad's pickup like pieces of jagged ice. I saw the pickup swerve and almost go off the road, its rear end wildly fishtailing, but then Dad got it righted. As Dr. Lezander's gun hand passed over my head again, I reached up and grabbed his wrist, pinning that gun against the seat with all my strength. The Buick began to slew from side to side as he grappled with the wheel and with me at the same time, but I hung on.

The gun went off in front of my face, the bullet passing through the seat and out the door with a metallic *clang*. The sound and heat of it going off so close to me sent a shock and shiver through my bones, and I guess I let go but I don't remember and then Dr. Lezander hit me a glancing blow on the right shoulder with that gun barrel. It was perhaps the worst pain I'd ever felt in my life; it filled me up and overspilled from my mouth in a cry. Without the padding of my coat in the way, my shoulder would've surely been broken. As it was, I grabbed at it and fell back against the passenger-side door, my face contorted with pain and my right arm all but dead. I saw, as if locked in a cyclic dream akin to that in *Invaders from Mars,* that we were about to pass the dark plain of Saxon's Lake. And then Dr. Lezander jammed on the brake with his bare foot, and as the Buick slowed and Dad's pickup gained ground, the doctor threw his arm back again and this time he looked over his shoulder to aim. His face was slickly wet in the wash of the lights, his teeth clenched, his eyes those of the savage, hunted animal. He fired, and the windshield of Dad's truck suddenly had a fist-sized hole in it. I saw his finger tighten on the trigger, and I wanted to fight him with all the want in my body, but that pain in my shoulder had me whipped.

Something huge and dark and fast burst out of the woods on the other side of the road, near where I'd seen Mrs. Lezander standing that morning in March.

It was on us before Dr. Lezander even saw it, and it was headed straight for his door.

At the same instant, the gun went off and the beast from the lost world collided with us.

This, truly, was a noise like the end of the world.

Over gunshot and Lezanderscream and crash of glass and folding metal, the Buick was knocked up onto the two tires on my side and they shrieked like constipated banshees as the entire car was shoved off the pavement. Dr. Lezander, his door buckled in as if kicked by God, came tumbling into me across the seat and my breath burst out, my ribs in danger of snapping. I heard a snort and grunt: the triceratops, protecting his territory, was pushing the rival dinosaur off Route Ten. Dr. Lezander's face was pressed up against mine, his weight crushing me, and I smelled his fear like green onions. Then he screamed again and I think I screamed, too, because suddenly the car was falling.

We hit with a bone-jarring jolt and splash.

Dark water seethed up into the floorboard. We had just been received by Saxon's Lake.

The Buick's steaming hood was rising. As it did, water began to surge over the slope of the trunk and pour through the shattered glass. The window on Dr. Lezander's side was broken as well, but the water hadn't yet reached it. He was lying on top of me, the gun lost. His eyes were glassy, blood oozing from his mouth where he must've bitten his lip or tongue. His left arm, the arm which had taken the brunt of the beast's power, was lying at a weird crooked angle. I saw the wet glistening of white bone protruding from the wrist in the red silk sleeve.

The lake was coming in faster now, air bubbles exploding around the trunk. The rear windshield was a waterfall. I couldn't get Dr. Lezander off me, and now the car was turning slowly against me as the Buick rolled over like a happy hog and my side started to submerge. Dr. Lezander was drooling bloody foam, and I realized his ribs must've taken a wallop, too.

"Cory! Cory!"

I looked up, past Dr. Lezander to the broken window rising above me.

My father was there, his hair plastered flat, his face dripping. Blood was creeping down from his cut eyebrow. He started wrenching out bits of glass from the window frame with his fingers. The Buick shuddered and moaned. Water edged up over the seat and its cold touch shocked me and made Dr. Lezander start thrashing.

"Can you grab my hand?" Dad wedged his body in through the crumpled window and strained to reach me.

I couldn't, not with that weight on me. "Help me, Dad," I croaked.

He fought to winnow in farther. His sides must've been raked and clawed by glass, but his face showed no pain. His lips were tight and grim, his eyes fixed on me like red-rimmed lamps. His hand tried to part the distance between us, but still the distance was too great.

Dr. Lezander's body lurched. He said something, but it must've been a snarl of German. He blinked, his eyes coming into painful focus. Water sloshed over us, a touch of the grave.

He looked at his broken wrist, and he made a deep moaning noise.

"Get off him!" Dad shouted. "For God's sake, get off my son!"

Dr. Lezander shuddered and coughed. On the third cough, bright red blood sprayed from his nose and mouth. He grasped at his side, and suddenly there was blood on his hand. The beast from the lost world had staved his ribs right through his innards.

The water was roaring now. The Buick was sinking at the trunk.

"Please!" Dad begged, still straining to reach me. "Please give me my son!"

Dr. Lezander looked around as if trying to figure out exactly where he was. He lifted himself off me a few inches, which made me able to breathe without feeling like I was jammed in a sardine can. Dr. Lezander looked back at the sinking trunk and the water surging dark and foamy where the rear windshield had been and I heard him whisper *"Oh."*

It was the whisper of surrender.

Dr. Lezander's face turned. He stared at me. Blood dripped from his nose and ran down my cheek. "Cory," he said, and his voice gurgled. His good hand closed on my wrist.

"Up you go," he whispered. "Bronco."

He lifted himself up with an effort that must've racked him, and he guided my hand into my father's.

Dad pulled me out, and I flung my arms around his neck. He held me, his legs treading water and tears streaming down his heroic face.

With a great buckling and moaning noise, the Buick was going down. The water rushed around us, drawing us in. Dad started kicking us away from it, but the pull was too strong. Then, with a hissing noise of heat and liquid at war, the Buick was drawn down into the depths. I felt my father fighting the suction, and then he gasped a breath and I knew he had lost.

We went under.

The car was sinking below us, into a huge gloomy vault where the sun was a stranger. Air bubbles rose from it like silver jellyfish. Dad was kicking frantically, trying to break the pull, but we were going down with Dr. Lezander. In the underwater blur I saw the doctor's white face pressed up against the windshield. Bubbles were streaming from his open mouth.

And suddenly something had drifted up from below and was clinging to the trunk. Something that might have been a big clump of moss or rags somebody had dumped into Saxon's Lake with their garbage. Whatever this thing was, it moved slowly and inexorably into the Buick through the broken rear windshield. The car was turning, turning over like a bizarre ride at the Bran-dywine Carnival, suspended against darkness. As my lungs burned for breath I saw the blur of Dr. Lezander's white face again, only this time the ragged mossy thing had wrapped itself around him like a putrid robe. Whatever this thing was, it had hold of his jaw. I saw a faint glint of a silver tooth, like a receding star. Then the Buick turned over on its back like a huge turtle and as air bubbles rushed up again I felt them hit us and break us loose from the suction. We were rising toward the realm of light.

Dad lifted me up, so my head broke the surface first.

There wasn't much light up there today, but there was a whole lot of air. Dad and I clung together in the choppy murk, breathing.

At last we swam to where we could pull ourselves out, through mud and reeds to solid earth. Dad sat down on the ground next to the pickup truck, his hands scraped raw with glass cuts, and I huddled on the red rock cliff and looked out over Saxon's Lake.

"Hey, partner!" Dad said. "You okay?"

"Yes sir." My teeth were chattering, but being cold was a passing thing.

"Better get in the truck," he said.

"I will," I answered, but I wasn't ready yet. My shoulder, which would become one swollen lump of bruise in the next couple of days, was mercifully numb.

Dad pulled his knees up to his chest. The sleet was falling, but we were already cold and wet, so what of it? "I've got a story to tell you about Dr. Lezander," he said.

"I want to tell you one, too," I answered. I listened; the wind swept over the lake's surface and made it whisper.

He was down in the dark now. He had come from darkness and to darkness he had returned.

"He called me Bronco," I said.

"Yeah. How about that?"

We couldn't stay here very much longer. The wind was really getting cold. It was the kind of weather that made you catch your death.

Dad looked up at the low gray clouds and the January gloom. He smiled, with the face of a boy unburdened.

"Gosh," he said, "it's a beautiful day."

Hell might have been for heroes, but life was for the living. These things happened, in the aftermath.

When Mom got up off the floor from her faint, she was all right. She hugged both Dad and me, but she didn't cling on to us. We had come back to her a little worse for wear, but we were back. Dad in particular; his dreams of the man at the bottom of Saxon's Lake were ended, good and truly.

Mr. Steiner and Mr. Hannaford, though dismayed that they had never even gotten a finger on Dr. Gunther Dahninaderke, were at least satisfied with the outcome of rough justice. They had Mrs. Kara Dahninaderke and her birds of human bone in their custody, however, and that was a great consolation. The last I heard of her, she was going to a prison where even the light lay chained.

Ben and Johnny were beside themselves. Ben jumped up and down in a fit and Johnny scowled and stomped when they realized they had been sitting in front of a movie while I'd been battling for my life against a Nazi war criminal. To say this made me a celebrity at school was like saying the moon is the size of a river pebble. Even the teachers wanted to hear my tale. Pretty Miss Fontaine was enthralled by it, and Mr. Cardinale asked to hear it twice. "You ought to be a writer, Cory!" Miss Fontaine said. "You surely know your words!" Mr. Cardinale said, "You'd make a fine author, in my opinion."

Writer? Author?

Storyteller, that's what I decided to be.

On a cold but sunny Saturday morning toward the end of January, I left Rocket on the front porch and got into the pickup truck with Mom and Dad. He drove us across the gargoyle bridge and along Route Ten—slowly, all the time watching for the beast from the lost world. Though the beast remained loose in the woods, I never saw him again. I believe he was a gift to me from Davy Ray.

We reached Saxon's Lake. The water was smooth. There was no trace of what lay at its bottom, but we all knew.

I stood on the red rock cliff, and I reached into my pocket and pulled out the green feather. Dad had tied twine around it, with a little lead-ball weight on its end. I threw it into the lake, and it went down faster than you can say Dahninaderke. Much faster, I'm sure.

I wanted no souvenirs of tragedy.

Dad stood on one side of me, and Mom on the other. We were a mighty good team.

"I'm ready now," I told them.

And I went home, where my monsters and my magic box were waiting.

Five

Zephyr as It Is

I T HAS BEEN A long, cold winter, and I am going home.

South from Birmingham on Interstate 65, that busy high-way leading to the state capital. A left turn at Exit 205, and then following the road as it narrows and winds past drowsing towns named Coopers, Rockford, Hissop, and Cottage Grove. No sign spells out the name Zephyr anymore, but I know where it is and I am going home.

I am not going alone, on this beautiful Saturday afternoon at the beginning of spring. My wife, Sandy, is beside me, and our own "young'un" in the back, curled up wearing a Birmingham Barons baseball cap on backward and baseball cards scattered over the seat. These days there might be a fortune back there, who knows? The radio—pardon me, the stereo cassette player—is on, with Tears For Fears coming out of the speakers. I think Roland Orzabal is a fantastic singer.

It's 1991. Can you believe it? We're poised on the edge of a new century, for better or worse. I guess we'll all make up our own minds which. The year 1964 seems like ancient history now. The Polaroids taken in that year have turned yellow. No one wears their hair like that anymore, and the clothes have changed. People have changed, too, I think. Not just in the South, but everywhere. For better or worse? You can decide for yourself.

And what we and the world have been through since 1964! Think of it! It's been a faster, more brain-busting ride than ever could be devised by the Brandywine Carnival. We've lived through Vietnam—if we've been fortunate—and the era of Flower Power, Watergate and the fall of Nixon, the Ayatollah, Ronnie and Nancy, the cracking of the Wall and the beginning of the end of Communist Russia. We truly are living in the time of whirlwinds and comets. And like rivers that flow to the sea, time must flow into the future. It boggles the mind to think what might be ahead. But, as the Lady once said, you can't know where you're going until you figure out where you've been. Sometimes I think we have a lot of figuring out to do.

"It's such a lovely day," Sandy says, and she leans back in her seat to watch the countryside glide past. I glance at her and my eyes are blessed. She wears sunlight in her blond hair like a spill of golden flowers. There's some silver in there, too, and I like it though she frets some. Her eyes are pale gray and her gaze is calm and steady. She is a rock when I need strength, and a pillow when I need comfort. We're a good team. Our child has her eyes and her calm, the dark brown of my hair and my curiosity about the world. Our child has my father's sharp-bridged nose and the slimfingered "artist's hands" of my mother. I think it's a fine combination.

"Hey, Dad!" The baseball cards have been forgotten for the moment.

"Yeah?"

"Are you nervous?"

"No," I say. Better be honest, I think. "Well . . . maybe a little bit."

"What's it gonna be like?"

"I don't know. It's been . . . oh . . . let's see, we left Zephyr in 1966. So it's been . . . you tell me how many years."

A few seconds' pause. "Twenty-five."

"Right as rain," I say. Our child gets an aptitude in math strictly from Sandy's side of the family, believe me.

"How come you never came back here? I mean, if you liked it so much?"

"I started to, more than a few times. I got as far as the turnoff from I-65. But Zephyr's not like it was. I guess I know things can't stay the same, and that's all right but . . . Zephyr was my home, and it hurts to think it's changed so much."

"So how's it changed? It's still a town, isn't it?" I hear the baseball cards being flipped through again, being sorted by team and alphabetized.

"Not like it was," I say. "The Air Force base near here closed down in 1974, and the paper mill up on the Tecumseh shut down two years later. Union Town grew. It's about four or five times the size it was when I was a boy. But Zephyr . . . just got smaller."

"Um." The attention is drifting now.

I glance at Sandy, and we smile at each other. Her hand finds mine. They were meant to be clasped together, just like this. Before us, the hills rise around Adams Valley. They are covered by trees that blaze with the yellow and purple of new buds. Some green is appearing, too, though April's not here yet. The air outside the car is still cool, but the sun is a glorious promise of summer.

My folks and I indeed did leave Zephyr, in August of 1966. Dad, who had found a job working at Mr. Vandercamp's hardware store, sensed the changing winds and decided to search for greener pastures. He found a job in Birmingham, as the assistant manager on the night shift at the Coca-Cola bottling plant. He was making twice as much money as he'd ever made when he was a milkman. By 1970, he'd moved up to be the night-shift manager, and he thought we were in high cotton. That was the year I started college, at the University of Alabama. Dad saw me graduate, with a degree in journalism, before he died of cancer in 1978. It was, thankfully, a quick passing. Mom grieved terribly, and I thought I was going to lose her, too. But in 1983, on a cruise to Alaska with a group of friends from her church, Mom met a widowed gentleman who owned a horse breeding farm near Bowling Green, Kentucky. Two years later, she became his wife and she lives on that farm still. He's a great guy and is very good to my mother, but he's not my dad. Life goes on, and the roads always lead to unexpected destinations.

ROUTE TEN, reads a sign pocked with rust-edged bullet holes.

My heart is starting to beat harder. My throat is dry. I expect change, but I'm afraid of it.

I've tried my damnedest not to get old. This in itself is a tough job. I don't mean age old, because that's an honorable thing. I mean attitude old. I've seen guys my age suddenly wake up one morning and forget their fathers forbade them to listen to those demonic Rolling Stones. They've forgotten their fathers demanding that they get out of the house if they're going to wear their hair down on their foreheads. They've forgotten what it meant, to be the bossee instead of the bosser. Of course the world is tougher now, no doubt about it. There are harder choices to be made, with more terrible consequences. Kids need guidance, for sure. I did, and I'm glad I got guided because it helped me miss making a lot of mistakes. But I think parents aren't teachers anymore. Parents—or a whole lot of us, at least—lead by mouth instead of by example. It seems to me that if a child's hero is their mother or father—or even better, both of them in tandem—then the rough road of learning and experience is going to be smoothed some. And every little bit of smoothing helps, in this rough old world that wants children to be miniature adults, devoid of charm and magic and the beauty of innocence.

Well, my last name's neither Lovoy nor Blessett, so I ought to get off my pulpit now.

I've changed somewhat since 1964, of course. I don't have as much hair, and I wear glasses. I've picked up some wrinkles, but I've gained some laugh lines, too. Sandy says she thinks I'm more handsome now than I ever was. This is called love. But as I say, I really have tried to hold off the attitude aging. In this regard, music came to my rescue. I believe music is the language of youth, and the more you can accept as being valid, the younger your attitude gets. I credit the Beach Boys with getting me interested in music to begin with. Now my record collection—excuse me, my CD collection—includes artists like Elvis Costello, U2, Sinéad O'Connor, Concrete Blonde, Simple Minds, and Technotronic. I have to say, however, that sometimes I feel the classics pulling at me, like Led Zeppelin and the Lovin' Spoonful. But with all this choice on my platter, I have a feast.

I drive past a weeded-up road that cuts through the woods, and I know what ruin lies at its end fifty yards away. Miss Grace and her bad girls folded their tents right after the Blaylocks went to prison. The house's roof was blown off during a windstorm in July of 1965. I doubt if there's much left at all now. The kudzu vines around here have always been hungry.

Ben started college at the University of Alabama the same year I did, majoring in business. He even stayed to go to graduate school, and I would never in a million years have thought that Ben would actually enjoy school. He and I got together from time to time at the university, but gradually he was more and more involved with his business fraternity and I didn't see a whole lot of him. He joined Sigma Chi social fraternity and became vice president of the chapter. He lives now in Atlanta, where he's a stockbroker. He and his wife, Jane Anne, have a boy and a girl. The guy is rich, he drives a gold-colored BMW, and he's fatter than ever. He called me three years ago, after he read one of my books, and we see each other every few months. Last summer we drove down to a small town near the state line between Alabama and Florida to visit the chief of police there. His name is John Wilson.

I always knew Johnny had the blood of a chief in his veins. He runs a tight ship in that town, and he accepts no nonsense. But I understand that he's a fair man, and everybody there seems to like him, because he's in his second term. While we were there, Ben and I met Johnny's wife, Rachel. Rachel is a stunning woman who looks like she could easily be a fashion model. She hangs all over that guy. Though they have no children, Johnny and Rachel are perfectly happy. We all went deep-sea fishing off Destin one weekend, and Johnny caught a marlin, I got my line tangled up under the boat, and Ben got the sunburn of his life. But we sure did do a lot of laughing and catching up.

It is there before I realize it. My stomach tightens.

"Saxon's Lake," I tell them. They both crane their necks to look.

It hasn't changed at all. The same size, the same dark water, the same mud and reeds, the same red rock cliff. It wouldn't take much effort to imagine Dad's milk truck parked there, and him leaping into the water after a sinking car. It likewise wouldn't take much effort to remember a Buick wallowing there, water flooding through the broken rear windshield, and my father straining to reach me with a glass-slashed hand. Not much effort at all.

Dad, I love you, I think as we leave Saxon's Lake behind.

I remember his face, washed by firelight, as he sat there in the house and explained to me about Dr. Gunther Dahninaderke. It took us both—and Mom, too, and just about everybody in town—a long time to accept the fact that he and his wife had done such evil things. Though he wasn't evil through and through, or else why would he have saved my life? I don't think anyone is evil beyond saving. Maybe I'm like Dad that way: naive. But better naive, I think, than calloused to the core.

It dawned on me sometime later about Dr. Dahninaderke and his nightly vigils at the shortwave radio. I firmly believe he was listening to the foreign countries for news on who else in the Nazi regime had been captured and brought to justice. I believe that under his cool exterior he lived in perpetual terror, waiting for that knock on the door. He had delivered agonies, and he had suffered them, too. Would he have killed me once he had that green feather in his fist, as he and Kara had tortured and killed Jeff Hannaford over blackmail money? I honestly don't know. Do you?

Oh, yes! The Demon!

Ben told me this. The Demon, who had demonstrated later in high school that she was indeed a genius, went to college at Vanderbilt and became a chemist for DuPont. She did very well at that, but her strange nature would not let her alone. The last Ben understood, the Demon has become a performance artist in New York City and is locking horns with Jesse Helms over an art piece she does in which she screams and rants about corporate America while sitting in a baby pool full of . . . you can guess what.

All I can say is, Jesse Helms better not get on her bad side. If he does, I pity him. He might find himself glued to his desk one fine day.

I follow the same curves that scared the yell out of me when Donny Blaylock flew around them. And then the hills move aside and the road becomes as cleanly straight as a part made by Mr. Dollar and there is the gargoyle bridge.

Missing its gargoyles. The heads of the Confederate generals have been hacked away. Maybe it was vandalism, maybe it was somebody who would get a thousand dollars apiece for them on the art market as examples of Southern primitivism. I don't know, but they are gone. There is the railroad trestle, which is about the same, and there is the shine of the Tecumseh River. I imagine that Old Moses is happier, now that the paper mill has closed. He doesn't get pollution in his teeth when he bites a mouthful of turtle. Of course, he doesn't get his Good Friday feast anymore, either. That ended, Ben told me, when the Lady passed over her own river in 1967 at the grand old age of one hundred and nine. The Moon Man, Ben said, left town soon afterward, heading for New Orleans, and after that the community of Bruton began to dwindle, getting smaller at even a faster rate than Zephyr. The Tecumseh River may be cleaner now, but I wonder if on some nights Old Moses doesn't lift his scaly head to the surface and spout steam and water from the twin furnaces of his nostrils. I wonder if he doesn't listen to the silence beyond the sounds of water sloshing over rocks and think in his own reptilian language. "Why doesn't anybody ever come to play with me anymore?"

Maybe he's still here. Maybe he's gone, following the river to the sea.

We cross the gargoyle-less bridge. And there on the other side is my hometown.

"Here we are," I hear myself say as I slow the car down, but instantly I know I am incorrect. We may be in a particular place in time, but this place is no longer Zephyr.

At least not the Zephyr I knew. The houses are still here, but many of them are tumbling down, the yards forlorn. It's not totally a ghost town, however, because some of the houses—a small, small number, it appears—are still being lived in, and there are a few cars on the streets. But already I feel that a great gathering—a wonderful party and celebration of life—has moved on somewhere else, leaving its physical evidence behind like a garden of dead flowers.

This is going to be a lot tougher than I thought.

Sandy senses it. "You all right?"

"We'll find out," I tell her, and I manage a feeble smile.

"There's hardly anybody here, is there, Dad?"

"Hardly a soul," I answer.

I turn off Merchants Street before I get to the center of town. I can't take that yet. I drive to the ball field where the Branlins made their savage attack on us that day, and I stop the car on the field's edge.

"Mind if we sit here for a minute, kids?" I ask.

"No," Sandy says, and she squeezes my hand.

About the Branlins. Johnny supplied me with this information, being an officer of the law. It seems that the brothers were not of a single nature after all. Gotha started playing football in high school and became the man of the hour when he intercepted a Union Town High School pass right on their goal line and ran it back for a big TD. The acclaim did wonders for him, proving that all the time he only craved the attention his mother and father were too stupid or mean to give him. Gotha, Johnny told me, now lives in Birmingham and sells insurance, and he coaches a peewee football team on the side. Johnny told me Gotha needs no peroxide in his hair anymore, since he has not a strand of it left.

Gordo, on the other hand, continued his descent. I'm sorry to say that in 1980 Gordo was shot to death by the owner of a 7-Eleven in Baton Rouge, Louisiana, where he'd fallen in with a bad crowd. Gordo died trying to steal less than three hundred dollars from the register and all the Little Debbie cakes he could carry. It seems to me that once upon a time he did have a chance, but he didn't listen to the poison ivy.

"I'm gonna get out for a minute and stretch my legs," I say.

"Want us to go with you, Dad?"

"No," I answer. "Not right now."

I get out and walk across the overgrown baseball field. I stand on the pitcher's mound, caressed by cool breeze and warm sun. The bleachers where I first saw Nemo Curliss are sagging. I hold my arm out with my palm toward the sky, and I wait.

What would happen if that ball Nemo Curliss flung to heaven suddenly came down into my hand after all these years?

I wait.

But it doesn't happen. Nemo, the boy with a perfect arm who was trapped by all-too-imperfect circumstances, threw that ball beyond the clouds. It never came down and it never will, and only Ben, Johnny, and I remember.

I close my palm, and return my arm to my side.

I can see Poulter Hill from here.

It, too, has been allowed to deteriorate. The weeds are pushing up amid the headstones, and it appears that no new flowers have been put up there for a long time. That's a shame, I think, because there lie Zephyr's faithful ones.

I don't want to walk amid those stones. I had never been back, after my train trip. I had said my good-bye to Davy Ray, and he said his to me. Anything else would be a numb-nuts thing to do.

I turn away from Death, and walk back to the living.

"This was my school," I tell my wife and child as I stop the car beside the playground.

We all get out here, and Sandy walks at my side as my shoes

stir the playground's dust. Our "young'un" begins to run around in wider and wider circles, like a pony set free after a long period of confinement. "Be careful!" Sandy warns, because she's seen a broken bottle. Worrying, it seems, comes with the job.

I put my arm around Sandy, and her arm goes around my back. The elementary school is empty, some of the windows shattered. There is a crushing silence, where so many young voices whooped and hollered. I see the place near the fence where Johnny and Gotha Branlin squared off. I see the gate where I fled from Gordo on Rocket and led him to Lucifer's judgment. I see—

"Hey, Dad! Look what I found!"

Our "young'un" comes trotting back. "I found it over there! Neat, huh?"

I look into the small, offered palm, and I have to smile.

It is a black arrowhead, smooth and almost perfectly formed. There are hardly any cuts on it at all. It was obviously fashioned by someone who was proud of his labors. A chief, most likely.

"Can I keep it, Dad?" my daughter asks.

Her name is Skye. She turned twelve in January, and she's going through what Sandy calls the "tomboy stage." Skye would rather put on a baseball cap backward and run grinning through the dust than play with dolls and dream about the New Kids on the Block. These things will come later, I'm sure. For right now, Skye is fine.

"I believe you ought to," I tell her, and she eagerly pushes that arrowhead down into the pocket of her jeans like a secret treasure.

You see, it's a girl's life, too.

And now we drive along Merchants Street, into the center of the stilled heart.

Everything is closed. Mr. Dollar's barbershop, the Piggly-Wiggly, the Bright Star Cafe, the hardware store, the Lyric, everything. The windows of the Woolworth's are soaped over. The growth of retail outlets, apartments, and a shopping mall with four theaters in Union Town consumed the spirit of Zephyr, as

Big Paul's Pantry finished off the milkman's route. This is a going-forward, but is it progress?

We drive past the courthouse. Silence. Past the public swimming pool and the shell of the Spinnin' Wheel. Silence, silence. We drive past the house of Miss Blue Glass, and the silence where there used to be music is heavy indeed.

Miss Blue Glass. I wish I can say I know what happened to her, but I don't. She would be in her eighties now, if she is still alive. I just don't know. The same is true with so many others, who drifted away from Zephyr in the waning years: Mr. Dollar, Sheriff Marchette, Jazzman Jackson, Mr. and Mrs. Damaronde, Nila Castile and Gavin, Mrs. Velvadine, Mayor Swope. I think they are all alive, in other towns. I think they have kept part of Zephyr with them, and wherever they go they leave Zephyr's seeds in the earth. As I do.

I worked for a newspaper in Birmingham for two years after I finished college. I wrote headlines and edited other people's stories. When I went to my apartment in that big city after work, I sat down at my magic box—not that same one, but a new magic box—and I wrote. And I wrote. The stories went out into the mail and the stories came back. Then, out of desperation, I tried to write a novel. Lo and behold, it found a publisher.

I am a library now. A small one, but I'm growing.

I slow the car as we move past a house set back off the street next to a barn. "He lived right there," I tell Sandy.

"Wow!" Skye says. "It's creepy! It looks like a haunted house!"

"No," I tell her, "I think it's just a house now."

Like Bo knows football, my daughter knows haunted houses. She knows Vincent Price and Peter Cushing, the films of Hammer, the works of Poe, the chronicles of Mars and the town called 'Salem's Lot. But she knows Alice through the looking glass, too, and the Faithful Tin Soldier, the Ugly Duckling, and the journeys of Stuart Little. She knows Oz and the jungles of Tarzan, and though she is too young to fully appreciate anything but the colors, she knows the hands of Van Gogh, Winslow Homer, and Miró. She will listen to Duke Ellington and Count Basie, as well as to the Beach Boys. Just last week she asked me if she could put a picture in a frame on her dresser. She said she thought this particular dude was cool.

His name is Freddy.

"Skye," I said, "I really think havin' that in here is gonna give you night—"

And then I stopped. Oh-oh, I thought. Oh-oh.

Freddy, meet Skye. Talk to her about the power of make-believe, will you?

I turn the car onto Hilltop Street, and we rise toward my house.

I'm doing all right with my writing. It's a hard job, but I enjoy it. Sandy and I aren't the kind of people who need to own half the world to be happy. I have to say, though, that once I did splurge. I bought an old red convertible that called to me from a used car lot when Sandy and I were taking a vacation in New England. I think they used to refer to such cars as roadsters. I've restored it back to how it must've looked when Zephyr was new. Sometimes, when I'm alone out in that car, speeding along with the wind in my hair and the sun on my face, I forget myself and speak to it. I call it by a certain name.

You know what I call it.

That bicycle went with me when we left Zephyr. We had more adventures, and that golden eye saw a lot of trouble coming and kept me from getting into it on more than several occasions. But eventually it creaked under my weight, and my hands didn't seem to fit on the grips anymore. It was consigned to the basement, under a blue tarp. I imagined it went to sleep like a bird. One weekend I returned from college to find that Mom had had a garage sale, which included the contents of the basement. And here's your money a fella paid for your old bike! she'd said as she handed me a twenty-dollar bill. He bought it for his own boy, isn't that grand, Cory? Cory? Isn't that grand?

It's grand, I'd told my mother. And that night I put my head on my dad's shoulder and cried as if I were twelve again instead of twenty.

My heart stutters.

There it is. Right there.

"My house," I tell Sandy and Skye.

It has aged, under sun and rain. It needs paint and care. It needs love, but it is empty now. I stop the car at the curb, and I stare at the porch and see my father suddenly emerge smiling from the front door. He looks strong and fit, like he always does when I remember him.

"Hey, Cory!" he says. "How ya gettin' along?"

Just fine, sir, I answer.

"I knew you would be. I did all right, didn't I?"

Yes sir, you did, I say.

"Sure do have a pretty wife and a good daughter, Cory. And those books of yours! I knew you were gonna do well, all the time I knew it."

Dad? Do you want me to come in and stay awhile?

"Come in *here*?" He leans against the porch column. "Why would you want to do that, Cory?"

Aren't you lonely? I mean . . . it's so quiet here.

"Quiet?" He laughs heartily. "Sometimes I wish it *was* quiet! It's not a bit of quiet here!"

But . . . it's empty. Isn't it?

"It's full to the brim," my father says. He looks up at the sun, over the hills of spring. "You don't have to come here to see them, Cory. Or to see me, either. You really don't. You don't have to leave what is, to visit what was. You've got a good life, Cory. Better than I dreamed. How's your mom doin'?"

She's happy. I mean, she misses you, but . . .

"But life is for the livin'," he tells me in his fatherly voice. "Now go on and get on with it instead of wantin' to come in an old house with a saggy floor."

Yes sir, I say, but I can't leave yet.

He starts to go in, but he pauses, too. "Cory?" he says.

Yes sir?

"I'll always love you. Always. And I'll always love your mother, and I am so very happy for the both of you. Do you understand?"

I nod.

"You'll always be my boy," Dad says, and then he returns to the house and the porch is empty.

"Cory? Cory?"

I turn my face and look at Sandy.

"What do you see?" she asks me.

"A shadow," I say.

I want to go one more place before I turn the car around and drive away. I head us up the winding path of Temple Street, toward the Thaxter mansion at its summit.

Here things have really changed.

Some of the big houses have actually been torn down. Where they were is rolling grass. And here is another surprise: the Thaxter mansion has grown, sprouting additions on either side. The property around it is huge. My God! I realize. Vernon must still live there! I drive through a gate and past a big swimming pool. A treehouse has been constructed in the arms of a massive oak. The mansion itself is immaculate, the grounds beautiful, and smaller buildings have been constructed in its style.

I stop the car in front. "I can't believe this!" I tell Sandy. "I've gotta find out if Vernon's still here!"

I get out and start for the front door, my insides quaking with excitement.

But before I reach it, I hear a bell ring. *Ding . . . ding . . . ding . . . ding.*

I hear what sounds like a tidal wave, gaining speed and force.

And my breath is well and truly swept away.

Because here they come.

Swarming out of the front door, like wasps from the nest in

the church's ceiling on Easter Sunday. Here they come, laughing and hollering and jostling each other. Here they come, in a wonderful riot of noise.

The boys. Dozens of them, dozens. Some white, some black. Their numbers surge around me, as if I am an island in the river. Some of them run for the treehouse, others scamper across the rolling green yard. I am at the center of a young universe, and then I see the brass plaque on the wall next to the door.

It says THE ZEPHYR HOME FOR BOYS.

Vernon's mansion has become an orphanage.

And still they stream out around me, furious in their freedom on this glorious Saturday afternoon. A window opens on the second floor, and a wrinkled face peers out. "James Lucius!" her voice squawks. "Edward and Gregory! Get up here for your piano lessons right this very minute!"

She wears blue.

Two older women I don't know come out, chasing after the crowd of boys. Good luck to them, I think. And then a younger man emerges, and he stops before me. "Can I help you?"

"I . . . used to live here. In Zephyr, I mean." I am so stunned I can hardly talk. "When did this become an orphanage?"

"In 1985," the man tells me. "Mr. Vernon Thaxter left it to us."

"Is Mr. Thaxter still alive?"

"He left town. I'm sorry, but I don't know what became of him." This man has a gentle face. He has blond hair, and eyes of cornflower blue. "May I ask your name?"

"I'm—" I stop, because I realize who he must be. "Who are *you?*"

"I'm Bubba Willow." He smiles, and I can see Chile in him. "Reverend Bubba Willow."

"I'm very pleased to meet you." We shake hands. "I met your mother once."

"My mom? Really? What's your name?"

"Cory Mackenson."

The name doesn't register. I was a ship, passing through Chile's night. "How's your mother doin'?"

"Oh, just great. She moved to St. Louis, and she's teachin' sixth grade now."

"I'll bet her students sure feel lucky."

"Parson?" A wizened voice says. "Par son Willa?"

An elderly black man in faded overalls has come out. Around his skinny waist he wears a tool belt holding hammers, screwdrivers, and arcane-looking wrenches. "Parson, I done fixed that slow leak upastairs. Oughta lookat that ol' freezer now." His eyes find me. "Oh," he says with a soft slow gasp. "I know you."

And a smile spreads across his face like day following night.

I hug him, and when he grasps me his tool belt jingle-jangles.

"Cory Mackenson! My Lord! Is that you?"

I peer up at the woman in blue. "Yes ma'am, it is."

"My Lord, my Lord! Excuse me, Reverend! *My Lord, my Lord!"* Then her attention goes where it ought to: toward the new generation of boys. "James Lucius! Don't you get up in that treehouse and break those fingers!"

"Would you and your family like to come in?" Reverend Willow asks.

"Please do," Mr. Lightfoot says, smiling. "Lots ta talk about."

"Got coffee and doughnuts inside," the reverend tempts me. "Mrs. Velvadine runs a grand kitchen."

"Cory, you get on in here!" Then: "James Luuuuucius!"

Sandy and Skye have gotten out of the car. Sandy knows me, and she knows I'd like to stay for just a little while. We will not tarry long here, because my hometown is not our home, but an hour would be time well spent.

As they go in, I pause outside the door before I join them.

I look up, into the bright blue air.

I think I see four figures with wings, and their winged dogs, swooping and playing in the rivers of light.

They will always be there, as long as magic lives.

And magic has a strong, strong heart.

Rogers and Trigger; *X-Men;* Buffalo Bob and Howdy; the Brothers Grimm; Bela Lugosi; Paladin; *The Outer Limits;* Brigitte Bardot (I didn't spend all my time with *Geographic*s!); Basil Rathbone; Mister Dillon! Mister Dillon!; Sir Arthur Conan Doyle; *Invaders from Mars;* Gene Autry; Steve Reeves; Aunt Bea; Dr. Richard Kimble; the Who; Hans Christian Andersen; *13 Ghosts* and those weird glasses; Sergeant Preston of the Yukon; Mr. and Mrs. North; the Thin Man; Peter Lorre; Alfred Hitchcock; Here, Lassie!; Errol Flynn, the perfect Robin Hood; a man named Jed; the *Aquanauts;* Steve Roper and Mike Nomad; Clint Walker; Kookie, my hair's falling out!; *Gorgo; Rodan; Reptilicus;* Charles Laughton; Oral Roberts heal thyself; *The Gallant Men;* Victor Mature swinging that jawbone; Walt Disney; Mr. Lucky; Burt Lancaster; *Through the Looking Glass;* Bronco and Sugarfoot; the Mavericks, wild as the wind in Or-e-gon; Joe and Frank; *Fantasia;* that house on haunted hill; Guy Madison and Andy Devine; *The Mysterians; Dementia 13* (Yikes!); Captain America and Bucky; Harper Lee; Steve McQueen (Cooler!) on that motorcycle, jumping the barbed wire; Tom Swift and His; and so many, many more whom I will think of as soon as I believe I've finished writing this.

To two very special influences on this boy's life and writing: Mr. Rod Serling, for his talent and imagination that continues on far beyond the *Zone;* and to Mr. Ray Bradbury. Your lake will always be deeper and sweeter than mine, your jar hold greater mysteries, your rockets travel truer to the heart. Thank you so very, very much.

Well, I see by the old clock on the wall that it's time to go. Good-bye, kids!

Robert McCammon
April 14, 1990–September 23, 1990

Acknowledgments

No BOOK IS EVER WRITTEN without help and influence. *Boy's Life* is no exception. I would like to thank, then, some of the people and things that helped create *Boy's Life,* whether they're aware of such help or not.

My thanks to Forrest J. Ackermann; Roger Corman; Boris Karloff; Vincent Price; Lon Chaney Senior and Junior; Jungle Jim; Sky King and Penny; *Screen Thrills Illustrated;* Ian Fleming and Bond, James Bond; Eudora Welty; Bob Kane; Barbara Steele; Big Daddy Roth; the Boys from Hawthorne though a young man is gone; Clutch Cargo; Space Angels; Super Car; the Captain and Tom Terrrrific; Yancy Derringer; *Famous Monsters of Filmland;* Gordon Scott; Vic Morrow and the *Combat* squad; Jim Warren (sorry, Forry!); Boston Blackie; Zorro; Cisco Kid and Pancho; the Whistler; Kirk Douglas in *Spartacus;* the Rolling Stones; *Thriller* and those pigeons from hell; the Hammer Films bunch; Peter Cushing, the ultimate Van Helsing; Christopher Lee; Edgar Rice Burroughs; Red Skelton and the passing parade; *Creepy* and *Eerie;* Ray Harryhausen and the Ymir; Mr. Television, Milton Berle; *It's A Mad, Mad, Mad, Mad* (Did I miss one?) *World;* Edgar Allan Poe; Lester Dent or Kenneth Robeson or whoever cranked out all those great Doc Savages; Three Dog Night (hello, Cory!); Clayton Moore, the one and only Lone Ranger; Richard Matheson; Roy